Evangeline Clarion is a fiery artist and elemental witch. She dreams of opening a gallery in her small town of Arbor, but Eva's embrace of her own power and sexuality offends the pious sensibilities of the devout Arbor citizenry.

A gaggle Eva referred to as "Arbor's Most Moral" sets out on a witch hunt to ruin her and drive her out of town. They attack her in the pews, in the press, and in person. But instead of weakening her, the relentless barrage fuels the fire within her.

As her burgeoning magic is set aflame within Eva, so is her desire. While her neighbors plot against her, Eva falls in love—first with the mesmerizing heir of the Morgan Manor estate, and later with a beautiful Wiccan. Eva relies on both of them, along with a cast of magical cohorts, to help her combat the witch hunt. But when magical retribution goes too far, Arbor's salvation rests in the hands of a witch.

THE BURNING OF ARBOR

The Witches of Arbor, Book One

J.L. Brown

A NineStar Press Publication

Published by NineStar Press
P.O. Box 91792,
Albuquerque, New Mexico, 87199 USA.
www.ninestarpress.com

The Burning of Arbor

Printed in the USA
First Edition
April, 2018

Print ISBN: 978-1-948608-49-7

Also available in eBook, ISBN: 978-1-948608-45-9

Warning: This book contains sexual explicit content, which may only be suitable for mature readers, and depictions of sexual assault and attempted rape, graphic violence, death of an animal.

Dedication

This book is dedicated to all those who dare to be their authentic selves, to those who defy the naysayers in the tireless quest to realize their dreams, to those who lift others up, and to all those who refuse to be quiet about things that matter.

Special thanks

To all my friends and family, especially Ken, Aiden, Wyatt, Mr. D, Clair, Jenn2, Mike, Laurie, Barb, Erica, and all the amazing women who have my back and inspire me every day.

Chapter One

True magic has thrived in the world long before man documented such things. A spark of magic is present in every wish, at every birth and deathbed. It manifests itself in first kisses and first loves. It animates and inspires us. It abounds in the change of seasons, in the most remote forests and congested steel cities. Magic dwells within the rock of the mountains, and inhabits the waters of every stream and river and ocean. It exists both in the wondrous and mundane of every day. It is neither good nor evil. Magic bears no moral compass. The intention of the practitioner who wields it determines its use, for good or ill. And no one can escape magic's most essential rule: what one projects into the universe will return threefold.

The Wiccan Rede states, "An ye harm none, do what ye will."

I chose a different motto to live by. "Harm none, but take no shit."

I was never good at following the rules, and I learned my lessons the hard way.

SUNDAY

I refused to cower. I clenched my fists to keep from fidgeting and sighed at the twinge of pain where my nails left half-moon imprints in my palms.

"Isn't the bank usually closed on your Sabbath?" I asked, maintaining eye contact with the crotchety loan officer across the desk.

The woman could catapult my dreams had she the inclination, and I could tell she reveled in this power over me. My emerald stare seemed to unnerve her for a slim second, but she set her spine rigid. Her suspicious gaze rolled over me, and she twisted her wrinkled lips into a scowl.

"I thought it best not to delay the inevitable, Ms. Clarion. I'll be brief. You know as well as I that this little scheme will never get off the ground. Arbor is a quiet, wholesome community, not well suited for your kind of...

business venture." She scrunched up her nose as if the notion itself smelled foul. "However, I am nothing if not by-the-book. I reviewed your application, and after considering every factor, I must decline your request. Your excessive student loans, exorbitant debt-to-income ratio, and lackluster credit history disqualify you for a mortgage loan."

"What about my savings?" I asked. *This isn't happening. This can't be happening.* Panic spiked my veins, and sweat beaded along my forehead.

"Your... savings?" she snickered. "Woefully inadequate."

"It's twenty thousand dollars!" I said, shooting to my feet.

"I am sorry, Ms. Clarion. There is nothing I can do for you." But she wasn't sorry. Her smug expression made that clear. She enjoyed withholding the means of my success.

Of course this is happening. The decision shouldn't have shocked me, but it did, and it hurt. "So, that's it?"

"I'm afraid so."

I should've known better than to think anyone from Arbor would allow someone like me so public a platform. I might sully the well-crafted image of the town they so carefully portray to the world.

For as long as I could remember, I'd dreamed of owning a place to sell my artwork and designs, somewhere to perform. It would be a gathering spot for the creative, the different, the weird. I'd been saving for years.

This woman thinks she can crush my dreams in a single five-minute meeting? No fucking way. I'll figure something out.

The glare of the noonday sun blinded me as I emerged from the Arbor Savings & Loan. Squinting, I sat on the bank's steps to fish my sunglasses out of my bag. Once my vision adjusted, I took in the view along Parson Street, downtown Arbor's main drag. It bustled with a Sunday afternoon's lazy vigor. The Rockwellian cafés and shops teemed with the post–church-service crowd. Clusters of believers mingled and gossiped and bragged, decked out in their finest prim and proper attire. Arrogance and privilege marked their manners. Without a droplet of sweat on a single brow, the parishioners seemed somehow immune to the sun's crushing heat. The air hung stagnant and oppressive in the conservative hamlet, nestled as it was into the base of Gothics Peak.

A piercing "Keeee-aaar" sounded from high above. I looked into the crystalline summer sky at a red-tailed hawk swooping in circles, his wings spread wide. I'd know that bird anywhere. Rocky had been my faithful familiar for almost nine years, since I'd entered high school. Besides his no-

nonsense sagacity, Rocky granted me the ability to fly—when he was in close enough proximity for me to feed off his magic. He was the second familiar with whom I'd been blessed. Shasta came to me when I was eight, right after my mother died. Shasta never ventured into town, though. An abnormally large black bear walking amongst the masses wouldn't go over well.

"*Your meeting didn't go as planned, I judge.*" Rocky's sharp, stately voice echoed within my mind.

"*You judge correctly,*" I replied in the same fashion.

"*That backwards thinking pencil-pusher never had any intention of aiding you, and you know it. I'll never understand why you bother with the fools in this town. Your talents would shine down in the city. That's where you need to be.*"

"*You know I can't leave Maggie.*"

"*No. You don't want to leave your goddess-mother. Big difference.*"

"*I'm not going to argue semantics. I just want to get home and forget this entire morning.*"

"*Hate to break the news, but unless you plan on riding the wind with me, you face a delay.*"

"*I've already exceeded my maximum daily dose of aggravation, thank you very much. I'm done.*"

"*You don't have a choice. Have you seen who's planted in your path?*"

Halfway down Parson Street, between me and where I'd parked my truck, was a gaggle I referred to as *Arbor's Most Moral*. Mayor Doreen Crandall sat at a bistro table outside of Ebenezer's Café. Beside her lounged Reverend Cudlow—pastor of the First Ecclesiastical Church of Arbor, the town's only house of worship—and his haughty wife Gladys.

"*Hurry by them, Evangeline, and do not dawdle. Shasta's got her fur in a bunch.*"

Without waiting for a reply, he caught the wind and headed back to our cottage.

I threw my heels in my bag, grabbed my well-worn paperback of *Pride and Prejudice*, and jogged down the bank steps. Barefoot, I hurried along the blistering sidewalk. With my head buried in my book, I scanned the lines inked along the faded, dog-eared pages. Keeping my attention fixed on the trials and tribulation of the Bennet sisters gave me the cover I needed to avoid the sneers directed at me by the sanctimonious flock.

"Harlot! Heathen!" Two elderly ladies hissed from the flower shop doorway.

With a quick side-eye glance, I caught their judgmental expressions, brows drawn tight, lips pursed.

My presence alone offended the pious sensibilities of the devout Arbor citizenry. The delicate, black blouson dress that I'd made myself grazed just a bit too high along my pale thighs. Its neckline plunged an inch or two too low for propriety. My tiny naked feet were tipped in black polish, and my long, dark pigtail braids hinted at an innocence my reputation contradicted.

The matriarchs of each clustered brood clutched their pearls and progeny as I passed, as if to shield them from my malevolence. The men's eyes snaked greedily along my silhouette, but their tongues cursed me. They didn't label me simply a sinner, but a demon from Hell; a vile deviant sent by the Devil himself to corrupt and defile my good neighbors. No one cared that I didn't even believe in Hell or the Devil they accused me of worshipping.

Harassment was nothing new. I'd dealt with it since I'd moved to Arbor as a child. Being raised by my goddess-mother—a powerful witch who'd been my mother's lover prior to her untimely death—didn't lend itself to a conventional childhood. After so many years, my indifference to the niceties of general society was fixed. I was no wild-woman. I had no lack of sense or intelligence. I simply had no desire to please those who'd as soon see me hanged as prosper.

I increased my pace, my short legs heel-toeing it double-time. I prayed to the Goddess that I could make it past the café without incident.

Keep your cool, Evangeline. I cheered myself on as I tried my damnedest not to take off in a full sprint. "Please leave me alone. Please just leave me alone," I muttered.

"Good afternoon, Ms. Clarion! How lovely to see you on this fine day," Reverend Cudlow greeted me with his usual note of sinful sincerity. "I don't believe I saw you in the pews. I would've remembered." He tipped his sunglasses down the bridge of his nose and looked me over. "Such a shame, really, to deprive the church of your wonders."

His lecherous smile made me want to hurl. I stepped back, out of reach. "My absence is for your benefit, Reverend, and for the benefit of your parishioners. My presence below your steeple could be dangerous. We wouldn't want lightning to strike."

I tried to continue along past him, but he sidestepped me and blocked my path.

"I hope I've made it clear that you and your godmother are welcome in our congregation. I'd hate for you not to join us because you felt... unwanted."

"Because you're definitely wanted," a menacing voice rasped from a darkened alleyway beside the café. Stuart Cudlow, the Reverend and Gladys Cudlow's only son, smirked as he stepped out of the shadows.

Even standing ten feet away, he made me physically ill. I fought my body's instinct for self-preservation. I refused to flee. I wouldn't run from this man—if such a beast could be called a man. He was lanky and ginger like his mother, with his father's unquenchable appetite for sins of the flesh. Since his early teens, Stuart had been groomed to take up the mantle of preacher from his father. Every seminary school he attended, however, expelled him on charges of cruel and licentious behavior.

I knew from personal experience just how wicked he could be. And I knew responding to men like Stuart, whether civilly or with anger, only gave them more power. Any reply would show he'd gotten a rise out of me. And I wasn't taking the bait.

Ignoring the son, I returned my attention to the father. "Here's a quick review, Reverend, just to catch you up. I acknowledge the Goddess not your God. Therefore, Maggie is my goddess-mother not my godmother—as you are well aware. So, while I appreciate your invitation to worship, on behalf of myself and my goddess-mother, I respectfully decline. Now, I'm in no mood to spar with you, so please move aside and let me pass."

But he didn't move. Not a single wispy white hair so much as quivered upon his wrinkled, pasty head.

"My dear, I have no desire to spar..."

"Don't bother with that hussy, *my dear*. She isn't worth your time...or the Lord's." Gladys sneered with a huff, lifting her nose high. The gaunt and florally festooned First Lady of the Church considered herself the town's preeminent authority on all things moral. "Even the Lord knows a lost cause when He sees one."

"Correct as always, my good friend," Mayor Crandall chimed in.

Ah, there she is.

"It isn't worth bothering the Lord with the likes of Evangeline Clarion, Gladys."

The voice I dreaded more than any on the Goddess's great Earth was that of Doreen Crandall, Arbor's despotic mayor and mother of my sleazy ex-boyfriend, Jay. I represented everything the mayor railed against, or so she enjoyed reminding me. But ever since she kicked off her campaign for the state legislature, her viciousness and disdain for me increased tenfold.

"I knew you couldn't stay out of such a public confrontation."

The blonde bureaucrat moved in so close I could smell the chai tea on her breath—and the bourbon it was meant to hide. "I will not let you get away scot-free."

"Get away with what?" I railed.

"Prancing around town like Jezebel, with a flippant disregard for decency or decorum."

"I haven't done a damn thing wrong, and you know it, Doreen." I refused to back down to the venomous bitch.

"Let me tell you something, little miss," she said, poking her manicured finger into my chest. "You show me some respect, or I'll have Chief Harrison haul you down to lock-up before you can say, 'thank you very much, Madam Mayor.'"

Just as she finished speaking, a sun-kissed hipster burst out of the café door flanked by pastel-clad sorority girls. He'd given one bubbly debutant the privilege of holding his left hand, while he sucked down a green apple slushy in his right.

"If it isn't Evangeline Clarion, the love of my life!" Jay Crandall bellowed as he flashed his baby blues and his bad-boy smile.

"Jay Crandall, the bane of my existence. My day is complete," I said, deadpan. "Graduation was two weeks ago. Still dallying with freshmen?"

"Excuse me, I'm a sophomore at NYU cosmetology," the twit on his arm hissed at me. "Who's she, baby? I thought I was the love of your life!" She whined as she clung desperately to my ex's arm.

"Of course, you are…" Jay reached unsuccessfully for her name.

"Lauren."

"Lauren, yeh, thanks. Don't know how I forgot that," Jay said as he leisurely—unapologetically—checked me out. His crooked lips puckered, and I knew some juicy memories of the two of us stormed through his mind.

Jay had a model's face, an athlete's physique, and was a porn star in bed. He also oozed hubris from every orifice. I loathed him.

"No. Way!" His arm candy squealed as she looked from him, to me, and back to him, grasping the connection between the two of us. Jealousy flashed in her eyes. She flung her arm out, smacking his, and knocking the green slushy from his hand.

I lived the next few moments in surreal slow motion. The cup and lid flew one way, hitting Mayor Crandall in the head. The contents of the slushy flew the other way, coating me from head to toe. The shock of the bitter freeze stole my breath. The cloying, sticky sweetness tinted my skin green. My sopping dress caused a wet T-shirt effect that only made my endowments more flagrant. Slushy dripped from my braids and splashed into puddles at my feet.

All but the mayor and I burst out in mocking cackles. The sneers and pointed fingers clawed at my thinning self-control, but the mayor's worries were far greater than snickering townsfolk. As her son's cup hit her in the head, the press popped out of nowhere, cameras flashing. They swarmed like rats to raw meat, capturing more than one break-the-internet shot of Mayor Crandall. Candidate Crandall.

This sucks for her campaign, and it's all too much for me. I need to get out of here.

I was lucky. Even though I resembled a drowned leprechaun, most eyes—and lenses—were trained on the mayor. Her mouth popped wide in shock, she clutched her head. A single green trail trickled down her cheek from the straw caught in her hair.

Grateful for the distraction, I headed for my truck.

I barely made it three paces before Gladys Cudlow stepped in my path and shrieked, "Repent!"

"Are you fucking kidding me? What's wrong with you people?"

I tried to push past the pompous pastor's wife, but the crowd had swollen. Folks congregated to gawk at the melee occurring between the mayor and the press. I couldn't duck her.

Gladys's eyes burned with religious fervor. "Accept Jesus as your Lord and savior or leave!"

"I'm trying to leave."

"Repent or leave Arbor; you and your godmother."

"Goddess-mother. She's my…never mind. Why should we leave Arbor?" I knew it was foolish to encourage the zealot, but the audacity it took to lord over me like some pampered dictator astounded me. "This is our home. Magdalena Maramma and her family have owned that cottage and land for more than two hundred years. It is sacred ground to us."

Gladys recoiled. "How dare you presume to understand the nature of sanctity!" she spat.

And then, she actually spat. Her thick glob of muddy yellow saliva landed on the cover of my book. My favorite book. And I don't mean my favorite story. I mean that that particular copy of that book was my favorite; the one that had just miraculously survived a slushy attack. Now Gladys Cudlow's spit covered Elizabeth Bennet's face.

I closed my eyes for a moment in an attempt to marshal my rage. No good would come from lashing out, and well I knew it. But I was tired of the bullshit. I'd put up with it for too long. Adelaide Good, high priestess of the coven to which my goddess-mother and I belonged, always said, "Don't let 'em bait you. Let Karma do the dirty work." These echoed words gave me focus. A calmness blanketed me. The corners of my mouth lifted into a menacing grin.

Panic spiked across the church lady's face.

I called on the power within, reached my arms out wide, and recited the spell.

> "Upon you I place a karmic debt,
> So you will not too soon forget.
> All actions, thoughts, and words of hate
> Become your own decided fate.
> I return your villainy back to thee.
> As I will it, so mote it be."

As I spoke the words, every cruelty Gladys had ever perpetrated, every incident of brutality, every occasion of callousness, played out before her eyes. And I made sure she knew, in her heart, in her blood, to expect swift justice should malice be her guide again.

"Have a lovely afternoon, Gladys. I'll send my goddess-mother your good wishes."

Chapter Two

I lived with Magdalena Maramma in a cheerful thatched-roof cottage. It stood on ten acres of fertile land in the outlying rural area of town. Twisted grapevines arched into a fifteen-foot-tall arbor marking our river-rock driveway. Sweeping lavender fields lined a full five acres of the property. Eight beehives capped the end of the lavender. A crooked, gnarly stream snaked along a hundred yards from our violet-stained front door and wound through the dense woods that edged the cottage. Wildflowers and peppermint grew around the perimeter of the cottage's stuccoed facade. A slate patio, complete with wicker rockers, a wrought-iron table and chairs, and a sage-green umbrella, offered a lovely spot for soaking in the Goddess's wonders.

When I finally made it home from my trek into town, I collapsed on the sofa in the gallery—what others might call a living room. The room functioned as a library, music room, and art studio. It also passed as a waiting room for the patients who visited Maggie for her tonics and healing touch. The space rioted with a clash of patterns, colors, and textures. With its exposed beams, fluffy pillows, and rich fabrics, it was both lush and comfortable. Haphazard stacks of sheet music and art supplies cluttered the space. Stringed and woodwind instruments, an upright piano, and a varied assortment of other music makers vied for pride of place among the painted canvases and floor-to-ceiling bookshelves. The room bubbled over in joyous, creative chaos.

"Hey, Mags," I called out. "I'm home."

"I'm in here," she hollered back. "But you better head to the woods to see Shasta. She's been in a tizzy waiting for you."

As it turned out, I didn't need to go anywhere to see Shasta. I heard her approach outside the cottage door, her teeth gnashing in anxious agitation.

I called out to her within my mind. *"Hey there, Momma Bear."* I propelled myself to the door and was snatched up into the bear's shaggy embrace before I took a single step outside.

"You never said goodbye before you left this morning. I've been on pins and needles. Rocky wouldn't say a word. But I feel your disappointment. Things went poorly at the bank?"

"It didn't go well."

Shasta lifted a large, black paw to stroke my cheek. *"This is not what I wished for your birthday."* She tilted her broad head, and her rounded ears bent with concern.

"Well, you can't always get what you want..." I said with a smirk.

"But if you try sometimes, you just might find, you get what you need." Shasta was a huge classic-rock fan. *"Tell me, what is it you want, more than anything?"*

I thought for a moment. *"The Goddess blessed me with the ability to create. I'm an artist, a designer, a musician. I can't be content with creating in the shadows. Selling my work at the Arbor Community Market isn't enough. So, I guess, to answer your question, I want what every artist wants: to make a living, to make a life doing what I love."*

"You have spoken your will, and so it shall be. Today's troubles are just that, today's. Tomorrow brings new opportunities."

"And new troubles."

"Things will work out, dearie. You mustn't lose hope.... Trust me."

"Always. Love you, Momma Bear." I squeezed her tight, buried my face into her fur, and breathed in her familiar musk.

"I love you, too. Now go to Magdalena. Let her be a balm for your spirit. Off with you." Shasta dropped down on all fours and barreled into the woods.

The decadent aroma of dark chocolate led me by the nose into the cottage's rustic kitchen. A cast-iron caldron hung, bubbling in a fury, from a river-stone hearth. Across from it blazed a brick oven. A twelve-inch-thick butcher block, concave from decades of use, sat beside a 1910 Bridge Beach & Co. antique cookstove. Culinary, medicinal, and magical herbs hung drying from the rafters and filled hundreds of glass jars in the well-stocked pantry. There was echinacea, St. John's wart, and ginseng root that went into the tinctures and salves Maggie prepared for the sick. We used the likes of henbane, mugwort, elderflower, and angelica root for potion making. Marjoram, basil, thyme, and at least thirty other cooking herbs were available to make any cuisine imaginable. All told, more than a hundred herbs, spices, roots, and flowers crammed Maggie's pantry stores. Homemade pastries and Mason jars of honey filled the wrought-iron baker's racks that lined the far wall. In the center of it all, I found my goddess-mother with her steady hands clasped around a piping bag. The blue apron she wore over her boho-chic dress was splattered in puffs of flour. Shafts of afternoon sunlight pierced the kitchen window, illuminating Maggie's wild waves of blonde hair, ice-gray eyes, and lean figure. She formed a striking vision.

"Oh, Eva!" She gasped with a guilty grin and jumped to hide a delicately decorated dark-chocolate cake. "You weren't supposed to see it yet. I wanted to surprise you." She leaned down and kissed my cheek. "Happy birthday, sweetheart."

"Thanks. Cake looks amazing." I swiped a finger along its bottom edge. "Tastes divine," I mumbled as I savored the chocolate.

"Thank you," she said and paused. "So..."

"So, what?"

"Buttons." She couldn't help herself. "Are you going to tell me why you're all sticky? And green?"

I filled Maggie in on my adventures with Arbor's Most Moral and Jay's cosmetologist as I washed the slushy from my hands and face in the porcelain farmhouse sink.

"I feel every slight like a lash on my back, but there's nothing they can do to me that I won't take into myself and use as fuel," I professed.

Maggie shook her head in frustration. "Sometimes, I think I'll never understand this town. Most folks are kind and good-natured when we chat one on one. But when they get together...forget it. And why should they hate us? We've never sought to convert them. We've never ridiculed their faith. I quite like their Jesus. I wish they acted more like him." She smiled softly and brushed my hair away from my face. "I'm sorry you had to go through this on your birthday."

I wasn't alone in attracting the contempt of our Arbor neighbors. Maggie had her own set of allegations with which to contend. Her "homeopathic remedies" were celebrated throughout Arbor and the surrounding county for their efficacy. So many folks in the area were opposed to signing up for *government-run* healthcare, that they were left without the ability to visit a doctor or hospital. This put Maggie in high demand. She made no promises of miracle cures, but Arbor's Most Moral, and the sheep who followed them, denounced her as a charlatan and a snake-oil salesman. They wanted to see her shut down for good or, preferably, locked up. Through it all, Maggie remained perpetually optimistic. She chose to care for those who condemned her.

"The pain they endure must be great for them to exude such hatred," she said.

"I marvel at your level of empathy."

"Walking a mile in another's shoes is the only way to understand their motivations."

"Know your enemy."

"Something like that," she grinned. But the joy quickly slipped from her face. "You haven't mentioned your meeting at the bank. Should I take that as a bad sign?" she asked, concern wrinkling her forehead.

"What do you think?" I snapped and immediately regretted it. "According to the Arbor Savings and Loan, the twenty thousand I've saved is still not enough cash on hand. My credit's mediocre. And I owe too much in student loans. So, no mortgage, no property, no gallery."

Maggie lifted my chin. "Let me help. The cottage and acreage are equity. You've got a much better chance of getting a mortgage approved if I cosign."

"You know I can't do that." I shrugged my chin from her hold.

"Of course, you can!" she said as if it should be the most obvious thing in the world. "You will be a monumental success. As I will it, so mote it be."

While I trusted Maggie's wisdom and appreciated her faith in me, her blind optimism seemed naïve. "Even if I was able to get the property, there's a snowball's chance in hell the zoning board would approve my plans for the place. The bottom line is they'll never let *me* open a gallery in Arbor."

We brooded in silence for a few moments until Maggie nudged me with her elbow.

"You could always look somewhere else."

"And leave you? No."

"Sweetheart, you don't need to look out for me. I'm a big girl." She winked.

"Whatever I decide, I'm going to do it on my own. It's my dream, and I'll either make it happen or I won't. But thank you. I love you for offering to help." I shot her a pathetic excuse for a smile. "So, how's Adelaide?" I asked, changing the subject.

"She says she's fine."

"But..."

"She's not."

Her bluntness shocked me. "Compared to your average eighty-year-old, Adelaide's in astonishing health."

"She can hardly be called average."

Adelaide Good was spunky and outspoken and widely judged as one of Arbor's great eccentrics; a designation she wore with pride. Her quirks and idiosyncrasies were tolerated, but most folks considered her a joke. The Adelaide I knew was a bad-ass witch. She could manipulate nature, conjure elements at will, and coax glimpses of the future from her scrying mirror. When added to her irreverent wit, Adelaide was a force few on Earth could best. As the high priestess of our coven, a decline in her power would be devastating.

"What are you sensing?" I asked.

"She's slowing down. There's a shaking in her hands, and maybe some arthritis in her fingers. A deterioration in her motor functions could affect her spell casting. Adelaide's potent magic doesn't only improve her mortality rate with its many gifts. That level of power requires an equal measure of energy from the witch in return. I'll give her a check-up after your birthday dinner tonight if she feels up to joining us."

Blood or not, Adelaide was family, so I hated the thought of her health weakening. I hated that she insisted on living alone in her cramped apartment downtown, instead of with us. And as childish as it was, I hated that she might miss my birthday dinner. The day wouldn't be complete without her. Although, it had been fourteen years since I celebrated my birthday with much enthusiasm.

My mother, Lavinia Clarion, had died when I was eight. We'd celebrated my birthday the night before her passing. As usual, Maggie joined us for the festivities. My home had never looked more cheerful, strewn with balloons and streamers, with presents piled high. My mother had been young and healthy, but when I stepped off the school bus the next afternoon, she was gone. I had no interest in knowing her manner of death or the reasons behind it. I'd lost my mother. Her lilting voice would never again lull me to sleep. I'd no longer feel the strength of her hands as she brushed and braided my hair. Never again would I witness my mother's breathtaking, unparalleled magic. Since then, my birthdays were less about celebrating a new chapter in life and more about reflecting on whether or not I lived up to the mother I'd lost.

But Adelaide never let me wallow in the pain of the past. She taught that life was meant to be enjoyed and savored—in all its sweet bitterness.

"Adelaide is going to be just fine. As I will it, so mote it be," Maggie said, willing the words into being with serene confidence. "What about the boys? Are they going to make it for your birthday dinner?"

"No, unfortunately. I talked to Ethan this morning. He's got a few more performances before his summer break, so he's barricading himself in the dance studio to practice. Gregory is the guest chef at some Michelin-starred restaurant down in the city for the next few weeks, and the brothers are in San Diego. Nicolae's attending a conference, and I assume Luca is breaking hearts. I don't think we'll see any of them until Litha."

The boys, as the coven referred to them, were powerful witches in their twenties. Every one of them was drool-worthy in his own magnificent way. Ethan, who was believed to be part fae, was lithe and graceful with silver hair and sharp features. He could sweep a person off their feet, whisk them away, and have them forgetting their own name. Gregory descended from an ancient line of Druid priests. He was an imposing, seductive figure whose very presence could intoxicate. He wore his flaxen hair dreaded and his beard long, and the pungent scent of marijuana followed him. The Romani brothers, Nicolae and Luca Loveridge, were olive skinned with onyx hair and eyes. There wasn't a soul alive who could withstand Nicolae's powers of persuasion, and no one who could hide their truth from Luca. I'd known the boys since I'd worn diapers. Growing up, we all participated in the festivals and rites celebrated by the coven, and they visited the cottage often. My close friendship with the boys helped create my loose reputation in town.

Maggie dropped her pastry bag on the counter and wrapped me up in her arms. "I'm sorry, sweetheart," she said and kissed my forehead. "They all love you."

"I know. I love them too."

"Our Midsummer Litha celebration is only a few weeks away. We'll see the boys soon enough," Maggie said.

"I know. You're right," I agreed without much conviction.

"Now," Maggie began as she pulled a to-do list from her flour-splattered apron and handed it to me, "I need you to give me a hand with the chores this afternoon."

"Of course. Whatever you need."

"Excellent," she said with a sharp nod. "Give to the earth, and the earth will give back to you. Sustain it, and it will sustain you." She recited her personal motto as she nudged me out the back door and into the gardens.

A bit of everything needed tending. The first item on the list was jarring honey and caring for the beehives. I slipped into the white protective overalls, jacket, and helmet necessary for beekeeping—not that Maggie ever wore them. She held a deep affinity for the bees that kept our little slice of earth buzzing along. The queen bee, Hanna, was Maggie's familiar. The abilities Hanna gave to Maggie epitomized the phrase "busy as a bee."

The next task was weeding, pruning, and harvesting the small but bountiful vegetable garden that grew just outside the kitchen. Then I bundled herbs, reciting the uses of each as I worked. As much as I appreciated the importance of herbology, I preferred playing music, sewing, painting, and drawing. Magic worked differently through me than through Maggie. She was a great healer, whereas I was a catalyst for creation.

After the chores, I took a long shower. I let the stinging spray wash away the remnants of green slushy stickiness—and my ill temper. Once I freshened up, I made my way back out to the kitchen. I stopped short when I overheard Maggie speaking with someone. At first, I assumed she was on the phone. There were no other voices. But, no. She was curled up in her favorite armchair, staring out of the window and talking to my mother.

"Oh, Lavinia, my love," she said, releasing a deep sigh. "You'd be so proud of our girl. Twenty-two today, can you believe it? I wish you could see her magic. She's even more powerful than you were at her age. And there's a real fire churning within her. I think she's happy—most of the time. But there is something missing from her life. Adelaide believes it's a man. I think she's a flower hidden beneath a rock. She needs space to bloom, and the sun to illuminate her beauty. Please, guide me and guide our girl. We both miss you terribly."

Magdalena and my mother, Lavinia, grew up together from childhood, and they loved each other deeply. Together, they practiced their craft, tying the spiritual with the powers of the natural world, honoring and celebrating the Goddess, the Universal Energy that created all in existence. The magic they made together sang with the harmony of night and day. And although my mother no longer lingered on this plane, her spirit lived within us, those she loved most.

I cleared my throat to announce my presence. Maggie jumped a bit and hid her face to wipe away tears.

"Hey, sweetie. Thanks for helping with the chores. I know it's your birthday, but nature cares nothing for these celebrations." She looked at me tenderly. "Are you ready for your birthday dinner?"

"Sure...but where is it?" I asked, eyeing the empty kitchen.

"Outside, of course."

A patchwork blanket stretched out on the bank of the stream that ran along the edge of the cottage's front yard. On it sat a large picnic basket overflowing with all manner of savory delicacies. Alongside the basket were bottles of Prosecco and Lemoncello and Maggie's exquisitely decorated birthday cake.

"Oh, Mags, this is amazing, thank you." I reached up on tiptoe to kiss her cheek. "There's just one flaw in your plan."

"And what's that?" Maggie asked cautiously.

"There's so much food, we'll end up too full to touch that mouthwatering masterpiece you've been working on all day."

Maggie's eyes lit up. "Then it's a good thing a few friends dropped by."

From the side of the cottage emerged Shasta, Rocky, Hanna, Adelaide and her familiar Fledermous the bat, and my best and only mundane friend Gwendolyn Reed—aka Bunny.

"Surprise!" the humans shouted. *"Surprise!"* the familiars echoed in my mind.

A joyous sob burst from my throat before I could bite it back.

I was promptly tackled around the neck by my bubbly, blonde friend. Then she grabbed my face and slathered sloppy smooches over my cheeks. Some called her my shadow. She reminded me more of the Energizer Bunny, always going, always banging that damn drum; hence the nickname. Bunny never cared about my unconventional beliefs or the inexplicable happenings she witnessed when we hung out. She never looked too close or asked too many questions. That was how we'd stayed friends for so long.

"Hey, crazy lady," I said with love, and returned her affection with a small peck on her heavily made-up cheek. "I didn't think I'd see you for a couple days. You threatened—" I cringed at my slip. "I mean, you promised to take me to the spa and do some shopping later this week."

"Oh, don't you worry your wicked little head. I have oodles of plans up my sleeve. Your birthday week will be epic!" she squealed.

And that was just Bunny's way. She dragged me to every party and community event—decked out in her characteristic pastel hues, with her teased-out blonde curls and generous breasts bopping beside me. And the girl could work a crowd. Her bright smile and bubbly disposition drew a smile from one and all. Bunny's exuberance pulled me into the world, to live fully and with enthusiasm...just like Adelaide taught.

Yet I groaned inwardly at the thought of a birthday week full of Bunny.

"Epic. Yeah," I said with little enthusiasm.

Our relationship had turned stale of late. We'd never been thick as thieves as childhood friends. I'd never confided my deepest truths to her. A divide would always exist between us. Lately, however, I grew increasingly irritated in Bunny's company. She'd prattle away about local gossip and her ill-informed news of the day, and all I could think about was how tiresome and insipid it all was, how devoid of depth. Still, I understood that these were my issues, not hers. Bunny had always been a steadfast friend.

I kissed her cheek and thanked her before greeting another dear friend.

"You didn't have to come tonight, you know," I said to my high priestess, who'd somehow managed to blend into the surroundings despite her soft strawberry-orange curls frizzed out from the humidity and her unusual sense of style shown off with pointy-heeled Victorian boots, a long skirt, and bulky sweater. She'd been watching my exchange with Bunny with a curious expression that evaporated as I kissed her on each cheek. "Maggie said you're not feeling well. You should be resting. It would've been okay. I would've understood."

"You're a good girl, but no, no. I wouldn't miss your birthday for all the gin in Georgia. My old age does get the better of me on occasion, but I'm not ready to turn in my party hat quite yet."

"Here," Adelaide said, handing me a package wrapped in orange organza. "Happy birthday! Welcome to a new year of life! May all your days be joyous and all your nights hot." She shimmied her shoulders and raised a toast with an invisible glass and a celebratory smile.

What a strange bird you are, I marveled. *Like an Aunty Mame.*

Unwrapping my birthday gift revealed a three-inch oval amethyst, polished to a high shine, hanging from a slender silver chain. Amethyst provided serenity, a sense of balance. It also encouraged and enhanced matters of the heart.

"It's lovely. Thank you."

"Wear it well and wisely," she said with a wink.

The familiars all greeted me with birthday wishes. And when I embraced Shasta and Rocky, I felt my connection with them deepen further than ever before. They'd helped me survive and thrive another year on the earth, and I felt truly blessed to have such loyal companions.

I grabbed ahold of Maggie last and squeezed her tight. Every brittle, chaffed emotion in me went into that hug.

"Thank you—for the cake, for the dinner, for the surprise, for everything," I said with a tearful grin.

"You're very welcome," Maggie said and handed me a fork. "Now let's eat."

Chapter Three

MONDAY

I woke early the next morning. The larks hadn't yet begun stirring in their nests, and the dew still clung like glitter on the grass. The screeching cicadas promised a scorcher of a day. After making myself some coffee, I grabbed my laptop and checked my messages. The boys all sent birthday wishes, apologies for missing my dinner, and promises of expensive gifts to make it up to me.

When I clicked over to the online version of our local newspaper, *The Messenger*, the headline and photo almost knocked me on my ass. The image showed a horrified Doreen Crandall with that straw stuck in her hair and a dribble of green slushy running down her cheek. Jay and his ladies stood beside her, laughing and pointing. Over it, the headline read:

COLD CRANDALL ICED BY PETULANT PLAYBOY

Shit. This is not good.

There was nothing I could do about it, however. I had work to do, and neither the mayor nor the press was going to pay my bills. So I finished my coffee and got ready for the day.

Less than an hour later, I had loaded up my truck with boxes of my handmade clothes, half a dozen paintings, jars of honey, and bushels of dried lavender bundles. Then I headed to the Arbor Community Market. Maggie and I ran a stand at the open-air marketplace. I usually worked the stand, but Maggie lent a hand when she wasn't tending to the cottage gardens, beehives, and lavender fields, or caring for the sick. The market offered me the opportunity to display my talents and earn a little money. The pragmatist in me was grateful for the modest opportunity. The artist within was left woefully unfulfilled.

The sprawling locale at the end of Parson Street was more than a humble farmer's market. High-end antique dealers and artisans of every medium regularly drew thousands of deep-pocketed shoppers from all over the state. The market boasted more than two hundred permanent vendors, and another twenty booths were open to nonprofits and political organizations. Groups with broad appeal like the Red Cross were tolerated, but the conservative leaning of the town welcomed Tea Partiers, climate-change deniers, creationists, and end-times prophecy proponents with open arms.

I'd just finished setting up my stand when I noticed some commotion coming from a nearby booth. Doreen Crandall stood before an ostentatious display of political propaganda. Banners, ablaze in red, white, and blue and baring her visage, waved from every spare surface of the mayor's campaign booth. The slick politician descended upon the unsuspecting market patrons to press the flesh. She shook every hand that passed by and cooed at every baby. She laughed along with the children who played at her feet. She even answered a question or two. I had to hand it to her. The mayor almost came across as genuine. Her bid for a seat in the state legislature amped her up like nothing I'd seen before. As much as I abhorred the woman, I couldn't deny she was a damn good politician.

As usual, the mayor's most loyal acolyte, Gladys Cudlow, glommed onto her side. Gladys appeared downright maniacal, with her eyes bugged out and bloodshot and her fuchsia-slicked lips stretched into a devious grin. She rubbed her hands together feverishly as she hissed into the mayor's ear.

Before long, the nature of their conniving became clear. Gladys set up a podium and microphone in front of the mayor's booth and lined up a group of *supporters* behind the podium. Once the reporters converged upon the market, the mayor got down to business.

"Ladies and gentlemen, I thank you all for joining me on this glorious morning. As you know, I've had the privilege of being the mayor of Arbor for over five years. I am now fighting for the opportunity to bring the same grit and dedication to the state legislature that I've brought to our fine community.

"I am no meek maiden. I understand campaigns can be cutthroat. That's exactly why I've come before you today. I am compelled to address a scandalous report that a certain publication chose to splash across their front page this morning. I must set the record straight!" She pounded on the podium.

"*The Messenger* professed with great aplomb that I was cold-natured—which, as anyone who knows me would attest is simply hogwash. And they accused my only son, my flesh and blood, of being a petulant playboy. This is nothing more than slander and disgusting, irresponsible journalism."

At this, the assembled press grumbled their disapproval.

"So let's clear things up, shall we? Yesterday afternoon, my son and I, along with Reverend Cudlow of the First Ecclesiastical Church of Arbor, his wife Gladys, and their son Stuart had just come from church services. We'd stopped to enjoy a respite at one of Arbor's delightful eateries. Members of the press happened upon us while we were being harassed by an unfortunate member of the Arbor community, a young woman by the name of Evangeline Clarion."

The locals in the crowd shot wary glances in my direction before returning eagerly to the mayor's speech.

"This disturbed individual accosted us with her vile professions of witchcraft and devil worship. The heinous female's blasphemy so overcame my deeply devout son that he lost control of his beverage. That's the 'why' behind that silly photo. Now, I enjoy a good joke as much as the next gal, but I refuse to have my name, or my son's name, besmirched by so-called journalists hankering for a juicy story."

Again, the press muttered.

"But there *is* a wretched tale in all of this that must be told; one so pervasive it is even found here in our upstanding community of Arbor. Witchcraft. It has vexed us since our forefathers stepped foot on our nation's soil, and it is as prevalent today as ever. More so even because of the ease of indoctrination via e-books, movies, and the internet.

"The woman who accosted us after our church services, this *Ms. Clarion*, has a long history of contemptible behavior, specifically a history of corrupting and tempting men. Yet she is but one godless heathen among the many who have infiltrated communities across this great state in an attempt to bring more souls to Satan. It is just such evil I vow to battle in the legislature should the citizens of our fair state elect me to do so.

"To attest to the level of depravity to which Ms. Clarion is willing to stoop, is our own Gladys Cudlow."

A smattering of polite applause introduced the reverend's wife.

Gladys stepped to the mic, her face a mask of serene piety. "Good morning, my dear friends. Just last week, my husband and I were the unfortunate recipients of a disturbing report. It was a tale no parent wants to hear. Our poor son Stuart barely escaped the talons of this wicked witch, thanks to his inability to maintain an erection. She did everything she could to seduce Stuart, to stoke his manhood. But thanks to his deep devotion, Stuart was able to remain flaccid and thus survived her siren song.

"The seduction of our men by Jezebels like Ms. Clarion is an ever-growing threat. But I have faith that with prayer, the men of Arbor—and all men throughout this great state—will be able to overcome these temptresses just as my son has."

The crowd's hysterical peals of laughter drowned out my own gagging disgust at having the horrific incident she referenced so nauseatingly misrepresented. The *real* truth behind Gladys's tale was simple. Stuart had assaulted me. I'd given him no encouragement, no reason to believe I was interested. I hadn't been intoxicated in any way. I could say I wasn't dressed provocatively, but my view of what was and was not risqué vastly differed from that of most people in town. None of the callous excuses so many use to blame victims of sexual assault could be applied. Stuart cornered me, backed me against a wall. He crushed me, grinding his skeletal frame against my body. He forced his hands up my shirt and groped my breasts. His rancid, panting breath clogged my nose.

No intrinsic powers came to my aid. No magic saved me. At that moment, I wasn't a witch. I was just a woman, shocked immobile. My brain shut down. The fact that Stuart had no opportunity to continue was only due to Gladys arriving on the scene. Stuart cursed me and pushed away quickly as if I'd been the one on the attack. But before he fell dutifully in line behind his mother, he had vowed to finish what he'd begun.

Mayor Crandall again took the mic. "Thanks to the good Lord, Gladys's son was saved from the town slut, unlike so many others. And thanks to the good Lord, she doesn't have to be shackled with the knowledge that *that* piece of trash soiled her sweet boy."

Some in the crowd shouted, "Praised be!" But others seemed deeply disturbed by the mayor's blunt accusations. Her words smacked of bitterness, considering the locals all knew her son Jay and I had once been a couple.

How long will it take that little nugget to find its way to the press?

"So, you see, there is the truth of it," the mayor announced as if she'd bleached away the newspaper's headline—and its backlash. "I have no doubt the press will be diligent in rectifying these onerous falsehoods. I thank you for allowing me the opportunity to set the record straight. Now, all that remains to be said is...vote Crandall!"

There was no way in hell I could allow those women to twist my assault into a tool to tear me down. I couldn't let them humiliate me in public—and to the press!—without repercussion. I flicked my wrists discreetly and whipped the light summer breeze into a torrent. Aiming the gust with pointed fingers, I sent the whistling wind sweeping toward them. Gladys's enormous floppy hat lifted off her head. She tried in vain to catch it as it skipped along down the rows of tables. Mayor Crandall's political propaganda flew from her fingertips. The banners blew away. Her bumper stickers and campaign buttons scattered and were trampled by the bustling market crowd. But when the mayor's skirt caught the wind's upward draft, wrapped around her face, and flashed her granny panties, my revenge was complete and satisfying. And the cameras caught it all.

The press is going to have a field day with those shots. I knew it was an inappropriate use of my magic, but I felt, naively, that it was worth the risk.

Not wanting to attract any additional embarrassing attention, the mayor waited until the press and snickering spectators moved on before berating me.

"You think you're so damn cute, don't you, Ms. Clarion? Your wicked behavior and flagrant disregard for propriety demonstrate precisely what is wrong with society today," she ranted. "Well, I've had it with your games. I refuse to put up with your tricks while I'm in the middle of a campaign. I will not permit my agenda to be derailed by the very evils I'm fighting against parading right under my nose. If that Sapphic heathen you call a *goddess*-mother is unable to rein you in, I will be forced to take action myself. For once, do what's right and stay the hell out of my way."

"I have no idea what you're talking about, mayor," I said with a straight face.

"Don't play coy with me," she scowled.

"Are you accusing me of manipulating the wind? I wasn't aware that you believed in magic, Mayor. I'm sure that's something the voters would love to know."

I smiled as she squirmed. The ridicule that would bloom in the wake of such an accusation would forever remove her name as a serious candidate for any office. And she knew it.

"Don't push me, missy."

"Just for you, and for the sake of your campaign, of course, I'll keep my shenanigans to a minimum."

Crandall stormed away with her head high and a simpering grin plastered from ear to ear. I marveled at her ability to go from fire-breather to people-pleaser in two seconds flat.

Thankfully, once the mayor took off, the day passed at a quick clip. The steady flow of customers either didn't know or didn't care that I was the witch the mayor had just railed against. They bought most of the dried lavender and honey, as well as a few of my pieces, including two small oil paintings.

Adelaide stopped by, and it relieved me to see her out and about and up to no good. As always, she boisterously admired my creations for all the market to hear. She made sure any and all passersby knew just how spectacular she thought my creations truly were. She was particularly drawn to a thick violet shawl and insisted on paying me more than it was worth. Adelaide owned more of my creations than I did. She was my biggest fan.

She expressed her opinions about the spectacle I'd caused with equal sauce, although she turned down the volume. A bit.

"I enjoyed your work with Doreen and Gladys. Impressive nature manipulation, and so inconspicuous. I wouldn't have known you had a hand in it if I wasn't so terribly clever. Next time, I'd go for the full monty with the mayor, if I were you. No one in their right mind would elect someone so incredibly droopy."

"Adelaide!"

"Oh, don't pretend to be so missish. You know it's the truth. And that malicious old bag has it coming to her. I'd have done her in myself long ago if I wasn't so content with my idleness. I mean, seriously, who has the time or the muscle to hide a body these days? Not to mention the fact that Magdalena would be heartily disappointed in me. For some reason, she thinks I'm a good person. I'd hate to disavow her of that belief."

"Oh, Adelaide..."

"Oh no you don't. Don't you 'Oh, Adelaide' me. At my age, I can't afford *not* to say what's on my mind. Neither can you, for that matter." She smiled kindly. "I hope you're not overly offended by the mayor's libelous tirade. Not that I'm defending her, but I do understand her motives."

"You do? Because I sure as hell don't."

"Come now, think. That nasty headline and photo splashed across the news this morning undermined the mayor's ambitions. You and I know damn well none of it was your fault, but she needed a scapegoat to deflect attention away from herself. And you, my dear, are an easy target."

"I see your point."

"And let me give you one last piece of unsolicited advice. From now on, you stay as far away from the Crandalls and Cudlows as possible. They've made you their patsy, and they'll continue to do so if you give them a shred of ammunition."

"I have no trouble making that promise."

"Just keep it."

"I will," I vowed.

"Fine. Fine. Just fine."

"Mmm, honey," a male voice said behind me.

I couldn't stand that men thought they could call you whatever pet name popped into their heads when they caught a glimpse of a nice ass or a little cleavage. "What the hell did you say?" I snapped as I rounded to face the offender. "Dear Goddess..."

Even Adelaide was struck dumb by the Adonis who stood before my booth. Draped in the scent of leather and sandalwood, he had me salivating. The dangerously stunning creature loomed over me at an easy six foot. His dark, hooded eyes captivated me from behind the chestnut waves that licked his jawline.

Oh, to be a lock of hair... I thought I'd spoken to myself.

When his eyes widened suddenly, however, I realized I must have spoken my private thoughts aloud. A knowing smirk overtook the corners of his mouth, adding mischief to his already striking features. There was an ease about him, a simplicity in his stance, a quiet confidence that could only be described as cool. A simple white tee showed off the strength of his arms and stomach. Baggy cargo shorts fell low on his hips. My fingers itched to touch the scruff along his cheeks and chin. And he was barefoot, which I found sexy as hell. They didn't grow males like this in Arbor. I was shamelessly enthralled.

He was fully aware that I was checking him out and reciprocated in kind. Smiling softly, he held up a jar.

"Honey."

"Yes, dear?" I answered in an attempt at levity.

My snark earned me a grin so hungry it threatened to drop me to my knees. A deep, churning energy radiated from him; enveloping me as if he'd cast a spell. A light breeze could've tipped me over.

"Oh, yes. You'll do just fine," Adelaide whispered on a sigh.

"What's that?" he asked.

"Where have you been all my life?" Adelaide fawned, batting her mascara lashes and leaning on a popped hip.

"New Jersey, ma'am. Princeton, to be exact. It's a pleasure meeting you. I'm Alexander Morgan, and you are?"

"Smitten." Adelaide held out her hand, which he kissed. "Morgan, you say?"

"Yes, ma'am."

"You're Old Man Cain's great-grandson," she said.

"I am, yes. Did you know him?" Alexander's face lit with boyish joy at the mention of his great-grandfather.

"Yes, knew him well. I liked the crazy buzzard tremendously. Cain was a close friend, and I mourned his passing. I was disappointed to hear he hadn't wanted a service of any kind, but I drank to his memory nonetheless."

"Thank you, ma'am. That means a great deal." Alexander nodded in momentary reverence, his faraway expression like a snapshot in time. "I'm here in Arbor to settle my great-grandfather's estate. It's an unhappy undertaking, but I'm duty bound to attend to the task to the best of my ability."

His words were solemn and genteel, displaying the dignified manners of the highborn. But he no longer addressed Adelaide. He'd turned his gaze to me, and a question burned within his eyes.

"Anywho, I'd better be setting off. Have a pleasant afternoon, you two," Adelaide waved goodbye, though she barely registered in my view.

"I know you," Alexander said, his voice low, almost a whisper. "We've never met, but I can't shake this feeling…"

"I don't know you." I lowered my eyes to hide my lie. I didn't remember meeting him, but somehow, I recognized his face, his spirit. *Impossible. No one could forget a man like this.*

"Did you want… Did you have…" My vocal cords momentarily failed me. I gave a loud, honking cough to clear my throat, then gestured to the jar of honey in his hand. "Would you like some honey?"

"Most definitely. But is it any good?" he asked, his mien playful and predatory at once.

"The sweetest nectar you'll ever taste." The words trickled from my lips.

"I'll take two jars, then. And your name, if you have a mind to get to know me," he challenged with a cocked brow.

"Hhm? What? Oh! Yes, yes of course," I stammered. "Two jars will be eight dollars." I was compelled to look away—to break the spell and collect my thoughts. "And my name's Evangeline. You can call me Eva."

"It's a great pleasure meeting you, Evangeline. I look forward to tasting your honey. Shit! Sorry, that's not what I…" He shook his head. "I just meant, thanks for the honey."

I laughed lightly, and he responded with his own Hollywood grin.

Money changed hands, and he turned to leave. After only a few steps, he looked back.

"We *will* see each other soon," he said with a wink, before getting swallowed up by the market crowd.

Great Goddess above! Now that's the kind of man that makes me believe the Creator of All Things is a female. Only a woman could create such a perfect specimen.

Chapter Four

As I closed up shop for the day, my mind lingered over the mysterious, virile Alexander. Distracted, I lugged the remaining stock onto the flatbed of my truck. Turning abruptly to grab another box, I slammed into a redheaded beanpole. Stuart Cudlow glared down at me from a freakish height.

From within my mind, I heard Rocky. *"I'm just above you in the trees. Be careful! He's not here for pleasantries."*

"Don't worry. I'll be fine," I tried to reassure him. And myself.

"Can I help you with something, Stuart? Maybe interest you in a shawl? It's gotta get cold way up there," I asked with a saccharine smile.

Neither my grin nor my hubris lasted long. Stuart dragged me by the arm to the side of my truck, shielding us from the view of any lingering market staff. I tried belting out a scream, but he slapped his hand over my mouth.

"Evangeline! Let me help you!" Rocky called to me.

"No! I can handle this."

"You're not getting away this time. It's my turn for a taste. Everybody else had some."

"I'm not an all-you-can-eat buffet, you jackass," I mumbled from behind his hand just before I bit down on his fingers.

"You fucking bitch," he cried, spittle flinging from his lips. He yanked his hand back in pain.

I tried to run, but he was too fast. He grabbed me by the hair, wound it in his fist, and pulled me in close. His eyes darted around, nervous, frenzied. When he'd reassured himself of our seclusion, he slapped me so hard that pops of bright light burst behind my eye leaving me temporarily blind. My teeth crunched together—bone crunching against bone. I let loose a soul-shattering scream.

He slapped me again. "I said be quiet, you goddamn tease. Thanks to you, Crandall and my fucking mother told the world I can't get it up." Stuart threw me against my truck. He grabbed my hand and pressed it onto his erection. "Oh, but I can, and you're going to feel every inch." He took both my wrists in one hand and held me in place. With his other hand, he felt me up, digging his fingers into my skin. He pressed his greasy face into my neck. His fetid breath assaulted me. My stomach heaved violently, and I gagged on the bile that rose in my throat.

"It's okay, my little slut. I'm gonna give you what you want," he spoke, almost gently, into my ear. He reached under my sundress and ran his hand between my thighs. A shudder rocked through him as if he was ejaculating.

I was happy about one thing. My mind hadn't shut down this time. Before his hand could move any higher, I tried to knee him in the groin. I missed my target, but I did manage to get him to step back.

I watched Rocky dive onto a lower branch. *"Stay where you are. I've got this."*

"No, you don't," he replied, and ignoring my directive, the hawk swooped down. He pecked and clawed at Stuart. It seemed for a moment that Rocky was gaining ground until Stuart's fist landed a shot to Rocky's head. I felt my familiar's pain within my own head and buckled over.

"Rocky!" I screamed.

"I'll survive, but I'm hurt. I must retreat. I'm sorry I've failed you."

He took off before I could reply.

I thought for a second about using my powers, but I nixed the idea. There was no way I could control myself. It would be too hard to explain how Stuart ended up in a tree, twisted like a goddamn pretzel. But that didn't mean I couldn't keep fighting back.

As I shifted into full-on defense mode, Stuart was thrown aside. Powerful arms lifted me into the air, cradling me. It was Alexander, and he was pissed. He moved with speed, depositing me in the back seat of some swanky luxury vehicle. He crouched down and assessed me for injury. Momentarily satisfied, he stormed off toward the deer-in-headlights degenerate dirtbag. Stuart scrambled to his feet but froze as Alexander let one brutal right hook fly. Stuart dropped again. Alexander grabbed him by his prematurely thinning ginger hair and growled into his ear. Although I couldn't hear a word, Stuart's petrified face, splattered in blood, and the piss that pooled around him told me all I needed to know. Once Alexander stepped back, Stuart took off running.

My defender was before me in a flash, again examining me for signs of distress. The primary object of his inspection, however, turned out to be my breasts. Sweat had made the top of my sundress almost completely transparent. In one fluid motion, he pulled his T-shirt off and yanked it over my head.

"For God sakes, you've got to cover yourself better," he growled.

I shrunk back at the severity of his tone.

"You're too tempting. Foolish boys don't know how to control themselves around a creature like you," he snarled. "Or foolish men," he added under his breath.

"Excuse me, but it's not up to me, or any female, to temper their behavior or adjust the way they dress because assholes like that can't control their hormones," I snapped. "What a crock. And, for the record, I didn't ask for your help."

"Just tell me you're okay. Tell me he didn't hurt you too badly," Alexander demanded, though with a gentler voice. His face contorted, twisting between fury and frustration. The back of his hand grazed my cheek.

I cringed as he brushed the impact spots of the slaps I'd taken. "I'll live. It's not the first time. I doubt it'll be the last."

"I'm sorry," he said on a breath. Clasping my wrists carefully, he rotated my hands and skimmed his fingers down my arms. A shiver ran through me, but there was no lust in his looks. "Nothing seems broken, and I don't see any blood. Are you in much pain?"

Whether mesmerized by his expression of tenderness and sincerity or deluded by naive romantic notions, I reached out and laid my hand against his cheek. "Don't worry. I'm okay, now anyway. I guess you're my hero."

He leaned into my touch, and his eyelids fell shut. "I'm no hero, Evangeline." My name a caress upon his lips. "But I must ensure your safety, make sure you're all right. Can I drive you home?"

The gentle ferocity with which he spoke almost brought me to tears. "No, I really am fine, just exhausted." The gravity of the day had weakened my knees in earnest.

"Allow me to escort you to your car, then?"

"Yes, thank you."

Alexander placed a large, capable hand at the small of my back. Another shiver radiated through me, making me drop my keys. He tried to hide a grin, obviously amused he could so easily affect me. I didn't find it amusing at all. It freaked me out. We walked together the last few yards, and taking my hand, he helped me into my truck. But he didn't let go. Instead, he dropped his gaze to our hands intertwined. He traced each of my fingers, pausing at every knuckle. When he finally looked up, the riot of emotions that warred within him etched into the sharp angles of his face. He cleared his throat, kissed the back of my hand, and closed my door.

I steeled my expression before leaning out of the window to face him. "Thank you. You know, I was about to kick the crap out of that son of a bitch, before your serendipitous arrival. I'm perfectly capable of taking care of myself."

"I have no doubt."

As soon as I got home, I called out to Shasta and Rocky. I found them in the forest beside the cottage. We rested our spirits together within the womb of the woods. I cradled Rocky as Shasta cradled me, and they helped calm my violent heart. Although my Rocky sustained no lingering injury, I was a long way from whole.

"Go inside and take care of yourself, dearie," Shasta said. *"I'll look after Rocky."*

A scalding hot shower became step number one in removing the noxious remains of Stuart's assault. There were shelves of plush towels, loofahs, scrubbers, and all manner of soaps and sweet smelling oils beside the tub. I figured I'd need all of them if I was ever to be clean again. I could still feel Stuart's hands on me. His sweat clung to my thighs, and I scrubbed them until they flamed red and raw. I scoured the grease from his face off my neck. I disinfected every curve and crevice, every inch of skin. Yet, even then, the foul stench of his breath lingered in my nose.

It wasn't only my body that needed cleansing. My spirit needed purification. What Stuart had done to me, coupled with the lies and never-ending insults hurled at me from every corner of Arbor, caused such anger to flame within my belly and blood I was sure it would consume me.

Still naked, I sat in the tub and let it fill with clean water. Using a smoldering white-sage smudge stick, I blessed myself with its smoke. Then, while scooping the water over my arms and legs, I spoke.

> "I am a woman created in the likeness of the Goddess.
> I am powerful in the face of torment.
> My flesh and my spirit have been desecrated, but I will thrive.
> I will ascend from the ash as a phoenix.
> I purify myself, cleansing away all sorrow and fear.
> I purify myself, cleansing away all negativity.
> I will ascend wiser, more courageous, fierce, and resilient.
> I am a woman created in the likeness of the Goddess.
> The power within me is my own.
> I am whole."

Halfway through the spell, my tears gave way. But by the end, the strength of the Goddess within me overcame my sorrow. I was replenished, refreshed.

I'd just finished dressing when the unmistakable pungent smell of garlic beckoned me to the dining room. Bowls filled to overflowing with pasta and sauce, a garden salad, and the garlic bread filled the center of the table.

"I thought some comfort food was in order," Maggie said as she poured us each a glass of Montepulciano d'Abruzzo—my favorite Italian red.

"But before we eat, let me take a look at that cheek of yours," Maggie said with a small basket of medicinal odds and ends in her hands. She dipped a warm cloth into a tincture of calendula leaves and dabbed it onto my cheek while muttering an incantation under her breath. I could feel the bruised muscle healing the instant the cloth touched my skin. After a few minutes of her ministrations, the last of my lingering pain dissipated.

Once we gave thanks to the Goddess for her many blessings, we dug into our meal and I rehashed my day with Maggie as we ate.

She scolded me for abusing my abilities against Gladys and Mayor Crandall. "Oh, yes, I heard all about your little display from Adelaide. She thought it was fabulous. But you know the Law of Three. I've warned you a million times against letting folks rile you up and lashing out against them. That was incredibly foolish, however provoked you may have been. I know they're hateful people. I know they skewered you. That's still no excuse for your irresponsible behavior. The power you have requires discipline. You know this."

I wanted to argue. I wanted to explain that I'd grown tired of their lies, but she was right about the foolishness of flaunting my magic. I hung my head.

"How are you feeling about what happened with Stuart?"

I shrugged and stared down at my hands clasped in my lap.

"This is the second time he's put his hands on you. I'd like you to seriously consider pressing charges. I can't stand that some men walk around as if females should be at their beck and call, thinking they can sample whatever tidbit strikes their fancy. Disgusting." Maggie was livid. Her anger pulsed in waves from within her. "Stuart deserves any and all punishment the Goddess sees fit to bestow, but that doesn't mean he can't also face justice of a more corporeal nature. You say the word, and I'll have him brought up on charges by morning."

Maggie had a gentle, loving spirit, but by no means was she weak. This incident amplified the warrior within her. She'd protect me with all the ferocity of a swarm of angry bees, literally if necessary.

"Thank you, but no. The last thing I want to do is explain over and over in excruciating detail what that pig did to me. And I'd have to explain it to people who already hate me. They're more likely to turn it around against me than punish Stuart. And I guarantee it would end up in the press. I don't think I can handle that. I don't want to handle that."

"Chief Harrison doesn't hate us. He's a good man. He'd listen." A shadow of sadness marked her kind face. "But I understand. I'm going to take your lead on this. The moment you change your mind, though, I'm all over it."

"Thank you." I raised my head and captured the steel of Maggie's gaze. "I may not want to go to the police about Stuart, but that doesn't mean I'm going to sit on my hands. I'm not letting this go. I don't believe the Goddess would deny me justice." I was confident in my faithfulness. "Would you help me with a bit of spellwork?"

"Of course. I can give Adelaide a ring if you'd like. If she's free to lend a hand, her power will amplify the spell."

"Please. I'll get things set up outside. You two can meet me there."

The moon was waning. It would be another three nights before the dark moon; a perfect time for hexing. I brought out a large canvas bag I kept stocked with candles, oils, and other magical paraphernalia and spellwork sundries. Calling out to Shasta and Rocky, I asked them to join me as I set up our stone altar. Cleansing the space was my first task. With my besom broom, I swept away any negative energies. It was a traditional besom, made with birch twigs for the brush, ash for the handle, and willow for the bindings. When the space was cleansed, I laid out the ritual tools facing north. My chalice took up the top left corner, while white sage sat at the top right. Through the center of the altar, I placed a bell, a bowl of salt, a beeswax altar candle, and my athame.

Just as I completed my task, Maggie and Adelaide arrived with their familiars. Hanna the queen bee buzzed around Maggie's head, while Fledermaus the bat sat stoically upon Adelaide's shoulder.

Until, that is, Adelaide traipsed dramatically toward me, bellowing, "Evangeline! My dear, sweet thing, I have come to aid you in your time of distress!" Fledermaus flapped, fitful, into the air.

Adelaide hugged me quickly, and got down to the heart of the matter. "So, Stuart Cudlow strikes again, does he? Well, we can't allow him to make this a habit. That little pissant thinks he's the bee's knees. Let's disavow him of that belief, shall we?"

Adelaide took the altar bell in hand and rang it thrice from the north, east, south, and west points. Magdalena then took the bowl of salt and poured a thick circle around us and the altar. I used the athame to draw a circle in the dirt within the salt line. Together, we lit the altar candle.

Then Adelaide, Maggie, and I joined hands and spoke as one.

> "We are maiden, mother, crone,
> Magic forged in blood and bone.
> Hear us, Goddess, on this night
> Help us to set wrongs to right."

Adelaide handed me a fat, black candle and a silver pen.

"Around the tip of the candle, write the offender's name. Write along the candle's sides the nature of the justice to be served and then speak your will," Adelaide instructed.

After I wrote the spell on the candle's side, I spoke in a confident voice.

> "What is not yours, you shall not touch,
> Or rely you will upon a crutch.
> No longer may you violate,
> Or draw a most unpleasant fate.
> The rod that has led you astray
> Will fail you 'til your dying day—
> If with unwelcome hands you take,
> Fulfillment of this spell you make."

Maggie sighed. "Well done, my dear."

"Ha! Excellent!" Adelaide boomed, clapping her hands together. "Continue."

I anointed the black candle with oil and placed it in the center of the altar. Maggie and Adelaide lit incense and two white candles, which they placed on either side.

As I lit my candle, I spoke.

"In the name of the Goddess
Who holds the keys of life and death,
Let this man be caught by his own foolishness,
By his ego,
By his evil.
By the Law of Three Times Three,
As I will it, so mote it be!"

Flanked by our familiars, we sat before the altar in silence until the black candle burned down to nothing. I gathered up the beeswax and ash, the remains of the spell. Then my goddess-mother, high priestess, the familiars and I turned as one, and walked to the cottage. No one dared look back, lest the spell backfire and rebound.

After saying goodbye to Adelaide, I intended to go right to bed, but Maggie wasn't quite finished with me yet.

"I found a large men's T-shirt in the laundry. I wondered if you could tell me to whom it belongs." Maggie wiggled her eyebrows as she dangled the shirt from her fingertips.

Despite the darkness of the night, I lit up at the mention of the T-shirt's owner. Overwhelming feelings for this man—that I'd known all of fifteen minutes—rampaged my heart and brain and motor functions. I stuttered for a beat, unable to form anything resembling a coherent reply.

"It belongs to Alexander Morgan," I said finally, looking anywhere but at Maggie.

"And how did it find itself in our laundry?" she asked with a sternness that stood at odds with the pleasant astonishment glowing from within her.

"He took it off and gave it to me to cover up after my run in with Stuart." I chanced a peek, only to find Maggie wearing the kind of sly expression more frequently seen on Adelaide.

As it happened, she knew a lot more about my knight in bare feet than I did. Maggie's engaging bedside manner encouraged an easy rapport with her patients, so she was as in the loop as a barber or bartender. She wasn't a gossip by nature, but this news was too fascinating to pass up.

"The entirety of Cain Morgan's fortune, estate, and assets settled on his eldest male heir, in fact his only heir, Alexander! His father and grandfather would have inherited, but they both passed last year. And Cain's estate settled fast for one so massive. Apparently, Alexander is one hell of a businessman. He made quite the impression downtown, and not just with the ladies."

I cringed reflexively at the thought.

"Everyone's going on about how bright and sharp and in charge he seems," she continued. "Not even thirty and taking the reins of a billion-dollar estate."

"Wow."

"Yeah. Wow." She paused, and we each drifted away in our own thoughts for a few moments. "I wonder if he plans to live at Morgan Manor or sell off the property. I heard Cain dismissed all but three of the staff over the course of the last few years. Two of them have lived and worked at the manor since they were kids. If he sells, they'll lose their homes and their jobs."

"Then he should be persuaded to take ownership of the manor. I wouldn't want to see loyal staff thrown out with nothing." A wicked thought crept into my brain, and a sly smile played upon my lips. "I, for one, am not at all opposed to having Mr. Alexander Morgan as a new neighbor. Not one little bit."

Before collapsing into bed, I sent out a group message to the boys: *Missing my henchmen. AMM and their spawn have been busy. Need brotherly advice. Xoxo*

Within minutes, Ethan, Gregory, Nicolae, and Luca all messaged back with their love and promises to help. And each confirmed they wouldn't return to Arbor until the Midsummer Litha celebration. We'd keep in touch, but it would be a few weeks before I could see my boys.

Chapter Five

Tuesday

By the time the sun cracked the horizon, I felt like death warmed up. "Ain't no rest for the wicked," I sang in a grumble as the lifesaving aroma of good coffee lured me, zombielike, onto the patio. My brain still muddled by sleep, I rubbed my swollen eyes and scratched at the messy bun twisted atop my head.

Shielded behind bowls of berries and baskets of homemade muffins, Maggie sipped a glass of orange juice and scowled at her newspaper. She peeked over *The Messenger* at my approach and immediately brightened. Backlit in beams of sunlight, she was resplendent. Her hair danced wild as a lion's mane. With rosy cheeks and glittering eyes, Maggie's face required no artificial enhancement. Silver and stones, however, adorned her ears, neck, wrists, and fingers. I was amazed at her ability to function with all the jingling and jangling. And how that woman could accomplish all she did before seven a.m. was magic I'd yet to fathom.

"Morning," I mumbled, plopping onto the plump, floral cushion tied to the wrought-iron chair. "I don't want to adult today."

"It's a good thing I've got you covered." Maggie smirked from behind the lowered newspaper. "I switched a few patient appointments...so I'm working for you at the market. At least for the next couple days."

I sat bolt upright. "No, Mags. You have enough on your plate. Seriously."

"Trust me. I got this. Take some Eva time. *Seriously*," she teased. "I know you're tough, but with everything that's happening...you need time to process. Your spells and blessings will go a long way in mending your spirit. But you still need to take a step back. Breathe. Okay?"

I hated the thought of her taking on the added burden, but the market was the last place I want to be. "Thank you. Love you."

"Love you, too. Oh, Rocky and Shasta asked me to tell you they're hunting. They'll be gone most of the day."

"I was wondering where they were. Last night's ritual took a lot out of them. I'm glad they're fueling up."

"You need to do the same," Maggie said and poured me a cup of coffee—fixing it just how I like. She made me a plate of strawberries and a blueberry muffin with jam. Then she settled into her chair, took a sip of coffee, and tucked back into her newspaper.

I tucked into my breakfast.

"Still no rain forecasted this week," Maggie said from behind the spread pages.

"Gladys and the garden club must be in a tizzy," I garbled with my mouth full.

"They're not the only ones. The whole town's buzzing about the drought."

"Something else for them to blame on us."

"I, ah, I may as well show you the front page," Maggie said warily.

"Great. Peachy. Lay it on me."

CRANDALL & CRONY SWEPT AWAY WITH WITCH HUNT

The photo accompanying the headline depicted a panic-stricken Gladys attempting to catch her errant hat, while the mayor's undergarments flashed the crowd.

"This isn't going to go over well," I said.

"No, it's not. All the more reason I should be the one at the market. The last thing we need is for Mayor Crandall to confront you again—or the press for that matter."

We both cringed at the thought.

"Now that you have the day free, what are your plans?" she asked, moving on to more pleasant topics.

"I think I'll head out to paint. Maybe set up by the stream and let the water inspire me."

"Excellent."

Half an hour later, Maggie tossed her bag into her vintage light-blue Bug. Boxes of inventory, packed to the roof, weighed down the vehicle so much that the body almost scraped the driveway. She drove off in a joyful whirlwind, rocks and dirt kicking up in her wake.

I decided since I was indulging in Eva time, that a good dose of pampering was the best way to kick-start the day. I soaked in a milk bath and gave myself a facial. After shaving and lotioning my legs, I repainted my finger- and toenails a lovely shade of black. A touch of light makeup was sufficient for a day off. My hair fell in low pigtail braids. Finally, I threw on a pair of cut-off jean shorts and a black tank: no bra, no panties, and no shoes—my usual when at home.

Rummaging through the gallery, I gathered up my paints and brushes, easel and pallet. I lugged everything outside and across the lawn. The ideal position for my canvas had both the stream and forest in view. Before settling into my work, I slid my feet into the stream's cool waters. The wind began to swirl, creating ripples in the stream. I focused my energy. With no more than my will and the point of a finger, I lifted the ripples from their watery bed and churned them into mini cyclones. Wispy, white butterflies flitted like fairies to investigate the phenomenon. When my magic ceased, my winged friends splashed me with the swirling water. I couldn't stop a wild cackle from erupting. It felt amazing to laugh, to let the world fall away, even for a moment.

Centered and refreshed, I settled into my work. It wasn't long before I lost myself in the images I created. The stream acted as both muse and soundtrack, with the cascading waters gurgling over and around rocks. My canvas danced in shades of sapphire and jade. Never a neat freak, globs of paint found themselves on my cheeks, arms, legs, and clothes. My painting took on a frenzied and intense edge as the magic of the waters and mystery of the forest emerged from each brush stroke.

Hours passed. As the sun made its way across the sky, the shadows of the wood shifted, casting a veil over me. Stepping back from the canvas, I analyzed what I'd accomplished with a critical eye. It was good, really good. I couldn't remember ever painting anything so vibrant and rich, yet haunting. A loud rumbling in my stomach interrupted the self-critique and informed me that I'd missed lunch—by a mile. It was time to pack up and head back to the cottage.

Preoccupied with hauling my easel, paints, brushes, and wet canvas, I didn't notice the black Bentley parked in the driveway. Until, that is, I smacked full force into its fender with my knee. I buckled over in pain and landed on my ass. The load I was juggling scattered. I clutched my bleeding knee and channeled a drunken sailor.

"Goddamn, fuck, son of a bitch, motherfucker that hurts!"

Maggie arrived by my side in an instant.

"When did you get home?" I asked, struck by her sudden appearance.

She pecked a tiny kiss on my head as if caring for a child. "I've been home for half an hour. It's almost six. I guess you've been out there all day?"

"Yeah, actually." I shook my head to clear the fog. *How the hell have I been outside for so long without realizing it?*

Maggie set to work on the nasty gash on my knee. Magically, she had all the supplies needed to care for my wound at hand. With a cotton ball dipped in a blend of water and tea tree and lavender oils, she dabbed at the wound and cleansed the area of blood and dirt. She crinkled up a fresh yarrow root and pressed it into the injury. She accomplished all this while muttering incantations under her breath.

I looked around for my painting and discovered it lying face-up about fifteen feet away. It didn't seem to be damaged, thank the Goddess. As a matter of fact, it was tremendous; probably the best work I'd ever done. But my pleasure with the end product did nothing to ease my wariness. Somehow, I'd painted nonstop without food, drink, or bathroom breaks for over eight hours. I was good, but I'd never been that good.

My heart rate had just returned to a steady, even rhythm. Then I saw him, and it amped back up again. Alexander leaned against the fallen oak tree that marked the main footpath through the forest. Although his arms crossed casually, his anxious expression betrayed him. There was no denying the intensity in his eyes. He was worried about me. Again. He caught me staring and shot me an apologetic grin. I was mortified. Paint, sweat, and blood covered me. My hair shot out wildly from messy braids, and I was practically drooling at the sight of him. For Goddess's sake, I was sitting in the dirt, getting patched up because my knee busted his Bentley.

I'm such an ass.

Maggie's head popped up. "Right as rain," she announced with gusto. She leaned down, wound an arm around my back, and tried to help me up.

The moment I straightened my leg, a sharp pain shot through my knee. Cringing, I cursed again.

Alexander appeared like a bolt of lightning, whisking me into his arms. "I've got you."

"What are you doing here?" I blurted.

"You know I could drop your little ass...but I'd rather hold on to you for a while longer," he said with a wink. He carried me into the cottage and scanned the gallery for a spot to place me.

Maggie arrived to clear off a chair, and Alexander lowered me into it. The shuffling of sheet music revealed an ottoman, which he placed under my legs and feet. He jogged outside to collect my art supplies. When he returned and plopped them into a corner, I noticed he still held my painting.

"This is outstanding, truly inspired work," Alexander said with awe setting his face aglow. He placed it carefully on the coffee table and knelt by my side.

"Thank you," I said, my chest puffing with pride. "You, ah, you never answered my question. What are you doing here?"

"I wanted to see you... how you're recovering from yesterday. But now I've hurt you. I'm so sorry." His gaze slid up from my bare toes, over my smooth calves, and lingered on the knee that only minutes before had been cut and bleeding. It now showed only the faintest hint of an injury.

Maggie's flare for just such remedies was what made her so popular—and notorious—in town.

"It's not your fault. I wasn't paying attention. And I'm pretty sure I broke your car. I should be the one apologizing," I said, hoping to relieve his concern and deflect his confusion about my speedy recovery.

"No. It's only a car. But you...I can't get you—what happened to you, that is—out of my mind. I can't imagine what you must be going through. How are you feeling?" He inched closer.

"I'm okay," I said softly; his nearness drawing me in, ensnaring me. "Were you watching me paint?"

"Yes."

"For how long?"

"About an hour. I didn't want to disturb you. You were in the zone."

"What did I look...did I...was I..."

"Magnificent," he breathed as his gaze made its way from my knee up to my thighs splattered with paint and landed on a spot where my cut-off shorts gaped just enough to reveal nothing underneath. A serious blush rushed into his cheeks, and his head snapped up. Directly at his eye level, my breasts heaved. A light sheen of sweat broke out across his forehead.

I hadn't noticed that he still held my hand until his thumb began rubbing circles into my palm. The motion shot a jolt of pleasure to my core. I got hot fast and squeezed my thighs together to relieve the ache.

Recognizing my response to his touch, Alexander's eyes flashed, his pulse surged, and a ravenous growl vibrated through him. "Would it be out of line... Is it too soon to ask...would you join me for dinner? Tonight? Soon?" he asked, his voice thick and scarcely audible.

"I'd love to," I said on an exhaled breath.

His eyes lit up at my reply. "I'll be back at seven thirty to pick you up."

Then, with a sultry smile and a stiff nod, he left.

"Well, isn't he sex on a stick," Maggie said as she peeked her head around the corner where she'd been hiding.

"Quite," I muttered, still overwhelmed by the encounter.

Just then, my stomach grumbled—again. Maggie and I looked to each other and fell into a fit of the giggles.

"Okay, okay. Rest up a bit. I'll whip you up a snack. You're going to need your strength for your date." Maggie winked as she left for the kitchen.

Closing my eyes, I tipped back my head and took a deep breath. I could hardly believe I was going to dinner with this otherworldly creature.

Sudden panic shot through me. *Dear Goddess, what am I going to wear?*

Chapter Six

By seven twenty-five, I was scrubbed, buffed, and beautified. My dark hair hung loose around my shoulders and down my back. I wore my makeup heavier than usual, accentuating my wide green eyes and plump lips. My pale-pink sheath dress skimmed the middle of my thighs. Rose quartz decorated my ears, wrists, and fingers; the quartz opening the heart and inviting love. But the three-inch oval amethyst that hung from a delicate silver chain around my neck—my birthday gift from Adelaide—was the true highlight. Like the quartz, it too drew love.

I felt incredible. It wasn't just the work of the stones or because I looked damn good. Energy surged through my veins, and I knew my powers were intensifying. Events were shifting into place. I was where I needed to be. I could feel it.

"Thanks for your help, Mags," I said and kissed her on the cheek.

"Oh, my darling, my genes didn't create this exquisite vision." She sighed. "You've grown into a beautiful woman, inside and out. Your mother would be so proud of you. I know I am."

Maggie's gushing was cut short by a knock at the door. She gave my shoulders an encouraging squeeze, and I braced myself as she welcomed my date.

Nothing could have prepared me, however, for the enticing man that entered. With the scent of leather and sandalwood preceding him, Alexander arrived with a cheeky smile and a roguish twinkle in his eye.

He's up to something. "You're punctual."

"I'm smitten." He beamed, mimicking the words Adelaide had spoken the day we first met.

Maybe it was the confidence he projected, but Alexander seemed taller than I remembered, despite the fact that I had on heels. He had every reason for confidence. His jeans hugged him just right, and his white button-down dress shirt was left untucked with the top two buttons undone and his sleeves rolled up. He hadn't bothered with a razor, and his dark hair fell in waves, still damp from a shower. He was positively elysian.

An inescapable desire to feel him, to taste him rocketed through me. I moved until I stood within an inch of his chest. Balancing on my toes, I ran my fingers through his hair and guided him to my mouth. There was no hesitation in the kiss. It was a delicious blend of hard and soft and was frustratingly brief.

My actions were brazen, and the look he gave in response was not meant for polite company. "What was that for?"

"For saving me yesterday. For helping me today. And because I wanted to kiss you."

Humor lit his dark eyes. "Do you always do whatever you want?"

"Usually."

He smiled and stepped back to take me all in. "You're breathtaking."

"You look rather fetching yourself," I said with cheek.

Without warning, Alexander fell to his knees before me. With a hesitant gentleness, he brushed his knuckles across my knee where less than two hours before a deep gash had marred my skin. No sign of injury remained. His questioning eyes shot up to meet mine.

Maggie, having been forgotten, cleared her throat.

Alexander hopped to his feet. "Ms. Maramma, you work miracles. There's not even a scar. How's that possible?"

"Please, call me Maggie."

"Maggie. How?" The tenor of his voice commanded respect.

"I'm a miracle worker, like you said," she answered innocently.

He shook his head as if to remove the confusion and regain his decorum. "I promise to have Evangeline home at a respectable hour."

"Let me give you a piece of advice. Don't let Eva's appearance fool you. She may look like a pixie, but she's a powerhouse. Eva's perfectly capable of deciding when she'd like to come home." Maggie softened before continuing. "But your chivalry does you credit as a gentleman."

Maggie scooted us to the door before pulling me back for a moment. "Be yourself."

Alexander fiddled with the stereo and filled the car with Hozier's haunting voice. The music hummed and pulsed and stirred me, and the air in the Bentley crackled with desire.

"Where are we headed for dinner?" I asked when I realized we'd passed the only two decent restaurants in town.

"I thought a private dinner at the manor would give us a chance to get to know each other. I hope that's all right."

"Thank the Goddess, yes," I blurted. The words flew from my mouth before I realized what I was saying. I'd been uneasy about the Arbor gossips eyeballing us on our date.

My response elicited a dazzling, albeit puzzled grin. "Have you ever been inside Morgan Manor?" he asked.

"Yes, every year for the last fourteen years. Your great-grandfather hosted a masked ball for Samhain—um, Halloween—and the whole town was invited." I cursed myself for yet another slip of the tongue. I was usually much more cautious with my language. I kept my beliefs close to my heart and only revealed them when I believed I could trust someone—which was almost never. But everything about Alexander distracted me.

"I've only seen the first floor, and never without the scarecrows and pumpkins. But the art collection is spectacular."

"Then you know Morgan Manor about as well as I do. I haven't gotten the chance to explore the place yet, but I'm looking forward to it."

"That surprises me. I mean, that you're not familiar with the manor already."

As he navigated the Bentley's winding ascent up Red Hill toward Morgan Manor and its thirty-acre property, he explained. "I didn't know my great-grandfather well. When I was a kid, my father and I visited Cain at the manor a couple times a year—around the holidays and during tax season. Our visits were always brief, and we never stayed the night. I remember sitting with the old man in his study. It looked more like the lab of a mad scientist than a businessman's office. There were beakers and test tubes and Bunsen burners, the whole deal. I was disappointed to find that all gone when I arrived." He paused, lost in his memories. "He always surrounded himself with the craziest cast of characters: actors and artists and musicians. My great-grandfather was a nonconformist."

As he reflected, his face softened, but his happy reflection was swiftly tempered. "Those visits ended years ago. My father and grandfather grew tired of his attitude, and his...unconventional behavior." Alexander ended there, although it was obvious there was much more to that tale.

"From what I knew of him, it was clear Cain Morgan danced to his own rhythm. I think that's a good way to be, though. It's certainly more interesting. Don't you think?"

"I do," he said and shot me a glance. We held each other's stare for a long moment before he put his attention back on the road. "Here we are."

A ten-foot-high stone wall surrounded the Morgan Manor estate, breaking only for an arched iron gate that was guarded on either side by stone phoenixes. We buzzed in through an intercom system, and the iron creaked and squealed as it opened. The narrow drive wound between wildly overgrown hedges. Vines grew high and thick and bent the moonlight into menacing shadows. The drive eventually opened up to the pinnacle of creepiness, the manor itself. It looked like a castle pulled from a gothic horror flick, with seven stories of rough gray stone, battlements, turrets, and a bell tower. The only things missing were a moat and a drawbridge.

We drove up to curved stone steps that led to the manor's fifteen-foot-tall iron front doors. Alexander hopped from the Bentley and jogged over to open my door.

As he took my hand, he swept his unoccupied arm in dramatic fashion. "Welcome to my home, Ms. Clarion."

An ancient, bent butler greeted us, though he didn't look happy about it. "Good evening, Mr. Morgan." The butler scowled.

"Don't be so gloomy, Franklin. We have a guest."

"Ms. Clarion," he said, his nodded greeting barely perceptible.

I stepped through the doorway, and my breath caught. For as macabre as the outside appeared, the inside defined opulence. An alabaster hearth stood as the focal point of the entry. The banister of the sweeping, grand staircase was made of solid silver; its steps, black marble. The foyer floor was marbled in shades of gray, silver, and black. A ruby chandelier hung from the apex of several arches ornamented with vivid Bacchanalian scenes. A hodgepodge of realist, impressionist, post-impressionist, symbolist, and abstract paintings hung from ashen, damask-papered walls. Close inspection of each Manet, Renoir, Cézanne, Beardsley, and Kandinsky proved all were originals. Morgan Manor was just as exceptional as its former inhabitant. And its current one.

Alexander's words abruptly jumped to the fore.

"Did you just welcome me to your home?" I swung around to face him.

"Yes," he laughed lightly. "I decided to stay. It seemed a waste to allow the place to remain vacant. And I happened to be in the market for a new home." Alexander held out his elbow. "Come. I'll tell you more about it once we settle in. Shall we?"

I weaved my arm through his, and he escorted me through a large, formal sitting room. Along the far wall, french doors framed what once must have been meticulously manicured gardens, now growing wild, flourishing in a brilliant frenzy.

"I had a feeling you'd love the gardens," Alexander said.

"How did you..." I began.

"It's written all over your face."

"For a second, I was worried you could read my mind." *That would suck.*

"I can't deny that is a tantalizing thought. But before I let my imagination run wild, why don't we have a seat?" He gestured through the french doors.

I didn't simply step outside; I entered a fantasy. On a veranda tucked into the gardens sat a table topped with a delicate white cloth and a bouquet of pale yellow daisies in a crystal vase. A canopy draped with bolts of cascading sheer fabric framed the table. Blue thistles, pink peonies, and tiny tea lights decorated the side tables and knee-high garden walls. Light music and lightning bugs lingered on a gentle breeze.

"I...don't know what to say."

"I have a strong suspicion that leaving you speechless isn't an easy task, so I'm going to take it as a compliment."

"Yes, do. It's like magic," I said as my gaze darted around the veranda. "You set this up in, what, an hour?" I stopped and frowned. "You didn't need to... No one's ever done anything like this for me before. And we just met. We're practically strangers."

I scrolled mentally through a disappointing anthology of lovers, not one caring for anything except getting into my pants. Although at one point, I thought Jay Crandall loved me.

Alexander clasped my hands and pulled me to him. He lifted my chin so my wary gaze met the earnestness in his.

"I did need to do this. We are not strangers." He hesitated before continuing. "This is going to sound crazy, but the moment I saw you, my soul seemed to recognize yours. Images like memories, ancient and foreign, engulfed me. And though I don't know the origin of these memories, somehow I understand their meaning. I've known you forever. Always."

Alexander stopped and rubbed the back of his neck. It was clear he'd been more forthcoming than he intended. "Anyway, damn, I don't mean to freak you out."

"I didn't know you were a poet," I teased to ease him. "There's a lot we don't know about each other, regardless of our soulful connection. Why don't we rectify that?"

"Yes. Come. Sit," he said, more a plea than a command.

We settled in, and the wizened butler, Franklin, appeared with two tall glasses filled with a cloudy bluish liquid. He frowned disapprovingly at me as he delivered the curious drinks.

"Blueberry lemonade," Alexander answered my unspoken query.

Taking a tentative sip, I sighed in approval.

"I hope the rest of our evening elicits equally gratifying responses." Alexander allowed his fingers to skim mine. The gesture appeared absentminded, second nature.

I felt sure my face would remain forever blushed if I spent much more time with this man. I cleared my throat to compose myself.

"You seem young to be taking ownership of an estate of such magnitude. What made you decide to hang on to the property instead of selling it off?"

"I've been renting an apartment in Princeton, just off campus. I intended to purchase a home after graduation. I never anticipated inheriting all this. Like I said, I never spent much time with my great-grandfather. But with my father and grandfather gone, it seems only right to keep it in the family."

"Do you have other family joining you?"

"No. My mother died before my first birthday, and I don't have any aunts or uncles or cousins. As far as I know, I'm the last Morgan."

"I lost my mother too—when I was eight. I've lived with Maggie ever since."

"She seems like an extraordinary woman. If you don't mind me asking, how is it that she never married? She's certainly beautiful, smart."

"I used to think it was because of me. She was saddled with a child to care for who wasn't her own. Really though, it's because she has only ever loved my mother."

I awaited the inevitable barrage of questions about the nature of the love between Maggie and my mother, but the questions never came. Instead, a sad, haunted haze overtook Alexander's face.

"What about your father? Did he abandon you?" he asked in a clipped tone.

"I never knew him." I shrugged. "When I was a little girl, it was just my mother and I, and Maggie of course."

"My father supported me financially, but his idea of caring was to ship me off to boarding school. That ensured he only had to deal with me a few times a year when I came home for holidays. Even then, I was treated more as a burden than a beloved son." After a pause, he recovered his sensibilities. "Excuse me, I shouldn't complain. My life's a cakewalk compared to what most people have to deal with."

"No, it's okay. We all have our burdens to bear."

"I've spent my entire life doing what was expected of me," he explained. "I went to Princeton because that's what my father and grandfather wanted. Even after they died, I knew I needed to finish school. So I put my head down and kept working. Now there's no school and no one laying out their plans for me. I hate to admit this, but I have no idea what I want to do with my life. My business degree will come in handy when dealing with the management of the estate, but I feel like the world is wide open to me for the first time. And I have the luxury not to have to stress about it too much, in the short term at least."

"I didn't have a ton of money growing up, but I never wanted for anything." I told him what it was like growing up with Maggie at the cottage, about our bees and lavender and gardens. I explained how I loved to create through music, sewing, drawing, and painting. "I've been saving for years to buy a property I could set up as a gallery and performance space. Selling my artwork and designs at the market is fine, but I want more."

Before we could continue our conversation, two liveried female staff brought out our meal.

"Ah, good evening, Mrs. Marsh, Celeste," Alexander greeted them kindly.

Celeste, a slim wisp of a young woman, approached with a butcher-block platter in trembling hands. With demure eyes, she placed the assortment of cheeses and fruit in the center of the table for us to share. When she turned away, her hand brushed my shoulder. She allowed it to rest there for a moment. A quiet warmth radiated from her, like she was a daisy in the sunshine. And when she finally removed her hand, I felt curiously deprived of her touch.

Mrs. Marsh, a severe, graying woman, scowled at me as she presented plates of angel-hair pasta with lobster, summer vegetables, and crusty bread. I wasn't sure what I'd done to elicit such apparent disdain, but I wasn't going to let some crabby old bat ruin my evening.

Once their duty was complete, the austere Mrs. Marsh grabbed ahold of Celeste's arm and dragged her inside—but not before the prim maid leveled me with blazing eyes that didn't seem to match the sweet face they sat upon.

What the hell was that all about?

"I'm not sure what's come over the staff tonight. I hope they haven't offended you," Alexander said with anxiety deepening his voice.

"Not at all." I smiled brightly to reassure him.

The charms of my date and the delicious aroma of the meal regained my attention. Despite the odd behavior of the staff, the date was turning out better than I'd expected.

"Thank you for dinner. It looks and smells delicious," I said.

His face lit with pleasure. "At first I thought I'd cook for you myself but decided food poisoning wasn't the best way to impress you. Cooking is not one of my strengths."

"Maybe I can cook for you on our next date?"

"Oh, we'll be seeing each other again after tonight?" His lips dripped with sarcasm.

"Possibly. We'll have to see how well you continue to charm me."

We talked and laughed and learned about each other while we ate. I couldn't remember ever feeling so comfortable around any man. He asked me questions and listened to the answers. He was open and attentive with a healthy dose of humor. It was refreshing to spend an evening with someone who genuinely wanted to get to know me.

After dinner, we wandered through the gardens, overgrown with English ivy, ferns, and trumpet vines, with glorious bursts of color from the bluestar, pink milkweed, white anemone, and yellow merrybells. It would have been blissfully easy to get lost among them, and I was tempted to do just that. But a concern weighed so heavily on my heart that even the untamed beauty of my surroundings couldn't lift my suddenly despondent spirits.

"So...." I worried my words would send him careening away from me.

"What is it?"

"I like you very much." I stopped walking, tipped my head back, and took a deep breath.

"I like you too. So, what's wrong?"

"You just moved into Arbor. It's a small town with a big mouth. I don't have the greatest reputation, and frankly, neither does Maggie. Yeah, they call her when they need help with their chronic back problems or gout or whatever, but they just as quickly spit bile behind her back. With me, they're blunt about their contempt."

"So...you're worried I'll believe gossip?"

"A bit, I guess, but it's more than that. I don't want you to be tarred and feathered because of me. The mayor of Arbor, Doreen Crandall, is campaigning for a seat in the state legislature, and she hates me. Just yesterday, she smeared me at a press conference she held at the market. It's only going to get uglier."

"I'm sure I can handle a few bitter, jealous fools who have nothing better to do than spread tall tales about a beautiful woman."

Heat rushed to my cheeks, and there was that blush again.

"But, why don't you tell me what's really bothering you," he prodded.

We sat down together on a stone bench under a weeping cherry tree in full bloom. I wrung my hands, unsure how—or *if*—I should continue.

He hunched over with his elbows resting on his spread knees. "I want you to feel comfortable with me. You can talk to me, honestly."

"Okay, here it goes." I decided to throw it all out in the open. "I'm a witch. There, I said it. You can take me home now if you want."

Alexander didn't respond right away. He took my small hands in his, turned them over, and kissed the inside palm of each. Then he lifted his head and looked me in the eyes.

"You believe in the beauty and power of nature. I could never look down on you for that," he said with complete sincerity.

I had to keep going. I felt a deep need to share myself with this man. If I wanted this budding relationship to grow into something real, he had to understand who and what I was.

What the hell. I already told him I'm a witch. Yet I knew that was the easy part. Alexander's reaction to my next truth would be the real test of his character.

"I have powers," I blurted, lowering my eyes, too scared to see the inevitable horror in his expression.

To his credit, he didn't laugh or run away screaming. "I don't understand," he said, squinting as if the act could eliminate his confusion. "What do you mean you have powers?"

I decided it was better to show him than try to explain. I stood and faced both Alexander and the weeping cherry tree. I silently sent a prayer to the Goddess for Her blessing.

"Watch."

Raising my arms slowly and with infinitesimal finger movements, I changed the color of the tree's flowers from white to red to yellow to blue and back to white. With a swift flick of my wrist, I made all the flowers fall from the tree, turn into snow, rain, and then reattach to their branches. Finally, with a wide sweep of my arms, I made the weeping cherry burst into flames. I assumed this would make Alexander gasp or jump, but he just watched, stupefied. I snapped my fingers, and the tree returned to its original state.

"I have a hell of a lot more umph than your run-of-the-mill, girl-in-black next door. My magic is as real as the draw of the moon on water and women. That was no sleight of hand or trickery. Nature manipulation is one of the most difficult pieces of magic to attempt, and I've been studying it since I was a toddler." It was done. There was no turning back.

"Fuck," he cursed softly. "Can you do other things? I mean, do you have other powers?"

"Yes. Many."

He stood and pulled me into an embrace. "You extraordinary female…You captivated me long before this astonishing display. Now, I'm hooked. I have never been so shaken, to my very core, by anyone. No one has ever come close to the way you make me feel." His arms tightened their hold around me, and his breath kissed along the nape of my neck.

"And how do I make you feel?" I managed to squeak out.

His jaw clenched tight, and the veins in his neck pulsed. "Like a man possessed."

There was a desperate fury in the way he held me, like I was the only source for his next breath. His lips crushed mine. I ran my tongue around his and nipped his bottom lip. He groaned and deepened the kiss. When he broke away to sit on the stone bench under the cherry tree, I straddled his lap. I was on fire, not scorched but roiling like hot lava. Alexander tasted his way along my jaw, down my neck to my shoulder. I pulled him back to my lips and lost myself in the feel and the scent and the taste of him.

"Eva…Eva, we have to stop," he murmured into my mouth. I ignored him, desperately holding on. "Honey, stop." This time, his words had more conviction.

It prompted me to do something that I'd never done in my life. I pouted.

Alexander threw his head back and barked out a laugh. "If we don't stop right now, I'm going to fuck you here on this bench. And as much as I love the sound of that, it wouldn't be very gentlemanly."

Then I did it again. I popped out my bottom lip and flashed puppy dog eyes. *What the hell is wrong with me? Since when do I beg for a man's attention?*

"Oh, you are trouble. But don't worry. I'm up to the challenge."

"You know what? I believe you just might be." I kissed the tip of his nose. "But don't you need a bit of assistance?" I rotated my hips into him for effect. "I'd be more than happy to help you out."

He growled and bit down hard on my shoulder. My head lolled to the side, and a guttural moan escaped my lips. "Please, Alexander. Let me make you feel good."

"No," he said sharply and lifted me from his lap. "I just need a minute." He hung his head and paced, running his hands through his hair.

Being rebuffed by a man was unfamiliar territory. I knew he wanted me, but I conceded that it was best we slow things down. The desire between us was so palpable that we wouldn't be able to stop once we'd begun. And as much as I wanted him, I wasn't ready for that yet. So I stood patiently until he composed himself.

He placed a finger under my chin and guided my gaze to his. "I will have you. But not tonight. And not like this." Then he pulled me into his arms again and held me close.

My ear pressed against his chest as his frenzied heart eased into rhythm. And I realized in that moment that I'd never felt so cherished in my life.

After our heated encounter, Alexander behaved like a gentleman. He straightened my dress and smoothed down my hair. We took our time finishing our tour of the gardens, and eventually he took me home. Just before midnight, we walked to the front door of the cottage with our hands clasped.

"I can't wait long to see you again."

"Good. Don't." I stood on my tiptoes and kissed him once more before walking inside.

Chapter Seven

I closed the front door and leaned back against it, a slow, triumphant smile creeping onto my face. After kicking off my heels, I flew into a happy dance, like a jig, around the room. Maggie, woken by either the car doors or my crazed hysteria, stopped short at the sight of me.

"Evangeline Clarion! Are you drunk?" she asked, shocked by my frenzy.

"Ha! No, not unless you count gallons of blueberry lemonade. Maybe I have sugar shock. That's a thing, right?"

"I'm going to assume you had a good time." She hesitated. "I'm not sure how much I want to know."

I grabbed her hands and spun her around in circles. "You fabulous female, I always tell you everything."

"Mostly. Yes. I know," she said with a good-natured groan.

We collapsed onto the sofa.

"Mags, it was magic. But like no magic I've ever known."

My goddess-mother's sharp, gray eyes narrowed. "Explain this new magic."

I proceeded to tell her *almost* everything about my evening with Alexander. I neglected to mention that I jumped into his lap. And I sure as hell didn't tell her I pouted.

When do I pout?

I rewound the night, and as I recited the details of the date, I grew increasingly nervous. When Maggie's eyes welled up, my heart broke. She'd always been both mother-hen and friend, and her insight and advice were invaluable. She was irreplaceable.

But Maggie didn't say a word.

My stomach turned. *What did I do? I exposed our secret. I put us in harm's way. I allowed lust to cloud my judgment.*

"I will fix this," I vowed like it was the last thing I'd ever do on Earth. "I only told him about me. I didn't implicate you or Adelaide. I promise."

"No," she croaked and cleared her throat. "No, darling. You haven't done anything wrong. I'm just so happy for you." A small laugh erupted from her, and then she sucked in a sob. "Lavinia would have loved this. I wish your mother could see how her little girl has become such an exquisite woman."

I wrapped my arms around her. "Love you."

"I love you too, so very, very much. Why don't you settle in for the night, and I'll bring you a snack and some tea?"

"That sounds perfect. Thank you."

My bedroom was one of three in the cottage. A shabby-chic dresser, pale-blue painted end table, and a four-poster bed draped in swathes of colorful fabrics furnished the small space. A large bay window with a pillow-topped seat looked out over the cottage's lawn, stream, and forest. It was my favorite spot to sew and sketch. I also loved my en-suite bathroom. It was cozy and quaint. A Victorian-era claw-foot tub perched in the corner, but as tempting as it was, I was too tired for a bath. Instead, I washed up at the pedestal sink. And when I caught my reflection in the medicine-cabinet mirror, I noticed a faint glow beneath my skin. I leaned closer to my reflection, and as I stared, the glow faded away. My skin returned to its pale rosy hue.

I shook off the strange phenomenon and got dressed for bed in boxers and a T-shirt. My fluttering thoughts leapt to a pleasanter topic. Alexander. I grabbed my sketchpad and pencil, and settled into the window seat. I leaned my head against the cool windowpane. Pulling images from my mind's eye, I drew the untamed gardens, the weeping cherry tree, and the stone bench on which Alexander and I had kissed. My hand flew over the page at a frenetic pace. Even in black and white, the magic of the manor seemed tangible.

So engrossed was I in my work that I didn't hear Maggie's approach.

She spoke softly. "It's breathtaking."

I jumped, almost knocking the tea and cookies from her hands.

"Sorry! I didn't mean to startle you," Maggie apologized.

"S'fine," I said through a yawn. "Was lost in the garden and didn't hear you come in."

Maggie set my snack down on the bedside table. "May I?" She nodded toward my drawing.

"Of course." I handed over the sketch and hopped into bed. "Nice! Adelaide's famous cherry chocolate-chip cookies." I grabbed one, took a huge bite, and swooned. I washed it down with a sip of Maggie's tea, and a sense of relaxation and calm spread through me, washing over me from my head to my shoulders, lower back, stomach, legs, and finally my feet. Maggie truly performed miracles with herbs.

I looked over at her, perched on the edge of the window seat, staring at my sketch.

"What do you see?" I asked in a whisper, knowing it was more than my pencil lines on which she focused.

Maggie was quiet for a heartbeat and then spoke in a voice much lower in pitch than her own. "Two spirits of torment, pained and oppressed, are an ominous portent, until they find rest."

Her vision ended, and my sketch fluttered from her fingers to the floor. She blinked to clear away the revelation. "Morgan Manor must be freed from these discontented spirits," she said softly, her voice her own again. "There's malice, danger in that place that could pose a threat to Alexander. The home and grounds must be blessed and the spirits aided in their journey onto the next plane."

Then she kissed my head, said good night, and left.

With the exception of the peculiar behavior of the staff, I hadn't sensed anything *off* at the manor—although a bolt of lightning couldn't have distracted me from Alexander's charms. I wasn't fool enough to ignore Maggie's instincts, however. I promised myself I'd talk to Alexander in the morning to see if he'd allowed us to deal with these spirits.

I picked up my sketch and laid it in the light of the moon spilling in through the window. I shoved another cookie in my mouth, downed my tea, and snuggled into bed under cool sheets. The tea soothed my spirit and lulled my pulse. Sleep rolled over me like a great wave.

Rest, on the other hand, would prove much more difficult to come by.

A warm wind whistled through tall rows of lavender bushes. The heady scent ascended, curled on the breeze, and cascaded under the noses of a familiar collection of animals. Rocky perched on Shasta's shoulder, while Hanna and Fledermaus hummed and flapped above. Beside them walked a peculiar pair, a German shepherd with a viper coiled on its back. Together, they traveled toward an elder tree off in the distance. A deer, a crane, and a hare surrounded the elder tree and beckoned the other animals forward. They called out in muffled, echoed voices—human voices, drawing the familiars closer.

Before they could reach their destination, a pack of wolves surrounded them. The wolves snarled, spitting mad, with their muzzles drawn back over rotten, blackened gums and jagged teeth. Shasta raised herself up onto her hind legs and let loose a furious growl. Targeting the largest and most formidable foe, the wolves launched themselves onto the bear. They latched on to her flank and torso and whipped their heads from side to side, tearing at her flesh. Shasta swatted her razor-sharp claws at the wolves, landing blow after mighty blow, but the pack was relentless. They swarmed her in waves, wearing her down. After Shasta took a chunk out of one wolf's side, the canine countered with a series of quick bites to her hindquarters. And the bear collapsed in a thunderous heap.

The fight pitted the fearsome strength of a black bear against the wolves' swiftness and agility. And if they had been the only combatants, the fight might have ended there. As the pack prepared to descend as one upon the injured and bleeding bear, Shasta's companions charged in. The German shepherd sprang into the melee, and took on three wolves at once. The viper coiled itself around the pack alpha, repeatedly sunk its teeth into the wolf's legs, and left it writhing in the dirt. The rest of the pack squared off against aerial attacks by Rocky, Fledermous, and Hanna. The bat and bee proved ineffective on their own, but they joined forces to distract and disorient their canine adversaries. Fledermous blinded the wolves by feverishly flapping in their eyes, while Hanna shot up their nose and stung them. This left Rocky free to attack. His hooked beak and talons shredded the wolves' muzzles and hides.

It seemed the familiars were on the edge of victory when fanged teeth ripped through Fledermous's wing. He fell helpless from the sky and landed in a lavender bush. The German shepherd raced to retrieve the bat, but a wolf captured the prize first. With a vicious snarl, it shredded Fledermous to pieces.

Every creature stilled. Not even the wind dared to blow. When the rustling of leaves and branches subsided, the German shepherd lifted its head to the heavens and bellowed a mournful cry. As if he'd called it forward, lightning cracked from within the elder tree and shot out at the wolves.

Before I could see what happened next, I was shaken awake.

WEDNESDAY

"What the hell!" I shrieked, more than a little irritated by my inconsiderate and ill-timed rousing. "What's your problem?"

"Yeah, you're awake! It's about time. It's almost eight o'clock. Come on, birthday girl, we have so much to do today: manicures, shopping, lunch, and then we absolutely must... Eva, are you even listening to me?"

She's positively maniacal. "Why are you in my bed?"

"I had to wake your lazy ass up somehow. You sleep like the dead. So let's go, sleepyhead! Rise and shine!" Bunny squealed, babbled, and bounced.

"Seriously, Bunny, how old are you?" I asked, my voice groggy with sleep.

"Seriously, Eva," she mimicked, singsong. "We have to go, go, go. Maggie told me she's working for you, so you have no excuse."

"I don't need a manicure. I just painted my nails yesterday."

"They're black, like your soul, and it's up to me to save you from yourself," she said a little too seriously.

"You're cute."

"I know." Bunny beamed.

"Listen, I'm broke—" I began before she interrupted.

Her eyebrows shot up. "No, you're not. You have twenty grand. I think you can cover the cost of a shopping trip."

"That's not expendable cash. So if I need an outfit, I can make one or borrow one from Mags."

"Well, ya can't borrow mine. You'll stretch them out." Bunny stuck out her tongue and snickered.

"You're a bitch, and you couldn't pay me enough to wear the 1980s throwback, teeny-bopper atrocities you call clothes."

I swung my legs out of bed, stretched, and opened my window to a bucolic portrait framed by a cloudless blue sky. "How blessed I am," I whispered to the wind.

"Huh?" Bunny's head lolled to the side.

"Nothing," I shook my head, knowing it was pointless to explain how nature soothed my weary soul. She'd never understand. "Listen, I really am sorry. I'm just not up for going out." As much as I didn't want to hang out with Bunny, I also didn't want to upset her. She'd done nothing wrong.

"How about tonight instead? I can pick you up, and we can go to the lake or something? It won't cost you a cent."

"I'll think about it, okay? Text me later," I said and immediately regretted it.

"Yeah!" She clapped her hands and bopped up and down like I'd just given her a new puppy. "Oh. My. God. I have the juiciest gossip."

"Please, no. No gossip," I said, pleading.

But Bunny prattled on. "So, you know how you're on the mayor's shit list? Of course you do. It's all over the internet. Anyway, *The Messenger* ripped her again, and she lost it. They ran a story implying that Doreen Crandall's attacks on you stem from her belief in magic." Bunny whipped out her phone and pulled up the newspaper's online site. "Where is it? Where is it? Here it is! 'This editorial board concludes that Doreen Crandall, the mayor of Arbor, New York, and 2018 candidate for the state legislature, lacks good sense and judgment. Her recent twisted fascination proves she is unfit to serve and unable to fulfill her duties.'

"I saw the mayor downtown about an hour ago, freaking the hell out. She was waving the newspaper over her head and railing about her slipping poll numbers. I'm pretty sure she was drunk."

Someone's not having a good week. I almost feel sorry for her.

"But she's nobody to mess with, Eva. Take my advice and stay away from the mayor for as long as you can. It is inevitable, though. She's going to take you down one way or another, especially if her numbers don't rebound soon."

"Take me down? For what? Crandall brought this all on herself," I said, incredulous.

Bunny stared at me as if arms sprouted from my ears. "And they say I'm the dumb one. Do you really think it matters who set this in motion? Her persona is tarnished. She'll do whatever it takes to restore her reputation and get her campaign back on track. And since you're the poster child for evil, Crandall's going to make an example out of you."

"Contrary to popular opinion, I'm not evil."

"Helllooo." She dragged the word out like I was an idiot. "You attacked and cursed them. Everyone saw you do it."

"No. No one saw me attack them because I didn't."

"But, you cursed them?"

"No, not exactly." I fidgeted. For as long as Bunny and I had been friends, she had never realized I had real powers. It was one of the things I liked most about our friendship. She never asked too many questions. "After the press jumped all over the mayor, Gladys confronted me. She insisted that Maggie and I repent or leave Arbor. I guess you could say I prayed for Karma to land in its rightful place."

Bunny hit me with a quizzical look. "Just consider yourself warned, okay? Things are going to get worse." She glanced around my room at my broom and candles and crystals. "And you should hide your witchy shit. It won't look good."

Before I realized what she'd said, Bunny climbed out of my window.

"See ya tonight!" she squealed as she hopped into her Prius convertible and waved goodbye.

"Maybe!" I called out after her. "Text me first."

How am I supposed to enjoy a night by the lake when I've got the mayor breathing down my neck? What the hell am I supposed to do? Hide? Strike back?

I realized nothing could be decided without some coffee in my system, so I made my way to the kitchen. I expected Maggie to still be home, finishing breakfast before heading to the market. I'd hoped to tell her about my dream. The kitchen was empty, however, and all was quiet except for the gurgling of the coffeemaker. I made a beeline to my favorite mug—huge, green, and chipped. It had a note taped to the front.

> Morning. Eva! I had to get an early start today. I'm stopping by to see Adelaide before heading to the market. I brewed you up some coffee. I'll be home in time to make dinner. Have a lovely day!—Maggie

There was a P.S. at the bottom of the note, written in different handwriting—and hot pink lipstick.

> Morning, Eva! I'm about to go wake your sorry butt up. I hate coffee so I made myself some cocoa. I'll be upstairs in about two minutes. I can't wait to get our manicures! My nails look terrible.—Bunny

That crazy girl does make me laugh. I smiled to myself.

I grabbed the milk, cocoa, and sugar and put just the right amount of each into the mug. I topped it all off with 100 percent organic, fair-trade, shade-grown, bird-friendly Kona coffee—not a Kona *blend*, just pure Hawaiian Kona. Coffee purists would burn me at the stake if they saw what I added to the supremely eminent cup of java. I didn't care. It was sublime.

I believed we should appreciate the fruits of creation. I could never understand the Puritanical mindset. Why deny oneself of simple pleasures? Sugar and dark chocolate on the tongue? Sex? Wine! Why reject the creator's bounty? For the possibility of happiness after death? The earth provides these generous gifts in exchange for cultivation. And protection. Therein lies the bond between the earth and a witch—the great synchronistic bestowing of strengths.

I grabbed my steaming mug of deliciousness and headed out to the patio. I opened the front door, was smacked in the face by a wall of brutally dry heat, and immediately tripped over a USPS package. I flung out my arms to catch myself and, in the process, lost hold of my coffee. The mug shattered on the slate patio, and ceramic shards exploded.

"Shit, shit, shit!" I screamed and grumbled as I ran back inside the cottage for cleaning supplies. It took me the next half hour to clean up the glass and get another cup of coffee.

Finally, I settled into a cushioned wicker rocker and took a deep breath. Yielding to the power of nature's raw energy, I opened myself up. I let my eyes fall closed and welcomed the cool breeze as it enveloped me and banished the sun's ruthlessness. I could almost taste the honey in the air. The robins, thrushes, and skylarks offered their songs as the music of the morning. My silent prayers of gratitude to the Goddess curled up to the heavens like sage smoke.

I opened my eyes only to find my feathered familiar staring at me from his perch upon my table. Startled, I jumped up from my rocker and scared the crap out of Rocky. He took off, flying in swooping circles above my head.

He truly was a regal creature. With a wingspan of over four feet, he had broad, rounded, red-brown wings with dark bars along their edges. His tail feathers were short, and his underbelly creamy white. As he made his final descent, he let out a shrill "keeee-aaar" and landed gracefully next to me.

"Sorry." I laughed. "I didn't mean to scare you."

"No need for apologies. I should've announced my presence," his stately tenor resounded within my mind. *"I've come with an invitation. I thought you might like to fly with me. You've had a tumultuous few days. It seems a good time to reacquaint yourself with your power."*

No response was needed. As my familiar, he knew my wishes. As my friend, he knew my heart—and it soared at the mention of flight. I ignored my harried heart. The shedding of burdens was necessary for flight. Without casting off life's chains, the weight of one's soul tethered the body to the earth. So I released all that constrained me, all that diminished me. A surge of energy coursed through my veins, and I surrendered to it. The moment my bare toes left the earth was euphoric, a teeth-numbing adrenaline shot, the way sex should feel.

For as long as I could remember, I had abilities others did not. Yet nothing came close to the power within me thanks to this otherworldly bird. There was no freedom like viewing one's life from a hawk's perspective.

Rows of lavender bent and swayed like great waves in the wind, the blue-green waters of the stream rippled around the rocks, and the bees swarmed around their hives, dancing together like schools of fish.

I glided upward and slowed as I reached the cottage roof. Rocky rested on the cottage chimney, tapping his foot in mock impatience. At his nod, we took off like a shot toward the forest. I squinted against the stinging wind. We flew just high enough to skim the tree line. When Rocky spotted a break in the branches, we dove into the cool shade of the woods. We wove through tree trunks and brambles, darted over fallen logs, maneuvering faster and faster, five feet or so above the mossy, leaf-packed carpet of the forest. When we reached a clearing, I landed with a sureness of foot that elicited heavy praise from Rocky.

"Well done indeed! For not having practiced in weeks, you show no sign of rust. How do you feel?"

I felt fabulous. I wasn't even breathing heavy. "What do you think?" I said with a wicked grin. "Race ya!"

With the words barely off my lips, I flew into the thick of the woods back toward the cottage. I outstripped Rocky from the get-go. I looked behind for him as I passed the fallen oak at the mouth of the forest. And I flew right into Alexander.

"Oh!"

"Oh!"

We both grunted as I collided into his chest at ten miles an hour in midair. We crashed to the ground with me landing on top.

"Great Goddess, are you okay?"

"Holy shit, are you okay?"

We spoke in concert.

I leaned over him, keenly aware of every inch of my body that covered his. His stare drew me in, as did his lips—inches away—and the heat from his hands as they moved up my back. I felt myself falling under his spell again. He seized the opportunity to roll me over and take a position of power above me.

"Are you okay?" he asked, his voice low.

"Mhm."

Years passed, or hours. Whole fields of flowers could have bloomed and died around us, and we'd never have known. I didn't dare move for fear of breaking the spell. But Alexander moved. Ever so slowly, he moved his lips closer to mine. At the first brush of his mouth, I noticed a distinct noise growing louder around us.

So enraptured was I, that I didn't sense Shasta's approach until it was too late. She let out a deafening roar and charged. Alexander scrambled to his feet, dragging me with him.

"Run, Eva, run!" he screamed.

His abrasive tone only served to make Shasta angrier. Her roared reply even scared me, and I'd been snuggling with her for fourteen years.

"Stop!" I yelled at the bear in the most commanding voice I could muster, and she immediately halted her advance.

I turned my attention back to the man who, once again, intended to save me. *He needs to realize—and quick—that I'm not some fickle flower that requires constant tending.*

Alexander clutched my arm, trying in vain to pull me away from the bear. But all his valiant attempts proved futile. Thanks to Shasta, my muscles hardened. I could have overturned Alexander's snazzy ride with one hand if I'd wanted to. Tact was necessary, however. And showing off would've been plain arrogant.

"That's enough," I said, leveling him with a stare. "I need you to let me go and back up a few steps. Please, trust me."

To his credit, Alexander shut his mouth. He looked suspiciously from me to Shasta. With his brows drawn tight, he backed off.

"Shasta," I said. "That's enough."

She hurrummffed. *"I don't like the liberties he was taking, and I don't like the way he spoke to you,"* she scolded as if I was her cub.

"Momma Bear, you know I welcomed his advances, and I can scold him for his sass myself."

"I don't like this, but it's obvious you care for...this man." Shasta looked to Rocky and cocked her head to the side. They seemed to be communicating with each other, but for the first time, I was locked out of their discussion.

"I will stand down. For now," Shasta said, her voice sounding strained, like she was speaking through clenched teeth.

I decided not to call her out on her strange behavior. The situation had been defused. Temporarily. "Thank you."

Rocky, who'd been watching this little scene from a perch on the fallen oak, flew up and settled on Shasta's shoulder. Just like in my dream.

Speaking in a loud, clear voice, I made the precarious introductions. "Shasta, Rocky, I would like to formally introduce you both to my very good friend, Alexander. Alexander," I said, looking into his pasty, panic-stricken face, "these exceptional creatures are my familiars."

Then Alexander, an imposing figure in his own right, lost his battle with gravity. His eyes rolled back. His legs gave way. And he passed out on the lawn.

Chapter Eight

With the colossal strength Shasta's magic afforded, I carried Alexander into the cottage. I sat him in the same chair he'd placed me the day before. Crouching beside him, I dabbed his head with a cool cloth scented with eucalyptus. I lit a blue consecrated candle and spoke my will.

> "Magic mend and candle burn.
> Sickness end, good health return."

I repeated the incantation until his labored breath eased and his heart rate returned to normal. Slowly, Alexander came to and sat forward.

"What happened? You okay? There was a bear and a huge bird, and you were..." A violent cough seized him, cutting off his anxious rant.

I eased his shoulders back against the chair and ran the cloth over his forehead once more. "Shhh. It's okay. Everything's fine."

"I'm such an ass," he said with gravel in his throat. "I'm supposed to protect you."

I stood and planted my hands on my hips. "If you haven't figured it out by now, I can take care of myself."

"I know, but..."

"Besides, I wasn't in any danger," I said over my shoulder as I walked to the kitchen to grab him a glass of water.

I'd just stepped to the sink when he came up behind me. His signature scent filled my nose, and the warmth of his breath grazed my neck.

My body responded instinctually to him, but I refused to swoon.

"I know you're strong, and I can accept that magic is real, but..." He whipped me around to face him. "Can you really fly?"

I smiled. "Yes. Well, when Rocky's nearby. Rocky's the hawk you met. He's my familiar—one of them, anyway." I went on to explain how Shasta and Rocky came into my life at stages when I was most in need of their support. I described our method of communication, and how my familiars' inherent magic granted me even more power than already flowed within me.

"What else can you do?"

"I'm a decent spell caster. I can use herbs, stones, and candles to aid with common ailments—although that's Maggie's forte. I can manipulate nature, like the tree in your garden. My ability to conjure the elements—calling earth, air, fire, and water into being at my will—is growing by the day. But my most potent gift is creation. Playing new instruments comes remarkably easily, almost on the spot. I love to paint and sketch and sew, and as I breathe life into my creations, they breathe life into me."

Alexander wrapped me up in his arms, placed a kiss on my forehead, and tucked me under his chin. "Wow. You are a distraction. I almost forgot why I came over this morning."

"You mean it wasn't your intention to trick me into nursing you back to health so I'd smooch you?" I asked with an overly serious expression.

He barked out a laugh. "I couldn't wait to see you, so I decided to come over to ask if you'd like to join me for breakfast. I stopped into that little café in town and picked us up some croissants, danish, and muffins."

"Then why do you have that worried look on your face?"

"It occurred to me that you may have already eaten. Who has the energy to fly around with a hawk and argue with a bear unless they've already had breakfast?" A slow, soft smile grew as he spoke. "Then, I thought that if you are hungry, I'm going to have to make my way past those two outside. I left the pastries in the car."

"Well, I'm famished," I said with a chuckle. "So, why don't we go out there together? I'll check on Rocky and Shasta, and you grab the goodies."

Alexander took my hand and dragged me outside where he kissed me quick and jogged off to the car. I visited with my familiars. Shasta lounged on her backside against the cottage wall in the shade. Rocky perched, looking bored, atop the patio table umbrella.

"How are you two doing?"

"We're content," Rocky said, while leisurely preening his feathers.

"Sweet. Shasta, you know I love you, but to a stranger, you're quite fearsome."

"Such things you say." The bear lowered her fluttering black lashes over demure eyes.

"I believe Alexander's a good man. And I'd like us to get to know each other better. Can you try not to scare the hell out of him?"

"I'll do my best, dearie."

"Thank you. Well, Alexander and I are going to have a bite. Will you two be polite while I'm inside getting us coffee?"

They both nodded, but for some reason, I didn't buy their easy acquiescence.

Alexander walked back up with a cautious smile and his bare, muscled arms overflowing with boxes of pastry.

So much for a little breakfast, I thought with a grin.

Rocky and Shasta laughed in their way—a cackle and a hurrummff, causing poor Alexander to jump, juggle the pastries, and lose the color from his cheeks.

"It's okay. They won't bite," I said, laughing. "You're perfectly safe."

"You know for sure? I just met them," he said out of the side of his mouth.

"I could say the same about you." I winked. "I'm going to warm up my coffee. How do you take yours?"

"Black, thanks."

I didn't want to leave them all alone longer than necessary, so I ran inside and quickly made the two cups. I didn't want to push my luck. It was too soon to expect them to become pals. Returning with a mug in each hand, I smiled at my little group of companions. By no means conventional, but that worked just fine for me.

I set down the coffee, and its earthy notes wafted, intermingling with cinnamon and clove of the baked goodies. Too hungry to be polite, I piled one of each on my plate, tucked my legs underneath my backside, and dug in.

"This is so good," I mumbled behind a mouthful of danish. I finished chewing and sipped down coffee a bit too fast. I coughed and sputtered to clear my throat. *What a lady I am. Such class.* "Thanks." I made a feeble attempt to redeem myself.

When Alexander didn't respond, I looked up from my sugar-shock plate. He gaped at my drawing of the manor's gardens, the weeping cherry tree, and the bench where we'd held each other the night before. Then he turned to me in startling, wide-eyed adoration.

"This is unreal. It's like I could fall into it." The drawing claimed his attention again, and he examined it at a dozen different angles. "Have you submitted to galleries, magazines?"

"Many, and a couple liked my work. But nothing major's ever panned out. It's the same with every artist, I think. It doesn't matter the medium. We all work to be seen and appreciated, and we'd love to make a living from our passion. I don't just want to help myself. I want to own a comfortable space for painters and fashion designers and sculptors and photographers and musicians; a place where artists can showcase their passions and make some money in the process."

"I love your enthusiasm, but it makes me feel like a slacker. I wish I had your drive." He stopped and stared at me for a breath. "Maybe, after breakfast, you can show me more of your work? Unless you have other plans today. I know I just crashed your morning."

"I'd love to show you, and I'm glad you crashed my morning."

After we finished eating, we headed into the gallery. I curled up on the sofa as Alexander carefully inspected my paintings that filled the walls like Tetris. Every so often, he'd let out a soft gasp, but otherwise, neither of us spoke. The reverence with which he studied each piece was humbling.

"You have drawings and sewing projects too?" he asked.

I brought out my sketch portfolio and a few of the dresses I'd designed. Alexander skimmed the delicate garments with strong hands. His powerful flesh against the sleek cascading fabrics stirred me. I imagined him touching me where he caressed the dresses.

"Unbelievable." He stood back. "You've got enough instruments in here to start your own orchestra. Which of these do you play?"

"All of them."

"I'm sorry, what? I thought I heard you say that you play *all* of these instruments."

I smiled shyly. "I do." I stepped to the piano and brushed my fingertips over the black and white ivory without pressing a key. "Shall I?"

Alexander stood behind me, practicing great restraint as he slid his hands up and down my arms. He leaned in and whispered, "Show me what you can do."

I dropped a kiss to the scruff of his cheek before sliding onto the piano bench. I knew exactly what to play. The hauntingly seductive melody enveloped me before I played a note, but once I did, it surged through my fingers like lightning.

When I finished, he shot to his feet and cheered. "Magnificent! *Fantasie Impromptu*," he said.

"Yes, Chopin. You know it."

"I do."

"It's one of my favorites. Maggie's great-aunt sent her the record many years ago. She plays it often." I stood and ran my fingertips over the keys again, ever so softly, without dropping a note. "I don't need sheet music. Once I hear a song, I can play it."

I slipped into the chair behind my harp and curled into the instrument. My fingers danced over the strings. Then I took my violin under my chin. I played until I felt Alexander's hunger like static on my skin.

"Never in my life, Evangeline." He took my hands and brought them to his lips. "I've never met anyone so staggering to my soul."

"And I'm oh so sexy, too," I said, and motioned to the boxers and T-shirt I'd worn to bed. "I really know how to show off my assets."

Alexander closed his eyes for a moment. When they opened, they flashed with fury. He crushed me to him, and I trembled against his chest. His greedy hands clutched my back as he snarled.

"You're the most alluring woman I've ever known. Please," he begged, "please let me touch you."

"I believe you already are," I replied with an arched brow.

"More. I need more."

He moved my hair aside and kissed along my neck and shoulder. He placed his hands on my sides and moved them under my shirt, slowly upward.

An uncontrollable shiver rocked me. "Yes." I sighed.

He grabbed the bottom of my shirt and pulled it up over my head, revealing my heavy breasts. He cupped them and ran his thick fingers around my nipples, turning them into pink pebbles.

Recognizing the wetness between my legs brought me to my senses, and I backed out of his arms. I crossed my arms over my chest.

"I won't touch you unless you want me to," he said, his voice sharp. "I'd never... It can't be easy after..."

"No," I said, cutting him off before he traveled down a road I had no interest in revisiting. "It's just, are you sure you want to get wrapped up with me? I might be small, but I'm a lot to handle." I wanted him more than my next breath, but I needed to give him an out should he want it.

He didn't answer with words. Instead, Alexander lifted me into his arms and wrapped my legs around his waist. He walked me around the cottage until he found my room, his mouth on mine throughout the exploration. A savage hunger overtook us. He dropped me on the bed, and my legs dangled off the sides. He took off his shirt, and then kneeling between my knees, he tore off my shorts. I opened myself up to his hands and mouth as they made their way over my skin. I sat up, the need to see him, to touch him overriding every other inclination. I ran my hands over his hard, muscled chest and stomach, my touch cool against his feverish skin. I kissed his neck, shoulders, pecs, and his own small nipples.

"Stand up," I said.

Alexander obeyed with a question on his face. The look turned voracious as I undid the button and zipper of his shorts and pulled them off. Only black boxer briefs hid his thick erection, jutting forward, straining the cotton. I stared up at him from behind my lashes and removed his last piece of clothing.

"I want to taste you."

"And you always do what you want."

"Usually."

I held the length of him close to his abs, and licked the underside up to the tip. I rolled my tongue around him before slowly, smoothly, taking him all the way into my mouth. My lips wrapped around his base. Encouraged by his guttural groans, I repeatedly slid back and forward. Carefully teasing, I raked my teeth along him, and he grew larger in my mouth. Replacing my teeth with my tongue and wet lips, I bobbed faster. He held my head as he threw his own back in pleasure. He was quickening, and I knew his release was imminent. I continued my attentions even as the pulsing jet shot down my throat. When he finished, I licked him all over, savoring the salty taste, not wasting a drop. Then I leveled him with cherubic eyes.

"You, my dear, are wicked," Alexander praised as he fell onto the bed.

"It's been said."

He reached over and pulled me to him. I cuddled into the crook of his arm and listened proudly to the rapid rhythm of his heart.

Alexander looked down at me, his face glistening with sweat and satisfaction. "I hope you realize we're not finished yet."

"Oh?"

"Yes, my little temptress. You've got a lot coming to you."

Alexander rolled onto me. He kissed the tip of my nose, pecked my lips, and grazed my neck with his teeth, sending goose bumps prickling over my skin. He moved his hands to the inside of my thighs, gently spreading my legs apart. I couldn't hold back whimpers as he skimmed his fingers over me. When he lowered his mouth, a jolt of electricity charged through my body.

"Sweet Goddess above!" I shrieked.

Alexander stifled a laugh, but I was lost, consumed. He teased and rubbed as his mouth devoured me. I fisted his hair and held his head tight. I controlled him as much as he controlled me. When he took me over the edge, I shattered. My orgasm crashed in waves again and again until my body fell limp.

Alexander rested his head on my belly. "You're more delicious than I imagined."

"You've imagined how I tasted?"

"Mhm. And what your creamy skin would feel like under me. I've imagined...many things about you."

For a while, neither of us moved. Eventually, he curled me up with him. We recuperated in each other's arms and talked about absolutely nothing of consequence.

"I could use a shower," Alexander pronounced a few minutes or a millennium later.

"I have a better idea. Take a dip?" I said and motioned outside toward the stream.

"Perfect."

Chapter Nine

Alexander put his boxer briefs and shorts back on and lounged against a heap of pillows on my bed. With a smug smile, he crossed his arms over his bare chest. His bright eyes followed me.

"You look very pleased with yourself," I said behind a grin.

"You please me." He winked and grinned like a naughty schoolboy.

I puttered around my bedroom, stark naked, brazen and unashamed of my curvaceous figure. I took my time selecting a bikini, holding them up one at a time for his input. I was teasing him, and he loved it as much as I did.

We settled on a little pink number with black polka dots. I shimmied into the bathing suit, and he muttered, "I could get used to this." A faraway gaze set upon him.

After grabbing sunglasses and towels, we headed outside. We spread our towels out beside the stream, and I plopped down. I lay back, closed my eyes, and crinkled my toes in the lush grass. I thought of the once-emerald lawns in town, now crunchy, cornflake brown. The prize roses crisped up. The soil cracked and splintered. Our little patch of earth, on the other hand, flourished whether it rained four inches or forty over the course of a season. Maggie and I harvested an endless supply of produce from our vegetable and herb gardens. Our lavender bushes grew high and thick. If the weather be fair or foul, our land still produced an abundant yield. I tried to remember the last time it had rained. Forever ago, it seemed. Arbor was in desperate need of a deluge.

I peeked up from my ruminations and caught Alexander staring down at me.

"Come on. I really could use that swim," he said, grabbing my arms and hoisting me to my feet.

Alexander dropped his shorts and waded into the stream up to his belly button. I followed quickly behind, the cool water just covering my breasts. For the next hour, we laughed and played like children in the stream. Even Shasta and Rocky showed up to take part in the fun. Shasta splashed while Rocky swooped and dive-bombed us.

"I wish you could communicate with my familiars. I hate feeling like I'm leaving you out of the conversation," I said and waded closer to him.

Rocky and Shasta raised their voices as one. *"As you wish it, so shall it be."* Then they each addressed Alexander, though their voices were clear in my mind as well.

"I am the black bear, Shasta. I am Evangeline's familiar and companion. Through me, her strength is tenfold. I've pledged to do her bidding when it is in my power to do so. She has desired our communication, and so it shall be."

The poor man looked like he'd just gotten smacked in the back of the head with a two-by-four.

"I am the red-tailed hawk, Habrock. I am also Evangeline's familiar and companion. Through me, she has the power of flight. I will do all she bids if it is in my ability. She has requested ease of communication between you and I, and it is wise for it to be so. You, too, may call me Rocky, for I'm fond of the nickname."

When Alexander replied, his voice was thick, great emotion contorting his hard features. "Shasta, Rocky, I'm grateful for the trust you've placed in me, and I'll endeavor to deserve it. It relieves me to know Evangeline has such loyal companions to look after her."

After saying goodbye, my familiars retired to the forest and Alexander and I sat out on a rocky crag along the stream's edge. With our towels wrapped around us, we dangled our feet in the water. Alexander looked out over everything and nothing at all. His faraway gaze creased the corners of his eyes and between his brows.

"What is it?" I pressed.

"What was life like when Evangeline Clarion was young?" he asked, although I was pretty sure that wasn't the question foremost on his mind.

"Well, let's see... When I was very little, my mother and I lived farther upstate in a bungalow, clustered together with the other families in our coven. It was a close-knit community. The adults socialized. The kids all played together. That's where the boys and I got to be such good friends." I smiled softly.

"The boys?" Alexander's head popped up, and he eyed me curiously.

"Ethan and Gregory Massey, and Nicolae and Luca Loveridge. They're my best friends—besides Bunny, er, Gwendolyn Reed. But she's not a witch. Bunny knows nothing of magic. Anyway, Gregory's a chef down in the city. He doesn't have his own restaurant yet, but that's the plan. He's also a direct descendant of Druid priests."

"You're kidding?"

"I'm not." I grinned wider. "When he was five or so, he went on vacation with his parents to Ireland. While they explored some ancient forest, they found Ethan, a naked, ruddy toddler, abandoned in the brambles. Gregory's parents realized right away that Ethan had abilities. They adopted him, brought him home to the States, and raised him as their own. He's got the magic of the Good Folk."

"The Good Folk?"

"Fairies."

"You're kidding?" he said again, more incredulous this time.

"I'm not. There's infinitely more magic in the world than most people realize," I explained.

"So it seems." Alexander shook his head in disbelief. "What about the other guys?"

"Nicolae and Luca are brothers. They're Romani, what some call Gypsies. Most Romani don't practice witchcraft and consider it nothing more than trickery. But the Loveridge family descends from an ancient line of sorcerers who derive their power from the Goddess."

"So everyone in the coven has real magic like you?"

"Not all, but most. And magic manifests itself differently through each of us."

"But these guys all have powers?" Alexander asked as he took my small hand in his.

"Oh, yes. They're very powerful, each in his own way."

"I'm at a disadvantage from the outset then." He swept his fingers lightly along my temple.

"What? No. There's never been anything romantic, despite what the gossips say. The boys are like brothers to me, not to mention the fact that Ethan is gay, and Gregory, well, he likes to explore."

As we spoke, Alexander drew closer by degrees. It was getting harder for me to concentrate. He leaned in and nuzzled lightly along my neck. "Then I have another worry."

"What's that?"

"They might not approve of me."

"Ha!" I belted, making Alexander jump. "I'm sure you'll charm them as much as you've charmed me."

He smiled and tucked a stray bit of hair behind my ear. "Tell me more."

I shimmied closer. "I was precocious as a little girl. The boys and I ran wild in the wooded mountains, casting spells and causing a ruckus. With the coven, we could display our magic openly. And we did." I smiled at the memory of running around with the ruddy, dirt-kneed boys. "We were always getting into one mess or another. I was happy, for a time."

My good humor fled as my thoughts turned to my mother.

"But then your mom died," Alexander said. "What happened?"

How the hell does he do that?

I fidgeted, unsure how to explain what it felt like to have my heart torn from my chest when I was still too young to shave my legs or menstruate.

"I didn't speak for weeks and never cried. I retreated inward. In the meantime, Maggie made all the arrangements and organized every detail of my mother's funeral and Summerland Rite. I moved like a ghost, weaving aimlessly through throngs of mourners with my face stoic and gaze empty. Hordes of them, magical and mundane alike, invaded my home to offer condolences, with their tissues in hand to ensure they displayed the appropriate level of grief."

"What's Summerland?" Alexander drew his fingers along my arms as he spoke.

"We believe we're placed on Earth to learn lessons. From one incarnation to the next, we learn something new. We are energy—spirit. That energy leaves us when we die and eventually moves on to inhabit another form in another lifetime. While the spirit awaits a new form, it resides in Summerland."

His hand stilled for a second. "Wow, okay. So, the funeral? Maggie took care of you."

"She took care of everything. Thankfully, she didn't expect me to handle any task more challenging than my own grooming. I remember my dress was demure and black and I wore sensible shoes. I scrubbed my face and hands clean and neatly braided my hair. But my detached, unresponsive, almost catatonic demeanor disturbed all those who'd come to pay their respects. I heard their whispers, 'bizarre, oddity.' Yet even as a little girl, I understood that their indiscreet criticisms spoke more to their own arrogance than any impropriety in my manner of mourning.

"Two weeks after my mother's death, my home finally fell silent. The barrage of black-clad visitors ended. Only the noxious scent of decaying lilies and casseroles lingered. Maggie sat for hours on end at my mother's desk, finalizing her affairs and finances. She was granted custody of me, so

I moved in with her, into the cottage. And that was fine by me. I couldn't stand the looks and the whispers from the coven. Not that it got any better when I moved to Arbor."

Unabashed, I took Alexander's arms and wrapped them around my shoulders. I curled into him, soaking in the security he made me feel.

"My spirit was all but dead at that point. But if anyone could save my soul, it was Maggie. It was her hope that time spent cradled in the natural world would heal me—and my spirit. Maggie's most potent magic draws every bit of goodness from the earth and its creatures, myself included. She encouraged me to sketch, paint, sew, play music, anything that allowed for creativity and creation. She became my benefactor, my teacher, my protector, my friend. Together, we healed and we flourished."

Alexander and I hopped off the rocks we'd been lounging on and strolled along beside the water, hand in hand.

"And your mother? What was she like?"

"Her name was Lavinia. To call her a powerhouse would be a gross understatement. Animals flocked to her, often following at her heels wherever she went. Telekinesis and astral projection came as easy as breathing to her. It seemed like magic itself blazed from her emerald eyes. It's funny, my mother was the stark opposite of Maggie. She never reached five foot and had long, dark hair and curves for miles."

"Like you," Alexander said, curling a lock of my hair between his fingers.

"Like me." I sighed. "I'm blessed to have inherited my mother's looks, but I worry that the older I get and the more I resemble her, the harder it becomes for Maggie."

"She and your mother were...lovers?" Alexander ran his fingers almost absentmindedly along my shoulder, arm, the dip of my stomach, the rise of my hip.

I nodded. "Lovers. Soul mates. Their spirits have been connected through each and every one of their lifetimes. Their love will continue well beyond this life."

"You mentioned last night that Maggie has only ever loved your mother. That's why she never married."

"Yup."

Alexander stopped at the fallen oak, the mouth of the forest. He stared into its shadowed depths. "Have you seen today's paper?"

"Don't tell me they skewered Crandall again. The harder the press is on her, the worse it is for me."

"It's not so much about her as it is about you." He eyed me anxiously.

"Oh, for the love of the Goddess, how bad is it?"

"See for yourself." Alexander fished his phone out of his pocket, and pulled up *The Messenger*'s website. There in bold print:

VIXEN? OR VICTIM OF CRANDAL'S CRUSADE?

A picture of me, mercifully taken just prior to my dousing with the green apple slushy, sat below the headline. The article wasn't particularly damning. It explained my connection with the Crandalls, specifically my past relationship with Jay. Then there were the typical accusations from the more vocal Arbor residents. I was called a floozy with loose morals and an unrepentant temptress. The article also stated that I was an unapologetic, self-proclaimed witch. The paper noted, however, that according to the US Constitution, I had every right to espouse that belief.

"I guess it could be worse. The picture's not bad."

"You dated her son?" Alexander asked. The control necessary to hold back a growl, twisted his strained face.

I nodded. "For two years, until I found out he cheated on me with half the female population of the county and he found out I'd kissed my best friend."

"Bunny?"

I recalled the wistful memory vividly. *How lovely she looked that afternoon, stripped bare of her garish trappings.* "We shared a sweet moment, but nothing ever came of it. There was no romantic spark." My mood soured as I thought of how Jay Crandall and his mother had twisted that innocent experience to smear me. "Yeah, look, I'm not the slut they're trying to make me out to be."

"I wasn't implying—" he began.

"No, let me say this. I believe sexuality is divine, primal. I'm not some damn seductress preying on innocent men for my own fiendish amusement. I've dated my fair share. I've had a few lovers—male and female. But I don't sleep around. Yet every time I've taken an interest in a guy, he ends up regaling the town with elaborate tales of my wicked ways. To hear them talk, it's as if I have a magical vagina, a concept I find curiously amusing. It doesn't hurt. It pisses me off. And what truly infuriates me is that the reputations of the males in question never seem to tarnish." Violent adrenaline surged through me. I shook my hands out to release the energy. "I don't deserve this crap."

"What are you going to do?" Alexander asked, careful to keep his voice even.

"I wish I knew."

He and I rested against the fallen oak and stared down the jagged, forest path. A heavy silence fell between us, burdened by memories of yesterday and the uncertainties of tomorrow.

The sudden urge to take to the skies overcame me. I reached out mentally to Rocky. When I heard his caw, I knew he was close enough to aid my flight. Releasing the chains that weighed down my spirit was a bit more challenging than usual, but before long, I felt the familiar numbing adrenaline. I shot Alexander a wink and lifted off from the earth with a hop. The higher I rose, the heavier the air became, bloated with months of unshed rain. I thought the waters would spill out in a great gargling gush as I pierced the low-hanging clouds.

Alexander lit up as I soared high above him. He cheered me on, shouting and clapping. After a few minutes, I glided downward and landed with ease beside him.

"Unbelievable! You're even more stunning in the air." He whisked me up into his arms and kissed me with a fierceness that stole my breath and shocked my heart. Then he carried me into the cottage and waltzed straight into my bedroom.

And I let him.

He made me feel safe, protected. I wasn't ready to share this info with him, however. It was hard enough admitting it to myself.

We changed into suitable attire. Alexander put on his soft blue T-shirt, removed his wet boxers, and wore his shorts commando. I took off my bikini and threw on a navy tank and a floor-length, flowy purple skirt.

"Come on. Why don't we raid the fridge?" I asked.

"Hell yes," he said and smacked me on the ass.

I smiled and bolted toward the kitchen as he chased behind me. We stopped short when Maggie and Adelaide walked through the front door, both women's arms heavy with groceries.

"What a perfect time for a strapping young man to arrive!" Adelaide said. "My arms are about to fall off."

Alexander ran over, grabbed the bags from both ladies, and brought them into the kitchen. Adelaide followed closely behind so she could check out his ass.

Maggie pulled me aside. "What in blazes is going on?"

I offered a devious smile. "I've been letting Alexander get to know me."

"And are you getting to know him?" Maggie's brow crooked.

"A bit." I couldn't help the cheesy grin that lit up my face. I really liked him, and there was no reason to hide that fact from Maggie. But we had pressing matters to discuss. "How about Alexander and I help you and Adelaide with dinner, and then we can all talk? I could use her wisdom as well as yours."

The four of us worked well together in the kitchen, weaving around each other to set the table, open and pour wine, chop and sauté vegetables, and make risotto. Once the meal was complete, we all sat around the rough-cut mahogany dining table.

Adelaide raised her arms and called for us all to bow our heads. "Blessed are the seeds that grow the plants. Blessed are the wind, the sun, the rain, and the earth that nourish. Blessed are those who plant, tend, and harvest. Through these gifts, those around this table are sustained and enriched. We share this meal in grateful joy. Blessed Be."

We all responded, including Alexander, "Blessed Be."

Of course, Adelaide had to have the last word. "Let's dig in, cats and kittens!"

"I must say, Alexander," Maggie began after we'd all had a few minutes to eat, "I was surprised to see you here. Should I assume you've been here all day?" She directed her question to both of us, and we nodded our assent. "I understand Eva has told you a bit about herself. The cat's out of the bag, as it were."

"You mean the broom's out of the closet!" Adelaide said, cracking herself up.

With a tiny smile, Maggie continued. "As Eva explained, she is a witch. Adelaide and I are as well. While there are many witches in the world, we have a bit more...juice than most."

"You have powers too," Alexander said.

"You did throw caution to the wind, Evangeline. Well, well, it's quite all right. If he exposes us, we can just turn him into a horny toad," Adelaide said, deadpan.

Thankfully, Alexander caught her humor and laughed.

Maggie, on the other hand, maintained her serious demeanor. "Yes, the Goddess blessed us with great gifts. Those with true magic at their fingertips are a rarity. Eva's magic is exceptional, but her abilities are still evolving. She'll be more powerful than Adelaide and I combined soon enough. You may think she is cute and fun, but I assure you, our Evangeline is no one to trifle with."

"Ms. Maramma, I agree wholeheartedly that Evangeline is fun. But cute is not the word I'd use to describe her." He paused and took my hands. "It doesn't do her justice. Evangeline is the most mesmerizing, exhilarating, fierce female I have ever met." He sealed this declaration with a kiss upon my flushed cheek.

Maggie was floored and more than a little flustered. So was I. Adelaide just grinned, delighted by the magic sizzling in the air.

"Well then," Maggie continued after clearing her throat, "I only ask that you keep what you witness close to your heart. Our magic must not, cannot be revealed to anyone. It will never really be safe for us to practice openly. Half this town is looking for an excuse to run us out of here as it is. We can't give them one. Many of these folks have caught glimpses of the unexplained over the years." Maggie stopped to hit me with her signature disappointed *oh-Eva* look. "Lucky for us, they're so concerned that others would ridicule them for believing in magic, that no one admits what they've seen. We need to keep it that way."

"I understand, Ms. Maramma," Alexander said.

"Please, call me Maggie."

"Maggie." He smiled.

"So, my dear Alexander," Adelaide said, commanding the floor. "I hear you returned to the market the other day after we met and happened upon Evangeline getting attacked by that putrid pile of bull excrement, Stuart Cudlow. You ran him off."

"I did. I'd left the market with every intention of heading home, but I couldn't get Evangeline out of my head. So I drove back, hoping to catch her before she left. When I pulled into the parking lot, that asshole had his hands all over her. After I made sure Evangeline was out of harm's way, I dropped the guy. I told him I'd break his legs if he harassed another female again."

Adelaide was enraptured. She sat forward in her chair and rested her chin in her hands. "Then what? What did Stuart say?"

"Nothing. He pissed his pants and ran off to tell his mommy. From what Franklin, my butler, tells me, Mrs. Cudlow already called on me at the manor. Apparently, the Cudlows are threatening to sue. But they're going to have a rude awakening if they pursue legal action. Thanks to my great-grandfather, I have enough money to keep her lawyers busy until the end of days."

"Lawyers? Oh, this is all my fault." I dropped my face into my hands.

A flash of fury crashed over me. Alexander grabbed me gently but with a firm grip and turned me to face him. "You to listen to me. None of this is your fault." His voice was barely restrained. He was caged fury. "Now, don't think on this for another second," he said as his eyebrow twitched.

Maggie jumped in. "Let me caution you, Alexander. You do not want to get on the wrong side of Gladys Cudlow. She may be tacky, but she's an attack dog, a nasty piece of work. She comes across as a genteel matron of the church, but she's as much a woman of God as I am."

"I don't intimidate easily." Alexander dismissed the concern.

My Goddess, who is this man? My heart leapt. I wrapped my arms around him and buried my face in the crook of his neck. He hugged me close and ran his fingers up and down my spine.

A strange notion floated through my mind as I sat cocooned in Alexander's embrace. I felt cherished. It startled me to think that I could make such a deep connection with someone after so brief an acquaintance.

"Oh, I like you," said Adelaide. "Evangeline could benefit from a man like you beside her."

I caught the duel meaning of Adelaide's words and shot her a suspicious eye.

"You go ahead and spend as much time with Evangeline as she'd like."

I sipped my wine to hide my Cheshire smile.

"Has Eva spoken to you about my concerns with Morgan Manor?" Maggie threw out of left field, and I choked on my wine.

"Concerns? What's this about?" Alexander leveled his keen eyes on me.

"I'm sorry. I don't know why I didn't mention it earlier. We talked about so much, I guess it slipped my mind."

Saving me, Maggie explained the vision my sketch of the manor gardens had triggered, and she insisted Alexander allow us to aid the unsettled spirits onto the next plane.

"As strange as it sounds, that makes me feel better." Alexander took a swig from his wineglass, giving the cup's contents a wary eye. "I've noticed some strange things at the manor. It's good to know I'm not crazy. I'd be grateful for any assistance you could offer to, ah, guide these spirits to wherever it is they belong."

"Well, now that that's settled...Evangeline, you have the floor. We must hear about this prophetic dream you had last night. Get on with it, then," Adelaide prodded.

My eyes shot to the wise, wrinkled high priestess. "How did you know about my dream?"

"How dare you question the source of my knowledge." She placed a hand to her heart as if taking offense, before plastering on a grin. "Only the Goddess knows, dear. So spill it."

I explained the dream with as much detail as I could recall, having never gotten the chance to write down any notes about it.

Maggie interjected with an occasional question, but Adelaide remained quiet until I finished speaking.

Her face grew pale and pasty. "My Fledermous," she whimpered. "Dead?"

Just then, she went rigid, and her eyes tweaked awkwardly in their sockets. I knew the signs. She was having a premonition. It was different from the vision Maggie had. She could occasionally see images, scenes that had already taken place, but Adelaide could glimpse the future. Alexander, Maggie, and I waited until the color returned to the old woman's cheeks, until her focus returned to the here and now. She shook herself to release the premonition's hold.

"Do not take this dream lightly. We must unpack it. Shall we?" she asked and then continued without waiting for a reply. "The elder tree is known as the Goddess tree. It represents judgment, inevitability, and death. The animals around the elder tree were a deer, crane..."

"Lavinia," Maggie said in a whisper.

"What?" I squeaked, not expecting to hear my mother's name.

"Well, we know that the bear, hawk, bat, and bee in your dream are our familiars. It stands to reason that those around the tree would be familiars too. Lavinia, Evangeline's mother," Maggie explained to Alexander, "had two familiars, a deer and a crane."

"How could I have forgotten?" I mumbled softly to myself.

"Alrighty," Adelaide continued, "any idea about the hare, the other animal beside the elder tree?"

We looked to each other, eager for someone to make a connection, but it seemed no one had a theory.

"What about the German shepherd and the viper who showed up to help?" Adelaide asked.

Again, silence.

"Are the wolves familiars, too?" Alexander asked.

"I don't think so," Adelaide said. "How many were there, Evangeline?"

"Seven, I think."

"A plot," she suggested. And before I could question her, my high priestess pegged me with her oracle eyes. "Let there be no doubt, this threat originates with the Crandalls and Cudlows, and the presence of the press exacerbates the problem. You have challenging times ahead. Expect attacks from all sides. And you will not be the sole target of these attacks. What we need to know, Evangeline, is how you'd like to proceed."

They all stared at me, expectation carved into anxious brows and grim lips.

"I've been wondering what my mother would do." I paused to gauge Maggie's reaction to my words. Her mouth parted on an inhale, and she leaned forward. "Lavinia Clarion would not sit back; that's for damn sure. She'd be proactive. I think this requires a two-pronged approach. First, I need to speak up. Reporters can be brutal, but they can also be swayed. I'd like to call a press conference to address the accusations laid at my feet."

"Do you really think that's wise?" Alexander asked, consternation set along his clenched jaw. "As a last resort, maybe. But there are better ways of dealing with people like the Crandalls and Cudlows that don't involve subjecting yourself to further scrutiny."

"Like what?" I challenged.

"Like quietly suing them for libel, slander," he declared—as if it was such an obvious course of action, I should have thought of it first. "My lawyers will shut them up."

"You've got to be kidding. Bringing lawyers into the fray will only inflame the situation." *What is he thinking?* "It's guaranteed to incite retribution. Not to mention the fact that we'll have the press hiding among the lavender, snooping on us." My voice increased in pitch and volume as I defended my view.

"They're going to try to do that one way or another. But that's no reason to invite them in."

"I will do this on my terms," I insisted.

Adelaide looked back and forth at the two of us in amusement.

"Okay, you two, that's enough," Maggie called us to attention.

"My apologies, Ms. Maramma." Alexander nodded his head briefly in deference.

"Maggie," she corrected him.

He cleared his throat before addressing us all. "Here's how I see it. Evangeline is getting harassed, assaulted, and dragged through the mud by these people. This is criminal and should be dealt with as such." Alexander threw back a swig of wine in frustration.

Maggie searched my face. "Either way, we're shutting down the market stand until further notice."

"What the hell, Mags? No. I will not back down to threats and intimidation. Not to mention the fact that the market represents a good portion of our income. It's the only place I have to sell my work. We can't give in."

"It's not wise to instigate them, and you're too tempting a target."

I grumbled under my breath, knowing it was useless to argue.

"You said you had a two-pronged approach. Besides tackling things in the press, what else do you suggest?" Adelaide asked.

"Magic, of course."

"What? Is there some kind of *Bitch-be-gone* spell or something?" Alexander asked flippantly.

"Something like that." I smirked.

Adelaide beamed at us for a moment before apprehension crept into her eyes. "I cannot see the specifics of things yet, my darlings. But mark my words, there is ill fortune on the horizon." She took a labored breath. "I think it would be wise for me to consult my scrying mirror. With any luck, it will reveal the nature of the challenges ahead with more clarity."

Upon rising to her feet, Adelaide swayed, unsteady, and had to grab the edge of the table for support. The rest of us leapt to our feet, ready to catch her should she fall.

"Alexander, won't you be a dear and walk with me to the guest bedroom? I could use a strong arm to hold me up."

"Of course, Ms. Good. It would be my honor to escort you."

"Oh, my dear, your words are sweet as honeyed wine. Come, take my arm. Let us away to discern the future!"

Chapter Ten

Maggie's lips quivered, but she sucked up the frailty, squared her slim shoulders, and lifted a regal chin.

"You and I have a great deal to think on tonight," she said. "I'm going to spend some time with my grandmother's grimoire. Why don't you go save Alexander from Adelaide?" Maggie smoothed a wayward hair behind my ear and kissed my head. "Love you."

"I love you, too, Mags, but do you really think waiting to act is wise? Shouldn't we at least put up wards around the property?"

A text notification sounded from my phone, not giving Maggie a chance to answer. The message was from Bunny, and it was brief.

Pickin u up in 2.

Staying in. Another night? I responded.

Bitch was her only reply.

I didn't think anything of it. It had been a term of endearment between us for years.

I just don't have time to play with Bunny tonight. She'll get over it. She'll be fine.

"I think we're safe for one night," Maggie continued as if we hadn't been interrupted. "Our efforts will be more successful if we first practice a bit of thoughtful consideration. Acting rashly is not prudent."

I decided to follow Maggie's lead, but I had a bad feeling about it.

My goddess-mother walked off with a nod, her shine dulled, diluted. I hoped spending time with her grimoire and herbs would work its magic and soothe her.

I approached the guest bedroom where Adelaide slept when she visited. Hushed voices drifted from beyond the door that stood slightly ajar. Curiosity got the better of me, and I stopped to listen in.

"The two of you have known each other over the course of many lifetimes. There may have been lifetimes when you were lovers, sometimes even enemies, and lifetimes when you've been torn apart from each other. That's when you, Alexander, have been most dangerous. But your suspicion is spot-on. You and Evangeline are soul mates."

Soul mates? No. I'm not ready for that. I shrunk back at the thought.

I could hear Alexander pacing with his steady, measured cadence. "I'll be damned," he rumbled. "This has been a day for revelations. Frankly, these last few weeks have been insane. I finally finish school, and the next thing I know, I'm handed an urn of my great-grandfather's ashes, keys to a colossal estate, and more money and investments than I'll ever know what to do with, not to mention all the assets that go along with it."

"And ghosts," Adelaide chimed in.

"Ha! Yeah, and ghosts. One would think those things would rank pretty damn high up on the list of major life events, but no. Ms. Good, I had a conversation today with a bear and a hawk, as in an actual dialogue. Except I could only hear them within my mind."

"That is remarkable. Most familiars won't communicate with anyone other than a witch. They must consider you special."

"Evangeline is special," Alexander corrected and continued his pacing. "I've got this unrelenting desire to protect her, to please her. I'm compelled to be a better man to deserve her. Like I said, it's as if my soul knew hers on sight."

"It did, my boy, but I must caution you. Loving a witch is no easy task. Even being soul mates doesn't guarantee a happy life. You've spent innumerable lifetimes knitting together delicate strands of golden moments into life's tapestry. There are no assurances that this incarnation of your souls is one that completes the design." Adelaide paused to let the meaning of her words sink in. "No reason not to give it a try, though? Hmm?"

When Alexander didn't reply, she continued.

"Sit with your girl for a spell. Then go home and get some rest. Magdalena, Evangeline, and I have our hands full, and I'm sure you do as well. An estate of such grandeur doesn't run itself, you know."

"Very true. Thank you, Ms. Good. I appreciate your wisdom."

"Yes, yes. Well, that's the upside of being old as dirt. Now, get along with you."

That was my cue. I darted to my room. I couldn't let Alexander catch me eavesdropping. Sitting down casually on the edge of my bed, I waited. When a minute or two passed and there was no sign of him, I huffed to the kitchen to search him out. The image of Alexander standing beside the hearth and cauldron, his tortured brow drawn tight and creased, his jaw clenched, almost shattered my heart. I hated the anxiety I felt churning within him. I hated that I had caused it. Yet his presence brought me comfort. It felt almost selfish to want him beside me.

He turned at my approach but didn't move toward me. Instead, he reached out, beckoning me forward. In a moment, I found myself wrapped in his arms.

"You have bewitched me, body and soul," he said as he held me tight against his chest, his words feathering against my cheek. "You must allow me to tell you how ardently I admire you."

Dear Goddess, he's quoting Pride & Prejudice*!*

He spoke Darcy's words but left the quotes incomplete. He hadn't spoken of love. Part of me was relieved he wasn't outright declaring himself so soon. Another part was exceedingly jealous of Elizabeth Bennet.

"I think highly of you too. I greatly esteem you. I like you very much," was all I could stumble out, with my thoughts in a muddle. It wasn't until after I'd spoken that I realized I'd paraphrased *Sense and Sensibility.*

Is it possible to read too much Jane Austen?

"I'm worried about you and about Maggie and Ms. Good. These threats are not going to let up. And if Ms. Good's interpretation of your dream is to be believed, there's serious danger ahead."

"I agree we need to be proactive, but Maggie wants to take the cautious route, focus on determining the nature of their attack on us, and avoid acting rashly. So, while she's doing research, I need to prepare a response." I paused to pull my thoughts together. "You need to know I'm not backing down about going to the press. And I'm keeping lawyers out of it, unless they're absolutely necessary."

"Fine. But may I make a suggestion?" He heaved a sigh.

"Of course." My curiosity was piqued.

"You need professional help."

Alexander said the words with such a serious, straight face, that I hoped I'd misunderstood his meaning. But it still pissed me off.

"Fuck you!" I sneered and flipped him off.

"Huh? Whoa! That's not what I meant." He laughed, and that just pissed me off even more—which only made him laugh harder. "What I mean is that you need help from someone who knows how to handle the press, someone who can help you get your message across."

"I think that's an excellent idea." I knew exactly who to ask, but I decided to keep those details to myself for the time being.

"Great, I'll..."

"I've got this one covered."

"Okay," he conceded. "But what if there's a way to keep you all safe while you work out this plan?"

"What do you mean?"

He took hold of my hands and brought them to his lips. "I want you to stay with me at the manor. It's the only way I know you'll be safe. The three of you can take care of the manor's spirits and stay protected until things blow over."

Whoa there. I backed up a step.

"The walls of Morgan Manor won't keep the inevitable at bay. And I'm not a fan of being locked away—even in a castle, even for my safety, even with you."

"You're not being rational!" he said, exasperated. "Anyone can barrel on up to this cottage whenever they damn well please, Evangeline." Alexander took hold of my shoulders. He looked me in the eyes, determined to stress his point. "The press is going to hound you. Religious zealots are going to badger you. They could storm up here any minute with their fucking pitchforks. You're not safe here!" He paused and took a calming breath that did little to temper his anxiety. "I can protect you at the manor. Let me help you."

"You know I can't do what you're asking," I said in as steady a voice as I could muster.

"No, I don't know that. Why? Please, explain why you're better off here than at the manor," he challenged.

"Because this is my home. This is Maggie's home. Potent magic surges through the earth and waters and trees here. We're connected to this land and its magic viscerally, concretely."

"So this land and its magic can protect you better than me and my lawyers and my walls?" He turned his back, incredulous.

"Your money, you mean." I shook my head. "I'm sorry. I know you're trying to help, but we're a lot stronger than we look."

"I don't doubt your power, but you're sitting ducks here." His shoulders sagged in resignation. "I think it's best if I go now." Alexander made it as far as the next room before returning. He gathered me up in his strong arms and kissed me like I'd never been kissed before in my life. When he let me go, I sagged, almost losing my legs.

"Goodnight, Evangeline," he whispered. And then he was gone.

"He's right, you know," I said to Maggie and Adelaide who'd snuck into the room behind me. As shaken as I was by Alexander's departure, I didn't have the luxury of weakness. I pressed on. "Anyone can sneak onto the property, can bang down the door whenever they please." I turned to face my mentors. "Adelaide, have you gleaned anything of our troubles from the scrying mirror?" It was everything I could do not to mention what I'd overheard. Although, knowing Adelaide, she probably knew I'd listened in.

"Unfortunately nothing of consequence, nothing concrete we didn't already know," she answered in a huff.

"If you'd just give me more time to look through my—" Maggie began before I cut her off.

"The answers we seek won't be found in your grandmother's grimoire. We must invoke the elements, speak to them. We need to see what they see, hear what they hear. Besides Adelaide's scrying, they are our best chance to glean the nature of the plot against us. Then, wards must be put up around the property, every square inch." I waited a moment to see if they'd argue. When both women stood at attention, I continued. "If you gather up supplies, I'll meet you outside. I've got a bonfire to start."

It didn't take me long to get our ceremonial fire blazing. And with Shasta, Rocky, Fled, and Hanna beside me, I scanned the property for unwanted intruders. When the familiars and I made it back to the site of the evening's rituals, I took a moment to speak with them.

"Once the invocation of the elements is underway, Maggie, Adelaide, and I will be in a heavy, trancelike state until the spell is complete. This will leave us vulnerable. We're going to rely on you for protection."

Each familiar pledged humble allegiance to their witch and left to stand watch—or hover, as it was for some in the group—at their designated locations.

I was happy to have a moment alone. My nerves were frayed, and I knew the only way to invoke the elements was in a concentrated state of mind. So I turned inward and focused on the magic churning inside me. I recited a simple protection and calming chant.

> "I am at peace. I am strong. The Goddess protects me from all harm.
> I am calm. I am strong. The Goddess protects me from all harm."

By the time Maggie and Adelaide emerged from the cottage through the back kitchen door, peace had settled upon me. I was ready.

The moon hung hazy, a misty glow in the heavens. And all was still. No trees rustled. The stream ceased to flow. Bird and beast and bug sat silently as if all of nature held its breath, knowing we might have need of it and waiting for our call.

"Please, set the corners," I directed them. I walked the circumference of the fire with even, measured steps as the women placed representations of the elements at the northern, southern, eastern, and western directions. Maggie, Adelaide, and I then held hands, and spoke as one.

> "We are maiden, mother, crone;
> Magic forged in blood and bone.
> We invoke thee, Northern Earth,
> Flesh and bone of mortal birth.
> We invoke thee, Southern Fire,
> Sizzling pulse of love's desire.
> We invoke thee, Eastern Air,
> Breath of life and trumpets blare.
> We invoke thee, Western Water,
> Ocean tides and blooded daughter.
> As above, so too below.
> Within, without, does spirit flow.
> To hear and taste, to touch and see.
> As we will it, so mote it be."

Over and over and again, we recited the spell until each word became indistinct from the next.

Rocky's screech and Shasta's booming growl broke through my trance. *"The fire's growing out of control!"* Rocky warned.

I tried to open my eyes but could only manage to peek out through thin slits. Gray soot clouded my vision. I opened my mouth to call out to Adelaide and Maggie, but my lips were caked with ash. The thick sulfur air coated my nostrils and filled my lungs.

The bonfire had grown ten times its original size, and its tendrils threatened to spread into the forest. Violent flames licked at Maggie's arms and legs and clothing. Still deep within her trance, Maggie did nothing to avoid the fire that swirled around her. Her lips moved as she continued reciting the invocation. Her arms were outstretched, and her head turned to the sky when hot embers caught the hem of her dress and surged upward.

I didn't have to think. Instinct drove me. I swept my hands toward the stream and drew the waters out of their gurgling bed and through the air. I directed the deluge at the blaze that tormented Maggie and threatened the woods beyond. The fire retreated instantly, as if chastised. Once the great wave extinguished the flames, I returned the waters to their brook with a thunderous splash.

What remained of Maggie's dress fell charred and loose from her soot-streaked frame, doing little to cover her. I rushed to her side and wrapped myself around her nearly bare body. I expected she'd be cold after getting soaked with all that water, but her skin was hot, almost scorching to the touch. I'd been so distracted by the flames that it wasn't until I embraced her and my head lay in the crook of her neck that I noticed Maggie's hair. Her wild blonde mane had turned red. And not like Adelaide's wispy strawberry-orange locks, but a deep, rich, blood red.

What the fuck?

When her foggy eyes cleared and I could see the sallow color of her cheeks abating, I knew Maggie had returned to me.

"Mags, what happened?"

"The elements...they showed me what will be. A great burning. A deadly blaze." Her voice was hollow and cold.

"Because of the drought? Will there be a forest fire?" I asked.

"I...I don't know."

Adelaide and our familiars reached us in time to hear Maggie's cryptic revelation. My wary gaze met Adelaide's.

"We must summon the rain." If we alleviated the drought, it would be one less thing the mayor and the rest of Arbor could blame on us. And hopefully, it could thwart this great burning.

Adelaide nodded. "Give me a moment."

I turned back to Maggie, amazed as Hanna and her swarm whizzed around and around in an attempt to cloak her. Adelaide returned with an oversized upholstered bag in one hand and a bundle of clothing in the other. She handed me a towel. I held it up so Hanna would understand my intentions and pull back the swarm. I wrapped the towel around Maggie's shoulders, removed the charred remains of her clothing, and dried her off. Adelaide handed me one of Maggie's loose dresses, and I pulled it over her head.

"I'm fine, really," Maggie whispered in a cracked voice as she finished dressing herself.

"Good," I said. "Then let's begin."

Adelaide opened up her bag. First, she withdrew a large crystal jar of sea salt, which she poured out in a thick circle around us. Next, she removed a satchel of stones. She arranged moss agate, associated with the element earth, to the north; hematite, linked with fire, to the south; tiger's eye, an air stone, to the east; and lapis lazuli, the water stone, to the west. Within an earthen bowl positioned in the center of the circle, Adelaide placed a tall black candle. Around the candle, she poured enough diamonds to rival the crown jewels. Adelaide poured consecrated water into the bowl over the diamonds, then allowed four feathers from an albino raven to float above the water. Finally, she lit the candle.

Hand in hand, all at once and as one, we began to chant.

> "We are Maiden, Mother, Crone
> Magic forged in blood and bone.
> Water, Fire, Earth, and Air
> Defend your daughters. Heed our prayer.
> Draw down your waters; make it rain.
> Until the rivers swell again.
> Draw down your waters; make it rain.
> Until the flowers bloom again.
> Draw down your waters; make it rain.
> Until the earth is rich again.
> By the law of three times three,
> As we will it. So mote it be."

Again and again, we recited the incantation with our heads bowed and hands clasped. When chilling winds began to churn and stinging sprays of rain erupted from fat black clouds, we raised our eyes and hands to the heavens. Our recitation continued undaunted, swelling with fevered resolve...until the wail of sirens ripping the air broke our trance and heralded our bombardment.

I stood by in horror as Shasta charged from her watch at the forest's edge toward the police cruiser that had torn up the cottage driveway. A searing pain coursed through my head as a frightening premonition overcame me—Shasta with a bullet in her head.

"*No!*" I cried out to my beloved familiar, and she halted her advance in an instant. "Hide!" I commanded. And I fell to my knees, praising the Goddess, as the black bear disappeared into the woods unharmed.

Mayor Crandall and Chief Harrison, Arbor's top cop, stepped from the vehicle, immediately crouching under the onslaught of near hurricane-force rain. I turned to my goddess-mother and high priestess for guidance, but Maggie did not look well. The color had drained from her cheeks again, and she slumped, weak, against Adelaide. Conjuring the rain had taken a great toll on her, having come so quickly on the heels of our last spell.

"Hurry! Take her inside, Adelaide. She needs to lie down. Make her some tea. There is a jar of mint, hyssop, marjoram, thyme, and ginseng already blended, labeled as a restorative, on the right-hand side of the cupboard. I need to see what the hell is going on."

"I've got her. Don't you worry. Go on now."

Before I could take a step, Maggie grabbed my wrist. "Whatever happens, do not underestimate that woman. She is powerful in ways we are not. It'll take more than a summer storm to fend her off."

"I don't underestimate Mayor Crandall, Mags, but I refuse to let her rule me. We can't allow her to intimidate us. We have done nothing wrong."

I approached our uninvited guests with a calm spirit and clearness of mind that surprised me. With the chaos of the evening, nerves would have been normal. I intended to receive the mayor with an even temper, but as I held out my hand in greeting, she charged past me and squared off with Maggie.

"Hold it right there! Not so fast, Magdalena. You too, Adelaide Good. Where do you think you're going?"

My goddess-mother sagged in Adelaide's arms. I rushed to Maggie's side to help and grabbed a hold of her free arm.

"She's not well. She needs to rest." I faced off with the seething, sopping-wet mayor.

Crandall threw her wagging finger in my face and sneered. "She seemed healthy enough to join you and the hag in your wickedness. We've got it all on video! And the chief and I saw you with our own eyes."

What the hell? What does she mean she has it on video?

Chief Harrison, a kind, portly man in his mid-sixties, approached, nodding to each of us in turn. Though he walked with quiet steps, his jovial greeting boomed. "Good evenin', Ms. Maramma, Ms. Good. Evenin', Ms. Eva."

"Sir." I nodded back.

The rain pelted harder. I folded in closer to Maggie and fought a bout of the shivers.

"Just to clarify, Doreen," the chief began, "I didn't see nothin' more than three women with their arms lifted to the sky. Considerin' these are the first drops of rain in months, praisin' the heavens seems a logical thing to do."

The chief smiled over at me. "I don't wanna keep you ladies out here too long in all this weather, so I'll make it quick. Mayor Crandall here seems to believe you've been engagin' in some kind of satanic ritual. Now, you are well within your rights to believe what ya will, but I frown on sacrificin' and the like."

"Oh, can it, Harrison," Adelaide snapped. "You know darn well this Satan talk is a load of bunk." She threw a glare at Crandall.

"Then ya won't mind me taking a peek around?" the chief asked, hands planted firmly on his hips, looking every bit the long, *long* retired superhero.

"I don't care what you do, ya old codger, as long as you let me get Magdalena inside and out of this rain." Adelaide turned before the chief had the chance to reply.

"Of course, of course." He waved them off and began taking a critical eye to the scene of our evening's rituals.

"What the hell are you doing, Harrison?" Crandall screeched.

Ignoring the mayor as much as the rain, Chief Harrison walked carefully around the yard, examining every detail.

"Why aren't you arresting them?" She clawed at the officer's arm until he finally addressed her.

"Doreen, it doesn't look to me like they've been up to no good. I see no evidence of sacrificin', nothing out of the ordinary. I'm really not sure why you bothered draggin' me out here."

"Nothing out of the ordinary? Are you blind?" Crandall took in the scene around her, looking for something—anything—incriminating. She caught sight of the earthen bowl with the black candle in the center. The bowl of water with the albino raven feathers. And the diamonds. She charged over and snatched up the bowl.

"You better take a look here, Harrison. Diamonds. Lots of diamonds." Crandall slowly dipped her hand into the waters and cupped the jewels. Her eyes flashed.

Seething, I stepped up to the mayor and stared her down. Fear cracked her hardened expression. She lowered the bowl, showed me her diamond-free hands, and took a step back.

"Chief Harrison, sir, those belong to Adelaide," I explained, now ignoring Crandall. "I know you're aware of our beliefs. Look around the circle. There are other stones, lapis lazuli, tiger's eye. These are part of the way we worship. We've done nothing illegal. We are well within our rights."

Crandall, now closely resembling a waterlogged sheepdog, stepped between me and the chief. "She and those women are a cancer. They are a stain on this town. Their evil must be stopped."

"Listen here, Doreen. I didn't agree to come out here on some fishin' expedition. Shoot, this is a witch hunt, and I won't be part of it." The chief stepped around Crandall to address me. "Ms. Eva, I do apologize for keepin' ya out in all this nastiness. The mayor and I are gonna get outta your hair now."

"Watch how you address me, Harrison, especially in public," Crandall snapped. "And Ms. Clarion most certainly is coming downtown for questioning."

In a feat of epic stupidity, Crandall reached out and tried to snatch the chief's handcuffs that dangled from his belt. Unfortunately for the mayor, the chief was faster than he looked. He caught Crandall's wrist firmly. He hit her with a warning eye and released her.

The chief stood toe to toe with the mayor. "I don't work for you. I work for the people of Arbor. And it seems you need remindin' that no one is above the law. That stunt you just pulled was the only law broken here tonight. Now let's leave these women alone. You better hope they don't press charges...or turn ya into a toad!" He cracked himself up. "I'm gettin' out of this rain. Good night, Ms. Eva. I sure hope Ms. Maramma feels better."

"Thank you, sir. Good night."

"Oh, and please tell Ms. Good I wish her a pleasant evenin'," Chief Harrison said before turning back toward his police car.

Mayor Crandall stood frozen, stunned, with the pelting rain streaking her heavy makeup down her cheeks. "I'm not finished with you. Not by a long shot," she vowed and trudged away through the puddles and mud.

I stood alone with the stinging waters pouring over me, nature doing Her best to cleanse me. For as much as the night's rituals had accomplished—we found out about the great burning and called forth the rain to combat it—even greater concerns persisted. Maggie was right. It would take more than a summer storm to fend off Mayor Doreen Crandall.

Chapter Eleven

The deluge created a swamp where there once was lush, green lawn. By morning, the magic that breathed within the land would bring balance, but until then, muddy puddles sprung up every few feet. My ears vibrated with the rain's incessant static. I gathered up the discarded remains of our rituals: the stones and bowl, the scorched strips of Maggie's dress, and Adelaide's upholstered bag. I placed everything just inside the kitchen door. I said good night to Shasta and Rocky and wished them sweet dreams. Exhaustion threatened to overwhelm me. The weight of the day eroded the armor that guarded my spirit, and all I wished for was a soft bed on which to rest.

But something kept me outside, something left unsettled, a needling up my spine of something sinister prowling in the shadows. The drenching rain no longer mattered. I couldn't possibly get any wetter. And I knew I'd never be able to rest if I over-worried about bumps in the night. So I walked through each row of lavender, along every bend of the stream, allowing my bare feet to soak in the wisdom of the earth, willing the elements to guide me.

A rustling drew my attention down the length of the driveway to my left. Then once more, but ahead and to the right. I scanned the trees and underbrush that lined the drive but nothing seemed out of the ordinary. I thought about calling Rocky to check things out from above, but I didn't want to wake him. I walked a few feet more before deciding to head back to the cottage.

As I turned up the driveway, I caught Rocky's faint outline cut out of the haze. He was a rocket, headed straight for me. Fatigue had dulled my senses so that my familiar's panicked warnings registered as no more than garbling I couldn't quite comprehend. In my attempt to decipher Rocky's urgent message, I missed the approach of the two men who wrenched me from out of the darkness.

Under the cover of night and our magically forged downpour, they dragged me beneath a canopy of oaks and hurled me into the nettle and thistle. The briar swallowed me up, biting my flesh. Pinprick streaks of blood striped my body in crimson. Every muscle clenched from the sting, and I thought I'd freeze in that position.

And I thought I knew what fear was.

But I'd never known the kind of fear that Stuart Cudlow evoked in me that night. When I first saw his rabid expression—all fevered skin and pasty pallor; eyes wild, mad—I recoiled. My stomach convulsed, and I gagged on the bile that filled my mouth.

It was clear Stuart took great pleasure in my captivity, lording over me with a self-congratulatory smile like a hunter with his downed prey. Hunger juiced him up, and he licked the rain and sweat from his lips.

"Keep watch," he called to his accomplice as he pulled down the zipper on his pants. "You already fucked the witch. It's my turn."

His bluster distracted him long enough for me to nail him in the balls with the heel of my bare foot. He buckled over, and I seized the opportunity to detangle myself from my bed of brambles. But my second assailant was on me in a heartbeat.

I mentally withdrew from my surroundings, focusing instead on the power of the Goddess within. I called on the brambles to free me from their grasp and encircle my attackers instead. They immediately followed my directive, winding around the men's legs. But they weren't fast enough. Neither was I.

Clutching a large, jagged rock, Jay Crandall raised his hand high above his head.

I heard a shrill "keeee-aaaw."

And then...

Nothing.

And then...

A crash and blast and light and electricity rushing up my toes. Warm arms around my shoulders. Harsh rocks along my back. And pain—lancing, throbbing pain.

No rain, though. The rain had stopped.

When I heaved my eyes open, Alexander crushed me close. "Oh, thank the Goddess," he wept. "You're alive." Tears clung to every word. "I'm sorry. I'm so, so sorry" became Alexander's mantra as he laid my head on his lap and stroked gentle fingers along my temple. "Maggie will be here soon. I promise. You're going to be okay."

"No. Maggie's not well," I scratched out.

"Shhh, it's okay. She's okay."

"You came back." We hadn't parted on the best terms. I didn't understand why he was even there.

"I was an ass. I couldn't sleep knowing how I left things between us."

"I didn't think that kiss was so bad," I teased in a harsh whisper.

He smiled wide. "No, that kiss wasn't bad." He leaned down and placed another on my forehead.

Panting, stomping shadows caught our attention. I almost didn't recognize Maggie, having forgotten all about her fiery new locks. Adelaide lumbered a few steps behind her.

"This is not how I planned my evening," Adelaide groused. "I would turn both those beasts into toads and roast them up with a little rosemary if I didn't think they'd burn me at the stake for it."

"I've got her, Alexander," Maggie said, sitting down beside me.

"I won't be far, okay? I'm just going to talk to Adelaide for a minute," Alexander said softly before tucking me into Maggie's arms.

"Hey, my girl." Maggie eased me into a sitting position.

"What the hell happened?" I asked, my mind cotton-filled and foggy. "The last thing I remember is...shit, where's Stuart? And there was someone else... Jay!"

"Okay, relax. I need to tend to your injuries. We'll have plenty of time later to work through what happened," Maggie said as she examined my bleeding head, the scratches that covered my skin, and the scorch marks on my feet. I melted into my goddess-mother's capable embrace and let her work her magic.

Alexander and Adelaide's conversation, a few yards away, floated over to my ears.

"I didn't want to move her too far without knowing the extent of her injuries."

"That's just fine, son. I don't know how you did it, and you will need to explain that to me later, but you protected our girl well. Now, let's give Magdalena time to work; then we'll see where we are." Adelaide spoke calmly, but I knew her too well not to sense her agitation.

"Yes, ma'am, of course."

He protected me? From Stuart and Jay? Why's Adelaide so anxious? What the hell happened? My brain spun with questions.

It took Maggie another ten minutes to care for my wounds. My head hurt worst of all. Clearly, even with Maggie's healing magic, some of my wounds would take longer to heal than others.

"You're well enough to be moved," Maggie said. "But I need you to remain as still as you can, okay?"

"Yeah, okay." *Not like I'm looking to go for a jog.*

"She's in no danger," Maggie called out to the huddled duo.

"Let's move this party up to the cottage, then, shall we?" Adelaide suggested before starting up the drive.

"Okay, here we go," Alexander said as he lifted me effortlessly into his arms.

Maggie headed back up to the cottage, but Alexander planted his feet. Not a muscle on his solid frame quivered for a good minute or two. Then Alexander turned his head toward me, and his dark eyes met my green and held for an eternity.

"I thought I lost you," he croaked and cleared his throat. "I've just found you, and I...I...I can't lose you yet." He blinked long, damp lashes.

"I'm alive and in your arms because you came back for me." My eyelids fluttered, and I fought fiercely to keep them open.

"I've got you. You're safe." Alexander took his time walking us back to the cottage. "I see your eyes drooping. Go ahead and rest... I won't leave you."

His voice soothed me. I allowed my eyes to close. There wasn't an ounce of give left in me. I was tapped out, done. I paced my breath with his and finally allowed myself to let go.

I dipped in and out of consciousness, but my pain proved too great to allow me to linger long in the conscious world. When I finally came to, my body ached and my head was still killing me, but the scorch marks on my feet and most of the scrapes were gone. A few yellowish-purple bruises lingered. I looked over to my window, only stars glowed in the night sky, so I knew I hadn't been out for too long.

My long skirt—torn, damp, and caked in mud—twisted uncomfortably around my legs. I propped up the pillows behind me and worked on untangling the fabric. That's when I finally noticed Alexander slumped, snoring lightly, in a chair beside my bed.

My jostling roused him, and his head shot up. "Hey, you're awake," he slurred, his voice thick with sleep. "You okay? I should go tell Maggie and Adelaide you're up."

"No, wait. I'm sure they're sleeping. Please don't wake them."

"Do you need anything? A glass of water? Tea?" He was halfway out my bedroom door before I could say a word.

I coughed to clear my throat. "No. Thank you. Just a shower, I think."

Although I could smell my own body odor, I had other motives for wanting to get clean. Stuart's hands had been on me. Again. And Jay Crandall...

"That son of a bitch bashed me over the head with a rock," I said, hoarse and just above a whisper. "It's going to take a whole lot more than sage and candle magic to temper me now. They fucked with the wrong witch." I seethed inside. I railed. I cursed the energy of the Universe out of sheer indignation.

"Please. Let me take care of you." It was a request heavy with meaning.

It took me a moment before I could muster a reply. "I don't need anyone to take care of me. I don't want that. But I appreciate your support." *In other words, I have a few more tricks up my sleeve than your average Harry Potter Ministry of Magic employee. But I'm far from indestructible.*

Alexander helped me to my feet and dropped the softest breath of a kiss on my lips. He walked with me into the bathroom, sat me on the edge of the tub, and started the shower. Careful not to brush against my injuries, he removed my dirty, battered, blood-splattered clothes. I stood before him without a stitch, wholly unashamed of my nakedness. Once I stepped into the shower, I figured he'd leave me to wash up on my own. My heart squeezed at the prospect of being alone with my thoughts. But Alexander didn't leave. Instead, he stepped out of his own clothes and got into the shower with me.

An involuntary cringe drove me back to the shower wall. Fear shot adrenaline through my veins, and pain lanced my flesh in a hundred slivers. The warm shower water sizzled as it hit my skin.

"Easy, I'm just going to wash you," Alexander said with his open hands raised before me. When I gave no further resistance, he lowered them to my shoulders. "Turn around."

I submitted to his simple request with clenched fists. I faced the shower wall, and Alexander stood behind me. He gathered up my hair and twisted it into a knotted bun. Beginning with my neck and working downward, he ran a soapy washcloth over my tender skin. I tried to hide my flinching when the rag crossed sore spots, but he caught it.

"You don't have to hide anything from me. Set your mind at ease. I offer myself to your service."

My pathetic sense of humor chose this inappropriate moment to blurt out a laugh. "Sorry, you're just so very proper sometimes. Chivalrous almost."

"Almost?" His dark eyes widened with humor. "I must try harder."

Standing below the spray, I stretched and released a soul deep sigh. "Why do they keep trying to turn me into a victim?"

"Let's take one existential crisis at a time. Right now, our mission is to get you clean."

Alexander washed away the dirt and unwelcome fingerprints with reverence, like a soulful prayer. The humility and care he put into his attentions soothed my heart.

When we finished, grass and mud and sticks and thorns littered the bottom of the tub.

Alexander wrapped towels around each of us and helped me back to bed. "Feel a little better?"

"Much. Thank you."

Alexander threw his clothes on and then helped me dress in a pale blue T-shirt and boxers he'd rummaged out of my drawers. He sat behind me and gently ran my brush through my hair. I couldn't suppress a shudder. The last person to brush my hair had been my mother. I could almost feel her presence, smell her orange-blossom perfume. Alexander pretended not to notice when I wiped away the hot, reluctant tears that streaked my cheeks. Instead, he pulled back the sheets, laid me down, and tucked me in with a kiss.

He dropped back into the chair beside my bed and looked as wretched as a demigod or Calvin Klein model could possibly look—fatigue washing the color from his cheeks and heavy circles puffing under his eyes.

I curled onto my side to face him, bundling my crocheted blanket under my chin. "Would you tell me what happened? Tonight. I need to connect the dots."

Alexander hung his head, chestnut waves casting his tormented profile into shadow. "I couldn't sleep." He sighed in a huff. "I was pissed at myself for walking out, and I was still really worried. I thought I could change your mind about staying at the manor. The desire to keep fighting with you drove me to hop in the car and head back here." He gave me a quick, sad smile. "When I turned up the driveway, something in the bushes caught my eye. The rain was so heavy, I assumed I imagined it. But when I got to the cottage..." Alexander paused and shook his head. "Maggie and Adelaide descended on me, neither in good health or spirits. They hadn't seen you in over an hour and begged me to search for you. So, I headed back out. I didn't bother with the car. I just ran." Alexander rubbed the back of his neck.

"I didn't notice you right away. First, I found Rocky attacking Stuart and Jay. They were tucked into the trees, a few feet in from the driveway. Rocky clawed at them and tore at their skin with his beak. I called to him mentally to let him know I was there. 'Protect her,' he answered, and his words repeated like an echo in my mind. When I finally saw you, you were lying in a bundle of thorn bushes a few yards away from them. Blood streaked your arms and legs and gushed from that gash on your head."

I didn't think it was possible, but he hunched over even farther. He bore the exhausting events of the night like a physical burden on his shoulders.

"I panicked," he confessed. "I should have charged in and helped Rocky beat the shit out of those guys. Instead, I fell to my knees and called out to your Goddess."

"Wait." *What did he just say?* "You prayed to the Goddess?"

Alexander nodded, and when he lifted his eyes, they blazed with fear and awe. "I asked Her to help me protect you, and I felt a surge of energy shoot through me. The rain stopped, but a thunderous storm cloud boiled and swelled overhead. Rocky's pained caw drew my focus back to earth. He'd been hit by one of their blows and was huddling in the crook of a tree. Jay stood below, trying to shake him loose. Stuart turned from them and locked eyes on you. He trampled through the underbrush toward you."

Alexander paused and stared out of my bedroom window into the framed darkness beyond.

I wondered what he saw there. Was it only the blackened sky and its splattering of stars? Or was he watching the scenes he described? I wanted to reach out, to ease him, but I kept still. I needed to know more.

"I was just so fucking angry," he continued, "and scared. I stretched my arms out and imagined a bolt of lightning cracking from the storm cloud overhead...and striking Stuart and Jay."

"Dear Goddess, no." I slapped my hand over my mouth.

"It struck between them, no more than a couple yards from you."

He called down lightning! By himself. With no spell. How? I looked at Alexander in horror. "What about Rocky?"

"He's okay. Rocky's fine."

I thought my heart would burst in relief. "What happened with Stuart and Jay?" I needed to know where things stood in order to move forward.

"They're both still breathing." He gnashed his teeth. "The lightning strike caused a small fire. I called out to Shasta for help. Thankfully, she arrived quickly and stomped it out. As I pulled you from the thorns, she dragged the guys out of the brush and up to the cottage. Rocky took off ahead to alert Maggie and Adelaide. I don't know what would've happened if I hadn't been able to communicate with your familiars."

"Where are they now? Stuart and Jay, I mean."

"Maggie worked her magic with Jay, but Stuart was a mess. There was only so much Maggie could do. So she called Reverend Cudlow to pick the guys up and suggested he take Stuart to the hospital."

"How did you do it? How did you call down the lightning?"

"I...I have no clue. Like I said, I prayed to the Goddess for Her help protecting you. I imagined the lightning striking, and then it did."

"Wow." *What the hell does this mean?*

"Yeah, wow."

I dropped my eyes. "Thank you for saving me. Again," I added in a grumble. I hated being seen as weak, so to have any man save me twice in less than four days was hard to swallow. "How are you holding up? Are you okay?" I asked him. He looked like he'd aged ten years since I'd last lost myself in his dark eyes.

"Really? After all you went through tonight, and you're worried about *me*?" He shook his head and smiled softly. "I'm fine, just tired. Is there anything else you need before I get some shut-eye? Maggie put out some blankets and pillows on the sofa. I was going to crash here at the cottage tonight if that's all right with you."

"Of course. I feel safer knowing you're here." There was a truth bomb I never expected to think, let alone say aloud. "Would you mind grabbing my laptop before you head to the sofa? It's over on my dresser."

"Uh, sure." He brought it over and laid it on the bed. "What's so important it can't wait until sunrise?"

"I'm taking your advice," I said, smirking, but Alexander just squinted in confusion. "I'm getting help to deal with the press, like you suggested earlier."

"At this time of night, er, morning?"

"I'm messaging the boys," I said, typing as I spoke. "They won't mind the time. They *are*, however, going to be pissed that I haven't told them what's been going on. But I need their help, so I'll incur their wrath if I must." I continued to tap over my keyboard.

"I still don't get it. What are they going to be able to do?" Alexander's brow pinched.

Is he irritated that I'm turning to other men for help? "You never know what they'll come up with. But the bulk of this request is for Nicolae and Luca. I'm hoping they'll catch the red-eye and be here by noon tomorrow."

I finished the boys' messages and hit send. When I looked up over my laptop, Alexander stood at the end of my bed, confusion once more wrinkling his forehead.

"They're in San Diego," I said by way of explanation.

"And…"

"And, what?"

"They're just going to drop everything and hop a flight home because you asked them to?"

"I hope that's not all they do. Hopefully, Nicolae will use his flight time to plan my press conference. I'm only doing this once, so I need it to be effective. I'm hoping Luca's tech-savviness can unearth something that'll shed light on their plans. When the mayor was here earlier tonight, she said they had us on video. Maybe Luca can get his hands on it. And the Crandalls and Cudlows have dirty secrets. We need to uncover and, if pushed, expose them. What's the saying? The best defense is a good offense."

I closed my laptop and set it on my bedside table.

Alexander scowled. "You're digging in your heels? You're staying here?"

"Of course I'm staying here," I said, matter-of-fact.

His jaw dropped. That was clearly not the answer he had hoped to hear.

"How the fuck can you still want to stay here after all that's happened tonight? You're not safe!" he roared. I cringed at his outburst, and he checked himself. He took a breath. "I'm sorry. I can't always be here, Evangeline. I've neglected my responsibilities at the manor. I need to head back first thing in the morning. And yet I can't stand the thought of leaving you here alone, unprotected."

"I am never alone or unprotected. Don't ever underestimate me," I warned, flashing furious heat. "I'm a hell of a lot stronger than you realize, Alexander."

"I wish you'd let me help," he said, exasperated.

"You're helping me right now. You're here."

"I want to look out for you. Is that such a bad thing?"

"No one fights my battles for me."

"I can't stand by and watch." He shook his head, sounding more resigned than indignant.

"You don't have to." I wasn't going to force him—or even cajole him—to stay with me. That decision was his and his alone. "The Goddess blessed me with powers that allow me to look after myself." Which, though technically true, smacked of BS considering the evening's events.

Alexander knelt on the bed. Hovering over me, he leaned in close and whispered, "This is where we may have a problem."

"How so?" I peeped, more than a little affected by the nearness of his lips.

"Because every cell within me seems hardwired to take care you." He punctuated his words with a kiss so deep, I felt it in my soul.

"You're playing dirty," I rasped, when a massively unsexy, wide-mouthed yawn erupted.

"Okay, enough fun for one day," he said. I pouted, and he laughed lightly. "We can argue about it more in the morning. I'll stay with you until you fall asleep."

I scooted over, and Alexander curled into bed beside me.

He smoothed away wisps of hair from my cheeks. "Close your eyes. I'll sing you a lullaby."

His statement had the opposite effect of what he intended. I sat bolt upright and shrieked, "You can sing?"

Alexander smiled and guided me back into the comfort of the bed and his arms. "I can carry a tune. Now relax and rest."

I followed his gentle command and was lulled to sleep with his sweet song.

> *"Caro amore,* (Dear Love,)
> *Tu sei la luce delle stele* (You are the light of the stars)
> *Tu sei vento dolce* (You are sweet wind)
> *Tu sei piovuto dal cielo* (You rained from the sky)
> *E nessuno tranne te potrebbe mai riempire il mio cuore* (And no one but you could ever fill my heart.)
>
> *Caro amore,* (Dear Love,)
> *Possiamo amare di nuovo* (We can love again.)
> *Possiamo cantare di nuovo* (We can sing again.)
> *Possiamo sentire di nuovo* (We can hear again)
> *In modo che nessuno tranne te potrebbe mai riempire il mio cuore* (That no one but you could ever fill my heart.)

Ti prego, segui il tuo cuore (Please follow your heart)
E ascoltami (And listen to me.)
Balliamo alla luce della luna (We dance in the light of the moon.)
Balliamo sotto gli alberi. (We dance under the trees.)

Chapter Twelve

Waking beside Alexander electrified my drowsy heart. I imagined we existed in another time—one where I could ignore the outside world and stay curled in his embrace. I indulged this sweet notion a moment longer and ran my fingertips over the scruff along his jaw, careful not to rouse him. I pressed my lips softly to his and rose to greet the new day.

After drenching us so thoroughly the night before, the rain was back in force. It whipped against my windows, an ocean of blades striking the glass, threatening to break through. A dove-gray sky peeked out from behind the torrential sheets.

I wonder if we put a little too much umph behind our conjuring spell. Maybe we didn't need quite as many diamonds.

I decided to let Alexander sleep in a while longer and readied myself for the day ahead. I washed up, got dressed, and sat down to throw on some makeup. Carefully, I peeled back the three-inch bandage covering the gash Jay's rock sliced into my forehead. I gasped at my reflection in the mirror. Whereas my scrapes and bruises and scorched feet had healed completely, thanks to Maggie, my head looked like something out of a low-budget horror flick. I leaned in and examined it. There was no way Maggie worked her usual magic. She dressed the wound with only basic antiseptics. I just couldn't understand why. Avoiding the spot, I threw on a bit of light makeup, then applied a fresh bandage.

It'll have to be good enough.

I grabbed my laptop and clicked over to *The Messenger* website. Relief rushed through me as I read the headline praising the miraculous arrival of rain, without a scrap of mention about me or the mayor. I hopped over to check my messages, eager to read the boys' responses to my late-night correspondence. They all tore me apart for not having filled them in earlier about my issues with the Crandalls and Cudlows. Ethan and Gregory both promised a gift to aid me in my troubles and sent me their love and blessings.

Luca's note was brief. "I'll be there soon, baby girl." Typical Luca.

Nicolae's reply proved to be a mixed bag. He apologized that he wouldn't be able to rush back right away. His conference would keep him in San Diego for at least another day or two. He vowed to make it to the cottage as soon as he could. But he didn't leave me high and dry, not by a long shot. In his stead, he sent his business partner, a high-powered attorney turned marketing executive. Ayo Kehinde was a Nigerian Yoruba aje, or witch, of considerable abilities. Nicolae raved about her often, but we'd never met. She was already en route with Luca and would arrive by mid-afternoon. I was more than a little relieved to be gaining such a potent ally.

"You're a vision," Alexander whispered as he snuck up behind me, making me squeal like a schoolgirl.

"You're the Devil," I teased, laughing.

"I didn't think you believed in the Devil," he said as he dotted kisses along my shoulder.

"If I did, I suspect he'd be just like you; staggeringly handsome with soft lips and dark eyes that could make a virgin lift her skirt."

"Such things you say." With his chest pressed against my back, his arms encircling me, Alexander nuzzled into my neck.

I turned and snuggled into him. His mass of muscle and strength could have been intimidating, frightening after all I'd been through, but I'd come to equate Alexander with safety.

"Your head. I thought Maggie took care of that." He ran his finger gently along the edge of the stark-white cotton square.

"She did, sort of."

"Does it hurt?"

"A little, but I'm sure Maggie will take another look at it and fix it up right." I hoped. "If you're ready, we can raid the kitchen together. Right now, I've got one objective: coffee."

"I have to get back to the manor...but sure, I can stay for a cup."

We were all smiles as we entered the kitchen.

"Good morning, you two," Maggie said brightly. She glanced over at the folded blankets and untouched pillow on the sofa and then back to Alexander.

"Sleep well?" she asked with a cocked brow.

"I know I did." I jumped in to save Alexander from the awkward line of questioning that threatened. "Alexander sang me to sleep."

"Did he, now?" She lit up brighter.

I nodded. "It was a sweet Italian lullaby. He has a beautiful voice."

Poor Alexander rubbed the back of his neck. "It's more of a ballad." He squirmed in embarrassment.

"You speak Italian, Alexander?" Maggie asked him.

"I do. I've never known much about my mother, but I know she was Italian—right from Italy. As a kid, I used to play one of her old records over and over again. That was my favorite song."

"Well that's very sweet, dear. What was your mother's name?" Maggie asked.

"Teresa. Teresa Aradia."

"I'm sorry, what?" Maggie asked again sharply, clearly agitated by Alexander's response.

What the hell is wrong?

"Teresa Aradia. Did you know her?"

"No. No, I didn't," Maggie said.

My goddess-mother didn't lie, but this was not the total truth either. I sensed that Alexander caught her obfuscation too.

He paused for a beat, and suspicion crept onto his face. But the look faded as he lowered his eyes to mine. "I know I said I'd stay for coffee, but I really do need to head back. There are a million things I've been avoiding."

"Oh." A pout threatened. *That pout's becoming a nasty habit. Don't be such a pushover, Evangeline.* "Okay. Sure. We'll catch up soon."

"Of course we will. Please, you call me if you need anything," he said, impressing the importance of his words with a searing look. Then he dropped a sweet kiss to my bandaged head, thanked Maggie for her hospitality, and left. And he sucked the life out of the room as he went.

I craved his company and mourned the loss of it.

But what is the deal with Alexander's mom?

I rounded on Maggie and began my interrogation. "Do you want to tell me what that was all about?" But before I could really needle her for info, there was a knock at the door.

"I'll get it," Maggie said, and she spirited away, avoiding my question. A minute later, she returned with two packages in her arms. "They're for you."

"Oh, I bet they're from..." I examined their packing labels. "I was right. They're from Ethan and Gregory. They work fast. They promised to send me something to help with my press conference." I was all smiles now. I loved getting gifts.

"Something to help?" Maggie said with a quizzical grin. "Knowing those boys, I should probably have a fire extinguisher and a reversal spell at the ready before you open them." She was partly joking.

"The best things come in small packages, so I'm opening the little one first."

I tore open the wrappings. Inside was a delicately carved wooden box with a hinge on one side. Opening it revealed a two-inch cross-shaped stone, midnight blue, covered in intricate black symbols. The symbols looked to be part of the stone itself, not engraved upon it. It hung from a long black-silk cord.

"It's amazing. I've never seen anything like it. Do you know what it is?" I asked Maggie expectantly.

"I think I might, but let's see." She picked up a small note fitted into the lid of the wooden box and read it.

"A fairy stone is rarer than gold, more precious than any gem. For the magic it brings the wearer draws power from root, leaf, and stem. When the fairy stone lies upon your skin, no malice shall dent your armor. But rebound upon your aggressor it will; a stone of infinite karma."

Maggie paused, and we both drew deep breaths.

"Well, that's certainly helpful," she said.

"Or dangerous. Wait, there's something written on the back of the note." I turned it over.

"'*You can't be broken by any bitch. You're a powerful, Goddess-blessed witch. Love, Your Fairy Brother, Ethan—*' I do love that man."

"He certainly revels in his ancestry."

"If you got it, flaunt it." I shrugged.

"So..." Maggie handed me the second package and rubbed her hands together in excitement. "Now for the big one."

Her smile was contagious, and I beamed as I ripped back the wrappings. But at the sight of the black box with gold embossed letters: YSL, I dropped the silliness.

"Dear Goddess. Gregory sent me Saint Laurent," I whispered.

I removed the box's lid to find a black floppy-brimmed fedora. My jaw dropped. It was stunning. My pulse quickened as I carefully set the hat aside.

"Saint Laurent Spring/Summer 2013 collection," I said, awestruck.

I lifted the dress by the shoulders. It was slim and black. Its hem wouldn't fall below mid-thigh. The sleeves were long and narrow and capped in white cuffs. But the wow factors that clinched the dress's trademark look were the starched white bib, pointed white collar, and voluminous, delicate, black-knotted tie. It had obviously been tailored to fit my petite height and curves. I couldn't believe I held *the* dress that epitomized the chic modern witch in the fashion world. It was better than a power suit.

How the hell did Gregory pull this off?

"There's a note," Maggie picked it up and read.

> My dear little sister,
>
> If I've learned anything in life, it's that we must always embrace and celebrate our unique selves and never shrink from detractors. If you're going to stand before the press and cameras, if you're going to take on those whose greatest desire is to see you suffering and humiliated, you better look damn good doing it. This little number, which I know you will recognize, is simultaneously demure and sexy, and screams, "I'm a badass witch!" I'm sorry I can't be by your side as you wage what is sure to be the first battle in a long and arduous fight. But know that I'll be there in spirit.
>
> All my love, your ever-proud brother,
> Gregory

"They're amazing," I said as I gently placed the dress and hat back into the box. "My boys are seriously amazing." A sudden realization hit me. "Oh! Mags, I'm so sorry. I didn't tell you that—"

"That Luca is coming today with Nicolae's business partner, Ayo Kehinde?" Maggie cut me off with an indulgent smile. "Yes, I know. It's okay. Nicolae called me early this morning and explained that they are going to help you set up a press conference and dig for dirt on the Crandalls and Cudlows. They should be here in a couple hours."

"Good. The faster I can get this press conference over with, the better." I plopped down on a kitchen chair. The thought of standing in front of the press was nerve-racking. The whole situation sucked. My diminishing adrenaline gave way to the insanity of my circumstances.

Maggie sensed my mindset's morose trajectory. "Why don't you take a walk in the woods. The rain won't be as bad under its canopy. I'm sure Shasta and Rocky are eager to see you."

I took her advice, and after grabbing an umbrella, I headed into the forest. It was cool and damp but a glorious respite from the storm beyond.

Shasta had headed out early to hunt, so I spent the next hour with Rocky. But instead of searching for serenity, I drilled him for details from the night before. And he delivered. Although Alexander had given me the bullet points, many questions remained.

"Neither of those deviants who consider themselves men simply due to their wrinkly, dangling appendage left the grounds with life-threatening injuries. The blond, overgrown man-child was stunned by the lightning strike and sustained some injuries from my beak and claws," Rocky said, lifting a proud head. *"But Magdalena was able to set him right. The sadistic ginger, on the other hand, was in far worse shape. The lightning severely damaged his leg, and blood puddled around his groin. He wasn't able to walk on his own. Magdalena did what she could, but she suggested he be taken to the hospital."*

"What about Adelaide's confrontation with Reverend Cudlow?"

"When that lecherous, slithering excuse for a man of the cloth arrived to collect his vile spawn and that narcissistic preener, Ms. Good warned him, 'You better make sure those two keep their hands off Evangeline, or so help me Goddess, I will rip them apart with my teeth and serve them up for dinner to the creatures of the forest.'

"The reverend appeared genuinely amazed that you hadn't yet sought legal action. 'After tonight, Reverend, maybe she will,' she said to him. 'Just back off. We don't tell you how to worship. Give us that modicum of respect. You walk your path, and we'll walk ours,' she told him."

"I wonder why she was so easy on him."

"You call that going easy?"

"She let him off with a warning. Why would she do that?"

"I'm sure she understood the gravity of the situation and the need for temperance and tact."

"Rocky, we're talking about Adelaide here. I love her, but she's not exactly known for temperance and tact."

"Well then, it was her obvious compassion for a man who is caring for an ailing loved one."

"I doubt Adelaide had much sympathy for Stuart's health at that moment."

"Not Stuart. Mrs. Gladys Cudlow. She was taken ill after speaking at the mayor's press conference. After Stuart attacked you at the market and had his run-in with Alexander, Gladys's health declined further. I believe the high priestess showed the reverend some compassion."

"How did you come to know all this? If you don't mind me asking."

"A hawk sees many things, and from a singularly unique perspective." In other words, he wasn't saying.

"Where's Adelaide now? I haven't seen her all morning," I asked.

"Your goddess-mother drove the high priestess home before the sun rose this morning. I understand from speaking with Fledermous that Ms. Good desired her own environs. The lingering energy of Magdalena's patients that frequently convalesce in the cottage's spare bedroom interferes with her powers. She needed to rejuvenate."

"Or she didn't want us to see her weakening," I speculated. "Well, thank you for the chat. You've given me a lot to think about. I'm going to head back to the cottage, grab something to eat, and get started on my statement for the press conference."

"A piece of advice, if I may, Evangeline. In case you're considering treading lightly, I suggest you stomp."

The rain stopped as I polished off my speech. I felt good about it, but I wanted to run it past Nicolae's partner, Ayo Kehinde. She'd sent me a brief professional message as a greeting while she and Luca were in transit from San Diego to Arbor. We worked together online for about an hour, formulating a strategy forward. Ms. Kehinde would facilitate the media connections necessary for the conference. She would represent me to the press and public and act as legal counsel.

Alexander should be pleased.

By the end of our conversation, my chest loosened and my muscles relaxed. I felt so incredibly grateful and privileged to have such a powerhouse stand up for me. And I hadn't even met her in person yet.

Luca, meanwhile, would organize the tech setup of the conference and manage my online presence. And as always, Luca would be there to help me find the truth. That was just his way.

I looked out of my window at a gradually clearing sky as an electric-blue El Camino peeled up the driveway, spitting rock. It skidded sideways to a stop. I ran out of my room and barely made it to the kitchen before Luca overtook me. He swooped in, grabbed me around the waist, and swung me in circles.

"I've missed you, baby girl."

"Missed you, too," I said and kissed his smoothly shaven face.

Luca was as dangerously dapper as ever. He had a sharp jaw and keen eyes. And he wore black Armani from his sixteen-button vest to his polished, buckled boots. He could've walked straight off the pages of *GQ*.

"Don't you look delicious," I teased with the easy familiarity of long acquaintance. "Where have you left Ms. Kehinde?"

"Please, call me Ayo." I heard her deep feminine voice behind me.

I turned and was momentarily struck dumb. Just shy of six foot tall, the regal Nigerian smiled kindly down at me. She wore a tailored emerald-green suit, which accentuated her full, hourglass figure, and a patterned scarf intricately wrapped around her head.

"It's nice to meet you finally," I said, fighting the impulse to curtsey. "Nicolae raves about you."

"You and your goddess-mother too," she said, smiling easily. "I feel as if I know you both already." Ayo's rich Yoruban accent rolled like a warm melody from her lips. She stood with an unforced straight back and naturally squared shoulders. Her regal presence commanded respect, but she had an affectionate manner and a softness in her eyes that drew one closer.

Potent combination.

"Nicolae neglected to mention how beautiful you are," Maggie said as she breezed into the kitchen. "Welcome to our home."

She and Ayo shook hands, and I could have sworn I saw actual sparks flying between them. Their eyes locked. They neither spoke nor released their clasped hands until Luca cleared his throat.

"I stand corrected," Ayo purred. "I don't believe I could fully know you, Magdalena, if I spent every day until my last on the endeavor. But I'm certain I'd enjoy every moment."

"You have quite a way with words," Maggie said with a flirtatious glint in her eye.

"I have a way with many things." Ayo grinned.

Luca cleared his throat again, and the two women finally awoke from their mutual enchantment. Maggie regained her composure, though the blush in her cheeks lingered.

I didn't see this coming.

My goddess-mother had had many suitors over the years, both male and female. However, she never sought more than friendship from any of them nor welcomed their advances. I'd never seen Maggie's spirit shimmer as brightly as the moment Ayo Kehinde first stood before her.

"Luca." Maggie greeted him with her arms open wide for a hug. "It's wonderful to see you." Luca gave her a good squeeze. "Thank you," she said and chanced a look at Ayo. "Thank you both for flying out to help."

"I would have been here sooner had I known what was going on." Luca hit me with a stinging glare. "I wish you'd told us. Not that you two aren't capable of handling things, but I hate that you had to deal with this on your own."

"We weren't alone," Maggie corrected him. "Adelaide was here and Evangeline's new beau, of course."

If I didn't know better, I'd have sworn she was purposely deflecting attention from herself onto me.

"A new beau? Here helping you two?" Luca aimed his query at Maggie, but I answered.

"Yeah... and?" I planted my hands on my hips and copped an attitude.

"You left that bit out of your messages," he sniped.

Luca's keen eyes bore into mine, and he locked my gaze to his. I couldn't look away if I tried. I knew what he was doing. He'd been pulling this bit of magic since we were kids. But I had nothing to hide, so I opened up my psyche for his perusal. I allowed him to root around in my head and heart. The object of his search was always the same—the truth. I knew the moment he found what he was looking for. His whole body tensed up but only for the briefest of moments. Once he clamped down, I was unable to get a read on his feelings at all.

"Wow. You, ah, you really like this guy." Luca rubbed his chin, looking anywhere but at me.

"I do. It's shocked the hell out of me too."

And that was the truth. I'd always been cautious, suspicious of the motives of those who showed me even the smallest manner of kindness. Yet with Alexander, I'd lain myself bare. I'd opened myself up in a way I'd never done with anyone. Alexander had drawn me out of myself. Inexplicably, I felt a sense of freedom with him, even as he lobbied to lock me behind the walls of his manor.

"How can you be so foolish?" Luca thundered with such outrage, I thought my heart would stop.

What the hell? I flinched. I hadn't expected this reaction, and it completely threw me.

"You trust this *Alexander*?" Luca spoke the name like a curse, the name he found written on my heart. "After knowing him less than a week? Not only did you tell him you were a witch, but you showed him your powers! How could you be so stupid?"

"Now that's just rude!" I couldn't believe his nerve, speaking to me like I was an imbecile.

"Eva, you trusted some rich snot you've only known a couple days with the most sacred of Universal truths—that real, palpable, elemental magic exists and that you possess it. You trusted him so much that you exposed not only yourself but Maggie and Adelaide as well. This is crazy." Luca allowed his anger to flow freely, and it hit me with hurricane force.

But I hit right back.

"I didn't ask you to come here to lecture me—or to criticize the man who's saved me *twice* these last four days, the man whose spirit spoke to mine the instant we met, the man whom Adelaide has concluded is my true soul mate. No. I'm sorry. I've got much bigger fish to fry. I asked you here to help me." I paused and looked at Maggie. "To help *us* deal with the very real threats we're under from the Crandalls and Cudlows. This is serious shit." A sob suddenly threatened to erupt, but I held it back.

"Stuart Cudlow has put his hands on me three times in less than two weeks. I know I should press charges. I just...I just can't bring myself to regurgitate what I want so fucking badly to forget."

Luca ran his hands back over his sleek hair in frustration. "Shit, Eva," he cursed, then pulled me into a bear hug. "I'm sorry. I'm an asshole. I can't imagine how hard this has been for you. I'm so, so sorry." He rocked me gently as he spoke, and I felt like a little girl again. Even though Luca was the second youngest of the boys—only three years older than me—he'd always been the most paternal, simultaneously protective and indulgent.

I stepped out of the hug and looked him in the eyes. "I'm sorry too. I'm a mess. In the span of a week, I've been insulted, assaulted, slapped in the face, smashed in the head with a fucking rock, and humiliated in the press. I was slushied in the middle of a crowded sidewalk, for the love of the Goddess!" I threw my hands in the air in frustration.

Ayo stepped before me. She took my frantic hands in hers, instantly settling me.

"For the love of the Goddess, indeed," she said. "All of your trials and the manner in which you bore them have been for the love of the Goddess."

I looked down at my small pale hands held firmly within Ayo's dark grasp. Sparks like those I saw when she greeted Maggie, though not as bright or lively, crackled from Ayo's elegant fingers. The sparks surged up my arms to my heart, which leapt joyfully at the connection.

"The Goddess's magic animates your flesh and bone and blood more than any witch I've ever known, Evangeline. You have been mightily blessed. You've born great challenges, true. And I suspect your troubles are only beginning. These struggles will lead you to a tremendous unity with the Goddess. I know this as surely as I know you will not bear these burdens alone."

Ayo lowered my hands and guided me to sit beside the dining table. She walked to the kitchen and maneuvered through it as if she'd walked those floors for years. Somehow, Ayo knew exactly which cabinet held the mugs and the tea, the sugar and lemon. I sat, enthralled, as she prepared a perfect tea service for us all to share. She placed the ornate, polished silver set in the middle of the table and invited us all to partake.

When Maggie neither blinked nor flinched a muscle, Ayo stepped in close to her. She captured her gaze. "Take your rest. Allow me to help, Magdalena. I am quite capable—and eager—to assist you and Evangeline and Ms. Good too, of course." Ayo took hold of my goddess-mother's arms. Ayo's skin, smooth as melted chocolate against Maggie's milky paleness, struck as stark a contrast as the tea service to the mahogany of the dining table. There was a firm tenderness in Ayo's touch that awoke Maggie, returning the light to her eyes and the blush to her cheeks.

"Thank you, my friend," Maggie said. Then she took Ayo's hand, kissed it, and let it go. She smiled and sat down at the table. "I will be forever in your debt if you're able to help us through this."

"I'll do everything I can."

Maggie, Ayo, Luca, and I spent the rest of the afternoon reviewing, in detail, the ins and outs of recent events. Ayo and Luca wanted—needed—to hear it laid out in order to help us effectively. It was cathartic to release all the pain and anger and frustration to people who could understand, who were like me. For as easy as I found speaking to Alexander, he'd never fully understand the burden of having powers, yet still feeling so powerless.

Chapter Thirteen

"I'm fucking starving," Luca blurted. "There any decent restaurants left around here? I saw they closed that killer Italian place downtown. What was it called?"

"DiFabio's," I answered.

"Yeah, that's the one, DiFabio's. That place had the best lasagna, and their sauce with the pork chops, you couldn't beat it," Luca said, practically drooling.

"They were Catholic, and this town doesn't like them any more than they like witches," I explained. "Their beliefs are just as arcane and therefore dangerous. Reverend Cudlow and the rest of Arbor's fundamentalist flock even tried to drive away the Catholic sisters from the Franciscan convent up the way. Those nuns may be tough cookies, but really they're as harmless as a Girl Scout troop."

"Cudlow and his flock don't like Girl Scouts, either," Maggie quipped. "Mother Hildegard, the Superior in charge at the convent, doesn't scare easily. She'd never let vile hypocrites like Cudlow chase her and her sisters off."

"You speak as if you like this Hildegard," Ayo said with a question in her voice.

"I do, very much. She and I work together often. We organize food drives and look in on a few of the elderly folks in town who prefer to remain in their homes rather than languish in a hospital. She is a strong, caring woman. We may not worship the same deity, but we still work together to look after our neighbors."

"While Mother Hildegard sounds like a kick-ass lady and an important ally, she's not going to cure my grumbling stomach," Luca whined.

"Let's hit the café downtown," I suggested. "Their food's pretty good, and you can see where I got slushied."

As the four of us headed through the gallery to leave for dinner, a sharp pain shot through my eyes and my knees went wobbly. I buckled over, and Luca caught me before I could smack my head on the upright piano. Within my mind, I heard Shasta and Rocky calling out, pleading for help. I turned to Maggie in a panic, but she was no better off than I was. She leaned, weak, in Ayo's arms. That meant Hanna was in trouble, too.

Screw this. Adrenaline catapulted me outside just in time to see the back of a Prius convertible skidding down the driveway.

When I turned back to the cottage, I went numb.

Luca gasped. "Holy shit."

The cottage's façade was covered in red spray-painted graffiti. Crude images of hangings, badly drawn pentagrams, and vulgar curses: "Burn the witches," "Go to hell, dyke," and "Satan spawn," marred our home.

"Bunny," I hissed with a sour blend of confusion, anger, and bile on my tongue.

"Your buxom blonde friend?" Luca asked with his lips drawn thin and his brows knitted together tight.

"Yeah, I just saw her Prius pulling out of the driveway." My voice sounded dead to my ears. *Why the hell…? Who helped her? No way she did this all on her own.* "But right now, I don't give a shit about Bunny or the fucking cottage. We need to find the familiars," I cried out. "They're hurt."

Maggie and I called out mentally, only to receive faint echoes of anger and pain in reply.

"Let me help. I can search out their energies," Ayo offered.

"Find Hanna first," I said. "She's the smallest."

Ayo took Maggie's hands in her own and closed her eyes. A moment later, tremors rocked the aje's body. When she settled, she spoke in a whisper.

"The queen is alive. She's close by."

Ayo broke her hold on Maggie's hands and darted toward the lavender. Stopping suddenly, she scanned the ground.

"Magdalena, here!"

Maggie hurried over and fell to her knees. She scooped up the queen bee into her hands and rushed her to the hive.

"Ayo," Luca called. "You've got to help Eva."

Ayo took my hands and closed her eyes as she'd done with Maggie. The tremors overcame her. It seemed to take forever, and I started to worry. Then Ayo jerked her hands away and took off running toward the forest. I tried to run after her, but I was too weak. My connection with my familiars was as physical as it was visceral and spiritual. Their suffering was my suffering, and I had no strength from Shasta to aid me.

Luca hoisted me up onto his back, wrapping my arms around his neck and my legs around his waist like we did when we were kids. He raced us into the woods until we caught up to Ayo. When I found my brazen hawk and momma bear writhing and gasping for air on the forest floor, I hopped off Luca's back and fell to my knees beside them. There was a stinging, astringent odor hanging in the air—pepper spray. On closer examination, I saw not only had they been maced, but beaten. Rocky's wings were bent, feathers tattered and splashed in red. Thick blood oozed from gashes on Shasta's head and chest and arms.

"Ayo, Luca please," I shrieked. "We need Maggie. Hurry!"

I looked back down at my familiars, my poor, sweet, devoted friends. They blinked in a frenzy, vainly attempting to clear away the spray.

I have to rinse their eyes. But I can't draw water from the stream all the way through the forest, too much in the way from there to here. I need to conjure it. It's the only way.

Before I could dither over the staggering task of conjuring an element from nothing into existence, I let instinct rule me. With magic's raw power pulsing through my veins, I threw my hands forward over my injured friends. Immediately obeying my will, crisp clear water poured from the palms of my hands onto their faces, into their eyes, washing them clean of the poison that tortured and tormented them.

"Where the fuck is Maggie?" I hissed into the wind.

I lifted Rocky gently into my arms and curled us into Shasta's coarse, wet fur. Their wheezing, labored breaths eased. But instead of the water reviving them, their pulses became slower and slower still, until their heartbeats grew so faint, I could no longer detect them.

"No." I refused to believe it. "This isn't happening. No."

Grief and blind fury engulfed me. My heart seized, contracted, and a flame ignited within my chest. The blaze swelled, scorching as it spread into my limbs and head until it licked every inch of dermis from the inside. A guttural scream ripped from my throat, and I wailed into the wood and stratus beyond.

Get your shit together, Evangeline Clarion. Stop screaming. Take a breath. Breathe. Breathe. It's okay. Everything will be okay. They will be okay.

And then, I prayed. No grand spell came to my lips, just ceaseless, mumbled pleas to the Goddess, to the earth, to the energy that flowed within every rock and river, to heal my faithful familiars, my friends. I don't know how long I lay there, but when the sweet scent of orange blossoms washed over me, l jolted to attention. I popped my head up and bore witness to an astounding sight. Every woodland beast and creepy crawly that called the cottage grounds their home surrounded us in a great sweeping circle. The collective hum of the creatures resounded into a symphony of life, for the forest was alive and it sang to the heavens. The bear and hawk were well loved by these assembled friends. And the warmth radiating from them—from every squirrel and chipmunk, every spider and beetle, every cardinal and robin and thrush—swept away the damp chill. And the woods were warm and dry again.

A stirring in my arms and a shudder along my side caused my heart to leap, but it restricted just as quickly. I didn't dare hope that my dear companions survived their attack. A thought struck me suddenly. I'd felt their suffering, but I'd never felt them pass on.

Can I hope?

Then two massive furry arms wrapped around me and squeezed. Shasta's hot breath huffed along my neck. The edge of Rocky's beak slid along my wrist, and he stretched—spreading his wings wide. Their wounds had healed, and not a single bloody blemish marred their fur and feathers.

"Blessed Be!" I shouted with undiluted joy, and all the creatures of the woods joined me in praise.

I pulled Rocky tight to my chest and showered him with kisses.

"Yes, yes, I'm quite all right. That's enough, now. Please, go slobber on Shasta. She loves that kind of thing," Rocky grumbled with all his usual haughty snark.

And I did. I squeezed Shasta's bristly girth and gave thanks to all the powers of Nature for returning my beloved familiars to me.

Luca came bursting through the trees with Maggie hot on his heels. Maggie skidded to a stop and drew in a lungful of the orange-blossom scent that permeated the wood.

"Lavinia was here," she breathed, though I wasn't sure if it was a question or a statement of fact. She looked around in slack-jawed astonishment at the creatures that encircled us—just as they used to do when my mother was alive. Redirecting her attention, she fell upon me in relief, just as I'd done with my familiars.

"Is Hanna okay?" I asked.

She nodded and kissed my head and cheeks.

"Luca, please take Eva back to the cottage while I look over Shasta and Rocky," Maggie directed.

Luca bent down to lift me up, but I shook my head. "No, please. I'd like to walk," I said. "My strength is returning now that these two are on the mend."

"You got it, baby girl." Luca took my arm instead, and together we walked back to the cottage.

The vandalism and attacks on the familiars forced our hand. After Hanna, Shasta, and Rocky gave us their account of the afternoon's events, it was clear that Adelaide's interpretation of my dream had been spot-on. The Crandalls and Cudlows were plotting against us. That they'd colluded with Bunny to take us down added insult to injury.

How could she do this to me? Why?

Mourning my friend's betrayal would have to wait, however. We needed to take action, and not only a press conference, but legal steps were unavoidable. I refused to suffer in silence a moment longer while Doreen Crandall manipulated the public narrative and the spawn of *Arbor's Most Moral* tormented me and those I loved.

That evening, everyone hunkered down over bottles of wine and Maggie's homemade brick-oven pizza to formulate the details of our response and get the plans in motion. Ayo checked over the statement I'd written and offered a few notes of improvement. Then she went to work contacting the press and sending out the restraining orders and cease-and-desist letters to the Crandalls and Cudlows. Luca set up the chairs, podium, microphones, lighting, and the like. He also contacted the rest of the boys and gave them an update. They insisted that security equipment be installed, all manner of cameras and alarms—and not only in the cottage itself but all throughout the property. They planned to set it all up sometime after the press conference—scheduled for 10:00 a.m. the next morning.

After a long and frustrating discussion, I begrudgingly agreed with Maggie that we should tell Chief Harrison about the attacks on me and on the familiars. Maggie gave him a call, and he was over in less than an hour to hear what we had to say. Ayo, now officially acting as my attorney, sat beside me, glaring at the gray-haired officer as if daring him to put a toe out of line. But I knew Harrison was a fair man, so I related the recent events with as much clarity as I could. He listened patiently as I told my tale, interrupting only rarely to ask for clarification on a point. Once I finished, he took a handkerchief from his back pocket and patted away the sweat that beaded on his forehead. He shook his head.

"This is bad business, bad business, I tell ya, Ms. Eva. I wish you'da come forward right away with all this, though I understand your reasonin'. These are hefty accusations, and a lot of 'em. And more than a few rely on the testimony of animals. You can see how I might be in a pickle if I send this to the district attorney."

Ayo cleared her throat. "Ms. Clarion is prepared to waive all charges on two conditions: that Doreen Crandall and Gladys Cudlow publically retract their statements with the same fervent vigor with which they were made, and that Stuart Cudlow and Jay Crandall abide by their restraining orders in perpetuity. Ms. Clarion does not wish to drag this out. She desires nothing more than to have her good name restored and to be left to live in peace without any interference from the mayor, the church, or their conspirators."

Chief Harrison nodded. "Very well then. A record of the complaint and deposition will be passed along to the counsel for the accused. I will be in touch." Before leaving, he turned and took my hands in his. "On a personal note, I'd like to apologize for all the sufferin' you've been through. No one deserves to be treated the way you have. You're a good girl. I will do everything in my power to see that justice is served. You can bank on that."

I kissed his sweet, wrinkled cheek. "Thank you," I said, choking back tears. *He really is a good man.*

After my meeting with Chief Harrison, I went out to the woods to check on Rocky and Shasta. My visit didn't last long, however, as my fully recovered familiars were setting off to hunt. Upon my return to the cottage, Maggie sent me off to bed with a cup of her magical tea. And sleep was upon me in an instant.

FRIDAY

The morning arrived with the smell of bacon and the cacophony of boisterous male voices. I heard Luca and Alexander in the kitchen arguing over the Mets and Yankees. I decided to take the fact that they'd met over breakfast and hadn't killed each other as a positive sign. But, for some reason, I was hesitant to get up and face them—or anyone. I pulled my covers over my head.

Maybe if I huddle down far enough, everyone will forget about me.

"There's no hiding from your troubles, dear. It's time to face the world," Adelaide boomed from a few feet away, scaring the crap out of me and making me jump and scurry from my bed.

"What the hell? For the love of the Goddess, Adelaide, you almost gave me a heart attack."

"Not that I'm one for retribution, but that's what you get for keeping Alexander and me out of the loop yesterday. Did you ignore us on purpose? Have we done something to upset you?" she asked with overly dramatic puppy-dog eyes.

"What? Goddess, no. Of course not! I just...I don't know. It was a crazy day. I'm sorry."

"You're having a lot of those lately. And there's no need to apologize." Adelaide made herself comfortable on my window seat and looked out at the sparkling blue sky as she spoke. "Alexander was kind enough to come at my call quite early this morning. I knew something was amiss. So, he picked me up, and we hastened here to aid you." When I didn't reply, she continued. "Are you okay, dearie?"

"No. No, I'm not okay. This is fucking crazy. All of it. How the hell did we get here?" I shook my head.

"Now, now, here's what we're going to do. You're going to have some breakfast with your friends and your lovely man. You are going to take a nice, long shower. Then I'm going to help you get ready. Maggie told me about the gifts Ethan and Gregory sent. They are perfect and will suit you well today. They'll help you embrace the witch that you are. That's what this press conference is about—not backing down. Marshal your power, Evangeline. That's what is most important. Do not let these ignorant bigots dampen your fire. Do you hear me?"

"Yes. And you're right." I threw my shoulders back and stood up straight.

"Okay then. Let's get this show on the road."

I worried that Alexander would be angry with me, but my concerns were ill-founded. He jumped up as I entered the kitchen, ran to my side, and pulled me into a huge hug. "Are you okay? How are you feeling? Did you get a good sleep? I talked to Rocky and Shasta this morning. They seem okay. But, really, are you okay?"

"Dude." Luca cut Alexander off with a laugh. "Give the woman a chance to speak." And I knew from his easy banter that he had found Alexander's truth just as he'd found out mine.

I looked up into Alexander's warm, dark eyes. "I'm going to be okay. I'm glad you're here."

"Me too," he said with a smile. But his grin was quickly replaced by a stern brow and ridged lips. "Now sit down and eat. You need your strength for today."

I sat dutifully, and Alexander rewarded me with a plateful of bacon and blueberry pancakes, some juice and a cup of coffee. I devoured my breakfast as Ayo went over what we should all expect from the morning. Then I set off to prepare, feeling like I was dressing for a firing squad.

Two hours later, I stood in the gallery, peeking out of the window at the mass of reporters and cameras that had descended on our lawn.

"This is not at all what I hoped for," Ayo fretted, letting her nerves show. "Friday's a news-dump day because so few people watch. A Monday morning news cycle is best, but we're just going to have to make the best of it. At least the rain held out." Ayo then turned to give me a once-over and nodded her approval. "You look amazing. Are you ready?"

"Yes. I'm ready," I answered and prayed, *Great Goddess, see me through this.*

Flanked by Adelaide, Maggie, and Ayo, I faced the mass of reporters and cameras that filled my front lawn. The cottage's graffiti offered a harsh but pointed backdrop. Alexander and Luca stood behind the last row of press chairs, each offering me an encouraging smile. I stepped behind the podium, adjusted the microphone, cleared my throat, and began.

"Good afternoon. I'd like to thank you all for coming. I'm going to make a statement, and any questions you may have can be directed to Ms. Kehinde when I'm through."

I gestured over to Ayo as the crowd of reporters murmured their approval of the stunning, sophisticated female. I took a deep breath and touched the fairy stone that hung from my neck before speaking again.

"My name is Evangeline Clarion, and I am the target of a witch hunt. I have no doubt you recognize my name. This past Monday, Doreen Crandall, the mayor of Arbor and candidate for the state legislature, held her own press conference. Ms. Crandall dedicated the bulk of her time defaming my character.

"I would like to begin by addressing the charges she laid at my feet. The accusation of devil worship is *pure hogwash*, to borrow the mayor's term, and there isn't a shred of evidence to support such a claim. I do not worship Satan. I don't even believe in the existence of the character. What I do believe in is the intrinsic power of Nature. This is not a new belief system.

The worship of Nature is as old as humanity itself, far older than the two-thousand-year-old Christian construct, older than the Jewish or Muslim faiths, older than the monotheistic Zoroastrianism from which they all derive.

"The charge of witchcraft is an age-old device used to silence and ostracize powerful women. One might assume that the persecution of suspected witches ended in Salem, Massachusetts, in the 1600s, but that couldn't be further from the truth. The United Nations has estimated that the murders of those individuals—men, women, and even children—accused of witchcraft around the globe each year as numbering in the thousands, while assaults and exiles could reach into the millions annually. These well-documented cases of heinous brutality, beheadings, and burnings are growing in number and severity the world over. Although the vast majority of these incidents occur outside of the United States, the hatred, ignorance, and religious zealotry that spark them knows no boundaries or national borders.

"We don't live in the 1600s. We don't live in Saudi Arabia or Indonesia where the governments sanction the arrest and lashing and beheading of accused witches. We don't live in Kenya or the Central African Republic where villagers have been known to burn their own family members alive under the guise of spiritual warfare. And unlike most of the poor victims who are persecuted across the globe, I *am* a witch."

I paused, letting the gravity of my statement sink in.

"We live in the United States, a nation that prizes freedom and the free exercise of religion. This means I have the right to believe and practice whatever stirs my soul, without fear of intimidation or reprisal.

"Another allegation, made by both Mayor Doreen Crandall and Gladys Cudlow—wife of Reverend Cudlow of the First Ecclesiastical Church of Arbor, is the abhorrent claim that I am a sexual predator, a temptress of men. This is such a disgusting lie, it deserves no explanation. I suggest, instead, that you investigate Stuart Cudlow, son of Reverend and Gladys Cudlow, the man they accused me of assaulting. You will find his history stands in stark contrast to the upstanding, pious character his mother described. You will find that he is the sexual predator. And I should know, because he has assaulted me on three separate occasions over the course of the last two weeks."

A shocked murmur rustled through the crowd.

"The first incident occurred two weeks ago and was the basis for the tall tale woven by Gladys Cudlow at the mayor's press conference. The second incident happened only a few short hours after Mrs. Cudlow spoke. Although Stuart acted alone on these first two occasions, he was joined by Jay Crandall, the mayor's son, for my third attack. He is to thank for the nasty gash on my head left by the rock he cracked into my skull. I hesitated to press charges because I hoped to avoid regurgitating the details of my assaults to people who'd rather see me silenced than safe.

"But after the most recent..." Here I motioned to the graffiti-covered cottage backdrop. "I was left with no other choice but to seek legal support and lay the facts before the world. My attorney, Ayo Kehinde, has sent cease-and-desist letters to both Ms. Crandall and Mrs. Cudlow, informing them they each have twenty-four hours to publically retract their statements. Ms. Kehinde has also filed restraining orders against Stuart Cudlow and Jay Crandall. If they should refuse to comply, we will be forced to take further legal action.

"I want to make something very clear. I have done nothing wrong. I've committed no crime. I do not deserve the vitriol with which I've been treated. I wished, rather than believed, that my neighbors and I could resolve our differences amicably. Instead, I have been threatened with imprisonment. I've been told I must repent or leave Arbor. And my goddess-mother and I have had our home defiled. But I will. Not. Bow. To threats."

I pounded on the podium and needed a deep breath before continuing.

"My goddess-mother, Magdalena Maramma, and I are leaving the cottage, but only for a brief period while the vandalism is removed and security equipment is installed throughout the property. When the work is complete, we'll return home. Make no mistake, Arbor is our home, and it is where we're going to stay.

"I thank you sincerely for allowing me the opportunity to speak with you today. And now, the only thing left to say is... Blessed be."

I put on my sweetest smile and stepped back from the podium. Maggie gave my hand a reassuring squeeze, and Adelaide leaned in and whispered, "That, my dear, was spectacular."

A cacophony of shouted questions erupted from the press, but as soon as Ayo replaced me at the microphone, the crowd hushed. A palpable humming sizzled from the stately figure. She held the assembled enthralled. And a little scared, truth be told.

"Any questions for Ms. Clarion must be submitted in writing and sent to the contact information I provided upon your arrival. And one final note: This is private property. It is off-limits to any and all unless personally invited by the family. Trespassers will be prosecuted to the fullest extent of the law." Abruptly, the energy surrounding Ayo contracted, and she allowed a shadow of a smile to lift her lips. "We thank you again for coming and wish you a lovely day."

The four of us turned and filed into the cottage; leaving Luca and Alexander outside to get rid of the reporters and break down the conference chairs, podium, and tech gear. When I closed the front door, we collapsed on the sofas, heaving great sighs of exhaustion and exasperation. Within the confines of the cottage, all was still, all but our labored breaths. Words were not necessary. Adelaide, Maggie, Ayo, and I spoke instead with knowing looks. And we understood each other.

The press conference had been a success. We'd won the battle. But the nature of the retaliation was far less certain. And those who sought to ruin me—and my loved ones—*would* respond. Their retribution was inevitable.

The cottage is no longer safe.

I hated admitting this truth, hated placing my security and autonomy in another's hands. Still, I gave in and agreed to stay at Morgan Manor. I hung my head, refusing like a child to raise my eyes to the potent women surrounding me.

"I'll stay behind Alexander's walls only as long as it takes to clean the cottage, install the security equipment, and strategize—but not a minute longer."

I was pissed off as I lugged my suitcase out from under my bed and flung it open. I threw in some shorts and tops and skirts and dresses without much thought, then loaded in my makeup and toiletries. Before I closed up the bag, I decided to add my ceremonial robes, just in case. Then I moved on to packing the tools of my trade. My candles and oils, ceremonial wand, athame, chalice, black onyx mortar and pestle, holy water, sea salt, sewing needle, white thread, and a lighter all fit snug in a medium-sized backpack. I didn't need any herbs. Maggie would pack those. So once I grabbed my besom broom, I was ready to go.

But I wasn't happy about it.

I hauled my luggage into the kitchen and was immediately overcome by my goddess-mother's wrath. Her fury filled the room. She growled and groused as she rummaged through the pantry, flinging jarred herbs and tinctures into her bag. Her flaming red hair matched her mood. I'd never seen her in such a fitful state.

"Hey." I spoke as softly as I could, not wanting to agitate her any further.

Maggie's head shot up, ready to snap at whoever dared disrupt her raging. But seeing me, she instantly cooled. She dropped her bag, and pulled me tight into her arms.

"What is wrong with these people?" she lamented, knowing I had no good answers to give. She leaned back and looked me over. "You okay?"

"Yeah," I said reflexively.

But when I unconsciously lifted my hand to the bandage on my forehead, she inhaled and grabbed her heart. "Oh, my sweet girl, all that's been done to you... You've been through hell this week."

"I told you. There's nothing they can do to me that I won't take into myself and use as fuel."

Maggie nodded, sadness and frustration aging her care-worn face. "Here, let me fix that," she said. Within minutes of her ministrations, not a trace of the wound remained.

Magdalena Maramma personified empathy, but everyone had their breaking point. "I'm so sorry I haven't been able to protect you."

No other words could have brought me to my senses quicker than those. I plucked out the slightest weakness and weary whine within me and shook it off. For a moment, at least, every distraction faded.

I refuse to let Maggie feel responsible for the hatred of these people.

"That's enough lollygaggin', cats and kittens," Adelaide called from the gallery. "Let's get this show on the road. We can bitch about our collectively crappy circumstances once we get safely behind Alexander's walls. Right now, we gotta hustle, people! So let's move!"

Chapter Fourteen

We began our ascent up the winding Red Hill Road to Morgan Manor beneath a scorching, late-afternoon sun. But by the time we passed the estate's iron gates, boiling black clouds rolled in a furious tumult from the west. Lightning cracked across the sky, and the rain crashed upon the earth as if a dam had burst in the heavens. The wretched weather did nothing to improve the manor's sinister, melancholic aspect.

Leading the others in our caravan, Alexander pulled his Bentley up beside rounded gray stone steps below gargantuan iron doors. Franklin emerged at our approach, as dour as ever, with a liveried young man by his side. They held black umbrellas over their heads as they jogged down to meet us.

Franklin opened my door and helped me from the car. "Good afternoon, Ms. Clarion," he said with a small, stiff nod, a gesture he repeated a moment later as Alexander arrived to take my arm. "Mr. Morgan, sir. This is Elliot, the footman you asked me to hire."

Baby faced and broad shouldered, the new footman seemed better suited for farm work than domestic service. He had shaggy brown hair, suntanned skin, and an apple-pie smile. I liked him immediately. He was a ray of light in the gloom.

"Once Elliot escorts everyone inside, he'll attend to the luggage," the stern, gray butler said with calm competence.

"Very good. Thank you, Franklin," Alexander replied with equal decorum, though with more authority. He owned the place, after all.

Alexander dropped his dark eyes to mine and pulled me in tight. "These walls are here to protect you, not imprison you. I need you to understand that." Keeping my gaze under his control, he grazed his palm over my cheek and kissed me.

"I do," I replied. And I did.

My answer earned me one of Alexander's dazzling, joyful smiles. And right then and there, I was lost for good. That was the moment he stole my heart. I could no longer deny it, so I gave my heart permission to be happy.

It was a dangerous move, but I had no desire to play it safe. I stood on my tiptoes and kissed him hard and quick.

Beaming, Alexander grabbed my hand. "Let's go."

We raced through the downpour up the steps to the grand foyer, with Elliot feebly attempting to shield us from the dastardly drops with his umbrella as we ran. We bolted inside, puddles forming on the marble at our feet. Maggie, Adelaide, Ayo, and Luca sloshed and sputtered in behind us a minute later.

With the alabaster hearth in full blaze at their backs, the severe Mrs. Marsh and the pretty young maid, Celeste, greeted us at the apex of the entry. Not a tendril of silver hair wavered out of place from Mrs. Marsh's tightly coiled chignon. It tugged her wrinkled cheeks up into a menacing, lipsticked grin, the flash of rouge upon her lips the only color that adorned her. She stood yardstick straight with a sour face hidden beneath her false gentility. Celeste stood beside the domineering old dame, quiet as a dormouse, with her eyes lowered in deference. Yet there was a alluring energy reverberating from her. She intrigued me. Pink cheeked, she handed us each a warm towel to dry off, without ever once addressing us.

Mrs. Marsh took on that responsibility.

"Welcome home, Mr. Morgan. Good afternoon, ladies, and a good afternoon to the gentleman too, of course." She gestured to Luca. "Welcome." A shiver shot up my spine as she spoke. The cordiality of her words stood at odds with the frigid shoulder she presented. "I'm Mrs. Marsh, head housekeeper of Morgan Manor. Franklin and I, along with Celeste and Elliot, will be looking after you for the undetermined duration of your stay. We'll endeavor to make your brief visit as pleasant as possible."

I glanced at Adelaide, eager for her reaction to such passive-aggressively insulting behavior. Like another of my favorite characters, Adelaide was a connoisseur of human folly. She normally enjoyed mocking this type of arrogance, but Adelaide was apparently in no mood for games. Her knowing eyes flashed at Mrs. Marsh, and her wrinkled cheeks flamed red.

What the hell is that all about?

"If you would all follow Celeste into the music room. Elliot will be in shortly with refreshments," Mrs. Marsh said tersely before she turned and marched away.

"Isn't she just a bucket of rainbows and roses," I teased in what I thought was a hushed tone. Unfortunately, given the acoustics of the foyer, my snarky comments echoed. "Shit, sorry."

Luca busted out laughing, and Alexander snickered. "It's okay. I'm pretty sure even Marsh knows she'll never win Miss Congeniality."

Celeste bustled ahead and led us into the music room. All but Alexander stopped short a few feet in. We gaped, stunned at the grandeur of the palatial space. The ceilings vaulted at least thirty feet high, and were riddled with intricate ornamentation. The walls and floor were made entirely of swirling white and gray marble. A magnificent black grand piano adorned with two lit candelabrum and an arrangement of pink peonies dominated an entire corner of the room.

There wasn't a soul alive—nobility, gentry, or rabble—that wouldn't stand in awe.

Alexander walked up behind me and dropped a soft kiss on my shoulder. He ran his fingers lightly along the length of my neck and down my back. I tried unsuccessfully to hide a shiver.

His large, warm hands rested on my hips. "It's a Steinway, fully rebuilt model C, 1890," he whispered, his lips brushing along my ear.

I marveled at the craftsmanship involved in creating such a spectacular work of art. The piano *and* Alexander. "It's exquisite."

Alexander led me over to a cluster of love seats where the others had already made themselves comfortable. He chose a large leather armchair and pulled me down onto his lap. A trembling Elliot arrived to offer us all a glass of red wine, but he hadn't opened any bottles yet. The poor young man fumbled through the process so haphazardly, I feared for his safety. After he managed to successfully twist the corkscrew into the cork, a polite little cheer rose up. And then the poor dear not only broke the cork, but managed to drop the other half into the wine bottle. Before he could pour, Alexander hopped up, crossed the room, and grabbed the bottle from his hand. With his eyes harsh, he growled something too faintly to catch. Elliot offered a swift bow and rushed off. Alexander brought over six glasses and a different bottle, this one a white.

"Here we are," he said. "Please, enjoy a glass of Sancerre as an aperitif. I sent Elliot to grab a few special bottles of red from the cellars for us to have with dinner. They'll take some time to breathe. I hope that's okay?"

"Dear boy, it's been a hell of a day for everyone. If it's alcohol, it'll do," Adelaide said as she took her glass from Alexander.

"It's delicious, thank you, Alexander," Ayo replied.

"Yes, thank you," Maggie said.

"Luca, would you prefer whiskey or a beer?" Alexander asked.

"Wine's fine. Thanks, though."

"Alexander, I can't tell you how much I appreciate your generosity and hospitality." Maggie thanked our host.

"Of course, I'd do anything to keep Eva safe and happy," he said as he kissed me on the top of my head and handed me a glass of wine.

"I wonder, Alexander," Maggie began with trepidation, fiddling her fingers. It was a nervous twitch, uncharacteristic for her. "Do you realize how haunted this estate is? Morgan Manor has more spirits inhabiting it than any place I've ever stepped foot. Oddly enough, most of them love it. But there are two spirits here that are incredibly violent. I'm not certain, but I'd say they're both female."

Adelaide, Alexander, and I wore the same expression: *FUCK*.

I took a large sip of the wine and then another. My last mouthful killed the glass. It was too much. All too much. I didn't think I could handle anything else.

I need a time-out. I can't take any more shit. Bed can't come quick enough. I yawned and stretched out like a cat.

"I'm sorry, you know what, I've had enough for one day. Would you mind if I skipped dinner? I'm sapped and in desperate need of a shower and a bed."

"Hell yeah. I'm right there with you, baby girl," Luca blurted.

"Excuse me?" Alexander snapped and growled at my friend.

"No, back up, my man." Luca raised his hands defensively. "I just meant I agree with Eva. As in, yeah, I'm hungry as hell, but I'm too fucking tired to care. Between flying out here in the Goddess-forsaken hours yesterday morning, the attack on the familiars, the press conference...shit. The last two days have felt like a fucking week."

"Luca, watch the language. Your mother taught you better," Maggie scolded. But unable to leave him in distress, Maggie softened her tone. "You're right, though. I think we could all use a good night's rest."

Alexander rubbed his eyes. "Maybe you're right."

"I'd hate to waste the lovely dinner your chef's prepared for us, though," Maggie said.

"The manor's running without a proper chef these days, Ms. Good. I'm grateful to Mrs. Marsh for keeping me fed since I moved in. She'll whip up something delicious, I have no doubt. If everybody would rather head to their rooms, I can have trays made and brought up," Alexander suggested.

Adelaide popped to her feet and looked as if she'd sprint to her room if she could. "Yes, my darling man, do. Just make sure they include one of those lovely bottles of red you mentioned. I wouldn't want them to go to waste, either."

"Your wish is my command, madam," Alexander said with an exaggerated bow.

"Oh, I do like you more and more every day." Adelaide winked.

We all agreed to retire early, and Alexander called for Celeste to show Maggie, Adelaide, Ayo, and Luca to their rooms. Then he charged Franklin with bringing us each a dinner tray and bottle of wine. Everyone went their separate ways, and Alexander and I were left alone.

"And who's going to show me to my room?" I asked with faux innocence and fluttered lashes.

"I thought I'd do the honor. If the lady approves, of course." He offered a slight bow and a smirk.

A switch flipped within me. With predatory eyes, I stalked around my prey, taking in every taut muscle, every inch of chiseled masculinity. "Hmm," I purred. "The lady approves. And I'm suddenly not so sleepy." I grazed my fingertips over his back and arms.

Alexander stood at attention, allowing my fingers full access. And that's exactly what I wanted. But I didn't get a chance to move in. He took me first. A swift, agile maneuver angled Alexander over me, his arms planted solidly against the wall, capturing me. He lowered his mouth to my neck and bit down. Shivers tingled through me, and I sighed. Alexander kissed along my shoulder and up my neck, then nipped my earlobe with his teeth. He pulled back, his eyes shielded by his dark chin-length waves.

"I love that you're here. The manor's still new to me. Somehow you being here makes it feel more like home."

We both blanched at this declaration. The notion that my presence made him feel at home scared and excited me equally. And by the look on Alexander's face, he hadn't meant to be so forthcoming. But he didn't give me an inch. In fact, he moved in closer so his body pressed flush against mine. He held my hands in his.

Dropping his lips to my ear, he whispered, "Would you allow me the honor, Ms. Clarion, of escorting you to your room?"

"Yes," I breathed.

We turned toward the doorway, only to find Elliot standing frozen to his spot. He balanced a tray in his hand, obviously intending to clear away our wineglasses.

"I am so sorry, sir. I didn't think anyone was still in here," the young man rattled his apology. But he didn't hurry off. He just stared at us in wide-eyed wonder.

"No worries, Elliot. We were just leaving," Alexander said in his commanding tenor. "Have Franklin bring up two dinner trays, wine, and two glasses to Ms. Clarion's room, please." He took me by the hand and led me past the footman and out of the music room.

I skimmed my hand along the silver banister as we made our way up the arching marble staircase, glittered with red sparks of light reflected from the chandelier overhead, and I once again marveled at the opulence of the place. It was one thing to visit during Samhain, when the staggering architecture and unconventional décor added to the whimsy and eccentricity of the event, but witnessing Morgan Manor on an average day stunned my senses.

It's strange that Alexander can fit in so effortlessly here while also seeming so laid-back and comfortable in the cottage's modest surroundings.

"I was brought up in places like this my whole life," he replied to the thought I hadn't spoken aloud. "The home my father lived in wasn't as large as this one, but it was equally ostentatious. And my boarding school was filled with guys who grew up the same way. But that's not really me. I couldn't give a shit about money."

"Says the man who's never had to give a shit about money."

Alexander stopped at the top of the stairs and turned me to face him.

"You're right. I've never had to worry about money. But I don't need all this. I'm not like them."

"I know. I wouldn't have spent five minutes with you if I thought you were a spoiled brat," I teased. "Now, will you show me to my room before I collapse from exhaustion?"

"Of course."

We walked, hand in hand, down the emerald-carpeted hall until Alexander slowed his steps.

"Here's your room," he said, pointing to a door with a sly grin. "And there's mine." He motioned to the door across the hall. "Convenient, no?"

"Why might that be?" I planted my hands on shifted hips and popped up an eyebrow; enjoying the banter.

I could tell Alexander did too. "You might get scared. There are ghosts here remember."

"Spirits don't frighten me."

"You might have a nightmare, then."

"And you'll come running at my call, will you?"

"Lightning quick."

"And help me fall back to sleep?"

"Something like that," he said with rakish charm. He opened the door to my room and welcomed me inside with a grand sweep of his arm.

The room was pleasant and feminine with smoky-blue damask walls. A pale-yellow comforter and pillows covered a queen-size four-poster bed. Along one wall stood a massive armoire and, beside it, a mirrored dressing table with a cushioned bench. My luggage sat on the floor between the two. Three large windows displayed a remarkable view of Arbor. I walked to one and peered over the quaint town below; quite pretty from high atop Red Hill.

"Is the room to your liking?" Alexander asked expectantly.

"It's lovely." Just then I noticed a door tucked into a corner that I assumed led to an attached bathroom. It had been a very long day, and I felt grubby. "Do you mind if I change and wash up a bit?"

"Not at all. I'll wait out here for our dinner."

I grabbed my suitcase and opened the door to the bathroom. "Sweet Goddess above!"

"What? What is it?" Alexander ran to my side, checking me over like he was taking inventory of my limbs and sundry body parts. "What's wrong?" he asked once he determined I wasn't in mortal danger.

My voice caught in my throat. When I regained my power of speech, I squeaked, "This is the most amazing bathroom I've ever seen."

Alexander barked out a laugh. "Is that all? Don't do that to me. You're going to give me a damn heart attack."

"Sorry. But I think I might have to live right here forever."

"I wouldn't argue with that."

The bathroom looked nothing like the sweet room to which it was attached. It nestled into the curve of a turret, surrounded by thick-paned windows and bare stone walls. The ceiling vaulted overhead at least twenty feet high, and from it hung a black crystal chandelier. An iron claw-foot tub—like an enormous cauldron, large enough to fit four adults comfortably—was the focal point of the space. To the right, a stone shower, with more showerheads than I could count, seemed carved into the wall itself. What passed as a sink looked more like an ornate birdbath, and above it was, quite possibly, the actual evil queen's mirror from Snow White. Lush fabrics of every shade and hue hung through iron rings that dotted the perimeter of the space. The fabrics brought out the subtle hints of color in the slate floor, though I hadn't the foggiest idea of their intended purpose.

"You use them as towels," Alexander whispered into my ear.

"Okay, how the fuck do you do that?" I snapped and rounded on him.

"Do what?" He laughed.

"I'm serious, Alexander. How do you answer questions I haven't said out loud? You do it all the time. It's freaking me out."

"You do a whole hell of a lot of things I can't do. In case you forgot."

Before we could continue our bickering, there was a knock on the bedroom door.

"That's probably Franklin with our food. Go ahead and wash up. But don't take too long or the food will get cold," he said before slapping me on the ass and walking away.

I threw my hair up into a messy bun, scrubbed my face and hands, and changed into boxers and my soft Ramones T-shirt. I'd just begun brushing my teeth when I heard a frantic, frightened scream. I ran out in time to see Alexander bolt into the hallway, only to be dive-bombed by a swooping red-tailed hawk. A shivering Mrs. Marsh cowered behind him.

"Rocky! That is enough," I admonished him as he perched atop the wardrobe. "How dare you scare the daylights out of poor Mrs. Marsh! Show respect to our hosts."

In a voice only Alexander and I could hear, Rocky expressed his regret for the indelicacy of his approach. *"Alexander, please accept my sincerest apologies for frightening your amiable housekeeper. I became sidetracked in my travels and was eager to report all I've seen. It is of great import, sir."*

"Of course, Rocky. Please, perch anywhere you'd like and tell us your news." Alexander spoke respectfully to the hawk.

Mrs. Marsh eyed me and then her employer with abject horror. She ran off, tossing something behind her as she fled. It was my besom broom.

It must have gotten left behind when Elliot brought in the luggage. I retrieved it and placed it by the bed.

I peeked out into the emerald hallway. Finding it empty, I shut the bedroom door. "The last thing we need is another set of ears," I said in a slight whisper.

"Would you mind leaving the door open a few inches?" Rocky asked. *"I'd like to be able to make a quick getaway should the need arise. I see you haven't eaten yet,"* he said and nodded to the dinner trays. *"Please, enjoy your dinner while I fill you in."*

"That's fine. Just keep it down." I opened the door and, once more, peeked out. Satisfied, I left it open about six inches, just enough for Rocky to scoot through. I crawled onto the bed and snuggled under the covers. "Can your news wait until I've eaten?"

"Of course. As you wish."

Alexander leaned over and kissed me gently. Then he brought over a dinner tray. He lifted the silver lid, revealing chicken Kiev slathered in sauce, boiled baby carrots, and mashed potatoes.

"Thank you," I said and immediately dug in. *Not exactly a light summer dish, but I'm famished.*

Alexander fussed with a dusty bottle of wine.

"So what is it we'll be drinking?" I asked. "That bottle has so much dust, it's probably older than me."

"This bottle is eleven years older than you, to be precise. It's a 1985 Caymus Cabernet. One of the best vintages for California Cabs in the last forty years."

"Alexander, you don't have to waste that on me. There's no special occasion."

"You, my dear, are worth anything and everything I could possibly conceive to lavish upon you. And this is a special occasion. It may not be the first time we're sleeping under the same roof, but it is the first time you are sleeping under my roof. And truthfully, for as hard as these bottles are to come by, there happens to be six cases of them down in the wine cellar begging to be drunk. Too much longer and they'll turn."

"That's serendipitous. Lucky us. Although, I shouldn't drink. I need to keep my wits about me."

"One glass won't hurt. And it is a spectacular vintage. It would be a sin to let it go to waste."

"I'm beginning to think you really may be the Devil. Certainly the only one I've ever believed in."

"Your statement indicates that you believe in me, so I'm going to take that as a compliment."

He handed me a delicate, crystal goblet. Swirling the wine smoothly, I admired its legs that clung to the glass, reluctantly cascading. The rich claret glistened ruby in its depths and mahogany at its edges. I leaned into the glass and breathed deeply. The aroma alone was intoxicating; a heady blend of black cherry, currant, cigar, and vanilla. Taking the first sip, raspberries, lead pencil, cedar, and dark chocolate teased my taste buds. I took another drink, a bit bigger this time, and allowed my eyes to close. I could almost taste the sun on the vines, the rain that refreshed them, their nurturing soil.

With my head tilted backward, I called to Her. "My Goddess, the majesty of your creation is astounding to behold. I am grateful to those who planted the seeds, tended the vines, crushed the grapes, and bottled this wine. I am forever thankful. Blessed be."

As my eyes opened, they fell upon Alexander—staring at me.

"Blessed be," he said.

Chapter Fifteen

Alexander turned away, hiding the blush that crept over his cheeks. He grabbed his dinner, situated himself next to me in bed, and began to devour his meal.

After he'd hoovered half his plate, he encouraged my familiar to continue. "So what's the news, Rocky?"

Rocky had been watching our exchange with detached amusement, but when Alexander addressed him directly, he grew flustered.

"Yes, there is news. And I will tell you. Yes, very good, then. Well, no, it's not very good news. Not very good news at all. But, as I said before..." he prattled.

"Let's make *expeditious* the word of the night, shall we?" I prodded him along.

"I do apologize, Evangeline. It's just that I find it difficult to break this to you. It's involves Ms. Gwendo... pardon me – Bunny."

"We already know my former friend was involved with the vandalism and your attack," I threw out.

"Well, yes, but that's only a portion of her duplicity."

The moment Bunny's car peeled out of the driveway, I knew she'd turned her back on me. I just never anticipated the depth of her betrayal.

"On our way here, I was flying behind Master Luca's stellar mint-condition '69 SS 390 El Camino, when I noticed Bunny. She was driving alone, and I took the liberty of following her. She parked her pathetic excuse of an automobile outside an overpriced caffeine peddler. She spoke to no one inside save the pimply-faced overgrown child who poured her beverage and took her cash.

"As she exited the café, Bunny was confronted by that sanctimonious tripe, Gladys Cudlow, wearing a flamboyant floral dress and an obnoxiously large purple hat. Gladys hid the evidence of poor health—her dark circled eyes and splotchy skin that hung loose from fragile bones— under her floppy brim. Mrs. Cudlow bombarded Bunny with questions regarding your whereabouts. I must say, Mrs. Cudlow did not use polite

language. She said, and I quote, 'You promised to bring me dirt on that skanky witch.' I assumed she was referring to you."

Alexander snickered, and I shot him a look that shut him up quick.

Rocky carried on with his tale. *"'No,' Bunny said. 'My deal is with Crandall. And I already taped that...that...that ceremony thingy I saw. And Eva's press conference.' So then Mrs. Cudlow replied, 'Yes.' She laid a skeletal hand upon Bunny's heart. 'And Doreen was grateful for your videos of that unholy ritual and the tramp's attempt to manipulate the media. But I need more. The mayor needs more.' Once she vowed to uncover more information, Bunny stormed off.*

"After witnessing this encounter, I flew with all haste to inform you of my findings. I hope I have been of assistance."

"Yes, thank you." *I am blessed to have such a loyal, tenacious familiar— especially since my only nonmagical friend turned out to be so disloyal.* "You're welcome to hunt for your dinner now. It may take you a bit since this is new territory."

Rocky nodded, but before he took wing, he added yet another note. *"And so your heart can rest easy, know that Shasta is well healed and sends her love. She has obtained the assistance of Alexander's familiar, Archimedes, in guarding the estate grounds. He's a down-to-earth sort of fellow, without the excessive preening typical of purebreds. Archie, as he's asked us to call him, gave us a quick review of the layout of the estate. He and Shasta have been monitoring the perimeter of the manor since your arrival. Shasta plans on reporting to you in the morning unless anything urgent arises. In which case, she will most likely burst through the door. You may want to warn the good housekeeper. Well then, that's that, I believe. Good night, all. Pleasant dreaming."*

Rocky flew from the room, squawking and causing as much ruckus as he possibly could, determined to drive Mrs. Marsh crazier.

It couldn't be. No. That would mean...

"What did he just say? What does he mean my familiar?" Shock and trepidation lanced through Alexander's words.

"I can't believe it, either. You're a descendant."

"A descendant? Of what?" he croaked.

"A pure-blooded witch, of course, with magic in your veins. A conjurer of the elements, one who communes with the powers of Nature. Technically, the magic could have come from either parent, but in your case, I think it's safe to assume it was your mother."

"My mother?" he croaked again. "It just doesn't make any sense."

"Alexander, your familiar is a German shepherd," I said by way of explanation. "Just like in my dream. The one who fought alongside Shasta, Rocky, Hanna, and Fled."

As shocked as I was, somehow this revelation made complete sense—a puzzle piece I didn't realize I was missing.

"But what does this mean? No. You know what?" Alexander scrubbed his face with his hands and got out of bed. "I'm done. I'm spent. I can't ingest another thing." He heaved a great sigh. "I need a good night's sleep, and then maybe you can help me wrap my head around all this in the morning." He leaned down and gave me a soft, lingering kiss. "Is there anything I can do for you? Anything else you need before you settle in for the night?"

Mmm, I can think of a few things you can do for me. You could start by settling in beside me. "No, I'm good."

"Then enjoy the rest of the wine, and sleep well," he said with a knowing grin. And after another brush of his lips, he was gone.

I got out of bed and took my glass of wine in a walk about the room. I marveled at the luxury of it all. And I allowed a moment of fantasy, imagining myself as the mistress of Morgan Manor. It wasn't a life I'd ever envisioned, but the possibility intrigued me. I sipped as I wandered about the space, eventually making my way over to the fairy-tale bathroom. *Yeah, I could get used to this.*

A great yawn crashed over me in a wave. *Bed. Sleep. Now.* I downed the last of the wine, turned off the Victorian-era lamp on my bedside table, and burrowed into bed. The fluffy comforter and down pillows cocooned around me. But as cozy as it was, I couldn't get settled in. I flipped and flopped and changed positions again and again, my mind churning, my anxiety level spiking.

I cursed, turned the light back on, and hopped out of bed in a huff. I grabbed my sketchpad and pencil, dragged the vanity bench over to the windows, and plopped down. As flustered as I was, it was impossible not to appreciate the view. Arbor was nothing if not picturesque, especially from high atop Red Hill. So I drew—the tree-lined streets, the town clock, the quaint storefronts.

But the more detail I added to the picture, the more shocked I was. Details I would typically flub through, like the ridges on roof shingles and individual tree leaves, I rendered in startling minutia. My hand sped across the page faster and faster. In minutes, I completed such a striking image of Arbor that it could have been mistaken for a black-and-white photograph.

What the hell?

A gentle rapping came from my bedroom door, and I jumped in surprise. Maggie poked her head inside. "May I come in?" She held a steaming mug in her hands.

"Of course."

"Thanks. I'd like to... Dear Goddess, Eva, this is a masterpiece!" Maggie took my sketch, and examined it. "How long have you been working on this?"

"Almost half an hour."

"Half an hour! Your powers are growing at breakneck speed." She paused and searched my eyes. "This hasn't been easy, on top of everything else."

I didn't want to talk about how I was feeling. I didn't want to hash things out. But Maggie had given me everything. The least I could offer in return was some girl time. So I hopped into bed, enveloped myself once more under the billowy comforter, and mentally prepared for a heart-to-heart.

Maggie set the steaming mug down on the bedside table. Cocoa and cinnamon wafted toward me. "Are you okay? This has been hell, I know. How are you holding up?" Maggie smoothed my hair and ran her hand gently over my back, soothing my tattered spirit.

She really is too good to me. "Mags, there are patients— average Arbor residents— whose health conditions are going untreated because Arbor's Most Moral ran their only source of care off her own property. They defaced your home. They attacked Hanna and Rocky and Shasta. These holier-than-thou hypocrites, emboldened by far-right rhetoric, are hell-bent on our collective destruction. And Bunny is their accomplice! You know, Rocky found out she wasn't just involved in the cottage attack. She's been working for Crandall."

"For the mayor's campaign?" Maggie asked with a straight face.

"No. Crandall's been paying Bunny to spy on us."

"No!"

"That's why Crandall dragged Harrison out to the cottage the night we drew down the rain. Bunny was pissed that I ditched her. Again. She must have come over to the cottage to have it out with me and saw us performing the ritual. She knew the mayor was after me, so she tipped her off."

"Oh, how awful. What a fool I am!" Maggie cried out.

"You? You didn't do anything wrong. Others are culpable, Mags, not you."

"Adelaide warned me to keep an eye on Bunny, but I brushed her off. You two had been thick as thieves. I simply didn't believe Bunny would turn her back on you."

"She turned her back on all of us. How many times did you take her in when her mom went on a bender? Yet she didn't hesitate to throw you to the wolves."

"The poor girl," Maggie lamented.

"Poor girl? She conspired with the enemy!"

Maggie cocked her head to the side and seemed to be crafting a measured reply. "Have you stopped to think how Bunny must have felt when she realized we possessed true magic? The poor dear has never been the brightest bulb, so it's no surprise it took so long for her to understand what's been going on under her nose all these years. But you were her best friend. However essential it was to protect our powers from the public's prying eyes, at the end of the day, you hid a major part of yourself from her. That's got to hurt."

"I guess," I grumbled.

"No, Eva. Do not take the pain of others lightly," Maggie scolded with an unusually stern voice. "You wounded Bunny deeply. You put that out into the universe. Don't think it won't come back to bite you."

Great. Add that to the pile. "You know, Bunny's not the only one who has had their world shaken. Rocky dropped another bomb earlier tonight. Apparently, Alexander has a familiar."

"Does he?" she replied, somehow not appearing the least bit surprised.

"Yes. Meaning— "

"Meaning Alexander's a descendant," Maggie answered for me. "How... curious." She went silent for the breath of a heartbeat, until she changed the direction of the conversation. "I'm surprised Alexander's not here with you."

"He's had a long day."

"Yes, he has. He's stood beside you, beside all of us."

"Maggie, I... I think I love him," I confessed. "For the first time, I feel a true connection with someone. But I don't want to rush things, especially while we're in the midst of chaos."

"There's something to be said for delayed gratification. But you must remember, chaos is inevitable. That's life. And we're an innately social species. These tumultuous periods aren't meant to be endured alone. They are shared endeavors."

"So you like Alexander? You approve?"

"If he is your choice, then yes. There's a fire in that young man's eyes when he looks at you, which is anytime you're near. But it's more than that. He's sincere."

I couldn't help but smile.

"Do you know what I love most in this entire world?" Maggie asked, tucking an errant lock of hair behind my ear.

"What?"

"Seeing you smile like that. Hold on to that feeling. You will need to harness those positive emotions when trouble is at the door."

"I will try. I promise."

"Good. I feel much better now that we've spoken. I worried about you."

"And now?"

"Now? Now I know you're keeping as cool a head as possible with the hurricane of bullshit swirling around us."

"Maggie! Such language," I teased.

She chuckled and continued. "But if you ever feel like you're losing control, you come to me, for anything, okay?"

"Yes, I will," I said and kissed her cheek. "I love you."

"Love you too. And now that this has cooled," she said, gesturing to the mug. "You can go ahead and drink it down. You will have lovely dreams and a restful night's sleep."

I downed the drink and turned off the light. As the last drops of the brew trickled down my throat, I succumbed to a deep slumber.

Sometime later, a shrill scream ripped me from the sweetest dream. My dreams were so vivid, I thought I might still be in one. But when another wail struck like lightning to my heart, I shook myself fully awake. The clock read three a.m., the witching hour. A third scream jolted me out of bed, and I rushed from my room. I entered the hallway as Maggie emerged from her own room.

"It's Adelaide," she said with ice in her voice. She took off down the hall, and I followed. When we arrived at her door, Maggie tried to open it, but it was locked.

Alexander ran up to us with Mrs. Marsh in tow.

"Please, help. It won't open." Maggie was close to tears as she tugged on the door.

"I've got the master keys. I'll get it," Mrs. Marsh said, sounding bored and more than a little irritated. But when key after key refused to budge the lock, her expression turned to panic.

Another ear-splitting cry came from the room.

"We're right here, Adelaide! We're trying to get in," I called out to my frightened friend.

Alexander ordered the housekeeper to the side. He took a few steps backward, and rammed the door with his shoulder. Nothing. Again and again, he threw himself against the door in a valiant, but vain, attempt to break the damned thing down. When it became clear his efforts were futile, I asked him to stand back. He was wise enough not to question why a female over a foot shorter and far less muscular would think she could use brute force to break down a door—one that he couldn't budge. I mentally called out to Shasta and Rocky, and requested as much power as they could send. Instantly, a rush of raw energy burned through me. I stepped back from the door a few feet and rushed at it with my shoulder—the same way Alexander had attempted it. The door burst off its frame on my first try.

We rushed into the room, and the scene that confronted us was straight out of a nightmare. My high priestess crouched, crumpled and trembling, in the corner of her room. Blood gushed from a large gash on her temple. Leering over her was the semitransparent figure of a very angry old woman. The spirit turned at our approach and, with the flick of her hand, sent a large ceramic water pitcher straight at my head. I ducked just in time, and the pitcher shattered on the wall behind me.

"Amelia, stop!" Adelaide shrieked. "Your quarrel is not with the girl."

"Oh, but she's just like you, isn't she? An evil enchantress set on corrupting a Morgan man," said the specter of Amelia Morgan, wife of the late Cain Morgan, Alexander's great-grandmother, as she hovered inches away from Adelaide's fear-stricken face.

The apparition whipped back to me again. Once more, she flicked her wrist, this time sending the ceramic bowl that complemented the pitcher careening in my direction. Imbued with Rocky's magic, I rose into the air, grabbed the bowl, and sent it spiraling out of harm's way.

"Eva!" Adelaide called with her arms open wide.

Still airborne, I rocketed to my fallen mentor's side. Maggie reached us a moment later, and we all joined hands.

"No!" the specter screeched. "You must not defile Morgan Manor with your malevolence!"

"Repeat after me, and with intention," Adelaide directed in a rush. "*Ad requiem tuam. Derelinques nos in pace.*"

Words that had never before left my lips, in a language I'd never learned, poured from me in a commanding voice. My invocation melded with those of the wise women beside me. We were maiden, mother, and crone, united to banish the spirit of Alexander's great-grandmother from the earth and send her onward to Summerland. As we sent our supplication out into the universe, the apparition of Amelia Morgan spun above us, faster and faster, transforming into a living cyclone.

"To thy rest. Leave us in peace!" Adelaide cried out.

Swirling at blurring speeds, the vengeful spirit grew ever smaller and more faint until she was no more.

With the same jarring speed as it began, it ended, and maiden, mother, and crone collapsed into each other's weary arms. Alexander rushed to our side. He took Adelaide's hand in his and kissed it with great care and reverence. He leaned in close to Adelaide's ear, and whispered.

I strained to listen but couldn't make out a word. Glancing up, I noticed Mrs. Marsh standing in the doorway. Something about her blank expression disturbed me almost as much as the ghostly woman had. She caught me watching her and quickly turned to leave.

"Get back here!" Maggie screamed, her outcry drawing everyone's attention. "Why are you running off? To concoct another twisted plan? You called this spirit here tonight, didn't you? Amelia Morgan wasn't one of the unfortunate souls tethered to this place. But she certainly had a score to settle, didn't she? And you knew that."

"Ms. Maramma, allow me to assure you with the utmost vehemence, that I have never, and would never, dabble in the dark arts. I was merely going to fetch some tea, and some warm water and bandages for Ms. Good. Is there anything else you require?" she replied with false sincerity.

"We don't need your tea, and we're perfectly capable of tending to our friend's wounds." The poison in Maggie's voice surprised all, herself included, if her wide-eyed, slack-jawed expression was any tell.

"Yes, ma'am," Mrs. Marsh replied and ducked away into the safety of the hall.

I rounded on Alexander. "That woman is up to something, and I doubt she's acting alone. You'd better figure out what the hell is going on under your roof, Alexander. Fast."

"What the hell?" Alexander replied with his hands raised defensively. "What has Marsh done to deserve your suspicion?"

"Seriously? That old bat gives me the evil eye every time I'm in her presence."

"Just because—" Alexander began.

"Will you two shut it already and help an old lady up?" Adelaide snapped.

Alexander and I helped Maggie lift Adelaide back into bed.

"Are you okay?" I asked as I pulled the sheets up to her chin.

"Oh, I'll be just fine. You did well, Evangeline." Adelaide patted my hand. "One disgruntled spirit down, one to go," she pronounced on a yawn.

"Hmm, maybe," Maggie muttered to herself.

"Are you okay?" I asked Alexander, whose pinched brow deepened at the question.

"Ha!" he barked out a sarcastic laugh. "You're asking if I'm okay?" He shook his head in disbelief.

"It's not every day a guy sees his girl take on the vengeful spirit of his great-grandmother," I said with a shrug.

"I'm learning to expect the unexpected with you." He offered up half a smile before a yawn overtook him. His whole body clenched and released in a stretch, and I fawned over his taut muscles and the glorious vee at his hips.

Thank you Goddess. I cleared my throat. "Go on, head to bed. We're good here. I'll see you in the morning," I said.

After ensuring that Maggie had all she needed to aid Adelaide, Alexander said good night.

Not long after, I headed back to my own room, smiling all the way. Once again, I curled into the warmth of my bed. This time, sweet merciful sleep found me the instant I hit the pillow.

Chapter Sixteen

SATURDAY

A light tickling on my cheeks teased me awake. I grumbled and peeked my eyes open—hesitant, wary.

A mischievous grin greeted me. "Morning, sleepyhead!" Alexander bellowed. "Rise and shine!"

I cringed. "Are you always this boisterous in the morning? If so, I may need to reconsider this whole relationship thing."

Alexander's eyes flashed. "My little witch, that is something I prefer we not joke about." His voice was hard, and for a moment, I wasn't sure whether or not he was serious. Before I made up my mind on the issue, he pounced and tickled me until I lost my breath. I scurried to the edge of the bed, only to be mercilessly yanked back by the ankles. Hysterical laughter ripped through me. He lifted my shirt to expose my belly, leaned down, and blew raspberries.

I cackled like a crazed lunatic. "Stop!" I wailed. "Unhand me, vile beast!"

As my head flung back in tickle euphoria, I saw Maggie and Adelaide appear at my open bedroom door with their arms folded, smiling.

"Are you two going to just stand there gawking, or are you going to help a girl out?"

Recognizing the presence of the women, Alexander flung himself off me like a thief caught in the act.

"Alexander, relax," Maggie said breezily.

"Yes, don't stop on our account. That's the most action either of us has seen in years." Adelaide smirked.

And Maggie squirmed.

Wow. Okay then.

"But, you see, well, I just..." Alexander stuttered out a gibberish attempt at an explanation of his presence in my room, in my bed, on top of me.

"That's enough blubbering," Adelaide interrupted after indulging Alexander for a minute or two. "No one's upset with either of you. But you do need to get in gear. We have things to discuss, business to attend to."

"Yes, Ms. Good," he replied with a deferential bow.

Alexander lifted me to my feet, planted a kiss on my nose, and winked. When I tried in vain to pull him to my mouth, he whispered against my ear. "I can't get too close to your lips, little temptress. We'll never accomplish anything today."

"What a patently untrue statement. We'd get a good deal accomplished, I promise you."

"This is all very enlightening, but not exactly appropriate for present company," Adelaide chimed in. She wasn't just nudging me to maintain general propriety. Mrs. Marsh and Franklin had arrived, and it was clear by the horror on their faces that neither approved of me getting so close to the Morgan Manor heir.

Scowling his displeasure, Franklin took a half step forward. "Good morning, Mr. Morgan. Ladies." He nodded, avoiding our eyes. "Sir, you have several matters that you must attend to expeditiously. I will have Elliot bring your breakfast to your office so you can get an early start on the day." He stepped back again.

"Are you his boss or his butler?" I questioned the manipulative old codger.

"Little miss, you haven't the foggiest notion of the time and effort and attention necessary to run an estate like Morgan Manor," Mrs. Marsh countered in Franklin's defense. Clearly, she'd abandoned any pretense of deference. "Mr. Morgan has responsibilities that cannot be ignored for the sake of some tart."

"That's enough," Alexander thundered. "Show some respect, woman. Franklin, I will have my breakfast with the ladies. I can work while I eat. I'm sure the ladies won't mind. Will you?" He donned a quick, polite smile.

"It's your home," I said, folding my arms and popping a hip.

"And Franklin, Mrs. Marsh," Alexander addressed his employees with a firm and steady voice. "You are here at my request, not the other way around. Morgan Manor will receive anyone I invite across my threshold and will do so with dignity and competence. If that's a problem, you can find the door."

The maid and butler were starched as stiff as the formal livery they wore, sewn to the floor, motionless.

"That'll be all." Alexander turned his back to them, and Franklin and Mrs. Marsh plodded off down the emerald hallway, stupefied. "Ms. Good, Maggie, Evangeline, I apologize for the rudeness of my staff."

"No need to fret, dear boy," Adelaide piped up. "Those two could try the patience of the pope. Now, Magdalena and I are heading down for breakfast. We'll see you two...sooner or later, I'm sure." She winked.

Finally alone, I couldn't help thinking as soon as they were gone. And I blushed as Alexander turned his voracious gaze on me.

He closed the distance between us in a heartbeat and lifted my chin with a gentle hand. "We need to talk, but it can wait." He ran his hand lightly along my neck, sending shivers down my arms.

I shook myself and asked the question that had been on my mind from the moment I opened my eyes. "Are you completely freaked out? About last night, I mean. You're not angry with me, are you?"

He kissed me on the forehead. "There's nothing to be angry about. I admit, I was thrown by, well, everything."

"That's understandable. I mean, I busted down Adelaide's door, helped turn your great-grandmother into a cyclone and sent her on to the next plane. I can understand how you'd be shaken by all that." I hung my head, wondering for the millionth time why the hell this man wanted to get wrapped up with me knowing the insanity that tagged along.

"I'm going to have to get used to wild and magical things," he whispered, his lips just out of reach as he spoke. "But we can talk more at breakfast. I should let you get ready."

"Or you could stay and help." I fluttered my lashes and ran my hands over his solid, muscled chest.

"Now who's the Devil?" he teased. And then he kissed me as if the act itself gave him sweet sustenance long denied. "Get ready. Be quick." He left me breathless, weak kneed, and alone.

I wasn't quick. Adjusting to my new accommodations delayed my morning routine. And I wanted to look nice—for Alexander, yes, but really for me. So I dolled myself up. I applied my makeup with extra care. I left my dark hair down, so it flowed silken over my shoulders. The wispy, navy fabric of my strapless summer dress billowed around my smooth legs. The amethyst pendant and the fairy-stone necklace hung around my neck and rested just above my breasts. Feeling the need to go all-out, I unpacked my wooden jewelry box. I put on my silver and stone rings, bracelets and earrings, and an ornate silver cuff around my right upper arm. I slipped my feet into hand-embroidered ballet flats and walked to the full-length mirror in the bathroom.

I smiled. *I'm ready.*

By the time I made it down to the dining room, it was empty. I wondered if everyone had already finished eating until I heard a faint chortling of voices coming from outside. I exited through french doors and followed the voices. Weaving through a maze of greenery, I found a clematis-covered garden arbor. And a lively assemblage revealed itself on the other side.

The cabal I'd brought with me—Adelaide, Maggie, Ayo, Luca, and the familiars—had made themselves comfortable in Alexander's home. They lounged on an enormous Turkish rug amid mountains of pillows in shades of ruby, sapphire, and emerald. I marveled at my loved ones, reveling in the decadent delights around them.

The brunch delicacies were spread out, picnic style, in clusters on the rug. I gawked at the antique porcelain bowls of melons and berries and rosemary potatoes, the crystal platters of eggs Benedict, smoked salmon, sausages in puff pastry, crispy bacon, and baskets of croissants, danishes, and muffins. Trays of coffee, tea, champagne, orange juice, and blueberry lemonade sat on low tables at the outskirts of the banquet.

What a feast—and such company!—a scene impossible to duplicate.

Alexander raised his eyes to me as if I'd spoken aloud to him directly. "There you are. You are a vision." He beamed.

"Thank you." I blushed.

"It was such a nice day, I had Celeste move breakfast outside," Alexander pronounced proudly.

"I see that," I answered with a matching grin. "Good morning, everyone. You all look cozy." I hugged my way through each of the assembled and then curled up beside Alexander.

The ethereal beauty of the gardens awed me, left as they were to bloom unimpeded by the uninvited hand of man. The air blew sweet, without a trace of East Coast summer stickiness. And the late-morning sun beat warm on my pale pink skin and on the pink peonies bursting from the thick-vined trellises that lined the gardens.

"You're right. It's a lovely day, and this is sweet." I looked around at our picnic and at the friends and family that gathered. I felt the Goddess's blessings rush over me like a great wave. "Thank you." I sighed.

"It's my pleasure," Alexander said and brushed my cheek with his lips.

When he pulled away, I closed my eyes to steady my emotions. As I opened them again, I saw a powdery-blue sky had replaced the melancholy rain clouds. The grass grew greener and thicker, almost by the minute. I assumed the same could be said for the lawns throughout Arbor. And I was glad. I considered this proof of our effective spellwork.

We called down the rain. The grass is green again. We stopped the drought. The end.

"So we have you ladies to thank for all that rain?" Alexander said, offhand, as he chomped on an apple. "You're powerful enough to end a drought? Who knew!"

"Okay, that's enough. You stay out of my head," I snapped. Every eye turned to me, but I ignored them all. All except Alexander. "You can hear my thoughts. How do you do it?"

Alexander opened his mouth to speak, only to close it again. He repeated this fish imitation several more times. Then he rose to his feet, ran a hand through his hair, and began pacing. After several passes, he lifted his head, but before he could speak, he caught sight of something that drained all color from his cheeks.

I followed his gaze and couldn't resist a cackle. *Of course!*

"Dearest Archimedes, good morning. I hope you slept well." Shasta greeted the new arrival to our garden party.

"Archie," Rocky groused, *"you're looking well rested."*

"Hey, you volunteered for the nightwatch, bird. Don't give me a headache about it now," Archie said.

When the German shepherd caught sight of Alexander, he padded over and offered a slight bow. *"It's a great honor to officially meet you in this lifetime. The name's Archimedes. I'm your familiar, and you, sir, are my witch."*

And just like that, Alexander's eyes rolled to the back of his head, and he fell to his knees. Great jerking convulsions twisted and contorted his limbs.

I lunged to help him, but Adelaide called out, "Wait!"

Alexander's eyes popped open, and his muscles seized up rigid. He remained that way for over five minutes. It seemed as though he was watching some terrifying horror film, invisible to all but himself.

When I began to feel the last shred of patience in me slipping away, Alexander let out a howl of laughter. He fell from his knees onto his backside.

"Archie, you're one hell of a dog!" he bellowed.

The German shepherd bounded playfully onto his witch and proceeded to lick his face. Sitting in the grass, Alexander roughed up the dog's black, brown, and tan glossy coat. They chatted away, as natural as breathing. "Can Eva hear you too? Shasta and Rocky don't mind if I hear what they're saying, even though I'm not in the coven. I don't want her to feel left out."

"Of course." Archimedes nuzzled his head against my hand in introduction. *"Eva, it's great to see you again. Can I call you Eva? You can call me Archie or Archimedes, whichever you prefer. You're as lovely as ever. I've known you in each of your fourteen lifetimes, just as I've known Alex over here. Did you know?"*

"It's a pleasure to meet you, too, Archie. Yes, you can call me Eva. And, no, I wasn't aware that we've met in...what was it you said? Fourteen lifetimes?" I shot a piercing eye at Shasta and Rocky. "Something a witch might like to know."

Unexpectedly, Alexander stood, pulled me to my feet, and held my hands close to his heart. We stared at each other with a shattering recognition. The stirring of our souls, the instantaneous attraction, the ease with which we confided in each other, Adelaide's speculation that we'd spent lifetimes together, it was all real. There grew a sudden and unspoken understanding between us. There was nothing on earth we wouldn't do for each other.

Ignoring our gawking spectators, we embraced with a purity and reverence that had been foreign to me up until that moment. When our kiss ended, Alexander took my hand with a gentle smile upon his lips. He led me over to our little spot of rug. And we sat, viscerally connected, not only to each other but to the magical creatures that huddled around us.

A sudden thought struck me. "Alexander, what gift does Archie bring you?"

"What gift? I...I don't..." he stammered for only an instant. "Maybe..." Alexander ruffled Archie's fur. "Courage. Loyalty."

"Great, he'll be wearing armor by nightfall," Luca said.

"Can it, Luca," Adelaide scolded. "This is better than telenovelas."

Maggie fidgeted with her bracelets, and I knew she was brooding over something.

"This is remarkable, Alexander," Maggie said, "but your story is still far from complete. Adelaide, Ayo, and I have some pieces to add to your puzzle, if you don't mind us speaking about them here." Maggie's voice quivered with an uncertainty that underscored the gravity of her information.

Shit. This isn't going to be good.

Alexander obviously heard my thoughts. A wary shadow fell over him. "Of course, please," Alexander replied with his chin raised.

"Indulge me, if you will. I must begin by stepping back in time. When I was a young witch, my mother and I lived farther north with others of our coven. Every time we visited my grandmother's cottage here in Arbor— which was often—she'd beg my mother to stay. And every time, my mother declined. She had no interest in tending the land and preferred to be surrounded by our community of witches. When my grandmother's health began slipping, she again asked my mother to take ownership of the cottage and the ten acres of land on which it sits. And, yet again, she said no. My grandmother was furious. She begged my mother, threatened her, but to no avail."

"Why was it so important to your grandmother that you and your mother live there?" Alexander asked Maggie.

"The first Stregheria to cross the Atlantic from Italy settled there. This witch, otherwise known as la Strega, struck a magical bond that kept the land fertile and abundant and receptive to her magic. As long as la Strega of our bloodline inhabits that cottage and tends and protects the land, the land will protect and provide for the witch's well-being in return. An unbroken chain of succession was—is—imperative."

Maggie cleared her throat, looked nervously at Ayo, before continuing her tale. "My grandmother's health steadily declined. It was vital she find someone in the family bloodline to take over the cottage and the magical bond. So my grandmother contacted her family in Italy, namely, our matriarch Mia Aradia."

Alexander blanched at the name—Aradia.

"They organized the immigration of a young la Strega, my cousin, to take up my grandmother's post after her death." Maggie took a steadying breath. "My cousin's name was Teresa Aradia."

Goose bumps broke out over Alexander's skin. "I'm sorry, I...I don't understand."

"Are you saying Alexander's mother lived at the cottage?" I asked.

"No. That's just it. She never arrived. My grandmother waited and waited. She called back over to Italy, and Mia confirmed that Teresa Aradia had, indeed, departed at her scheduled time. They traced her from Italy to New York City, but no farther. Days, weeks, months passed. No one ever heard from her again."

"Guess I'm a bit slow this morning, but I still don't get it," Alexander said in a harsh, clipped tone.

"Well, I've done a bit of digging, with help, of course." Shyly, she caught Ayo's eyes, then looked away. "Ayo's legal expertise and Adelaide's love of gossip contributed greatly. We read through scores of documents, including testimony from former manor staff. The police thought they had him at one point, but there wasn't enough evidence to indict. All circumstantial."

Now I was lost. "Testimony? Evidence to indict? Maggie, what are you saying?" I prodded.

"You see...well..." Maggie began but faltered.

"You're killing me here," Alexander said through clenched teeth.

"Okay, okay. Not long after Teresa disappeared, there was word around town that your father, Charles, had fallen in love. What's more, he'd already married the girl, and she was expecting. You see, your father was a handsome, eligible bachelor. And though he was known about town— he was a Morgan, after all— he was new to the community. He'd only moved into the manor with his grandfather after graduating from Princeton. His relationship with his own father was so strained, that he flatly refused to move home with him. When he was offered his own house in the Hamptons, he turned that down, too." Maggie gave an uncharacteristic snort of derision. "He defied his father and moved into a castle instead."

Adelaide rose up, onto her knees at first. And as she raised herself to full height, her brittle, old bones popped and creaked. She brushed aside the hands that reached out to aid her and got straight to the point. "My dear, your father was not some deviant youngster just looking to poke his father in the eye. Oh no, not Charles. He was shrewd, cunning. That he was so pretty to look at helped, too, though not with what really mattered to him."

"And what really mattered to my father?" Alexander asked with a chip on his shoulder.

"You know the answer to that, foolish boy. Money. He believed that if he endeared himself to Cain, if he could prove himself a worthy successor, his grandfather would leave the Morgan Manor estate to him instead of his father. In his mind, the best way to do that was siring an heir. He wanted to secure his legacy, the next generation of Morgans. And he wanted to do that with as little fuss and expense to himself as possible."

When Adelaide's legs began to wobble, Luca shot to her side, lawn chair in hand, and guided her down onto the seat. She looked so frail sitting there; her shoulders slumped, her skin translucent. Yet the energy she emitted pulsed strong and true.

"Your father was admired throughout the community, you see," Maggie said, taking back the narrative. "There was no reason anyone at the time would have connected the two events—my cousin's disappearance and Charles's mysterious marriage. But the staff knew the score. Somehow, your father met Teresa upon her arrival in the States. He brought her here, to Morgan Manor. And here she stayed until her death—less than two years later." Maggie took a steadying breath. "I believe your father seduced my cousin into his home, into his bed. And once she bore him an heir and raised him past the need of mother's milk, he had her killed. Poisoned."

"Now wait, Magdalena," Adelaide interrupted. "We don't know if she was killed because she was no longer needed or because she was outed as a witch. I wasn't welcome at the manor in those days, so I don't know for sure."

"From everything I've read, it sounds like a bit of both," Ayo added.

"Hold on a goddamn minute!" Alexander snarled. "Are you telling me you think my father kidnapped this Italian witch, insinuated to his acquaintances that he had a new bride, and forced her to produce him an heir?"

"Yes," Maggie said.

"And you're saying I am that heir? That this witch is my mother?"

"Your mother's name is Teresa Aradia. You told me that yourself. It seems odd that two young Italian women by that same name were in Arbor at the same time. Don't you think?" Maggie asked in reply.

"And you believe—even in the absence of an indictment—that my father killed, poisoned, my mother?"

"Whether by his orders or his own hand, yes, your father was responsible for your mother's death." Maggie heaved a deep sigh. "I'm so very sorry Alexander."

Alexander's head dropped so low, his chin sat flush against his chest. He hunched over, and put his face in his hands. Then suddenly he blurted, "That's completely fucking ludicrous." His face blazed red. "Couldn't it be equally as likely that this woman, hungry for my father's money, forced herself upon him? Maybe manipulated him into her bed by way of magic?"

"And then, what, killed herself?" I scoffed at the suggestion.

"Sure! It seems feasible that once the spell wore off, and he saw her for what she was—a manipulative witch—he shunned her. Such a turn of events could have driven her to take her own life."

I recoiled. Alexander's words churned my stomach.

"Alexander," Maggie spoke with care. "You're speaking of your mother, remember."

"I know nothing of this woman you say is my mother."

"You're right about that. You don't know a damn thing about your mother," Adelaide added in a scolding tone she usually reserved for me.

"Look, my father was an asshole, but he was no murderer. And I'm not going to sit here and listen to any more of this sick, twisted conjecture."

Alexander turned to leave, but before he could walk off, Maggie took him by the hand. "I can't imagine how difficult this must be for you. But you need to understand what this all means. You have family. You and I are cousins. And you have some of the deepest, oldest magic on earth coursing through your veins. In her wisdom, the Goddess has brought your familiar to you—in your moment of need—to help guide you."

Alexander looked to me for the briefest moment. Then he retreated through the garden gate, Archie following dutifully at his feet.

"I'd say that went well," Luca joked to the collective groans of the other witches.

"Fuck," I cursed under my breath. I couldn't let Alexander go like that. I didn't care if he wanted to talk to me or not. He'd just been hit on the head with a ton of bricks. I needed to be by his side. So I kicked off my shoes and took off after him.

Luca chased after me. He was hot on my heels the whole way and grabbed my arm just before I stepped into the open foyer.

"Let me go!" I snapped.

"Hold up a second, please. You have to listen."

I took one look at his pained and earnest face and eased up. I flopped down into one of the stiff armchairs. "Fine. Go ahead," I huffed like a petulant child.

He knelt down in front of me and took my hands in his. "Look, the servants here hate us. They fucking hate us, Eva, every last one of us. But especially you."

"I know they hate me. They were nasty to me the last time I was here too, from the moment I stepped through the door," I admitted.

"I'm telling you, it goes a hell of a lot deeper than that. They know we're all witches, and the animals scare the shit out of them. They want us gone. They're not going to be content to grin and bear our presence here." Luca stopped and took a breath. "I read them, Eva. I read their truth." He paused again. "Mayor Crandall offered them money for dirt on you—on any of us. Franklin agreed that they'd be fools not to take the good mayor up on her generous offer."

Great. From the frying pan to the fryer.

"And there's more." Luca wrung his hands. "They worked here when Teresa Aradia lived here."

"No."

"Yes. They were involved in her murder."

"No!"

"Yes! Mrs. Marsh asked Franklin if he thought they'd have to take care of you the same way they took care of the last witch that dared entrap a Morgan man. And the butler said, 'The sacrifices we've made for this family, for this manor, will be for naught if we allow that hussy to weasel her way into the Morgan fortune. It mustn't be allowed to happen.'"

"What the hell?"

"Yeah, no shit. You're going to have to be on your guard, baby girl. They think you've got Alex under a spell, that you're manipulating him, and that you're after his money. These people are gunning for you."

Luca's power was finding the truth—the truth that lay deep within a person's heart. He carried these truths, these beautiful, burdensome blessings, heavily on his shoulders. Luca was a lifelong, invaluable friend. I loved him dearly, and I trusted him. And that's why I was scared.

I threw my hands up in frustration. "We came to Morgan Manor for sanctuary. We came because Alexander promised it would be a safe place to formulate a plan forward. So much for safety. We've been here less than twenty-four hours, and people already want to kill me."

"You can be a bit of a handful." Luca smiled and kissed my hand. "We'll get through this, okay? I've got your back, baby girl."

"And so do we," a familiar voice bellowed from the foyer archway.

"Boys!"

Chapter Seventeen

The arresting, primal presence of each individual man filling the arched entry could drop the most pious to their knees. When they stood together, shoulder to shoulder, their mingling magic amplifying their potency, there wasn't a soul alive that wouldn't cower before them. Until they smiled, that is, and their effervescent joy brightened the cavernous parlor.

"Hey dollface!" Luca's older brother boomed.

"Nikki!" I called out and ran into Nicolae's arms. He smelled of exotic cologne and the pomade he used to slick back his dark hair. Nicolae looked like Prince Charming, pressed into his three-piece business suit.

"Were you aware the press was trying to break down the front gate and scale the walls?" he asked with humor in his eyes, as if an attack by the paparazzi was nothing more than an amusing side show act.

"Oh no! We need to—" I began.

He squeezed me tight and then squared my shoulders. "It's okay. They're gone. For now, anyway."

"What did you do to them?" I asked, wary of his reply.

"I convinced them there was a juicier story over at the Cudlow household, so they took off. I bought you some time, but they will be back."

"Someone needs to warn..." I started to say before Nicolae planted a kiss on my head, and Gregory snatched me up into his arms.

"How ya holdin' up, little sister?" The thick-bearded, blond-dreaded chef asked in his deep baritone. He held me close, and I filled my lungs with his heady, dank scent of garlic, nag champa, and pot.

"Honestly, up and down. But right now, I'm great." I pulled back my shoulders and stood up straight, obeying an unconscious desire to demonstrate my declaration.

"That's why we're here. You need space to breathe and time to think, and we're gonna make sure you have it...and anything else you need. And it looks like Maggie's cottage could use a spit shine. We'll take care of that, too."

"Thank you, truly," I said and kissed his fuzzy cheek.

My favorite dancing fae promptly took me in hand. With a quick spin, Ethan led me in a waltz around the parlor, accompanied only by his off-key humming. A scant trace of iron hung in the air as we twirled. His silver-gray hair and luminescent skin glittered at my touch.

"No one is going hurt you while we're here. Do you understand?" Ethan punctuated his avowal—and the end of our dance—with a kiss, straight on the mouth and lingering. He leaned his forehead against mine. "You have my solemn oath. We're not letting anything bad happen to you or Maggie or Adelaide."

"Speaking of knights in shining armor," Luca cut in, "have you guys met Alexander?"

"We've not yet had the pleasure," Nicolae answered his brother. "The Crypt Keeper guarding the door was kind enough to inform us that the 'master of the house' was out on the grounds and unlikely to return before dinner," Nicolae mimicked Franklin's starched formality.

"What's he like?" Ethan asked with expectation hanging from a held breath. "Is he dreamy? He must be to make our Eva's heart go all a-flutter."

"He's beautiful," I answered. Yet, as I spoke, a dull, aching sadness washed over me. "And he's a little bit broken." The image of Alexander's stunned and angry face flashed before my mind's eye, and a small sob caught in my throat. "He just found out... and then Maggie told him..." I stuttered, unable to formulate the words needed to explain.

Once again, Luca stepped up. "Apparently Alexander is la Strega and was just blessed with a familiar, a German shepherd named Archie. Oh, and his dad killed his mom."

"Fuck," the boys responded in unison.

"Well, what the hell are you still doing talking to us?" Gregory asked. "Go get your man. Sounds like he could use a pretty shoulder to cry on."

"But you boys just got here. I..."

Nicolae stepped up and placed a comforting hand on my shoulder. "We're good. While you're gone we can tackle some business with Maggie."

"Besides," Gregory added with a note of mischief, "Adelaide's been chompin' at the bit to check out my newest batch of herb. For medicinal purposes, of course."

"Oh, of course." I feigned seriousness.

Ethan placed his hand on my other shoulder. "Once you take care of your man, take care of *you*. You need to *create*. That's where your truest, most undiluted magic lives. It may not give you answers, but it will keep you centered. Dive into it. Let it engulf you. We'll take care of you and...ya know...everything else." He waved his hand dismissively.

They knew me, like a left hand knows a right. We might not have been siblings genetically, but these boys were my brothers by the magic in our veins. I trusted them.

"You're right. Are you sure you won't hate me if I take off to find Alexander?" I looked at each of the boys in turn. I didn't want to give the impression that I wasn't a thoughtful hostess. Not that I considered the place my own, but everyone was there because of me.

"Hell no. Get ghost," Gregory spouted.

I've already had my ghostly experience for the day, thank you very much. It's not an experience I'd like to repeat. And it suddenly struck me as a sign of the depths of chaos into which my life had fallen that my encounter with the irate spirit of Alexander's great-grandmother had slipped my mind. Yet it ranked pretty far down on my list of important shit to deal with.

"We got ya covered, kid," Nicolae threw in, nodding his vow.

I looked at the four men, but instead, I saw my boys crossed-legged in a circle around me. We were in our tree house. Sitting on the floor, they took a pledge, a blood oath, to protect me. The sacred oath they swore was no child's play. It was ancient Druid magic. From then on, the boys believed they owed me their lives.

"Thank you for being here." My eyes welled up, and I swiped a finger under each to stop my mascara from streaking down my cheeks. "I feel so much better knowing you're holding down the fort." A snarky grin played my lips. "It *is* sad that it's going to take four of you to handle everything I do."

"Makes perfect sense to me," Luca said with a wink. "You're a fucking pain in the ass. It takes four of us to put up with you. Frankly, I'm glad you found Alexander. He'll take some of the stress off us."

I ran up to my room, threw my hair into braids, and packed a bag with my sketchbook, pencils, pastels, and charcoal. Then I headed outside on naked feet, to feel the spirit of the earth through my soles. Franklin had said Alexander would be on the grounds all afternoon, but the property was vast. He could be anywhere. On the plus side, the search for Alexander provided an opportunity to explore the overgrown acres and miles of wooded pathways, thick with nature's encroachment. They tempted me to venture into their winding walks. I was eager to get lost in their tangle. And even more eager to find my muse.

The path to my left became the starting point of my meandering journey, the path most gnarled with brambles and thickets. They caught and pulled at my skirt as I walked. With a bowed head and reverent heart, I asked them to pull back and clear the way. The prickly thorned vines and sandpaper leaves curled up into themselves in retreat, allowing me an unencumbered walk. Barbed foliage wasn't the only obstacle. Not ten yards in, the path weaved sharply westward, then arched hard to the east before guiding me up a steep incline dotted with brittle, rocky steps. I trekked along with care, and took time to appreciate the thick green canopy speckled with glittering diamonds of filtered sunlight, the gently pealing songs of thrushes huddled in their nest, and the sweet smell of honeysuckle on the wind.

As I reached the precipice, the path opened up into a wide, grassy clearing. A most remarkable sight greeted me. Alexander and Archie were playing. They romped and bounded around each other like long-lost pals reunited. Alexander got in a good swipe and ruffed up Archie's fur. Archie rounded on Alexander and wound himself through his legs, tripping him. An unintended chuckle burst from my throat, and Alexander froze at the sound. Taking advantage of his witch's distraction, Archie pounced, knocking him to the ground. The German shepherd placed a paw atop Alexander's chest and lifted his head high in victory.

"I concede," Alexander panted, grinning widely. "You've bested me this time, but don't get used to the feeling." He sat up and embraced his familiar around the neck.

Holy shit, Alexander's a witch. A powerful one, the earth-shifting turn of events finally sinking in. *Extraordinary. I've found my muse.*

I tucked myself back into the cover of the brambles. I found a soft spot to sit where I could hide but still bear witness to the forming of this new, magical relationship. My toes wriggled in the damp earth, and I got comfortable. I took out my pastels and opened up my sketchpad.

But before beginning my piece, I closed my eyes and sent up a prayer to the Goddess.

> *May your creation inspire my heart and my hand.*
> *May my endeavor prove worthy and good.*
> *Allow the magic of rain, sky, fire, and land,*
> *To reveal to me all that it should.*

Using the pastels as part crayon, part finger paint, I drew and smudged an abstract image of this exquisite, potent male witch and his familiar on their awakening day. Buttery yellow and coral and chestnut and burnt sienna all found their place within the piece. Kelly green and violet shocked across the background of the scene. My vision tunneled, allowing nothing but my muses and the page on which I recreated them in view.

Time wasn't just irrelevant, it ceased to be—within my little creative bubble, anyway.

After working for hours or days, I wiped the color from my fingers and onto my skirt, then rubbed my eyes. When I looked up at my pastel creation, a shudder rushed over me. Somehow, I managed to capture not only Alexander's budding magic and Archie's noble spirit, but the energy of the Goddess Herself.

"Is that how you see me?" Alexander asked, startling me from my reverie.

"Yes," I said, looking up into his dark, haunted eyes. "Today is your awakening. Today, you accepted your true nature. Meeting Archimedes was the impetus for this self-acceptance. That's what I captured in the pastel—you embracing your magic."

"So, what, am I like a wizard or something?"

I snorted out a laugh. "No. You're a true-blooded witch, just like Luca, Nicolae, Gregory, and Ethan. Although, they've been practicing the craft since childhood. Harnessing your gifts is going to take practice and lots of patience."

"I understand the boys arrived not long ago. Please, make my apologies for not welcoming them properly. I look forward to meeting them at dinner."

"Of course. Although, be warned, they're a raucous group."

We shared a soft smile. "You're lucky to have such a great family," he said, sadness filling his words.

I took his large, strong, smooth hands in mine. "Don't you realize, this is your family now, too? Maggie, a blooded La Strega witch, is your cousin."

"Knowledge hidden from me my entire life. But it shouldn't surprise me. My father and grandfather were control freaks. Anything that didn't fall into their definition of 'normal' or 'proper' was swiftly dealt with. My great-grandfather was as much a victim of their insatiable domination as I was. Did you know they tried to have him committed?"

"That's horrible! Why did they hate him so much?"

"They contended that no man in his right mind would give away thousands of dollars at a time to charities and fundraisers without batting an eye. Cain was a bit on the wacky side, but he was kind and generous. You know, during the Great Depression, he wanted to help the families in Arbor whose livelihoods had been devastated. Knowing the men would be too proud to take a handout, he created work for them. Those men are responsible for the tremendous stone walls that surround this entire fifty-acre estate. That project helped a lot of folks. Arbor weathered the Depression a hell of a lot better than most of the small towns around here. Much of the thanks goes to my great-grandfather."

"I'm sorry, maybe I'm missing something. How is that a bad thing?"

"To my father and grandfather, philanthropy was a waste. But I think what really infuriated them was that the entire Morgan family fortune was under their elder's control. Cain had to give his approval on anything and everything before a penny was allocated. Nothing could be done using Morgan capital without his knowledge. They loathed having to get approval from a man they believed to be deranged."

"Just awful," I said as I imagined Old Man Cain in a straitjacket.

"But in all honesty, the people who had the hardest time with the Morgan men have been the women they married." Alexander nodded. "Cain's wife committed suicide. She suspected Cain was having an affair—with Adelaide."

"What!" I couldn't believe it.

"My great-grandmother took laudanum to end her life. From what I understand, they actually weren't sleeping around. Although, I wouldn't doubt he had many other lady friends as well."

I dropped my head in my hands in shock. *No wonder the apparition attacked Adelaide!* I thought. *And no wonder she went after me. I'm another witch going after a Morgan man. Just like Alexander's mother. Just like Adelaide.*

"My grandmother wasn't much better off. I guess you could say she ended her own life too, just much more slowly. My grandfather was rarely home. He traveled all over the country and around the world, first during his military service, then later for business. And he was unfaithful, often and without remorse. There were times when my grandmother would be alone for three or more months at a time. The manor staff was her only human contact, and she frequently barred them from entering her bedchamber. Being shy by nature to begin with, she rarely had guests from town to visit. Lack of exercise, sunlight, and fresh air all took their toll on her over time. She lived like a hermit and took less and less care of herself. Eventually she stopped eating. Then one day a housekeeper found her, emaciated, dead in her own bed."

I gasped, and Alexander took a deep breath. I got the sense he'd never spoken to anyone about these things. It meant a great deal that he chose to share this history with me. I urged him to continue.

"And now, there's my own mother. So, you see, the women who marry Morgan men don't fare well. I haven't had the best role models in the relationship department. This is new to me. I'm winging it. And I'm going to fuck up."

I took a minute to let his words soak in. "Where was I when this marriage took place? Or the proposal, for that matter?"

Alexander laughed. "Yeah, I guess I'm rushing things. Sorry about that."

"Your future is not predetermined by the faults of your ancestors, long dead. It's the living you have to worry about." I fidgeted with my skirt, trying to decide how to fill him in on Luca's info. I decided just to go for it. "Listen, there's something you oughta know. Luca overheard something. He overheard a conversation between your staff."

"What have they said now?"

I took a deep breath. "He heard Mrs. Marsh and Franklin talking about the bribe they took from Mayor Crandall. She offered them cash to get dirt on Maggie and me. And they accepted it."

"Are you fucking kidding me?" he roared, and even Archie flinched at the fury. "I kept those morose bastards on my staff out of respect for their years of loyal service to my family, and this is how they repay me? By undermining the woman I love?" His eyes popped at the slip. It was the first time he'd ever used the word. But he only shrugged. "What? I love you. Is that a crime?"

When I didn't reply, his energy darkened. "There's more, isn't there?"

"Yes." Again, I hesitated to continue. I knew I needed to tell him, but I dreaded his reaction. "Luca heard Marsh and Franklin discussing whether or not to take care of me the same way they took care of the last witch that tried to ensnare a Morgan man. They're still deciding if they should kill me—just like they helped your father kill your mother. They think I'm after your money, that I've bewitched you, that you're under my spell."

Alexander froze, his face a mask of anger and disbelief. He didn't twitch or blink. He didn't fidget a fraction of an inch. Archie nudged him repeatedly to no avail. I grabbed a hold of the front of his shirt.

"Look at me."

Nothing.

"Look at me!" I demanded.

With his face still void of expression, Alexander tilted his head down to meet my eyes.

"I know this all sounds crazy, but—" I started, but Alexander cut me off.

"No. It's dangerous. I've put you in danger. This must be handled carefully. I'm going to head back to the manor with Archie now. This business needs my immediate attention, so I'll be in my office for the remainder of the day. I'll see you at dinner." He dropped a distracted kiss on the top of my head and walked off.

"It's been a pleasure, Evangeline. Until dinner, then." Archie nodded, before trotting after his witch.

Chapter Eighteen

I headed back to the manor as fast as my bare feet could carry me. Once inside, I rushed to my room to avoid running into Franklin or Marsh. The pungent scent of sage smoke greeted me as I entered my room. It was a smell I knew well and loved. But I wondered if I hadn't burned the sage, who had. I was pleasantly surprised to find the clothes I'd kicked off were folded and set aside. Fresh towels hung in the bathroom. The bed was neatly made. And on the bed sat three ornate boxes. Each box was a vivid display of creative mastery in itself, a not-so-subtle hint of the elegance of their contents. Beside the boxes, I spied a note in Gregory's swiftly fluid handwriting.

Little sister,

I wanted to give you an update, but I wasn't sure when I'd catch you alone. So you have a letter to read instead.

The boys and I spent the day setting up security at the cottage. We installed new locks on the cottage doors and windows. And we were careful with Maggie's beloved violet front door. Nikki and Luca installed motion-sensor cameras with infrared imaging and a high-tech alarm system. Ethan and I set up protective wards. We'll reset them before the coven convenes on Litha, but they'll hold until then. In the meantime, we need to secure the manor—wards around the perimeter of the estate and cameras, baby, lots and lots of cameras.

And do you know who else needs to be camera-ready? You do. Even though you are physically behind these walls, little sister, you are in the public eye. Nikki says the public is eager to see how you're holding up. So you need to show them that you're not cowering in fear. You're a bewitching woman. Own that shit. So, now you have a photo shoot to prepare for. And because we can't fucking help ourselves, Nicolae, Ethan, and I each bought you a little something. Choose your favorite and wear it tonight. The boys and I have a bet going over whose dress you'll pick, so make your selection wisely.

I rolled my eyes. *My boys...*

> Dinner's at eight, then we're performing the Summerland Rite for Teresa Aradia.
> I think that's everything to report. We love you—Gregory
>
> P.S. We still haven't met your new beau, but look forward to meeting him tonight!

I heaved a great sigh when I finished reading.

With security measures complete, the only thing that kept us at Morgan Manor was the blessing of the estate and grounds scheduled for the next day. Barring any unforeseen circumstances, we could go home in a couple days.

As that thought filled my mind, my gut twisted like the hand of the Goddess Herself clenched tight around my waist. I missed our cottage and the lavender fields, the gardens, the forest, the stream. I'd never realized just how much magic resided on the cottage grounds until being without it there at Morgan Manor.

But a rather large—and growing—part of me didn't want to leave Alexander.

No longer able to deny my curiosity, I turned my attention to the magnificent gifts my boys left me. I lifted the lid of the first box. It held an ethereal, rose-colored gown with feminine floral appliqués and a plunging neckline, created by Naeem Khan. The second box, by far the largest, held a voluminous, black gown with golden coral-like detailing by Andrew Gn. Both dresses were stunning, but I needed to see the last one before making up my mind.

I never knew one could experience love at first sight with a dress, but that is exactly what happened when I lifted the last lid. Every thread called out to me. The garnet Dilek Hanif gown wrapped around the waist and then up around the neck in a halter with a deep-vee neckline. A slit in the folds of fabric rose dangerously high and gunmetal-gray crystals encrusted the waist.

Completely. In. Love. I couldn't wait to put it on! If I wanted to look decent, I needed to hustle. A knock at the door derailed me before I'd taken off.

"Ms. Clarion? It's Celeste. Um, the maid. I'd like to give you a hand with dressing." Her voice began soft, nervous, but gained confidence as she continued. "I work miracles with hair, and I've got a steady hand for makeup. I won't disappoint you."

I opened the door and barely recognized the young woman on my threshold. *What a woman!* "Come on in," I said, and stepped aside to allow her through. I gawked blatantly at her. I couldn't help it. The starched, black uniform was gone, replaced by an airy, knee-length wrap-dress in the palest pink. Beatific blonde hair fell sleek in waves around her shoulders, held back gently by a band of satin. And she was steeped in secrets. You didn't have to be a witch to sense that. Celeste was rum-spiked cotton candy with porcelain cheeks and a cunning spirit. She fascinated me. She drew me in. I found myself curiously eager to reveal her mysteries.

"Mrs. Marsh fired me," Celeste said with her chin up.

"But you just offered to help me dress."

"Yes, I won't disappoint you."

"So you said. And you'd like to do this even though you're no longer employed by Morgan Manor?"

"Yes, I would."

I thought for a moment. "What do you want from me?"

"Let me work for you."

"Work—for me?"

"I can be your lady's maid. I'll set out your clothes, do your hair and makeup, organize your art supplies. I'm an artist too, you know," she said with an expectant smile.

"Celeste..." I sighed. "I'm not a lady, so I'm in no need of a lady's maid."

"A personal assistant, then. Call it whatever you want. I'm punctual, efficient, organized, and I have a keen eye, if I do say so myself." She curled sly lips into a smile. "I'm a woman of many talents."

My first thought was, *this female is dangerous*. My second was, *I think I'm in love*. The instant this entered my brain, I tried to shake it back out. But the more I tried to erase it, the more the thought needled me. *I don't even know this woman. Why the hell would I think that about her? Or about anyone, when I have Alexander?*

Unable to clear my mind, I cleared my throat and continued. "I can't hire you as an employee with no way to pay you. I don't even have an income now that the market stand is closed." I groaned.

The hope in her eyes vanished, and her rosy hue paled to ash. A pang shot through my heart at the crestfallen vision.

"You said you were an artist. What's your medium?" I asked.

"I make jewelry," she answered proudly, perking up a bit.

"Nice! I'd love to see your work. And I wish I could help you. Truly, I do. But I have no way of compensating you." The thought of not being able to help her struck me as a tragedy. "Too many artists and artisans with real talent wither with little or no opportunity to showcase their talents for any substantial compensation. My dream is to open a gallery where these artists like you can make a living from doing what they love."

"There, you see. You're definitely going to need help running an entire gallery. Until then, we can call it an internship; unpaid, on-the-job training. All I need is room and board. Once it's open—"

"Wait, wait, stop," I interrupted. "Does Alexander, I mean, does Mr. Morgan know that you've been fired? I'm sure if you spoke to him, explained your situation, he'd keep you on."

Celeste's breathing hitched. A dark shadow passed over her. And for the briefest moment, something akin to hatred flashed in her eyes. She recovered herself quickly, however, and replied with a request.

"Maybe you could speak to him? I'm not sure if he knows what's going on, and I don't want to be the one who fills him in. Believe it or not, I don't rattle easily, but Alexander Morgan intimidates me. Most of the time, I avoid being in the same room with him altogether. I'm sure he's agreeable among his social equals, but towards the staff, Mr. Morgan can be cold, dismissive." Celeste stared down at her hands and fiddled with the skin around her pale pink painted nails. "What did you think when you walked outside on your first date and saw the tea lights and the flowers and the table decorated so beautifully?"

What kind of question is that? I had no idea where she was heading, but I figured I'd follow along. "I thought it was lovely."

Celeste popped her head up. "Just *lovely*?"

No, it wasn't lovely. "It was magic."

She smiled softly at my reply. "Weren't you curious how he managed to pull that off in record time?"

"I had wondered about that, actually. Why?" I asked warily. *Please don't say what I think you're going to say.*

"Because Mr. Morgan didn't so much as light a candle."

Damn.

"He'd barreled into the kitchen just passed six o'clock, and said, 'Evangeline Clarion will be joining me for dinner,'" Celeste mimicked in a deep voice. I couldn't help but laugh as she teased, even though the situation was anything but funny. "'I expect the meal served promptly at eight on the back patio. And make sure it looks pretty.' And then he turned around and left. I scrambled to set up outside while Mrs. Marsh made dinner. We didn't see him again until we served your meal."

He'd taken credit for another's work. Or, at least, he hadn't contradicted my assumption that he'd been the one who decorated. *That's seriously messed up. Why the hell would he do that?*

My thoughts suddenly jumped to something he had said earlier at breakfast. *"It was such a nice day, I had Celeste move breakfast outside." He had her move that feast outside by herself? Did she carry that huge rug and all those pillows?*

"Why exactly were you fired?" I asked.

Celeste hung her head. "She caught me. Mrs. Marsh. She saw me," she said softly before lifting her eyes to mine. "We have more in common than art."

"Oh?" *Oh no.*

"I'm a Wiccan, too." Celeste paused, perhaps waiting for me to speak. When I said nothing, she continued. "Mrs. Marsh caught me casting a spell—here, in your room. She ran off and ratted me out to Franklin. They sacked me on the spot."

"So it was you who got busy with the sage. Why were you casting spells in my room?" I asked a bit too harshly.

After a slight cringe, Celeste explained. "It was a protection spell. I think, I *know*, you're in danger. Franklin and Mrs. Marsh have been plotting with the mayor and the reverend. I think... I think they're going to try to kill you. I'm sorry for casting a spell in your room, but I just wanted to keep you safe."

Shit. She got fired trying to protect me. "Do Franklin and Mrs. Marsh know of your suspicions? Do they know why you were casting a spell?"

"No, I don't think so. I don't know. Maybe," she shrugged.

"I'm so sorry you lost your job. I'll talk to Alexander and see what he says. I definitely can't let them fire you for looking out for me. Not without a fight." I offered a good-natured smile that withered away the moment I thought about my next revelation. "I do need to clarify something. I'm not a Wiccan. My goddess-mother, Adelaide, Ayo, and the boys—we're not Wiccan."

"What do you mean? I don't understand."

"We share many beliefs with Wiccans, but we're...well, we're witches with very real, Goddess-granted powers, abilities...magic." I knew it was dangerous to expose us, but I trusted her. As a Wiccan, Celeste no doubt faced the same discrimination. I wanted her to understand. And I wanted to help her. I figured a single flame would pose little challenge and make the point. I held out my hand and willed a small lick of fire into being. It sizzled and snapped and hovered a few inches over my palm.

"Unbelievable," she said, wide-eyed. "You must be a true favorite of the Goddess."

I eyed her closely, searching for signs of falsehood. She was hiding something, but I couldn't glean her genuine motivation.

But we all have secrets don't we? I thought of what I kept from Bunny all those years; the most consequential part of myself, my magic. *This is a job for Luca.*

"Okay, here's what we're going to do. You can help me get ready tonight, and we'll see how things go. I can't promise to take you on, but let's call it a trial run," I said. "How's that sound?"

She agreed and set to work preparing me for the evening's grand dinner. With Celeste's help, I bathed and had my hair and makeup done—all at warp speed and with dramatic results. My dark hair swept up in a delicate chignon with several strategically selected locks falling in gentle ringlets. The ebony makeup that highlighted my ivy-green eyes was heavy but chic, and my full lips popped with burgundy.

And then...there was *the dress*. It was the most elegant garment I'd ever worn. The gown slinked to the floor. The regal fabric rustled as I practiced walking on my four-inch stilettos. But something felt off, not quite right. It didn't fit the occasion. I looked over at the two other dresses on the bed. And then I looked at Celeste.

"Would you mind helping me try on one of the others?"

Celeste smiled but didn't speak. She walked around, stood behind me, and unzipped my dress down to the small of my back. She didn't allow the garment to fall to the floor. Instead, she held it low, and helped me step out of it. Celeste never asked me which of the other dresses I wanted to wear but chose my favorite anyway—the heavenly rose-colored gown. She helped me slip into it, and to my great pleasure, it fit beautifully.

Celeste and I caught each other staring in the full-length mirror. Without losing eye contact, she reached up and slowly pulled the pins out of my hair. Ringlets and waves fell over my shoulders.

"Perfect," she whispered. And then, as natural as breathing, she kissed me on the cheek.

Celeste and I walked together down to the dining room. Just as I had that morning, we found the dining room empty—and not only absent its human occupants. The dining table, chairs, and sideboard had been stripped from the room. I listened for the sound of voices and once again followed them out into the gardens. This was no brunch picnic, however. On the back lawn of the manor, beyond the canopy of clematis, the dining room's formal chairs surrounded a cream linen-covered table, long enough to seat the nine of us plus the familiars comfortably. Fine china, delicately hand-painted in shades of rose and violet, silver utensils polished to a high shine, and arrangements of bulbous pink peonies adorned the table.

The setting was lovely, but it was those gathered before me that put the frog in my throat. My friends. My family. I choked back a small sob and smiled over the familiar faces, each representing hundreds of moments and memories, both joyous and grim. The ladies clustered together, draped in haute couture gowns like royalty, sipping from crystal champagne flutes. Adelaide presided over their conversation while Magdalena and Ayo chanced furtive glances at each other. The boys, bedecked in their Ralph Lauren tuxes, chatted away with the familiars. None of them seemed to have the slightest concern for their highly irregular appearance.

My pleasure soured quickly when I noticed Franklin and Mrs. Marsh standing, starched, staring out over the crowd. *What the fuck are they still doing here? Why hasn't he fired them yet?* It was obvious in their expressions of disdain that the presence of the witches infuriated the elder staff, but it was the familiars that truly intimidated them. A pinch-lipped scowl of disapproval contorted Mrs. Marsh's face. Franklin's disgust was so great, his pasty cheeks flamed red. Neither moved against us or uttered a hostile word, however. The animals scared them too much, especially Shasta. And I wasn't sorry for it.

Then there was Alexander—set apart from the others, brooding beside the garden trellis. A thick burgundy swirled in his wineglass and worry settled deep in his creased brow. He looked every bit the dashing

Hollywood leading man in his expertly tailored tuxedo. He'd trimmed the ghost of a beard on his cheeks, turning his look from rugged to debonair, and his eyes—cast in the shadow of chestnut waves—held the confidence of a man comfortable in the most sophisticated surroundings.

I turned to Celeste to ask her what she thought of all this, but she'd vanished.

Turning back, I sighed, "What a sight you all are."

My arrival finally caught the attention of the rest of the party, and they greeted me with a deep, collective inhalation of breath. I blushed at their unspoken praise but didn't shrink from it. I stood as tall and formidable as my four-foot-eleven-inch frame would allow.

Five-three with the heels. I smiled to myself.

"Well, it's about damn time you showed up. At least you look gorgeous," Adelaide bellowed. Then addressing to the group, she continued, "Fashionably late is only acceptable if you arrive looking fashionable. There's an art to arriving in style, and our Evangeline is nothing if not an artist."

I smiled at her brash tribute and did a little twirl to show off my dress. "I have the boys to thank," I said with a nod.

"Give me your cash, gentlemen," Ethan said. "She's wearing the Naeem Khan."

Grumbling, Gregory and Nicolae handed over Ethan's winnings.

"And high praise must go to Celeste, of course," I continued. "I don't know what I would've done without her."

"Celeste?" Mrs. Marsh called out. Her eyes bugged, and her chin drooped.

Every head turned toward the source of the shrill outburst.

"Yes, of course. Celeste sculpted my hair and applied my makeup like a master artist. She helped me get into this scandalous beauty, and that was no small feat," I said, holding out my skirt a bit. "And she accomplished it all at warp speed." I couldn't help but smirk at Mrs. Marsh, the twisted hag, trying to wrap her brain around the situation. "Thank you for giving her some time away from her usual duties to lend me a hand. She's a treasure."

"What?" Mrs. Marsh gaped.

"That was awfully kind of you, Mrs. Marsh," Alexander said with no small measure of surprise. "I'm glad to hear she's working out well. Good help is hard to find," he leveled the housekeeper with a vicious glare.

Franklin stepped forward with a bowed, gray head. "Mr. Morgan, sir, I regret to inform you that Ms. Celeste Galehorn's employment has been terminated as of this afternoon."

"And why might that be? What could she have possibly done to warrant immediate termination?" Alexander growled at the cowering Franklin with barely sheathed anger.

"She's a witch," the old man muttered.

Alexander stepped up to his employee. "Say that again, a little louder this time. I think my friends would all like to hear."

"She was fired, sir, because she's a bloody demon witch from hell," the codger barked, showing backbone.

I worried Alexander might attack him. I expected he'd at least tell the guy off. But I was wrong on both counts.

Alexander only laughed. "Franklin, we're all witches here!"

For a moment, a suspension of time, my friends and I looked at each other in astonishment.

It was Adelaide, of course, who broke the tension with a riotous cackle. "This is why I love this boy! Calls it like he sees it," she blurted before turning to the staff. "My dear Mrs. Marsh, I am sure you and this old fart will get over it. You've served many worse characters in Morgan Manor than this lot. So suck it up."

No force on earth could've stopped the hysterical eruption of laughter from the party. We let loose a hurricane of hilarity that swept over poor Marsh and Franklin.

Eager to move the night along, I stepped forward. "I believe we have a photo shoot to attend to?" I asked, looking over at Nicolae.

"I think some candid shots during dinner would work best, don't you, Ayo?" Nicolae asked.

"I do. We need to show Eva's strength, but she must also come across as engaging and genuine. I think that'll come across better if it's unforced."

"Whatever you all think is best," I said and then turned to Mrs. Marsh and Franklin. "I believe we're ready for dinner to be served."

When neither moved, Alexander spoke up. "Ms. Clarion gave you direction, and as she is a guest of mine—a guest in my home—I expect you to comply with her requests. I will not remind you again."

First, he was funny, and then he was fierce, and I kept falling deeper.

Chapter Nineteen

Adelaide positioned herself at the head of the table and directed the rest of us to our seats. She cleared her throat and addressed the familiars. "I lack words sufficient enough to express my gratitude for your attendance tonight. And I thank you for opening yourselves up to all witches at this table. There are pressing matters that need attending, and your innate abilities, as well as the powers you grant to your witches, are immeasurably valuable assets that will no doubt be called upon in the coming hours, days, and weeks ahead."

Adelaide then raised her voice in prayer, and the entire party responded with a resounding "Blessed Be!"

Alexander stood, and the attention of the assembled turned his way.

"Before we eat, I'd like to say a few words." He paused and looked around the table. "I can honestly say this is the strangest collection of dinner party guests I've ever seen. If you told me a week ago I'd be having dinner with eight witches, I'd have said you were crazy. If you said there'd be a dog, a bear, a hawk, a bat, and a bee eating with us, I'd have driven you to the asylum myself. Yet here I am, about to dine with my new friends—including a Druid, a fairy, and a couple of Gypsies."

"It's Romani, darlin', not Gypsy," Adelaide corrected.

"Sorry, Romani," Alexander said.

"It's all good, Alexander, my man," Luca piped up.

"Luca, Nicolae, Gregory, Ethan, I am happy to have you here because I know how happy it makes Evangeline. So, to you and all of my guests, I say welcome, and thank you for sharing my table." Alexander lifted his glass high, and we responded in kind.

A parade of staff, carrying tray upon tray of the most glorious smelling fare, made its way around to encircle the table. In the orderly and practiced fashion of servants to the British aristocracy, each individual stood at attention until the rest were in position. At a cue unseen by the seated, the servers placed the trays onto the table with Olympic synchronicity. They departed with the same level of precision as they arrived.

"Where did all the servers come from?" I murmured to Alexander.

He smirked and nodded to Gregory. "Your boy works miracles."

Gregory shrugged. "I called in a favor, borrowed them for the night from a friend of mine who owns a high-end restaurant about a half hour from here. I got a couple of his sous chefs lending a hand back there, too."

Unbelievable. I love my boys.

Large platters of grilled salmon, shrimp, lobster, prime rib, zucchini and tomato casserole, cous cous, fresh fruit, and baskets of hot rolls filled the table to bursting. Famished and with mouths watering, the assembled began to grab for the trays. Before anyone could take a taste, Rocky let loose a clamoring squawk.

Everyone froze.

"If I may," Rocky announced, *"I'd like to have each item that has been presented for consumption this evening tasted before any of you eat."*

The rest of our party gasped at the accusation.

"You don't really think someone poisoned the dinner, do you?" Alexander asked, looking sick.

"One can never be too careful," Rocky said. *"It would not be the first time that there's been a poisoning at Morgan Manor, sir."*

"Yes, well..." Alexander shook his head. "Who do you suggest should put their life at risk to check the food?"

"Myself, of course."

"No!" I screamed and jumped to my feet, unceremoniously dumping my dining chair onto the lawn. "You will not risk your life for me, for us. I forbid it." I caught a quiver in my voice.

Rocky flew up, perched on my right shoulder, and nuzzled his head against mine. *"But that is my solemn duty—to protect you."*

I uprighted my seat and sat to the side, shielding my eyes. Alexander gathered a small bit of food from each of the platters onto one plate. He sat the food on the table and cleared a spot for Rocky to perch. After one final nuzzle against my cheek, he left my shoulder and landed beside the dish. No one spoke. No one moved. I watched Maggie to gauge the brave hawk's progress. I refused to look back until I saw relief slide over my goddess-mother's face.

"Once more with gusto!" Adelaide whooped. "Let's eat!"

The table turned its attention to the meal, but I'd lost my appetite. I was pissed off. I was mad at Alexander for allowing, for facilitating, Rocky's suicide mission. I was angry that Mrs. Marsh and Franklin, and much of the town of Arbor, would love nothing more than to see me destroyed. I was pissed that Bunny had stabbed me in the back. That my life had become online fodder for gossips just added insult to the injury.

"You okay?" Alexander asked quietly.

"No. No, I'm not. Excuse me. I need a minute," I said, frazzled, and walked without any direction other than *away*. I wove my way through the overgrown honeysuckle, clematis, and morning glories and dropped down onto a small tuft of grass beside the dirt path. Hidden from view and earshot of the diners, I put my face in my hands and wept. My sobs hid Shasta's lumbering approach.

"Dearie, may I sit beside you?" she asked.

I nodded.

The great bear plopped beside me. I leaned into her warm fur and continued crying.

"Rocky and I love you very much, you know. We have been with you in every one of your lifetimes. In each, it has been our obligation and our privilege to look out for you. I have always been there to give you strength and Rocky to set your spirit free. But we are charged to protect your heart as well. We would do anything in our power to spare you the pain you're feeling right now, but you must feel this."

I looked up, confused, and searched for meaning in Shasta's dark eyes.

"Do not let these things shrink you. Use them as your fuel."

I sighed. "You're right. I'm behaving like a child."

"Say nothing of it, dearie. If you hadn't shown emotion over Rocky's display, he would've thought you didn't love him. Silly bird." Shasta stood and pulled me up with her. *"And in future, be mindful of sitting in damp grass when wearing pale-rose haute couture, especially when there are cameras about.* She brushed off my backside. *Good. No damage. Now let us return to the meal. You must eat for your strength, and there is some very tasty-looking salmon I'd like to nibble on."*

"Thank you, my friend," I said as I gazed up into her sweet furry face.

"You are most welcome."

When we returned, I went around and kissed each witch at the table on the cheek. Then I dropped into Alexander's lap, wrapped my arms around him, and kissed him properly on the mouth.

Maggie watched our interaction and grinned. She gave me a small wink when I caught her staring.

"I made you a plate. I was worried everything would be gone before you came back. Archie over here has a huge appetite," Alexander said so only I could hear.

"Thank you. I'm starving."

As I ate, the boys passed a camera around, taking candid shots.

Yeah, me with my mouth full. That ought to make a pretty picture.

Alexander snickered, and I knew he must have heard my thoughts.

Once she saw I'd taken a few bites, my goddess-mother cleared her throat.

"Okay, now that we have gotten a bit of food in our bellies, I'd like to talk about the Summerland Rite for Alexander's mother, my cousin, Teresa Aradia." Maggie looked to her kin. "Alexander, when a witch dies, her coven guides her onto the next plane of existence, the place between the life they left behind and the next life they are to enter. The ritual involves a final celebration of the life of the departed. The loved ones say their goodbyes and express their wishes that a fulfilling next life awaits the deceased. When passing into Summerland, the spirit reviews their life's successes and failures. These determine in what form the spirit will be reborn. It is believed that in each successive lifetime, the spirit is often surrounded by those they have known and loved before."

"But what happens when a witch is not only denied her Summerland Rite but isn't mourned at all? What happens when her life is ended prematurely by one sworn to love and protect her?" Alexander asked.

His tortured expression nearly broke me.

"The spirit lingers," Adelaide answered. "Sometimes out of fear, sometimes sadness, and sometimes in order to enact revenge upon those who wronged them. These spirits are unable to move on to their next lifetime."

"I have no doubt Teresa is one of the unsettled spirits I sensed here," Maggie went on. "She certainly has just cause for her wrath. We will give your mother, my cousin, the proper memorial she deserves. And Alexander, it is imperative we perform the ritual this evening, so she isn't swept up in tomorrow's blessing of the manor."

Later that evening, just before midnight, we all met in a secluded spot tucked under one of the estate's many weeping cherry trees. In normal circumstances, the Summerland Rite would be performed by casting a circle around the body of the deceased. Since his mother had been gone for so many years, Alexander brought out a framed picture, a lock of her hair wrapped in a powder-blue ribbon, and a small jewelry box that had belonged to her as a girl. These items, along with a tall, white pillar candle, sat upon a cloth laid out on the ground. The boys stood with lit white candles at the north, south, east, and western points. Adelaide lit her sage smudge stick and allowed the smoke to billow. Then she raised her hands above her head.

> "As we all come from the Goddess to experience life, in death so we shall return to Her to experience peace.
> Teresa Aradia,
> By the element of Earth, you were grounded in the physical world.
> By the element of Air, you were open to knowledge and communication
> By the element of Fire, you were inspired with passion.
> By the element of Water, you dreamt your dreams.
> There is a time for everyone.
> Everyone has their place.
> May the Great Goddess guide you
> Beyond this impasse.
> By Earth, by Air, by Fire, by Water
> Shall you traverse the veil in peace, good daughter."

And we responded together, "As we will it, so mote it be."

Adelaide moved toward Alexander and handed him the lit pillar candle. He took a deep breath to center himself before he spoke.

"Mother, I never knew you beyond the comfort and succor you gave me as an infant. I wish I had at least those memories of you to hold on to. One thing I know for sure, you didn't deserve to die the way you did. So the pain and anger and vengeance that cling to you are understandable." He stopped a moment as his voice caught in grief. "But it's time to let go. Your peace is waiting for you. I want you to be at peace, Mother. You deserve to be at peace."

A blast of cold air encircled Alexander. His dark waves whipped wildly, and his eyes popped open wide. Yet underneath his shocked expression, a fierce, resolute spirit shown through. A spirit tested the very next moment when, from within the wind that swirled about him, a female voice resounded like a crystal bell ringing out from another plane.

"*Sta bene, figlio mio, ma guardingo. La gelosia manifesta una maledizione.*"

Around and around him, the cyclone wind grew warmer and gentler. Just before it faded to nothing, I caught the faintest outline of a hare.

From my dream!

"What in blazes does that mean?" Adelaide said, breaking the collective shocked silence.

"Be well, my son, but wary. Jealousy manifests a curse," Alexander answered in a morose voice.

"Well then," Adelaide said and gave a little cough. "We'll have to unpack that later. We must forge ahead. Teresa's passing is not complete." Adelaide handed Magdalena the candle. "It's your turn to speak."

"Teresa, my dear cousin, although we never met in life, we share a bond of blood and magic. You were stolen from the world. You were stolen from your son. I pledge my solemn vow to honor your life. It is my solemn vow to do right by your son. Understand that after all these years, the tragic circumstances of your death are finally known. You are free to move on, good cousin."

The gust that surrounded my goddess-mother began warm and instantly heated to a boil. In a crushing eruption, the scorching gale burst upward.

Alexander took the candle from Maggie and sat down among his mother's belongings. Gregory opened a few bottles of Alexander's glorious 1985 California Cab, and poured a glass for each of us. Maggie cut us all a slice of blueberry pie. For the next half an hour, we sat on the ground under the weeping cherry tree. We ate and drank and spoke in hushed voices about family and friends; all of us except Alexander. He spoke to no one. When we finished our wine and pie, Adelaide stood. She held her athame high.

> "Teresa Aradia,
> Merry we meet,
> And merry we part,
> Until we merry meet again.
> You are free, good sister.
> May your tomorrows bring more peace than your yesterdays."
> And we replied as one, "As we will it, so mote it be."

By the time we completed the Summerland Rite, the moon sat high in the heavens and peeked out through wispy clouds. Shadows of spindly, overgrown trees danced on the lawn to the melody of crickets. We were a quiet party as we walked back to the manor, our strength drained from the day's exertions. We returned, soul-weary, to our beds. The familiars stayed behind to protect us from intruders while we slept.

SUNDAY

"Good morning, Ms. Clarion." A female exhaled, and her soft breath brushed against my ear. "It looks like it's going to be a beautiful day."

I peeked out from under heavy lids. Celeste sat beside me on the edge of my bed, wearing a lovely smile and a navy blue sundress. First light split the clouds and shimmered through the windows, highlighting her lemon hair and peach mouth. She was summer sunshine.

"Mornin'," I grumbled, hoarse. My back felt stiff and ached as I sat up. I noticed a small glass of OJ in Celeste's slender hands. "For me?"

"Oh! Yes. Here," she said, handing me the juice. "Drink it down. There's a whole pitcher on the table, and some coffee… Oh, and breakfast, of course." She dipped her eyes, simultaneously shy and seductive. "I brought up breakfast."

My stomach grumbled obscenely at the mention of food. "And I'm positively famished."

Celeste's eyes brightened. "Don't you worry. I'll take good care of you."

She turned toward the sunlight and stepped away lithely. Her poise captivated me. She had a confidence about her that I coveted. With deft hands, Celeste lifted silver lid after silver lid, unveiling the most spectacular breakfast feast I'd seen in ages. Sure, the bacchanal picnic had been lavish, but this was my idea of pure decadence. Plump strawberries and bright red grapes, buttery croissants heaped beside eggs Benedict. Maple sausage and bacon—lots of bacon, blueberry pancakes, hash browns, peaches with mascarpone sauce, and what looked like a Spanish omelet.

"Uh, please tell me you didn't think I could house all this myself?" I asked.

"I guess it is a bit much," she said, smiling. "But I wanted to please you."

Oh my sweet Goddess. I took a sip of the orange juice, and it gave me the jolt I needed. I practically catapulted myself into the armchair beside the grub. Celeste looked to me expectantly for my approval.

"Divine," I sighed after sampling the Benedict.

Celeste beamed with pride and set about making me a cup of coffee while I dug into the omelet and hash browns.

"Please, sit, eat with me," I offered from behind a mouthful of food. "There's no way I can consume this much food on my own. Even with your help, it would take days to scarf this all down."

"No, thank you. It was prepared just for you. I couldn't."

"You will." The conviction, the authority, in my voice surprised even me.

Celeste let out a faint gasp and whipped back to face me. "If you insist."

"I do."

She scrutinized the breakfast items before landing on the peaches and cream. Slowly she dipped her fingers into the bowl, plucked out a plump, juicy bit of fruit, placed it between her lips, and slurped it down.

"You, my dear, are too enticing for your own good." I grinned and dug back into my breakfast with gusto—and very little respect for manners or decorum. "Sorry," I mumbled.

"Ms. Good said to remind you about today's blessing. She told me you'd need your white ceremonial gown. I took the liberty of removing it from your bag and getting the wrinkles out. It's hanging in the bathroom, whenever you're ready to dress for the day."

I eyed her with caution. "You went into my bags?"

She snapped to attention and stuttered a moment before answering. "Well, yes, I did. I wanted to make sure you had what you needed."

"While I appreciate your help, Celeste, we're going to have to lay down some ground rules. The first of which is: never go through my things without my consent."

I wasn't an idiot. Anyone could be bought. And Celeste would be easy prey for someone like Crandall. I had no reason to doubt her, but I couldn't afford to give the Crandalls and Cudlows any more ammunition. I decided to keep her close and watch.

Despite my misgivings, I found myself becoming more and more taken by Celeste. She puttered around the glorious bathroom, humming softly as I bathed in the caldron tub. We chatted as if we'd known each other all our lives. Her natural charm made the time sail by. I couldn't recall the last time I'd enjoyed myself more in the company of a female, even Bunny.

Once I finished bathing, Celeste dried me off with a large fluffy towel and helped me dress. The soft, stark-white fabric of my ceremonial gown, decorated with delicate gold and silver stitching, cascaded to the floor.

"You look like an angel," she said on a sigh as she stepped back to get a good look at me. "A naughty angel, mind you, but an angel just the same." She winked.

I did a final spin for her approval before grabbing my besom broom and heading downstairs for the blessing of the manor.

Chapter Twenty

Maggie, Ayo, and Adelaide gathered in the grand foyer wearing ceremonial garb, with Adelaide in the silver robe of a high priestess. They turned wary eyes to me; their hesitance unnerving.

Something's wrong.

"Good morning, sweetheart," Maggie said and kissed my cheek.

"Morning. Where's—"

"Great, the gang's all here," Adelaide cut me off. "Let's get this show on the road, shall we?" Her words reverberated through the cavernous space.

"Wait, what about Alexander, and where are the boys?" I asked, insistent.

The women looked nervously at each other. Maggie stepped forward, pity distorting her lovely features. "Alexander and the boys got into a little tiff this morning."

"What do you mean? I thought they were getting along."

Maggie shot a glance at Adelaide before continuing. "Alexander stumbled upon them setting up the cameras. The boys had explained their plan to Alexander last night. He'd agreed they could cover the manor and grounds in surveillance equipment. He'd consented because it was for your safety. But this morning, he flipped. He denied ever having made such an agreement. He suggested they were spies. He asked who they were working for!"

"What the hell?" I said in complete bewilderment.

"All I know is Alexander gave my boys hell for simply looking out for us. One would think, as owner of such an estate, Alexander would appreciate the additional security. They're his walls the press is scaling," Adelaide said with a sour face. "It was all I could do to stop myself from smacking him upside the head. I'm heartily disappointed."

Adelaide's admonition surprised me. She'd been Alexander's biggest fan since the moment of our first acquaintance. He must have behaved very badly to raise Adelaide's ire.

"Where are the boys now?" I asked.

Ayo stepped forward and took my hands. A buzz of electricity tingled at her touch. "There's been some news from town. It's Gladys Cudlow. Her health took a turn for the worse, and they rushed her to the hospital. They don't know if she's going to make it. The boys went to get details on Gladys's condition, ferret out information about the reverend and Stuart's movements, and to ascertain the mayor's intentions."

"Dear Goddess," I whispered in shock and sat on the steps to keep my knees from buckling.

Maggie reached out, took my hand, and hoisted me to my feet. "No sitting down on the job. There's work to do. But first, let's take a silent moment to offer up a blessing for Gladys' good health. She is a mother, after all, and voracious by nature; a fierce creature who is losing her fire. It is right to mourn the loss of such potent energy."

Both my goddess-mother's tenacity and empathy astounded me.

The four of us closed our eyes for a spell and offered up a blessing.

"Alrighty then ladies, let's get the show on the road," Adelaide said. "After Alexander's little tirade this morning, I wasn't sure if he still wanted us to go through with the blessing at all. He relented on the promise we stay out of his hair. So I suggest we get things going before he changes his mind."

What the hell is going on with him today? But I had no time for speculation. We had a job to do.

"Okay then," Adelaide went on, "the blessing is going to take some time. This home is enormous, as are the grounds, but we must be thorough. So I suggest we split up. Evangeline, you and I will team up and cover the lower floors and basement. Magdalena and Ayo, you two take care of the attics and upper floors. Once we've concluded with the manor itself, we will move outside. Beginning with the front door, we will move widdershins around the perimeter of the estate. Oh! I almost forgot! When we move on to the grounds, I want the familiars following along with us. Not only will they provide protection, but their presence will increase the power of our work. Okay, ladies, take hold of your brooms. Let's begin."

Holding out her athame in front of her—facing north—Adelaide began. "I cast this circle in the name of love and light. May it guide us and protect us from unwanted spirits!" She moved to the east, south, and then west, repeating the words with each turn.

Maggie, Ayo, and I followed her lead, sweeping out the negative energy with our besom brooms. With the athame still outstretched, Adelaide pointed it at the earth. Moving three times deosil—clockwise—she drew a circle in the air around us, before finally laying the ceremonial blade on a small makeshift altar. She handed a dried bundle of sage to each of us and lit a white candle from which we lit our dried-herb smudge sticks. Once we had them smoldering, we blew out their flames. Their mingled smoke curled and billowed.

Maggie and Ayo headed upstairs, while Adelaide and I began on the first floor. Focusing on corners, entryways, and windows, we worked the herbs in a circular manner.

> "Cleanse this house and make it clear.
> Only good may enter here.
> Bless and grace this home, this space.
> All joy and peace may it embrace.
> Infinite power of the Devine,
> Protect and bless this house through time."

We chanted through every room on the lower levels. With the exception of Alexander's office, that is. I figured we could hit that last.

"Now, for the basement," I said reluctantly.

"How delightful," Adelaide grumbled.

Adelaide opened the basement door, and it was as if we'd been smacked in the face with a block of ice.

"There are spirits here, many of them, and they are not thrilled we're snooping around. Brace yourself. We must press on," she commanded.

I followed her lead down the stairs, each creaking as we stepped. The basement was immense. Its stone floor spanned well over 6,000 square feet. Rows of wooden shelves took up a quarter of the expanse, most lined with freaky glass jars filled with what I presumed—what I hoped—were pickled items floating in murky liquid. The remainder of the basement was completely empty, to the point that it appeared to have been swept clean recently. I saw no cobwebs or dust. But it was damp, and a faint sound of dripping water echoed. Whatever spirits were there, they must have been convinced of our positive intentions or at least brought to heel by our incantations. No spirit found cause to attack or meddle with our work.

Our final task before meeting up with Maggie and Ayo and continuing outside was blessing the wine cellar. We hadn't been there more than a minute or two before I spotted something strange. Wedged between the fifth and sixth shelves of aged champagne, was a five-foot door, the trim of which protruded three inches from the wall. It was camouflaged to resemble a trellised garden gate. The gate's latch opened easily, without so much as a squeak from the hinges, suggesting it hadn't been long without use. A tunnel, six feet in circumference, stretched well past the gate's shadow. With our smoldering herbs in hand and the blessing chants on our lips, Adelaide and I made our way through the tunnel entrance.

For a half hour, we searched through what felt like miles of hidden tunnels with clammy walls and almost total darkness surrounding us. We encountered no overtly rascally spirits, but there were many cold spots and areas saturated in negative energy. We could only hope our blessings were powerful enough to bring peace.

As we made our way back to the wine-cellar gate, Adelaide caught sight of something glinting on the stone floor.

"Pick that up for me, dear, carefully," Adelaide said.

I knelt and took hold of a silver cross. Upon inspection, I noticed that the back side of the cross appeared to have remnants of hardened glue and a reddish leather.

"It looks like it was attached to something," I speculated.

"A Bible," Adelaide murmured. "It's the kind of cross one would see attached to the cover of a preacher's Bible."

"You don't think Reverend Cudlow has been here, do you?" I asked, but Adelaide had no answer to offer. She was too busy examining another strange phenomenon, a small wooden door fitted into the stone masonry. I didn't know how we'd missed it before. Adelaide pushed the groaning door open into what appeared to be a coat closet. Trying to squeeze into the tiny space, I lost my balance and knocked into Adelaide. We tipped over and fell through the closet door into the room beyond. Onto the floor of Alexander's office.

"Give me a fucking break!" Alexander cursed loudly. "Can't a man get a moment's peace? The incessant muttered incantations weren't enough? You had to bust down my door?" The office's dark mahogany-paneled walls, heavy navy curtains, and enormous desk exuded masculinity. As did the irate man who glared at us over mountains of files and ledgers. "I thought I was clear. I did not want to be disturbed. Do you people have no respect for privacy? This is my home, after all," he raged.

For once, Adelaide and I were both left dumbstruck. I hopped to my feet and helped Adelaide off the floor. But Alexander didn't move an inch to help us.

Who is this man? I didn't recognize his voice, his sour expression, or his cold, empty eyes.

"And what are you two doing in my closet? How did you get in there? Have you been spying on me?"

"No!" I hollered, offended by the accusation. "We were blessing the wine cellar, and we found a tunnel. There was a door in the masonry wall, and when we pushed through it, we found ourselves in your closet."

It was Alexander's turn to lose his words. He opened and closed his mouth, trying, I assumed, to wrap his brain around my explanation.

"You were blessing the wine cellar?" He hung his head and ran his hand back through his dark waves in frustration. "I'd like to say that's the strangest thing I've ever heard, but after this week, that just isn't true... But it's up there." The corners of his mouth turned down. "You okay?" he asked with the faintest hint of civility.

I nodded. "Yes."

"Good. Now you've got to go. I have work to do. I can't be disturbed," he said dismissively. He opened the office door wide and gestured for us to leave. Then he flung the door shut. I caught a glimpse of him dropping into the stiff leather chair behind his desk before the door slammed in my face.

"What a dick!" I yelled and searched for commiseration from Adelaide. But I received none.

"Come on. Let's go. We have to meet up with Magdalena and Ayo," Adelaide directed.

My feet wouldn't budge. *This is not the man I've been falling in love with.* "This is bullshit. He has no right to treat me like that!" I railed.

I flew back into Alexander's office, turned his chair to face me, and straddled his lap. I thought a glimmer of humor lit his eyes for a moment, but it vanished as soon as I caught it.

"What is your problem, Mr. Morgan?" I asked as I pinched his chin, forcing him to look at me.

"I'm fine. Look, I'm sorry. I don't have time for your games today."

"Games?" I let go of his chin, my arms dropping to my sides. "You think this is funny? You think this is a joke? You don't have time to deal with this?" All charged up, my voice rose in pitch and volume. "Did I have time to get my life splattered across the internet because of a neurotic, power-hungry zealot? Did I have time for my home—my body—to be defiled? Did I have time to sit beside the brutalized bodies of my friends, my familiars, and watch as they clung to life? You pushed for us to come here, to keep us safe. It was your idea. Don't you dare act as if I begged for this!"

He didn't recoil, or move at all for that matter. He didn't wrap his arms around me. He didn't smile or kiss me. His vacant eyes looked right through me. I didn't know this man.

Screw this. "I don't need this shit," I mumbled and slid off his lap.

"Don't pout, Eva. It doesn't suit you."

"Fuck you, Alex."

"Excuse me?" he shouted, his face turning red.

"You heard me, you grumpy prick. I don't have time for your attitude. I'm not beholden to your benevolence. I've done just fine without the help of a man this long."

"Ha! Have you?" he mocked me, rolling his eyes.

"Go to hell," I spat before storming from the room and slamming the door behind me. I marched down the long, dark hall in a tizzy. I was pissed, and I needed to get it out. I'd had enough.

"Leave the man alone for a while, dear. He's been through a rough couple of weeks." Adelaide tried reasoning with me.

But I was having none of it. "Oh boo-freaking-hoo. I have no patience for a man who thinks he can order me around, thinks he can talk to me like I'm hired help." I brushed past Adelaide and huffed through the foyer, completely ignoring Maggie and Ayo. And I disregarded their calls as I hiked up my ceremonial robe and took the winding marble steps two at a time.

Down another long hallway and into my room. I shut the door behind me and leaned back against it. I closed my eyes, and just breathed. It took some time to calm my heart. Just as I felt I'd begun to recuperate, a faint tapping startled me.

"Ms. Clarion," Celeste called out in a whisper. "Ms. Clarion, it's just me. Are you okay?"

Her voice stirred something within me. On an impulse, I flung the door open. And there she stood, the striking sprite with a bottle of wine in each hand. She was the noon-day sun, shining at midnight. And just as fantastical.

"I saw you were upset, and thought this might help." Celeste lifted the wine proudly. "One for each of us. I even opened them already. Oh, and I brought chocolate." She popped her hip to draw attention to her satchel, filled with sweets.

"How did you know exactly what I wanted right now?" I asked, and wondered if she understood the depth of my meaning.

"Because I know how to make a woman happy," she replied with an unabashed grin.

Her words threatened to undo me. I found myself pondering the differences in our body types. She, a tall waify blonde. Me, a short buxom brunette. Each equally lush. It reminded me of the contrasts between Magdalena and my mother. I explored the thought of her a bit longer. *We'd fit together. Her sharp angles cushioned by my curves.* At that moment, I wanted nothing in the world more than to take Celeste in my arms—consequences be damned. *But would I?*

I stepped aside to allow her entry. "Please, call me Eva."

"Come on, Eva. Let's have a drink."

I plopped down by the window, and she handed me a chilled bottle of pinot grigio. I didn't wait to give a cheer but lifted the bottle to my lips and took a long swig. I gave a soft moan of pleasure as the cool, tangy liquid filled my mouth and trickled down my throat.

Celeste heaved a sigh, and leaned back on the edge of the bed. She crossed her ankles, and casually tipped back her wine. "Did you want to talk about it? About whatever he did that threw you into a tizzy?" she asked.

"How do you know I'm upset with Alexander?"

"Because you're crazy about him. And because I heard you both screaming."

I took another long sip of wine. "No. I don't want to talk about him right now."

Celeste eyed me curiously. "Then what would you like to do?"

Oh, sweetheart, so many wonderful things. Then the idea came to me like a vivid vision. "I'd like to paint you."

The first thing we had to do was pick out something for her to wear. I wanted to capture her ethereal nature with something light and flowing. I rummaged through my bags, and flung dresses at her to try on. We didn't exactly wear the same size, so nothing seemed to work.

Frustrated by my futile search, I turned to apologize. As she was between outfits, Celeste stood beside my bed, cloaked only in my pale yellow sheets. She clasped them around her bare shoulders, covering herself but for one fine leg that parted the fabric.

"Don't move," I commanded. I pulled over my easel and paints, and went right to work. It didn't take long for the ceremonial robe I still wore to get tangled from my frenzied painting. In an impatient move, I stripped the robe off over my head, and cast it aside. I continued to paint in a tank and panties. Butter yellow, creamy peach, and fire-engine red splattered across my hands and arms and legs. And I couldn't have cared less. I thought of nothing, saw nothing; nothing but my muse.

How much time passed was unclear, but when I stepped back from the easel and laid down my brush, stars glittered in the coal black sky beyond the window.

Celeste shuffled over in the sheet. "May I look?" she asked expectantly.

"Of course," I said, and turned away, wary of her reaction.

I felt her move closer, and heard her breathing hitch. "Oh Eva. It's exquisite."

"I had an exquisite muse."

She stood behind me, close enough that I felt her warm breath on my neck. "Even the strongest need comfort," she whispered, "and he's not giving it to you. He only adds to your worries."

"And you can comfort me?"

"I'd like to try."

I wasn't a fool. I knew a physical relationship with Celeste would only add another complication to my already-complicated life.

I turned to face her. "You're right. I do need support. Just... not like that."

She remained stoic. Her face betrayed nothing, no embarrassment or shame. "You are magnificent, Eva. You deserve someone who will amplify your brilliance, not diminish it."

"What do you want from me?" I asked in frustration.

In a voice laced with sadness, she answered, "Everything." With the whisper of a kiss on my lips, she left with my sheet still wrapped around her shoulders.

It all hit me, in that one moment; Celeste's temptations, Alexander's attitude, the threats from the staff, and the main reasons I took refuge within Morgan Manor in the first place—the Crandalls, Cudlows, and the press. It seemed as if every time I'd begin to get a handle on the obstacles before us, new ones emerged.

Without warning, my head began to spin. My stomach heaved. I stumbled over to a waste basket in time to deposit what was left in my stomach in great spasms of acidic bile. Laying my cheek against the cool wooden floor, I lost myself to sleep.

I woke with Luca kneeling beside me. "I got ya, baby girl." He lifted me off the floor. Ethan rushed over to adjust my pillows so Luca could prop me up in bed. Nicolae tucked my comforter around me, and Gregory brought over a tray.

"I made you chicken soup with rice," Gregory said. "Then there are some crackers, a cup of Maggie's tea, and a glass of water." He kissed my cheek. "Love you."

"Love you too," I muttered.

One by one, the boys kissed me, then left me alone to eat. They knew better than to engage me in conversation.

I ate the simple but gratifying meal and drank down Maggie's tea. Willing sleep to draw me back, I curled up in the blankets and pillows, closed my eyes, and said a silent prayer to the Goddess. But even with the help of the tea, sleep was elusive. By the witching hour, I'd had enough of tossing and turning. My restlessness spurred me out of bed. I grabbed my broom and my bag of tricks and tiptoed downstairs. I made a pitstop in the kitchen for a green apple and another bottle of wine, and then snuck outside.

The night echoed with the songs of crickets and cicadas. A heady, earthen humidity saturated the air. Shadows from the overgrown gardens concealed me as I made my way to our weeping cherry tree. I don't know how long I stood there, staring down at our stone bench, but it was long enough to kill half the bottle of wine. I dropped to my knees before the bench and set up an altar. I lit a tall white candle and cast a circle. With my broom, I swept away any negative energy that threatened to invade. White sage burned beside my right hand and shallow dishes of consecrated water and sea salt sat on my left. Then I sliced the apple with my athame.

I opened my arms, trained my gaze to the heavens, and spoke in a clear voice.

> "Goddess of Wisdom with knowledge of old,
> Impart Your truths, let insight unfold.
> Direct my footsteps and brighten my path.
> Divulge Your vision, spare me Your wrath."

I ate a few slices of apple and washed it down with wine.

> "With fire and earth, with water and air,
> Justice fulfill as you see fit and fair.
> As above, so below, by the Law of Three,
> So do I will it, so mote it be."

With my athame, I dug a small hole in the earth. I took a bite of the apple, this time leaving it in my mouth. I sipped the wine, then spit it and the chewed apple into the hole. A swift slice on my thumb produced droplets of blood that I let fall into the mix. Then I stuck my thumb in my mouth and covered the hole back up. After a few minutes of contemplation, I blew out the altar candle. My spell was complete.

But as I stood to clear the altar, the candle relit on its own. The humid air turned frigid, and the wind began to gust. Suddenly, the flame of the altar candle grew ten times its size. From deep within the fire came a fearsome female voice.

> "She that once proclaimed good news,
> will see death wielded from the pews.
> He who should protect his people,
> will see life end below the steeple.
> She who seeks to harness love,
> Will see martyred spirits rise above."

With those words, the flame extinguished.

Shaken by the ominous message—and its inexplicable delivery—I gathered my things and hurried back up to the manor. I hoped I wouldn't run into anyone on my way to my room, but luck must have been busy elsewhere. I made it halfway up the stairs before I noticed Mrs. Marsh scowling down on me from the top step.

"Uh, hi. Just headed to my room," I muttered and tried to rush past her.

Her skeletal fingers gripped my arm. "Not so hasty, Ms. Clarion. Where have you been? Prowling around at this hour. And why are you carrying around an open bottle of wine?"

I faced off with the nasty old hag. "I find it funny that you think it's your business. Now kindly remove your hand, or I'll send my flying monkeys after you."

Scowling, Mrs. Marsh released her hold and shuffled off down the stairs.

The wine had clearly gone to my head, because I burst out in deafening cackles. My knee-slapping, belly-grabbing, tear-inducing laughter bounced and rebounded throughout the vaulted entry, and it followed me down the hall. The laugh caught in my throat the moment I stepped into my room.

Alexander stood beside my bed, his hands on his hips, his head hanging low, and his shoulders slumped. When he looked up, I gasped. His face was pasty white and sickly with dark, heavy circles under his eyes.

I set down the nearly empty bottle of wine and dropped my bag.

"What is it? What's the matter?" I asked, grabbing his hands and holding them to my heart—his earlier treatment of me pushed aside.

He sighed deeply and withdrew from my touch. "Oh, Evangeline, what am I supposed to do with you?" He turned and began pacing.

"What do you mean? What have I done now?" I was at a loss. What was so terrible that he'd felt compelled to come to my room in the wee hours of the morning to scold me about it?

He stopped his pacing and glared. "How long have you been playing me for a fool?"

"Excuse me?" I belted. "What are you talking about?"

"You deny it, then?"

"Alexander, please explain what is going on."

"Do you deny bewitching me?"

I snorted out a laugh devoid of humor. I felt nauseous again. "You can't be serious."

"Deadly serious! Did you ever care about me? Or has it all been a game from the start? And I'd love to know how you lured poor Celeste into your bed." He ranted with a clenched jaw and barely constrained anger. His nostrils flared as he trudged across the floor in sharp strides. "Unless Franklin is to be believed, and she's in on it with you. It's my money, isn't it? You need it to open your gallery."

I wanted to hit him. I'd never had so strong an impulse. Nothing had ever driven me like the desire to hurt this man. And yet, I stayed my hand.

"You said you were going to sack Franklin, that walking corpse. Now he's got you convinced I'm orchestrating some grand conspiracy to rip you off? I don't get it."

"I did sack Franklin. And Mrs. Marsh. They're out on their asses first thing in the morning. But their guilt doesn't prove your innocence. You've been playing me for a fool."

"That you'd entertain such a notion, even for a moment, is heartbreaking. You don't know me at all," I said in a small voice. I wanted to curse him. I wanted to rail and spit and break things. But I just shook my head in disbelief. "I've never cast a spell to make you love me," I said slowly and with conviction. "I've never deceived you. You pushed for me to come here, to protect me, to keep my loved ones safe. And I was so stubborn! It took the familiars getting attacked for me to concede. Now, as for Celeste... No. You know what, I am sick of being forced to defend myself against these accusations. I won't do it."

"How can you deny it? I saw you, just now, performing some spell out on our bench under the cherry tree. I saw Celeste leave your room earlier, wearing a very satisfied smile and your sheet wrapped around her. And then I find *this*." He took my painting of Celeste from the easel and hurled it across the room.

"You son of a bitch. I painted her. That's it. No, you know what? I'm done. If you loved me, you would never believe this crap. Please go. Now, if you don't mind, I'd like to get some sleep."

I turned and stared at Alexander's reflection in the darkened window. Over his shoulder, it seemed a bolt of lightning flashed. When I looked back, he was gone.

"Men!" I groused, and collapsed into bed. "I give up."

MONDAY

I moved through the morning in a fog. My eyes were blurry, my mind was fuzzy, and every muscle ached. I blindly threw on clothes and put my hair in a ponytail. I didn't bother brushing my teeth or putting on shoes. My bare feet slapped against the marble as I plodded down the steps, through the foyer, and into the dining room. For the first time since my arrival at the manor, people were eating at the dining room table—in the dining room. Yet every diner wore shocked, angry, sorrowful expressions. Adelaide, Maggie, Ayo, and the boys looked at each other, silently begging the others to speak up.

"What happened?" I asked, stunned by their reception.

Maggie stepped forward but couldn't find words.

"He's gone." My brain came to the conclusion my heart refused to even consider. "Dear Goddess, Maggie, Alexander's gone, isn't he?" I asked, beating a desolate fist against my chest. Because I knew her answer.

"Yes. He left before dawn. There's a note." She held out a small slip of paper.

I took it and read it aloud.

My Friends,

Please forgive my inability to say goodbye in person. Business calls me away. I sincerely appreciate your assistance in ridding Morgan Manor of its more troublesome spirits and for opening my eyes to so many new truths. I am fully aware that I offered my residence as a safe haven to you all during your time of distress. Unfortunately, as my absence is likely to be of considerable duration, I feel it is best that you return home. I have no doubt the newly installed security measures will prove adequate in ensuring your safety.

My Best Wishes,
Alexander Morgan

"What the fuck is this? 'Business calls me away.' What the fuck is that supposed to mean?" I felt every pulse of blood in my veins, every wretched heartbeat, and a hollow pain settled in my chest.

"Now, Eva, everything's going to be f—" Maggie began.

"No. Don't do that. Don't placate me. This is bullshit," I said, enraged. Unsure how to respond, I paced, as he would have. A traitorous sob overcame me, but I sucked it back. "You know what? Fuck him."

"I have had quite enough of the language, Evangeline Clarion!" Maggie scolded. "Since when do you let a man overthrow your sensibilities? I know about Adelaide's scrying-mirror visions and of what the familiars say of your many lives together with him. But remember, you've intertwined with him through many lifetimes, yet each had some major flaw or impediment to your happiness. There was never a guarantee that this lifetime would be the one to unite the two of you."

"And you must keep your focus," Adelaide jumped in. "You've got bigger fish to fry, my dear. The Crandalls and Cudlows aren't going to play nice because you've got an aching heart."

My mother, Maggie, Adelaide, Ayo—none of them needed a man. I didn't either.

"You're right. I've had enough of Morgan Manor," I said dully, and plodded off to pack my things.

I will never see him again.

Chapter Twenty-One

We kept busy after we left the manor. The boys decided to stay with us at the cottage until after our Midsummer Litha celebration. They set up an encampment tucked back into the farthest corner of the property, the de facto war room slash speak-easy. Along with the hours they devoted to uncovering my enemy's underbelly and protecting my online persona from trolls and hate-mongers, the boys helped Maggie work the land. When the sun went down, the wine flowed and tall tales were told back at the encampment.

Adelaide reluctantly gave up her apartment in town and moved permanently into the cottage's spare room. As was her way, she spent her days mentoring every witch in her charge and her nights staring into her scrying mirror. The biggest shocker came when Maggie stopped taking patients altogether. She played it off as if she was just taking a little summer vacation. But I knew better. She hadn't taken more than a few days off at a time since she took over the reins of the cottage. Her decision to close down her practice until the fall didn't go over well in town, either. For as much as they frowned upon Maggie's beliefs and lifestyle, many Arbor citizens relied on her for their care. But even with the powers granted her from Hanna and her swarm, Maggie was only human. She had to let her patients go. They deserved a caregiver's full attention, and she couldn't provide that. Instead, she split her time between feeding and caring for her guests, outreach to the witch communities and covens from coast to coast, gathering intelligence on *Arbor's Most Moral*, and Ayo. And when Ayo wasn't assisting in the orchestrated overthrow of my adversaries, she was by Maggie's side.

Celeste had asked to return with us to the cottage. And although my initial reaction to her request was positive, nagging suspicions remained. Seeing my uncertainty, she sought to assuage my conflicted feelings. Celeste offered to open herself up to Luca's psychic perusal of her truth. Yet, with all his digging, all Luca found within her heart was a deep, sincere affection for me – and that she didn't care much for Alexander. I chalked up her dislike of him to her earlier accusations that Alexander had been harsh and belittling to work for. That he'd hurt me so badly didn't help. So, I agreed to bring her along home.

Celeste bustled around during the day, lending a hand wherever needed. Sometimes, she'd go off on her own and collect rocks. When she'd return, she'd tumble and polish them to a high shine, then intricately wrap them in silver wire. If we ever opened the market stand again, I vowed to sell her beautiful creations right alongside mine.

Most nights, Celeste crashed on the gallery sofa. But some nights, when I was at my lowest, she curled into bed beside me and held me as I slept. Although we hadn't been intimate, the two of us grew close. She was smart and funny, and she distracted my heart, made hollow by Alexander's absence. Celeste was the only female I'd ever been friends with besides Bunny, and her friendship lessened the blow of Bunny's betrayal. As the days progressed, my physical attraction to her increased. But I never acted on the feelings. My heart shut down too quickly for any romantic attachment to solidify.

As grateful as I was to have the support of my friends and family, the simple pleasures of life no longer brought me joy. The food had no taste. Neither the earthy Kona coffee nor sweet honeyed wine offered the smallest shred of satisfaction. From within every reverberating instrument, I elicited haunted, melancholy melodies. Each painting and sketch, though enchanted, portrayed a shadowed muse. The scent of lavender that permeated the air around the cottage turned stagnant and sour in my nose. And although the clouds had lifted and the warm sun fell over summer flowers in every hue, I saw only in gray.

I refused to acknowledge my misery, however. When interacting at meal times and in the evening over wine, I wore a brave face and an easy grin. But my composure fooled no one. Everyone knew something in me had broken. They assumed it was my heart, but it was my spirit, burned to ash. At first, when I was alone, I thought the desolation that festered soul-deep would consume me, but I was too proud to give in. I would not languish in the emptiness that filled me.

Instead, I threw myself into work. I embraced my magic with a fervor bordering on obsession. Each day, I woke before the sun and retired long after the fireflies had found their rest. For hours at a time, I practiced conjuring the elements, manipulating nature, potion making, and spellwork. Thanks to my diligence, I'd managed not only to create flames in the palm of my hand but swell the blazes into veritable campfires. With just the right focus, the vegetable and herb gardens flourished at my command. And to Adelaide's great pleasure, I concocted a potion tasting deceptively similar to Pinot Noir, with none of wine's fuzzy effects.

Physical fitness had never been high on my agenda, but I threw myself into that as well. Shasta led me in strength training and conditioning. Every muscle ached from exertion, but I fed off the pain. And I spent more and more time in the clouds. Literally. There was nothing I loved more than soaring with Rocky above the forest canopy and dancing on the treetops. Flying was one of the few things that still brought me happiness, and my goddess-mother knew it. Normally, Maggie would have scolded me for being careless with my magic. But when she caught me one afternoon soaring high in the air on my besom broom, she just called for me to be careful and to hold on tight.

Through it all, we planned and we plotted. Adelaide frequented the downtown shops and subtly—discreetly—spread word among the local gossips that the cottage was to play host to a small midsummer celebration. She drew them in, tempted them with the prospect of pouncing on us in full witch mode. She knew there was nothing they'd love more than to catch us "in the act."

But this wasn't some little backyard barbeque we were planning. Litha celebrated the longest day of the year, light and life, and the turning of the wheel. These Midsummer festivities were both reverent and raucous. Celeste and I teamed up with Maggie and Ayo to coordinate and organize the celebration. Together, Celeste and I tackled everything from catering coordination with Gregory's crew and arranging entertainment, to weaving floral crowns and garlands. She and I worked in easy synchronicity. We had fun together. And the more time we spent in each other's company, the more I craved her closeness. I knew I couldn't resist my desire for her much longer.

Maggie and Ayo had a similar connection, supremely intimate, yet it didn't seem like Maggie had fully given herself over. But they supported each other. Maggie worked her connections to the magical communities around the country and promised the turnout for this year's Litha festivities would be unprecedented. Hundreds of witches, Wiccans, pagans, and their familiars were set to descend upon the unsuspecting community of Arbor and join us in our stand. Maggie hoped our numbers and our show of magical force would be intimidating enough to get them to back off.

And in case things went awry, Ayo had Maggie's back, as well as the press and Chief Harrison on speed dial. Ayo had been working with the chief to build a case against the Crandalls and Cudlows. They were a few pieces of evidence away from implicating both families in a host of illegal, unethical, and salaciously immoral scandals. Scandals so damning, they would mean complete personal and professional ruination.

The Sunday night before Litha, the boys arrived at the cottage with some dirt to spill. Our rag-tag family coven convened around the dining room table to hear the boys' tale. They'd split up to take on missions of their own; each requiring stealth and a healthy disregard for ethics. Ethan and Nicolae spirited in and out of the Crandall and Cudlow homes and both their downtown offices while the families attended church. The boys gained entry by charming the pants off the folks that worked for them. Everyone knew the boys were my friends, but they were too enticing to deny when they put on the charm and worked their magic.

"You should have seen them!" Ethan said and flared out his arms as if setting the scene at center stage. "Maids, cooks, secretaries, they practically begged us to look around. 'Come on in,' Cudlow's butler said. 'Have some iced tea. Hey, I know where the reverend keeps the key to his safe. Let's go check it out.'"

Nicolae shook his head. "It was almost too easy. But, we stole nothing. We did, however, record the whole adventure, and took photos of the evidence we found."

A murmur went through the group.

"Oh, just wait till you see the video Gregory and I picked up at church today," Luca said as he leaned back in his chair and balanced his wineglass on his knee. "Never thought I'd ever speak the words, 'at church today.' Anyway, the two of us started off the day's surveillance by attending Reverend Cudlow's service. And, let me tell you, the good reverend did not disappoint. He used his sermon to rail against the many sins of *the Witches of Arbor*— love the new moniker, by the way".

Gregory had the oration on his phone. "Gather round, kids. This shit's got to be seen to be believed."

We crowded around the video and shared our collective horror.

"We are waging a spiritual war," the reverend declared, pounding his Bible on the pulpit. "Exodus twenty-two verse eighteen decrees, 'Thou shalt not suffer a witch to live.' You know they're out there right now, castin' spells over our good and decent politicians so they will write more liberal laws. Oh, yes. Look what they did to the Supreme Court. These foul witches cast their spells upon those God-fearing justices, so they'd let the gays marry. Those sodomites and sapphists want all kinds of benefits that, up to now, have been rightly reserved for good, moral, Christian folks.

"These witches are out there casting spells on our writers and directors and entertainers, who then use their books and movies and music to tempt, indoctrinate, and defile our children! They're trying to convince our little ones that it's okay to carry a wand or lay with someone of the same sex. Yes, I said it. This is spiritual warfare! And we must act! We must root out the homosexuals, root out the witches, root out these hippie-dippy, liberal, voodoo sinners. We must cast them out like the demons they are!"

The reverend thundered, and great waves of exaltation rolled back to him from the congregation. They raised their hands in supplication. They closed their eyes and fell upon their knees. "Praise His name!" they shouted. "Amen!"

"If we do not cast them out," the reverend continued in a hush that grew louder as he charged onward. "If we do not march against these foes, mark my words, God's punishment will be severe. There will be more storms. There will be more fires. We're not going through climate change, folks. This is God's wrath. And His rage swells every day that these heinous affronts persist. Our inaction will spur God's swiftest and most mighty retribution. We must not be complacent! We must be swords of the Almighty's righteousness!"

The churchgoers roared with fanatical zeal.

It was appalling hate-speech that would have made the preachers of Salem proud. And the twenty-first-century churchgoers lapped it up.

The pews weren't the only places our Arbor neighbors shared this ugliness.

"So, after church," Gregory piped up. "Luca went over to Crandall's campaign rally, while I followed a haggard Gladys Cudlow into Ebenezer's Café. Despite her painful gait, thinning hair, and her skin's sickly purplish tinge, Gladys's penchant for gossip could not be squelched. The café was busy, so as she stood in line, she ranted. 'That dingbat, Adelaide Good, lost the last of her marbles when she threw in her lot with those foul she-devils.' The crowd's apathy obviously needled Gladys because when she spoke next, she turned the volume to eleven. 'Magdalena Maramma and Evangeline Clarion are black stains on our community. Their brand of evil requires sterilization.'"

Sterilization. The word froze my blood.

Luca downed his wine and sat up in his chair. "I think Doreen Crandall managed to deliver her bile to the largest audience. The mayor arranged a massive outdoor campaign rally at the Great Pavilion in the center of town. The Center for Holy-Civil Strategies, the extreme right-wing super-pac, sponsored the day. I maneuvered into the event with a little charm and witnessed the mayor spewing her own unique brand of hatred. I got most of this on tape, too."

We all leaned in around the dining table to watch the second video.

"I will not cower to the kind of political correctness that defines deviant homosexuality and pagans gallivanting naked in the woods as acceptable behaviors. They most certainly are not! It is our solemn obligation to rise above the refuse. I will not sit idly by while these degenerates defile our community. These perversions must not be allowed to spread. They must be eliminated, eradicated. We must become active participants in the spiritual cleansing of our nation. We have been charged by God to hold dominion over every segment of civil life until His return. When I am elected, I will make sure my first act will be to rid our entire state of this wickedness!"

We froze, unanimously appalled by the mayor's words. No one spoke for a full minute.

"She's out of her bloomin' mind!" Adelaide bellowed into the stillness with her eyes popped wide. "She's going to incite a riot talking like that. This cannot go unchecked."

"It's a good thing we've got government-level security in place, or I might actually be worried," Maggie added.

I walked to the window and gazed out into the darkness. It never ceased to amaze me that those who purported to adhere to a faith of love, were often the least loving.

"We should be worried. We're vulnerable. Because of my story, our story, *The Messenger* is selling more newspapers than they have since before the recession. Local businesses are thriving thanks to curious tourists hoping to catch a glimpse of the now-infamous *Witches of Arbor*. The town's profiting off of slandering us. I'm getting flogged online. I'm a national whipping post, the latest mass-media distraction. And all of your reputations are crumbling now, too. They've had a taste of blood. No one is safe."

I turned to find my friends staring at me, spellbound, with something akin to shock etched on to their frightened faces. It took me a moment to realize what transfixed them. My hands. Slivers of light shone from within them. I had squeezed my fists so tightly, my nails left crescent-moon-shaped imprints on my palms. And the moons shone, glowing a bright orange-red from underneath my skin. As the imprints faded, so did the glow.

"Are you okay?" Celeste whispered close to my ear. When I didn't respond, she took my shoulders with firm hands. "Please, sit down. You need to rest." Her voice was gentle but resolute.

I didn't speak right away. I didn't move. I couldn't. I was too focused on the nearness of her mouth. I had to remind myself we were not alone. Maggie, Ayo, Adelaide, and the boys were not eight feet away. Instead of lowering her cherub lips to mine, which suddenly became a desperate desire, Celeste dropped a sweet kiss on my shoulder. I instinctually tilted my head, offering myself up to her. And a great shiver rocked me when she nipped my skin with her teeth.

I bit down hard on my bottom lip to keep from shuddering a sigh.

"Please sit, Eva, relax and let me get you some tea? You don't look well."

"I'm fine," I said, a little too sharp. Then, deciding to ignore what I could only assume was yet another internal power surge, I turned my attention back to the boys. "Ethan, Nikki, what kind of evidence did you pull from their houses and offices? Spill it. We need every gory detail."

The boys looked to each other and, without a word spoken, came to an agreement.

"Fine." Nicolae rolled his broad shoulders and cracked his knuckles. "The worst of it involves the Reverend and Stuart Cudlow. They, ah... they've been hosting these parties; organizing what amounts to orgies in the church's basement rectory. It's seedy stuff, complete with girls of questionable age, strapping young men, cases of alcohol, and an urn of cocaine. Please don't make me elaborate on the kinky shit these sons of bitches are into. My stomach can't handle it. The point is, the good reverend is ripping off his parishioners by using their tithing for booze, drugs, and sex."

"Why does this not surprise me?" Adelaide asked everyone and no one.

And no one answered her.

I really didn't know what to expect, but nothing like this. I knew all too well the Cudlow men were depraved, but I'd never suspected it went to this level. "Tell me you're joking."

"I fucking wish," Nicolae said bluntly. "There's pictures."

"No," I said with a shiver of disgust. I felt an itching under my skin at the thought of those sick fucks getting a bunch of teenagers drunk and high and... I scrubbed my hands over my face.

"There's more," Ethan cut in, not even trying to hide the devious smirk that brightened his somber mien. "The good mayor has been naughty as well. With a staggeringly simple scheme, Doreen Crandall ripped off the citizens of Arbor to the tune of two and a half million dollars over the course of her five-year term. She set up fake businesses, then drafted fraudulent invoices from those companies, issuing them to the township of Arbor. All she had to do then was pay the bills."

My brain threatened to shut down at that point. A faint *waa waa waa* echoed throughout my cavernous mind. I shook my head to clear the cobwebs. "Is that it? Is that everything?"

"That's as much as we've been able to puzzle out." Nicolae's words were heavy with regret.

"And this is all true? You know these things as facts?"

"We confirmed every detail." Ethan's voice dropped low and cracked.

And these are the people who condemn me. Hypocrites who snort coke, fuck young men and underage girls, and rob the town blind. These are the righteous? The holy?

"So what do we do now?" I asked Ayo. "Go to Chief Harrison, the press?"

"Yes and yes," she answered.

"Good," I said with an approving nod. "Tomorrow is Midsummer. I think Litha should proceed as planned. No alterations. This new information changes nothing. Witches, Wiccans, pagans, and people of goodwill from across the country, will arrive before daybreak. We must remain focused and prepared."

I looked into the eyes of each of my closest companions. While I lingered over the brilliant faces of my family, another internal surge of power crashed over me. A red-orange light pulsed beneath my skin, and just as I grew accustomed to the sensation, it faded.

Maggie wrapped her arms around me, and I burrowed into her nest of blood-red hair. Neither of us spoke. When Celeste took my elbow, I stepped out of Maggie's embrace and joined her—instinctually and without hesitation. She accompanied me to my room and guided me to the bed. I sat on the edge as Celeste removed my shoes. She looked up from her knees—not with subservience or deference but with genuine concern.

"You've had a long day," she said, then stood, took my hairbrush from the dresser, and sat behind me on the bed. "Let me take care of you."

"I've had a long month," I corrected in a grumble. But I didn't stop her. I closed my eyes and let her brush my hair.

With gentle and efficient hands, she smoothed it free of knots, then rebraided it down the center of my back. "Is there anything else I can do for you?"

I yawned, wide and unladylike. "No, thank you. I'm going to turn in."

Celeste tucked the cool sheet around me and planted a light kiss on my forehead. "Tomorrow's a big day. Try to rest. I'll be just outside on the gallery sofa if you need anything."

When she turned to leave, I caught her hand. "Thank you for taking such good care of me. Thank you...thank you for everything."

Chapter Twenty-Two

By some Goddess-bestowed blessing, we completed the Midsummer Litha preparations before a single foot landed on the driveway. We'd never hosted so large a gathering, and the implications of the night's events weighed heavily on all of us. But every detail of the affair had received careful attention. We had a plan. We were organized.

Long, low tables adorned with tapestries of every color and design ran along the forest's edge. Small tables for two were scattered throughout the property. There were mismatched lanterns and candelabrum and sprays of lavender scattered about. A hodgepodge of pillows and cushions, the fairy circle of tree stumps down by the stream, the patio furniture, and an army of wooden folding chairs provided seating for our guests. But the focal point was the stone circle we'd erected, stacked with wood for our bonfire. It wouldn't be lit until the Litha ceremony commenced.

Our first guests arrived at dawn, and they continued to descend upon us throughout the morning. By noon, we played host to almost five hundred people, two-thirds of them true witches with incalculable powers. At least a hundred witches brought their familiars, so Rocky and Shasta took charge of helping them feel at home. But we'd invited the mundane as well as the magical. Folks mingled and mixed, and they came in every shape, size, hue, gender identity, sexual orientation, belief system, and magical ability— from age eighteen to eighty-eight.

Even Mother Hildegard and the sisters from the Franciscan convent came to join us, and not only in our celebration of the changing of the seasons. The Mother Superior was disgusted by what she considered the perversion of the Christian faith, from one of love to one of hate. She understood the intolerant fanaticism we were up against, and as fervent protectors of the oppressed, she and the Franciscan sisters insisted on standing beside us in our hour of need. There was a history throughout the ages of Catholic nuns protecting those practitioners of magic who used their powers in the service of others; witches accused of heresy by the Church and government alike. They vowed to honor this history.

The members of our coven were among the earliest to arrive. Mr. and Mrs. Loveridge, Nicolae and Luca's folks, were strong, steady, always able to calm my anxious heart—as well as everyone else's. Like their sons, their magic manifested internally—in the control of the heart. Mr. and Mrs. Massey were Gregory's parents, and they had raised Ethan as their own. Mrs. Massey, Amy, was a healer like Maggie. And Mr. George Massey was a great warrior, a decorated veteran, and a true gray witch if there ever was one. They'd seen me skin my first knee and cast my first spell. It made me smile to see the boys with their folks.

Mr. Ryan Finnegan and his wife Fanny were adorably short, rotund, Irish kitchen witches; all red hair and freckles. The illustrious Alastair Gant, a slender, bespectacled magician with unruly white hair upon his head and eyebrows, greeted me with a cracked-lipped kiss to each cheek. No one really knew whether he held true magic or if he was simply a master at sleight of hand. Not even Luca could see the truth of him.

Then there were the four Wiccans who'd joined our coven some seventy years before, three gray-haired crones and a wizened old man. They hadn't a lick of magical blood between them, but they held the wisdom of the ancients.

I stood clustered together with Maggie, Ayo, Adelaide, and Celeste. My goddess-mother and the magnificent aje—both draped in regal blue—held hands as they greeted our guests. Adelaide was acquainted with over half of those in attendance, and she introduced me to every witch worth knowing. Multiple times throughout these introductions, I found myself thanking the Goddess for Celeste. She helped me brave the crowd with a soft hand on my back to steady me. Though her feathered kisses on my cheek and neck and shoulders, which had become more frequent throughout the morning, weakened my knees.

Despite my nerves, a festive energy saturated the scene. There were witches reading tarot, some reading palms, and some gazing into spheres of quartz or obsidian to catch glimpses of the future. Fire twirlers, dancers, and magicians wove among the ever-teeming masses, wielding their magic in spectacular fashion. Local vendors—farmers, artists, and purveyors of the unique and obscure—peddled their wares before the backdrop of lavender fields and a seemingly endless sky. Lively mountain music filled the air. A fiddler, washboard scratcher, washtub bass plucker, and a burly, bearded man who blew the moonshine jug did their thing on a small stage set up beside the beehives. That was Adelaide's sinister suggestion. She had a twisted sense of humor. She figured the musicians would play and the revelers would dance with more energy, more abandon, if under the encouraging eyes of the honeybees.

The sun's position in the sky told me it was time to slip away. There was something I needed to do on my own before the Litha ceremony commenced. I whispered in Celeste's ear that I was going to check on the familiars and headed into the woods. Rocky and Shasta were expecting me.

"Are we ready?" I asked.

"Everything is in order," Rocky assured me, and Shasta nodded in agreement.

"Thanks, you two. I really appreciate the help—and the secrecy."

"Oh, dearie," said Shasta in a soothing tone. *"Rocky and I will always be here for you. You know this."* She wrapped her heavy arms around me and gave me a good squeeze. *"We love you."*

"I love you, too, Momma Bear." I kissed her furry cheek. "And you, Rocky."

"There isn't a witch, alive or dead, to whom I'd rather be linked," the regal bird replied with a bow.

A ring of boulders, each three to four feet high, had been erected within the forest clearing. Circling just beyond the stones was a growing mass of creatures of the wood along with the visiting familiars. In the center of the assembled was a flat stone altar. Upon it, I placed a white candle and lit it. Then I lit a white sage smudge stick and cast a circle.

With my arms wide and my voice clear, I chanted.

> "Earth, my body.
> Water, my blood.
> Air, my breath.
> Fire, my spirit."

Shasta handed me a long, wooden staff. With it, I tapped the ground three times, and called out, "Hear me, spirits of the north—spirits of patience and strength." I tapped the staff three times again and said, "Hear me, spirits of the east—spirits of wisdom and ancient knowledge." I tapped the staff three more times. "Hear me, spirits of the south—spirits of fire and commitment." I tapped three final times. "Hear me, spirits of the west—spirits of compassion." The animals, which had bordered the outside of the circle, huddled in closer. With the grace of the Goddess and the power within me to aid my magic, I voiced my intention.

"Earthen bone and winged beat,
Let my mother come to me,
Waves that crash and fire's heat,
Allow for now her spirit free,
I call her forth from time and space,
Permit me now to see her face,
When my queries are at an end,
Take her spirit home again."

I repeated my request twice more before I noticed the animals to the north began to move aside. My mother's familiars, a deer and a crane, stepped before me in corporal form.

"Midsummer Blessings to you, my lady," I heard the deer say from within the confines of my mind.

The deer and crane then bowed, and following their lead, every woodland creature genuflected. But it wasn't me to whom they bent their backs in reverence.

It was my mother.

She walked toward me not as some transparent apparition. Instead, she was flesh and blood, just as I remembered her.

"Hello, my darling. What a beauty you are! And fiercely powerful to have called me forth with such clarity." She spoke with ease and confidence.

"Mother," I prayed and fell to my knees.

"Yes, my love. I'm here. I wondered if you'd call. You've got your hands full these days."

"You know what's been going on?" I asked, shocked.

"I do, but please, unburden your heart."

"Now that you're here and there is so much to say, I'm not sure where to begin."

For the next hour, we spoke. I vented—about everything; about not having the money I needed to open my gallery, about the assaults and insults of the Crandalls and Cudlows, about Alexander and Celeste and my twisted heart, and how truly frightened I was of this ever-increasing power that surged within me. And my mother had a lifetime's worth of wisdom to impart. By the time we ended our conversation, I felt cleansed, purified. I'd never felt stronger or more sure of myself.

Before my mother left, she had one request. "Would you give Magdalena a message for me?"

"Of course."

"Tell her I love her. That I will always love her. But she must embrace the joy beside her."

Understanding her meaning, I took a deep breath before speaking. "She has and will always be faithful to you."

What looked like a tear fell from my mother's eye, but I knew that was impossible. Spirits can't cry.

"Please, please tell her. She must embrace joy. Be well, my love. Be strong."

She turned and, with her familiars beside her, walked back into the thick of the forest and disappeared.

I don't know how long I stood there, staring at the spot at which my mother vanished, but when I finally shook myself, I realized only Shasta and Rocky remained by my side.

"I've got to get back. I'm sure Maggie's wondering where I've been." My voice sounded hollow to my ears.

"Rocky and I need to have a word," Shasta said softly.

"Can it wait? It's almost time for the..."

"No, dearie, I'm afraid it cannot wait," she said more firmly.

"Okay. What is it?" *This can't be good.*

Rocky began. *"We have been with you at some stage in each and every one of your lifetimes, as has Alexander. As you know, in each lifetime there are lessons to learn. You have grown in grace and strength and bravery with each. Alexander, too, has overcome many obstacles. But one thing has been consistent... you and Alexander have been great loves in every single lifetime."*

"Except this one," I interrupted.

"No, Evangeline, you are wrong," Shasta said sharply.

Rocky continued. *"Although you have always been great loves, you've never ended up together. You have never grown old together. You never bore his children. And yet, this is what is meant to be. We cannot explain to you precisely the lesson that this lifetime is intended to teach Alexander. But you, dear one, must learn to trust and forgive—others as well as yourself. It is essential that you do so."*

It was Shasta's turn to speak. *"Think, Evangeline. There are those in Arbor who wish to do you harm. Why is that? Because they are envious, yes. You have beauty, talent, and confidence. But why else could you and Magdalena and Adelaide inspire such contempt? They see that you are different. You do not conform. And, what is more, you have no desire for their good opinion. It is human nature to react with fear to the strange and unconventional. Instinct dictates two responses to fear: fight or flight. And they are planning to fight. So, Miss Evangeline, it all comes down to fear.*" Shasta finished speaking, and while ruffling her paws through her furry head, she plopped down onto her backside.

"Are you saying Alexander left me because he fears me?" I extrapolated.

"*Oh, no,*" Rocky piped up. "*He has not left you. And he is not afraid of you. He is afraid for you.*"

"I'm sorry, I don't understand."

"*Isn't it possible that Alexander wanted you away from the manor to protect you? The staff there was surely working against you. His motivation is not clear to me, but I ask one thing of you. Give him the benefit of the doubt, please.*"

I sighed at the weight of everything. "Because I love and trust you both and I know you would never steer me wrong, I will do as you ask. I will reserve judgment until I am able to speak with Alexander face to face. If I ever see him again."

Realizing I'd been away for far too long, I took off out of the woods and toward the cottage. "Come on. We've got to hurry," I called to my familiars behind me. When I reached the mouth of the woods, I was tempted to stop a moment to take in the breathtaking sight before me. But I hurried to take my place within the inner circle, between Magdalena and Celeste.

The sky was ablaze with the reddening sun skimming the horizon. Our friends of other faiths sat at the tables, eating and drinking wine and waiting to bear witness to our Midsummer Litha ceremony. Our bonfire hadn't yet been lit, but around its base stood circle upon circle of witches and Wiccans. The perimeter of the bonfire was strewn in daisies and salvia. Adelaide stood at its north end before a white linen-covered table, upon which sat a bronze bell and a tall, fat, unlit white candle. At the southern end was a caldron filled with blessed water and an aspergillum.

As our high priestess, Adelaide raised her arms in welcome and addressed the crowd.

"Today, to celebrate Litha, Midsummer, the Longest of Days, we honor the earth itself. We are encircled by towering trees, fragrant lavender, nourishing vegetation, and potent herbs. Arching over us is a clear expanse of sky and, below our feet, rich fertile soil. We are connected to them all. We light this fire as the ancients did so long ago, as our fathers and mothers have done, as our sons and daughters will."

Adelaide lit the altar candle. Then each of us filed around to light our own candle from hers. One at a time, beginning with Maggie at Adelaide's right, we brought our flames forward and added our light to the bonfire. By the time we'd all made our contributions, the blaze flamed high and wide and furiously.

Adelaide went on. "Once again, the Wheel of the Year has completed its turn. For six long months until this day, the light has lengthened. Called the Light of the Shore by the old ones who came before us, this is a time for merriment and gratitude in equal measure. Tomorrow, the light will wane, as the Wheel turns on and ever on." Adelaide raised the bell from her altar and rang it three times.

As one, we turned to the east and said, "From the east comes the wind, with its life-giving breath, scattering seeds of new growth."

We moved to face the south and spoke again as one, "As the Midsummer sun shines high and bright upon the land, we embrace the new life it sparks into being."

Together, facing west, we recited, "From the west, the waters crash as hurricanes and creep as fog, nourishing all."

Finally, turning to the north, "Beneath our feet, the earth's fertile soil enriches and provides sustenance, from which life springs anew."

Adelaide rang the bronze bell seven times. We all threw our candles into the blaze before us. Adelaide walked to the cauldron and dipped the aspergillum into its depths. We paraded around the circle, each stopping before her to receive the blessing with water.

When our high priestess spoke again, it was to conclude the ceremony. "Whether called by the name Creator, the Great Spirit, Mother Nature, Danu, Morrigan, Kali, Frigg, Nana Buluku, or Diana, this primal force moves us ever forward. Go and celebrate life! Rejoice in simple pleasures. And be humbly grateful for the bounty with which you have been blessed." Adelaide's power was as undeniable as it was palpable. Her eighty years had done nothing to diminish her.

Once the ritual had ended, I expected the revelry to begin right away. But for a few moments, not a single person spoke. No one moved. The energy of the rite washed over us. Solemnity and reverence etched itself onto every face.

Still, one by one, eventually, the others moved on to dance and sing and drink honeyed wine. The bonfire cast dancing shadows on the revelers. Yet I found myself lost in the flames.

This fire churns within me.

I heard Celeste speak beside me, but her voice seemed miles away. "Destructive, true, but fire cleanses and purifies. As fire scorches a forest to the dirt, so too does it stimulate growth, a rebirth of the wood."

The blaze drew me closer and closer still, until it encased me in its forked tendrils. It lifted me high into the air, into its swirling coils, and burned down the walls I'd built around my spirit. But my flesh remained intact. I was no phoenix. It hadn't brought me to ash, but I was reborn. Once enveloped in the womb of the Goddess's light, now that light lived and breathed within me.

Painful, horrific screams wrenched me from my introspections. I blinked to clear my vision, but my mind refused to register what it saw. I was bathed in fire. My clothes had burnt away and lay in a smoldering heap below me. I hovered in midair, encased in searing power. The mass of awestruck witches cut off their cries and fell to their knees before me.

"Stand! You are powerful and beloved in the eyes of the Goddess. Bow before no one, for we all have Her spirit within us. Her imprint resides within us all."

My goddess-mother, high priestess, my coven, my friends, and my fellow worshippers began, as one, to chant.

> "Earth, Air, Fire, Water,
> In one, Crone, Mother, Daughter
> From acorn, spark, ripple, breeze,
> We began our lives upon our knees.
> To mighty oak and tidal wave
> To swirling cyclone and scorching blaze.
> Great Goddess within us from birth to death,
> Let your power compel us until our last breath.
> So shall we will it. So mote it be!"

Slowly, I descended until my naked feet felt the earth. Ayo rushed forward, wrapped an emerald shawl around my shoulders, and whispered to me. "You are blessed, Evangeline. I saw the Goddess within you tonight. *Ti o ba wa mi ga priestess titi mi ojo ikeyin.*"

And although I had never learned the West African language of Yoruba, I somehow understood and replied, "I will endeavor always to deserve such an honor."

She kissed my cheek and fell back into the crowd. Maggie and Adelaide approached me and wrapped me up in a group bear hug until I begged for breath. I couldn't help laughing.

"Oh, sweetheart, are you okay?" Maggie asked as she peppered kisses all over my face.

Before I could answer, Adelaide spoke up. "Of course she's okay. She's marvelous. You put on one hell of a show there, darlin'. I couldn't have enraptured the crowd any better."

"What did she say to you? Ayo, I mean," Maggie asked with nervous eyes cast down.

"She told me I was now her high priestess." I looked to Adelaide. "I...I'm sorry."

"Well, well!" Adelaide exclaimed. "Seems I've finally found someone to follow in my footsteps." She turned to Maggie. "Don't go getting jealous now, Magdalena. You don't want this blessing. It is a burden."

My goddess-mother beamed. "No. It's not what I want for myself, because I know I raised the one who'd fill that role." She turned her loving eyes to me. "I couldn't be happier for you. Lavinia would be so proud." Maggie wrapped her arms around me once more.

Through her waves of blood-red locks, I whispered in Maggie's ear, "I know she is. And she's proud of you too. She loves you so much and always will." My words surprised her. "The love you share is everlasting. Remember this," I said, and she stepped back. But I wasn't through. "I saw my mother today. I spoke with her."

It looked like Maggie had been struck by lightning. Her whole body jolted. "What? How?" Her brow pinched.

"The animals helped me draw her spirit to the forest. We talked. And she had a message for you."

Maggie's face twisted between wonder and trepidation.

"She wants you to embrace joy."

"Embrace joy? That's her message? She wants me to be happy?"

"Well, yes, of course she wants you to be happy, but no, that's not her message exactly." I looked over to find Ayo standing a few feet away, chatting with the boys and their parents. "Embrace joy," I said again and gestured to the striking aje. "In the Yoruban language, Ayo means joy."

Maggie glanced over at Ayo just as she looked back, and they held each other's gaze. When my goddess-mother returned her attention to me, she looked ages younger. It was clear the burden of guilt had been crushing her. Ayo had stolen her heart, but her soul belonged eternally to my mother. Now Lavinia had freed her spirit to embrace this new experience.

"Thank you," she said with watery eyes. "Your mother was wise to name you Evangeline—bringer of good news." She kissed my cheek. Then she went to Ayo's side and took her hand.

For once, Adelaide was speechless. I had no desire to explain. Instead, I asked for a drink.

"Of course! Come! Let's celebrate!" she called out. And our guests returned a ruckus cheer.

Chapter Twenty-Three

Celeste placed a glass of wine in my hands and a kiss on my lips. She smiled shamelessly as she lingered over slivers of bare skin that peeked out from under my emerald cloak. My thoughts traveled to the image of her standing beside my bed with that pale yellow sheet wrapped ever so gracefully around her naked shoulders. A blush brightened her porcelain cheeks, but it was no rouge of naïve innocence. No. I knew her better now. We'd spent almost every waking, and a few slumbering, moments beside each other over a period of weeks, a longer acquaintance than with Alexander. A trifling period of time in the grand scheme of things.

She and I didn't have the same kind of soulful connection that Alexander and I once shared. With Celeste, the draw was gravitational, a pull as irresistible as the full moon over ocean waters.

I closed the distance between us and brushed my fingers along her cheek. "We've grown close over these weeks."

"Yes."

"Become good friends."

"Yes."

"Is that all?" I asked and waited without breath for her reply.

"No," she whispered. "More."

Celeste took my hands in hers. They were gentle, warm, and velvety smooth. She drew me into her arms, and this time when our lips touched, I felt it underneath my skin, in my fingertips and toes.

Too soon, she pulled away, reminding me with a nod to the crowd that we weren't alone. "Come on." She laughed and led me into the throngs of wild revelry.

Hand drums, flute, and violin drove the revelers into rapturous elation. Celeste and I wove through them until we found the boys. They were, as usual, reducing every lady within a ten-foot radius into a puddle, and more than a few of the men. That they were skyclad made the reaction nearly impossible to avoid.

Looking to Celeste with mischievous eyes, I shed my emerald wrap. She followed without the briefest hesitation. Her robin's-egg-blue shift dress fell to the grass before my next breath.

And then we danced. I allowed the music—mystical and rousing—to swirl me into a captivated frenzy. I was spellbound as much by the driving rhythm and writhing bodies as the raw energy surging within me. It was savage beauty, and I allowed myself to be swept away in it.

Out of nowhere, Luca snatched me up from Celeste with a zeal I didn't appreciate. I was reluctant to remove my hands from her bare flesh for fear I'd never again feel its equal. And I didn't care for Luca's assumption that our history gave him permission to touch me however and whenever he got the itch. Luca was like a brother, however, so I forgave him. But as he drew me into a dance, I made sure he knew my feelings. I didn't need to say a word. He used his powers to delve into my heart in search of my truth. As always with us, I knew when he found it. I searched his eyes to gauge his reaction, but he gave nothing away. He simply kissed my cheek and handed me into the waiting arms of his older brother. And I danced with each of the boys in turn—without self-consciousness or shame, and without a stitch covering any of us.

After an hour or so, my ears began ringing, and my head throbbed. There was a searing heat within me, and I dripped in the collective sweat of the Midsummer celebrants. I made my excuses to Celeste and the boys and weaved out of the crowd. I had to clear my head.

Water. I need water.

But before I made it to the cottage door, I heard Adelaide welcome a late arrival. It stopped me in my tracks.

"Aren't you a sight for sore eyes!" she bellowed.

The music and merrymaking grew faint until all sound faded. Facing the cottage wall, my vision blurred. Unsure of my steadiness, I clung to my wineglass with two hands. I took a few calming breaths but still couldn't bring myself to turn around.

I sensed Alexander drawing closer. His intoxicating scent ignited me as sure as any torch.

A growl rumbled from deep within him. "Evangeline."

I didn't speak. I didn't move. I heard Alexander's trudging feet as he paced behind me. I imagined his head hung low with a brow pinched in deliberation and his hands clasped at the small of his back.

His footsteps stilled. "You're naked."

"You're observant," I answered with cold indifference.

"I'm not a prude, but this is a bit much, don't you think?"

"You made it abundantly clear that I was too much for you when you so valiantly ran off, leaving behind a note to make your excuses."

"Please, Evangeline," Alexander begged. His plea chipped my armor. He stepped closer. His breath caressed the back of my neck. "Look at me."

"I can't. I'm afraid."

His breathing hitched. "Oh, my sweet girl, please don't fear me."

I rounded on him in a fury. "How little you know me," I snapped. "I'm not some simpering child. And I sure as hell am not afraid of you." After a breath, my tone softened. "I'm afraid of myself." *Of my weakness.*

"I never meant to hurt you, Evangeline. You must know that."

"All I know is that you left," I said, resolute.

"Look, I didn't come to fight. I came to warn you. And we've wasted enough time already."

"What's this about, Alexander?" Adelaide asked, reminding us of her presence after hovering in the shadows while we bickered. "Warn us of what?"

"Gladys and the reverend are coming—tonight, soon—and half of Arbor with them. You guys have to get the hell out of here. Run." When he was met with silence, he persisted. "Seriously, you need to leave. Now!"

"Alexander, calm yourself," Maggie said sternly, buzzing in from out of nowhere. "We know they're coming. We're expecting them."

Alexander looked from Maggie's face to mine to Adelaide's and back to mine—incredulous. "What the hell do you mean? If you know they're on their way, why haven't you stopped celebrating?"

"Because then the terrorists win, dear boy. Don't you read the news?" Adelaide quipped.

Deciding to put the befuddled man out of his misery, I hastily explained our plan.

After the look of shock fell from his face, he barked, "Well, will you at least put some clothes on?"

"What the...who do you...oh, you're insufferable!" I stuttered in frustrated fury. Then I looked to Celeste. "Would you—?" I began, but she was already beside me. Together, we made our way into the cottage, arm in arm, hip to hip.

I huffed into my bedroom and collapsed facedown onto my bed. Celeste shut my curtains—which was a blessing, as the windows faced outward over the Midsummer festivities. Then she walked into the bathroom and ran the sink. Flopping onto my back, I stared up at the blank white ceiling until my vision began spinning and I got dizzy. I closed my eyes. I was alerted to Celeste's return by the patter of her feet and the slosh of water. I peeked from underneath heavy lids as Celeste dipped a cloth into a shallow bowl of water and wrung it out tight.

"Relax. Let me care for you," she said, her strong and steady voice at odds with the fragility of her countenance.

I obeyed and luxuriated in her gentle efficiency. She ran the cool cloth over every inch of my skin, cleansing me of soot and ash and sweat.

"Sit up," Celeste ordered, and again, I complied without complaint. She climbed onto the bed behind me and brushed out my hair with firm, capable hands.

"They're going to be here any minute," she said quietly.

"I know."

"Are you ready?"

"I will be," I said, and I meant it.

I got up and went to the bathroom mirror. The face that reflected back was not the one I'd known all my life. My skin glowed with the resolute confidence of fourteen lifetimes. The glow faded as I calmed my heart.

You have serious shit to take care of, Evangeline Clarion. Pull yourself together.

Celeste dressed in a delicate lavender shift and helped me step into a long, flowing deep-purple dress. She pinned up my hair in a loose but intricate bun atop my head.

Just as we headed back outside, we heard *them*. Singing.

> "Onward, Christian soldiers, marching as to war.
> With the cross of Jesus, going on before!
> Christ the royal Master, leads against the foe;
> Forward into battle, see his banner go!"

We hurried out of the cottage and took our positions beside our friends. Our coven, the boys and their parents, Ayo, Magdalena, and Adelaide stood beside us. Our line of power formed a protective barrier between our guests and Arbor's holy marchers. I briefly wondered where Alexander was, but then Celeste took my right hand. She looked me squarely in the eyes.

"You've got this," she said and kissed me hard and quick before returning her attention to the approaching throngs.

Dear Goddess. I sighed. I had to physically stop myself from pulling her into my arms. Not to keep making out with her, although that suddenly seemed like the best idea in the world, but just to have her close to me.

Why the hell can't I? Why shouldn't I? I wondered defiantly. She looked so lovely, so sweet. I loved the fiery, passionate soul that pulsed beneath her angelic exterior. She turned me on more than anyone I'd ever encountered—except for Alexander.

In a snap, just like that, with only the thought of his name, Alexander took the spot to my left. "Took you long enough to think about me," he said with a snide smirk.

It wasn't until then that I remembered he could probably hear everything I was thinking.

"Not everything, but almost." He wiggled his eyebrows.

"Excuse me?"

"The thoughts I read the clearest, are others' thoughts about me. It's one of the many things I learned in Italy."

"Italy! You left me to vacation in Italy?"

"It wasn't a vacation. I mean, not really. Look, when we have more time and privacy—" He paused to sneer at Celeste. "—I'll explain everything."

"I'm intrigued to hear about all you've learned, Alexander, but yes, it'll have to wait. We've got zealots with tiki torches to contend with."

"I can't believe you expect me to just stand by and watch them go after you."

I elbowed him hard in the gut, and he buckled. "Shhh," I scolded him and whispered, "this has to remain peaceful. Don't give them an excuse to lock us up. Just let us handle it."

Alexander growled, but before he had a chance to argue, Maggie chimed in. "Eva's right. Let's keep cool heads, everyone. We've done nothing wrong."

"Ha! That's never stopped bigots before," Adelaide said.

The figures marched in dissonant cadence up the driveway. There had to be over a hundred of them—holding their torches aloft, sneering as they sang their prayerful call to war.

"Holy shit," I said.

"That it is, my dear," Adelaide replied on a sigh. "That it is."

I caught Nicolae's eye and tapped the nonexistent watch on my wrist, hoping to wordlessly relay my directive, *Time to go*. I was relieved when he nodded, and one by one, the boys dispersed, heading to each corner of the property. From there, they would man the cameras, already in place, and make sure not a word or gesture was missed. If things got ugly between us and the crowd charging up our driveway, then Ethan would slice and dice the video, and send out clips to the Associated Press and splatter it all over social media.

"It looks like it's just the parishioners from the church. Gladys and the reverend are leading the charge. Oh my, she does not look well," Maggie murmured. "I don't see the mayor anywhere. If she were with them, she'd be front and center."

"Focus, everyone, focus," I commanded in a hiss.

The troop halted their advance twenty feet from our line of power, and their song ended. For a moment, all was quiet. Gladys and the reverend moved a few steps closer.

"Isn't this a motley crew?" Gladys grimaced with her nose in the air. "And just as I suspected. You've been drawing more demonic forces to Arbor. I'm physically attuned to these sorts of things, you know." She paused and glanced nervously down at her ailing form. "Well, we will not stand for it a moment longer. Your evil has been permitted to spread for too long in this town. We refuse to tolerate your wicked indoctrination of our community. We insist that you vacate this property, this town permanently. Mayor Crandall is giving you one day to pack up and head out. If you're not gone in twenty-four hours, the mayor will rain the Lord's justice down upon you. No mercy will be shown."

"Can't we just salt them and be done with it?" Adelaide mocked.

The reverend, scowling in reply, screwed his eyes shut tight and raised the Bible in his hand to the heavens.

"Don't you quote your book to me," Adelaide spouted at him. "Why don't you spend a little more time reading it yourself, especially the newer parts about that hippie who loved everyone and traveled around giving away free food and healthcare. I think we'd get along a whole lot better if you acted more like him."

Ignoring Adelaide, the reverend cleared his throat, and spoke out. "Through the power of the Almighty, we command you, instruments of hell, to release your hold over this land and the good people of Arbor. We are the righteous army of the Lord, and we are prepared to wage this spiritual war on His behalf. We will rid our community of your demonic influence. We will not succumb. We will not tire. We will be relentless in our blessed crusade. Repent! Repent and fall upon your knees in supplication to our Lord or remove yourselves forever from our faith-filled eyes."

"You have got to be kidding! First of all, you pompous nincompoop," Adelaide said, stepping within feet of the man of the cloth. "We don't even recognize the Satan character you like to pretend we worship. The Hell you speak of is a concept that has no place in our beliefs. Nowhere will you find the encouragement of evangelization, indoctrination, or coercion. The only ones I see employing those tactics are you, your wife, and the ignorant sheep behind you." Adelaide shook with anger.

Maggie placed a hand on the high priestess's shoulder and continued for her. "We believe in the power inherent within nature, and we praise the Creator of that nature. We celebrate the change of seasons, the glory of a sunrise, the mystery of the moon. We endeavor to use the gifts within us to improve ourselves, our communities, and the environments in which we live. We do not advocate harm to any creature, even those who wage war upon us." My goddess-mother spoke in a strong but calm manner in an attempt to temper the fury that simmered within us all.

"The poison you use to bewitch others drips in honey, but your sweetness does not fool us," Gladys hissed.

"Okay, I've had enough," I blurted. "I don't care how or to whom you pray. It has no bearing on any aspect of my life whatsoever. Just as my methods of worship have nothing to do with you. The glaring fact you so willfully overlook is that we live in a country that says I can genuflect every two hours to a toad or pray to a fish or prostrate myself before the image of a hollowed-out log and there isn't a damn thing you can do about it. This is our property, our land. Don't you get it yet? We mean you no ill will. We aren't a band of miscreants, nor are we demons hell-bent on sucking dry the souls of our neighbors. Yes, there are many of us." I motioned to the massive group that stood behind me. "There are many who follow our path. And there are many others who do not share our beliefs, who've chosen to stand beside us." I looked to Mother Hildegard and her habit-clad sisters with a grateful smile. "We've been able to find many areas of common ground with our neighbors of different beliefs. Caring for the poor, for example. My goddess-mother and Mother Hildegard, from the Saint Francis's Roman Catholic convent, coordinate food and clothing drives. They care for the sick and elderly together. Mother Hildegard and the sisters respect our right to worship in whatever fashion stirs our souls. And we respect them for their ability to balance sincere, steadfast devotion to their deity with peaceful coexistence and tolerance. I think I speak for all of us when I say that we'd love to find some common ground with you too. We don't have to be enemies."

At the conclusion of my speech, we collectively held our breath, awaiting a response.

"Let us pray," Reverend Cudlow called out. He and his congregation bowed their heads. "Through the power of the one true God, we bind every witch and call for the warrior angels to crush our enemies. In His name, we break down the walls of protection around these witches. We break the power of their curses, hexes, and charms. And if we must, we will saturate this land with His holy blood. We silence you in His name. In His name, we call for all witches to leave this land forever."

I was dumbfounded. *What the fuck is wrong with these people?* But as appalled as I felt, I knew I must offer a peaceful reply. So in a soft voice, I led an incantation of our own. And hundreds of voices repeated after every line.

> "We invoke thee, Northern Earth,
> Flesh and bone of mortal birth.
> We invoke thee, Southern Fire,
> Sizzling pulse of love's desire.
> We invoke thee, Eastern Air,
> Breath of life and trumpets blare.
> We invoke thee, Western Water,
> Ocean tides and blooded daughter.
> As above, so too below.
> Within, without, does spirit flow.
> To hear and taste, to touch and see.
> As we will it, so mote it be."

And then I continued, independent of the crowds. "We call on the energy and power of the elements to provide us with courage and strength of spirit, with the ability to overcome fear and hatred, with the humility to meet others with compassion, and with the gentle hearts required to greet our foes with kindness."

Their dumbfounded expressions made it evident the fanatical church faithful hadn't anticipated my conciliatory response, so I thought my next move would floor them. I walked a few feet to one of the tables filled with food and drink. I poured two glasses of honeyed wine and offered them to Gladys and the reverend.

"We don't worship the same way, but we are neighbors," I said, in as coaxing a voice as I could muster. "Maggie, Adelaide, and I have lived here just as long as any of you, and we love this town. Can't we find some commonality among us? Come, drink, join us. You are all welcome."

"Temptress!" Gladys shrieked.

"Get thee back, Satan!" boomed Reverend Cudlow.

"Seriously?" I threw my arms out in frustration.

"You and your kind have no sway over us. We will not be lured by your insincere overtures of friendship or your devil's brew. We've said our piece. You know our demands. It's your move," the reverend said and signaled the group to move on.

After almost ten minutes, their torches disappeared from view.

"So much for overtures of peace and a rally of supporters getting them to back off. Never let it be said that sabats are a bore here at the cottage!" Adelaide joked, sounding more like herself.

"Please everyone, stay as long as you'd like," Maggie called out. "We are so very grateful that you've all come to celebrate and stand with us. Enjoy the food and wine. But today's excitement has tired me. So goodnight, and may your journeys home be safe."

With Maggie off to rest—and Ayo along with her—I embraced the role of hostess and said farewell to each guest personally. A connection existed between us now, and I wanted them to know how much I valued that connection. These men and women had watched, first in horror then in awe, as the Goddess baptized me in fire. They'd witnessed the torch-lit threat of fanaticism. And they would be forever changed. As would I.

Chapter Twenty-Four

For Maggie, the colossal chore of post-festival cleanup would have been the work of an hour. But she, along with most everyone else, had called it a night. Alexander, Celeste, the boys, and I volunteered to stay and put the cottage and grounds back in order. I thought it was generous of Alexander to stick around to break down a party he'd attended for all of an hour. As we hauled away trash and stacked tables and chairs, I feasted on the sight of Alexander in flesh and blood—and muscle, bronzed from his adventures in sunny Italy. And when his wide, beaming smile fell over me, my heart split in two. My anger over his abandonment still burned, but every time I looked at him, my soul sighed relief.

Yet as the night grew longer and our tasks more tedious, Alexander grew more and more sour. I caught him more than once glaring at Celeste, poorly suppressing a snarl. And she took the bait and scowled back at him. I couldn't help but lament that, where there once was respect, animousity now poisoned them both. And I was the cause.

As soon as we finished cleanup duty, Alexander grabbed ahold of my hands and put them to his lips. "Can we go somewhere and talk," he asked softly. He shot his eyes over to Celeste. "In private?"

"Just say what you have to say," I said, impatient.

"Fine. Fine," he grumbled and began pacing. Every so often, he stopped and attempted to speak, only to hang his head and return to his brooding search for words.

After a minute, two, five passed without a word, Celeste lost her patience. "You don't need this asshole, Eva," she said without any attempt to cloak or temper her voice.

"Who the fuck do you think you are?" Alexander's words were like the cold, hard crunch of marble to the cranium.

"I'll tell you who I am. I'm the one who stood beside Eva when you walked out. I'm the one..." Celeste began as she charged toward him. I managed to hold her back before the slim wisp of a woman barreled right into his chest.

"You know what, I don't give a shit. Just keep your mouth shut and leave us the hell alone." He grabbed me by the arm and tried to drag me away.

I snatched my arm back again and steeled my spine. My familiars emerged to stand with me. Together, we squared off against Alexander and Archie. I offered Archie a look of apology, but he was just as loyal to his witch as my familiars were to me.

Celeste took her place at my side. "It's clear you don't give a shit, *Mr. Morgan*, but I no longer work for you. I'm under no obligation to follow your commands, no matter how much you growl at me. You punched a hole in her heart because you were too much of a coward to stand and fight beside her!"

"And you slithered right in to take my place."

"That's enough! Both of you! Celeste"—I turned and took her hands in mine—"go get some rest. You deserve it." I gently kissed her on the cheek. "I'd like to talk to Alexander."

Celeste crinkled her brow in frustration. "You have another long day tomorrow. Come with me. We'll rest together."

"So you're fucking her now?"

"I said enough! I'm done with the sniping. I've had it," I screamed.

With a leap, I took to the skies. I headed for the trees and landed effortlessly atop a sturdy branch deep within the woods. Rocky followed me and perched a few trees deeper in. Although he didn't speak or perhaps because he didn't, I knew he was pissed.

"Hey," I called to him with no reply. *"Heelllooo."*

Nothing. He stared right through me.

"You're giving me the silent treatment?"

"Of course not." He shook his feathered head as if it had been the most ludicrous thought in the world. *"I have no patience for games of that sort. I'm pondering the best way to get you to listen. And listen you must, and heed my words. It brings me no pleasure to say this…"*

"Rocky, for Goddess's sakes, spit it out."

"I am very disappointed in you. You've never been one to turn tail and run. Don't start now."

"What would you have me do?"

"Fight. In all things. Fight back. Yes, give Alexander the benefit of the doubt, but never back down—to anyone."

"There you are!" Alexander called from twenty or so feet below my perch. "Can you please come down and talk to me?"

Rocky took his cue and flew off.

"I'm kinda liking it up here. I think maybe I'll build a fort."

"Stop behaving like a child and get down here."

I jumped, landing lithely on my feet, inches from his nose.

"Thank you. Now maybe we can talk like adults," Alexander said, irritation poisoning his tone.

"Oh, I came down because I'd like to hit you." I lifted clenched fists, but the effect was more Jennifer Lawrence than Katniss Everdeen. He struggled to keep from laughing at my brazen hostility. I knew I was behaving like a petulant child, but I was angry and not yet willing to let go of the feeling.

"You're determined to make this difficult, aren't you?" he asked, shaking his head in frustration.

"Why should I make it easy? You didn't make it easy when you left that fucking note, when you took off without saying goodbye or telling me where the fuck you were going."

"Watch the language, Eva. It's vulgar."

"Are you kidding?" I stared at him, openmouthed. "You just asked me if I was fucking Celeste, and now you're going to stand there and scold me for using profanity? I wish I used it more often, maybe I'd have a better selection of four-letter vocabulary words with which to tell you to fuck off." I placed my hands on my hips and lifted a defiant chin.

Sorrow contorted Alexander's lips. "Look, I was wrong. I'm sorry," his voice rumbled. "I shouldn't have left the way I did. I shouldn't have left that note. I should've talked to you about what I was feeling instead of running off." He hung his head and ran his fingers through his hair. "It makes me sick that I caused you pain." He stepped closer and took my hands gently in his own.

The feel of his skin sent a jolt to my heart. *What the hell? Since when does he have a working man's hands?* I remembered him having the smooth, polished, manicured hands of the highborn, never having to do a moments worth of manual labor in his life. Now they were rough and callused and blistered. Cleaning up from Litha wouldn't have done that so quickly. And considering he'd only been gone a couple weeks, it was clear he'd been working very hard on something.

"Tell me what I can do to make things right," Alexander said, interrupting my thoughts. "Tell me how I can make it up to you. Please, please forgive me."

It pissed me off that I felt myself yielding to him. There existed a part of me that wanted him to suffer the way he'd made me suffer. But there was no denying the sincerity of his apology. His candor bled through every repentant word.

"Can you tell me why? What made you run?"

Alexander reverted to his standard practice of pacing. The waves of his hair hung against hunched shoulders. "I was just so fucking angry—at myself for shirking my responsibilities to the estate, at the mother I'd never known, at my father for being a calculating, manipulative, murderous prick, and at you for introducing chaos into my life. Since the moment we met, I've been consumed by an irresistible compulsion to protect you." He paused and cast his feverish eyes over me. "Yet even the walls of Morgan Manor weren't enough to keep the wolves at bay. Instead of sheltering you, my arrogance placed you directly into the line of fire.

"But the anger within me shifted the night of my mother's Summerland rite. She left that warning, and it triggered something within me. It's like everything went foggy except for a sliver of clarity. And what was clear was your betrayal."

"Excuse me?"

"Please, just listen." He took a breath and continued. "I was hyper-paranoid. I saw lies and betrayal on all sides. And I saw your scheming. I saw that you'd charmed me, seduced me, messed with my head, all to rip me off. I don't know what made me see this vileness, but it was all true. I was sure of it. And I was certain that a part of me loved you still, despite it all.

"What I didn't know for sure is who the hell I was. I couldn't see who I was supposed to be. I'd just learned my father wasn't only a prick, but a murderer, and he'd had my mother killed. I'd just learned that my mother was a witch, and that the magic in her blood flowed through me. And this magic had its roots in Italy, so that's where I went. I needed to understood my own magic, and my la Strega lineage. I had no idea what, if anything, I'd find in that seaside village in Italy, but it was a journey I needed to take."

"Did you find the answers you were looking for?"

"Yes, and some answers I didn't realize I needed."

"Oh? Like what?"

"The very first thing I learned after my arrival in Italy. I'd been cursed."

"Excuse me?"

"The fog that came over me, the severe paranoia, the rage, it was a curse. Unfortunately, who cursed me and why still eludes me. When that fog lifted, and I saw what I'd done, I wanted to come rushing right back to you. But I realized that I couldn't spend my life jumping in front of you at the slightest hint of a hazard, mainly because you could take on that hazard better than I could. I figured the best way to truly protect you was to learn as much about my magic as I could, so that I could fight beside you." Alexander struggled to control his emotions as he spoke. He locked his jaw, and a light sheen of sweat broke across his reddening cheeks and wrinkled brow.

I was proud of myself for making it through his little speech without blubbering. Too much resentment had calcified around my heart to allow the weakness of tears. With the absence of sorrow, the anger was liberating.

"So the fact that you thought I was screwing your maid had nothing to do with you running off?"

A growl thundered through him. "No. But there's something about her. I just... I can't stand that female."

"I'm pretty sure the feeling is mutual." A great war raged within me. My brain had had enough. My heart, though shattered, cared too much to let him go. And my soul was lost somewhere in between.

"Look, curse or not, I know how much I hurt you. Please, forgive me." He stepped slowly closer, never losing connection with my eyes, closer still until only thin fabric separated us. He rested his forehead against mine. His lips hesitated, trembling slightly.

I can't breathe.

"Me either," he said with a smirk.

Damn it, Alexander!

He laughed.

"I keep forgetting you can do that."

His lips curled, sinister. "Oh, my dear, I can't wait to show you all my new tricks."

"Showing off will have to wait," I said, throwing water on the spark he'd kindled between us. "Right now, I need some sleep." This time, it was his turn to pout, and I couldn't help but smile. "Sorry." Three words bounced around my brain: *Bed. Pillow. Now.*

I made a beeline for my bed with Alexander hot on my heels. It wasn't sex I had in mind. I needed to crash—hard. So I barged through the cottage, bypassing the kitchen, and forgoing a midnight snack. I trudged down the hall and through my bedroom door, ready to flop into bed. Instead, I sprawled out straight into Celeste's waiting arms.

"So you were the elephant I heard traipsing through the house," she reprimanded me, cloaked in her deceptively wholesome facade.

"You caught me," I declared and kissed the feisty Wiccan full on the mouth. Then I moved past her and curled into my bed. "I'm going to sleep now." I snuggled into my blankets and pillows and released a soulful sigh. "You guys can fight over sleeping arrangements on your own."

I closed my eyes and shut down my brain. Blissful oblivion engulfed me in an instant.

Celeste woke me early, and Alexander had already gone. Through the dense fog of lingering lethargy, I heard her prattling on about a breakfast picnic in the woods and documenting these events for posterity. She bustled here and there, preparing for the day ahead. I, on the other hand, felt trapped in mental molasses. I gazed out dreamily from my window. The sun peeked over the horizon, bathing the sky in great swathes of coral and violet.

"That's enough wool-gathering," Celeste whispered in my ear. "We need to start the day."

A shower and coffee went a long way in hauling me out of my morning sluggishness. Once rejuvenated, Celeste and I made quick work of packing a basket with fruit and muffins and a carafe of coffee. We hardly spoke but maneuvered effortlessly around each other with the ease of long acquaintance. In under half an hour, we passed the fallen oak and made our way into the woods. We laid out a picnic blanket in the clearing where I'd spoken with my mother only the evening before. After we finished our meal, Celeste pulled something out of her satchel I hadn't noticed.

"I thought you might like to document your first sabat, your first Litha, as high priestess," she said and handed me my mother's grimoire.

It wasn't aged or faded. No ancient family line revealed their secrets within its pages. My mother had begun writing in the book when she was six. Far from juvenile, even her most rudimentary spells and charms demonstrated a sharp wit, cleverness, and wisdom. She was an old soul. The coven—and the magical community at large—considered Lavinia Clarion a brilliant and accomplished witch by the time she was ten.

"Thank you," I said and dropped a kiss to Celeste's cheek. "Magic, you know, is as old as humanity itself." I ran my finger's over the grimoire's intricately etched leather. "Its earliest practitioners manipulated herbs and organic material imbued with the spark of spirit. They did this in order to bring about changes in weather, encourage crop growth, and the healing of illnesses. Their ways were shared mainly through oral tradition. Because of this, many of the lessons of the ancient ones have been lost or forgotten. Therefore, it is wise for every witch *and Wiccan—*" I nodded to Celeste. "—to organize their knowledge into a grimoire or Book of Shadows. Families pass down their grimoire to subsequent generations. Each learns from their ancestors while adding their own experiences to the ever-evolving tome."

"I'm sure your mother would be proud of you. Your magic is incomparable."

I couldn't recall the last time I'd written in the Book of Shadows, and that pained me. So for the next few hours, Celeste and I lounged together amid Mother Nature's splendor. She occupied her time by making jewelry, wrapping wire around stones in intricate designs. I filled my mother's grimoire with sketched images and detailed descriptions of our Midsummer visitors, my mother's visitation, the Litha ceremony, my blessing by fire, and finally, the threats from the Cudlows and their flock. The work was sweet catharsis. Unburdening myself onto the page left me physically lighter. A serenity of mind and body enveloped me.

My spirit, however, though eased, would not be lulled into complacency.

Celeste and I roused ourselves and headed out of the forest and back toward the cottage. Just as we passed the fallen oak, a thought struck me.

"Where did you and Alexander sleep last night?" I turned my eyes her way in time to watch her lips lift into a smile.

"We slept on either side of you," she said behind fluttering lashes.

"On either side of me?" I parroted, shocked by her reply.

She kissed my cheek. "Thank the Goddess you're tiny. Three in a queen-size is murder." She smirked. "We love you, Eva. Truth be told, we're *in* love with you. And though we've not discussed it, I think we agree that you need us both. So, I guess we have an unspoken truce in effect."

"How long's that going to last?" I asked, stunned by her admission.

"I guess that's up to you."

Chapter Twenty-Five

After churning Celeste's words around in my head for a while, I headed back to the cottage. I was halfway through the front door when I heard the crunch of tires on river rock. The vehicle took ages to appear. I waited so long with the door wide open that Maggie and Ayo came over to see what the fuss was about. Soon Adelaide, Celeste, and the boys joined us on the patio to greet this mysterious new arrival.

Finally, Alexander's Bentley emerged. It inched up the driveway as if protecting delicate cargo. I blanched at the sight of Alexander's face. Sweat coated his forehead and his knuckles were white at ten-and-two on the steering wheel. Archie sat in the back seat at full attention.

When they finally came to a full stop, Alexander sprang from the vehicle. I took a step toward him only to freeze when I realized he wasn't rushing to me. Instead, he opened the passenger door and offered his arm.

I hadn't even noticed anyone sitting on the passenger side.

A tiny, bent old woman of sturdy build unfolded herself from the sleek sedan and pointedly ignored Alexander's proffered arm. She shuffled up to us with the aid of a wooden walking stick carved into the shape of a viper.

Dear Goddess, the viper! An image from a dream flashed before me, a viper coiled on the back of the German shepherd and fighting off a pack of wolves alongside our familiars. I looked the crone over in search of her serpent, but it eluded me.

"Mia Aradia," Maggie whispered in awe. "What an honor."

Although I'd never met her, I recognized Maggie's great-aunt on sight. A new picture of her arrived every December with a letter and wishes for a blessed Yule. The crone had a round, ruddy face, wrinkled by primal wisdom and a life well lived. She wore a faded blue peasant's dress with a gray apron wrapped around her sturdy waist and a black shawl draped over her shoulders. Her white hair was swept up into a loose bun atop her head.

"*Buon pomeriggio.* Good afternoon. The honor is mine." Her words were short and thick. Her shrewd eyes appraised our formidable welcoming committee. "It is a privilege to stand upon such blessed soil, among such magical friends," she said and smiled at each one of us in turn. On spotting Maggie, she threw out her arms and flashed a toothy grin. "There she is, my Magdalena."

"Is it really you?" Maggie choked out through an ecstatic smile, unsuccessfully hidden behind her quivering, slender hands.

"In flesh, bone, and blood," the crone nodded, grinning with crooked, yellow teeth. She wrapped her arms around Maggie's slim waist, and the women embraced as both old friends and new acquaintances.

Maggie's eyes were wet, but she remained composed.

"This foolish cousin of yours"—Mia gestured wildly to Alexander—"felt the need to travel across an ocean to find answers that lay right here on our family's land. *His* family's land." She flung her shockingly swift arm toward Alexander, hitting him square in the gut. Then she shook a bony finger at us all. "I am thankful he did, however. I sensed trouble brewing but couldn't put my finger on the cause. Allessandro filled me in on this threat against you. I have come with the full force of Stregheria to support you in any way I can." She put her hand over her heart and offered a slight bow. "You're going to need it," she muttered.

"Thank you, Aunt Mia," Maggie said. "Please, let me introduce you to my family and friends."

As always, Maggie performed the duties of hostess flawlessly, orchestrating the introductions with easy poise. When she invited Mia inside, however, the crone declined.

"We will talk among the elements," Mia said and shuffled with her viper cane toward the stream. When she found a particularly fluffy plot of lawn, she plopped down, took off her worn boots and grey, thinning socks, and crinkled her bare toes in the grass.

We congregated around her, enraptured by the wise woman and eager to hear her speak.

"It was through my ancestral line," she began in her strong, accented tone, "Magdalena and Alessandro's line, that the first Stregheria stepped foot on American soil. This potent witch from the hills of Abruzzi made her way inland until the Goddess led her to this land. This la Strega was my grandmother. She made a pact with the very magic, the energy, the spirit that breathes life into the soil and waters and trees. The bond dictated that a Stregheria of the Aradian line would live upon this land and protect it, cultivate it. In return, the elements would serve the witch. Not only the lavender but crops of all kinds flourish here. The trees bear fruit and provide shade and warmth. The veil is thinner here. The creatures aid the witch. Spells succeed; their potency increases. When Magdalena inherited the cottage and its grounds from her grandmother, she also inherited this magical bond."

"And now, that bond is under attack," Maggie added, with sorrow thick in her voice.

My gaze darted over to Celeste. She kept fiddling with her cuticles. She seemed antsy, like she was on the brink of taking off. A low rumble of laughter from Alexander diverted my attention. He and the boys had obviously gotten over their disagreements and sat clustered together, a few feet away from the group. Clearly, they were conspiring, but it wasn't the time to ask too many questions.

I concentrated once more on the potent witch before us. Leaning on her viper cane for support, Mia rose from the lawn an inch or so at a time, ignoring all offers of assistance. Every eye followed her as she tottered over to the peppermint bushes beside the cottage's front door. A curious look of amusement, followed by dismay, crossed the old woman's expressive face. With painfully slow movements, she leaned down, and retrieved a package from the bushes.

Shit. That's the USPS box I tripped over. I forgot all about it.

Mia walked back and lowered herself down onto the grass. She turned to Maggie.

"Sensing trouble bubbling here at the cottage, I sent this package to you. I believe it arrived at your door more than two weeks ago. Somehow, it was disregarded." Mia cleared her throat as if she knew exactly what happened, but she didn't so much as glance in my direction. She unwrapped the box as she spoke. "Inside, there are objects that could have helped you avoid many of your troubles; objects that are still required for you to fulfill your mission in this life." She opened the lid, pulled out a parchment scroll, and handed it to Maggie. "This is one of the nine scrolls of Aradia, the original la Strega. Most of the scrolls contain ancient magic, but this one reveals the history of Aradia herself. Within it, Aradia predicts "the return of the daughter" who ushers in a return to the "old ways." She foretold of a witch of great empathy who would venture forth to heal and to teach the ways of the wise women. I believe that witch is you, Magdalena."

Maggie held the parchment with awe and reverence, and her eyes welled up. "Thank you, Aunt Mia. I will treasure this and learn all it has to teach."

Mia reached into the box again and pulled out a small silver charm. This time, she turned to me as she spoke. "This, Evangeline, is a Cimaruta, or "Witches Charm," and it wields great power to the witch who wears it. It bears six symbols: a rooster head to dispel the forces of darkness, a key to promote knowledge, a vervain blossom for protection, a dagger to draw down the Goddess's aid, a serpent to encourage cunning, and a crescent moon to strengthen your magic. Wear this charm about your neck, and trust that no power on earth can best you." She handed me the Cimaruta, and it felt warm in my palm.

Her focus next fell upon Celeste, who'd tucked herself into a darkened corner along the cottage's far wall until her shadowy presence captured Mia's eye.

"Come close, Wiccan, so I might see you better," she said and patted a spot of soft grass beside her. Reluctantly, and with downcast eyes, Celeste sat beside Mia and allowed the crone to take her hands. "It's a pleasure to meet you. You have strength within that has yet to be tapped, but anger stifles you. Only when you shed the shackles of resentment can you bloom into the dazzling female you're meant to be."

Mia lowered Celeste's hands and patted her cheek. "But it isn't only anger that has forced you from your path. Jealousy has done that, and the desire to control the emotions of others for your own benefit."

Celeste recoiled, and my stomach heaved.

"Never have I ever," Celeste began but stalled her speech as Mia pulled a small glass jar from her apron pocket.

"I know you recognize this," Mia said as she placed the jar on the ground in front of her. "The moment Allessandro arrived on my doorstep, I sensed a curse upon him. To release him from its hold took only a moment. However, it wasn't until I arrived at his home that I understood the reason behind the curse and the identity of the witch who cast it." She raised Celeste's chin and locked on to the young woman's eyes. "Inside that glass jar you buried on Allessandro's property are pins and needles and nails, meant to incite suspicion and paranoia and anger. There are strands of dog and cat hair to promote discord and quarrels. There is also hair belonging to both Allessandro and Evangeline, to direct the curse. But the most potent ingredient in this bottle is the hotfoot powder, obviously intended to drive Allessandro away from his love, his Evangeline."

No. No, this isn't true.

Celeste let out a guttural wail of grief. "He's doesn't deserve her! He's a pompous, privileged ass. He's only brought her heartache. But I can take care of her. I love her." She turned to me with true pain in her eyes. "I love you, Evangeline."

But I couldn't answer her. I couldn't look at her, this woman I'd opened myself up to, this woman I'd let into my heart. *How could she do this? How could she be so manipulative? I'm going to be sick.*

"Not much of a Wiccan, are you?" I sneered. "Hmm? Do no harm?"

"I never said I was a very good Wiccan. And in my own defense, I didn't physically hurt Alexander."

"Not *him*," I snapped. "Me. You fucking hurt me."

"I...I'm sorry. I shouldn't have intervened. I see that now. I saw it when Alexander left. I didn't honestly expect the spell to work. I don't have the kind of magic you have. My spells never work. I just knew he wasn't right for you, that you deserved better than some angry, privileged man who would never understand you, and who would only bring you pain."

"But you caused my pain. You made Alexander speak to me the way he did. You made Alexander leave." My face flamed red and blood surged through my veins.

"I didn't implant those thoughts in his head. I only amplified what was already present."

"No," Alexander interjected, his fury bubbling just under the surface. "There was anger within me, I won't deny that. But you didn't only amplify it. You twisted it. You redirected it."

"I'm sorry, Alexander, truly," she whimpered, but he turned his back to her. Then Celeste reached out to embrace me, but I recoiled. She dropped her head in her hands, and began to cry.

"My dear young woman," Mia said softly, regaining Celeste's attention. "Do not distress yourself so. You may not have Aradian blood in your veins, or that of the Yoruba aje or fae or Druid. But words spoken with conviction have power, as you have proven. Why else would they call it spelling? And besides, Evangeline will find it in her heart to forgive you. In time."

I will?

"Yes, you will," Alexander said in response to my unspoken thoughts. "Because you will see, however misguided and foolish and hurtful Celeste's actions were, she acted out of love for you," he explained.

This man never ceases to amaze me.

Mia continued with her attentions to Celeste. "It is the intention of the practitioner who wields the magic that determine's its use, for good or ill. We all act fools in love. Loyalty to Evangeline does you credit. We women must stick together at all cost." The crone glanced over at Alexander and shook her head. "You will give Allessandro a run for his money." She smiled conspiratorially. "And that is as it should be. He is a good man. Yet, he too acted a fool, yes? But let us forgive him this once. A life of magic is new to Allessandro, and men often take longer than women to accept their fate. Now that he is home where he belongs, his powers can be put to good use."

"What are these sensational powers, Alexander?" Adelaide asked. "Will you honor us with a demonstration?"

"Gladly," Alexander replied and raised his arms.

"Imbranato! Sei un pazzo? Are you out of your senses?" Mia scolded in a hiss. "Get out into the open, where nothing and no one can be harmed."

The fact that Alexander's magic was so potent as to require us all to get the hell out of the way, was an unsettling thought.

Alexander trudged out to the wide expanse of lawn. Once again, Alexander lifted his arms. He spread his hands and fingers open wide, and a vibration hummed around him. Specks of dirt and dust rose up. The air crackled with electricity. Low hanging clouds formed before our eyes. From those clouds a rumbling, groaning growl grew louder until a single bolt of lightning shot out with a deafening crack.

All but Mia and Alexander covered their ears and jumped a good foot off the ground. The grass struck by his lightning smoldered black and smoked. When Alexander closed his hands and lowered his arms, the clouds lifted.

"Great Goddess above!" I said in awe. I'd never seen anything like it. I'd been practicing magic since the toddler years. I could manifest fire and water, harness the wind, and direct the creatures of the earth. The rainstorm we caused took three experienced witches and elaborate spellwork. And yet Alexander, a fledgling witch with powers only a few weeks old, could conjure lightning!

"Ha!" Adelaide exclaimed. "Spectacular! I'd like to see Crandall, that sanctimonious, megalomaniacal bitch, try taking us down now."

"Speaking of Arbor's Most Moral, the church folk who dropped by last night threatened to return in..." I paused to check the watch I wasn't wearing.

"Approximately six hours," Luca helped me out.

"Thanks... In six hours. So, what's the plan here?"

I cast an expectant gaze over the group and waited. And waited. Until Maggie took mercy on me and chimed in.

"Well, we obviously have to concentrate on defense. We have the cameras and repellent magic in place already. But maybe a glamour cast over the grounds would help?" Maggie suggested.

"Great idea. Can you tackle it yourself?" I asked with impatient optimism.

"With pleasure. But maybe Ayo can give me a hand," Maggie proposed.

"I would, dear one, but I've got my hands full," Ayo replied with a sigh. "I have a meeting with Chief Harrison to turn over the evidence against the Crandalls and Cudlows."

"Excellent," I said and nodded my thanks.

Ayo kissed Maggie on the cheek before hurrying off with her phone already on her ear.

"I wonder, Magdalena," Mia interjected, "if you wouldn't mind if I took care of glamouring the property. I am particularly adept and enjoy creating a deceptive mirage."

Maggie looked a bit taken aback by the request. It was a great honor to have Stregheria magic woven into their ancestral land. She eagerly agreed and thanked the elder witch for her aid.

"I do have another request." Mia cleared her throat. "This one for the Wiccan." She turned her knowing eyes to the sulking blonde. "Would you assist me with the glamour? As proficient as I am, it is a large property. A strong young woman beside me would do me good."

A sad but grateful smile lit Celeste's face, and her tight shoulders eased. "Of course." Celeste took the crone by the arm and led her off to the farthest corner of the property, beyond the lavender, where Mia would begin to cast her magical veil.

When the women were out of sight, Luca stepped forward. Fidgeting with the collar of his tight black T-shirt, he looked back at the other boys and over to Alexander before he spoke.

"We're moving back into the manor."

"I'm sorry, what? Are you insane? I am *not* moving back there," I shouted, shocked.

"Not *you*, baby girl. Us," Luca said in a calm, soothing voice, obviously concerned with the severity of my reaction. "The manor's close enough to be able to get here quick should you need help. And as much as we all love sleeping in Mother Nature's wide expanse, the novelty of tent living has worn off."

I stared, unblinking, unable to respond.

Alexander stepped up close to me, and I tilted my head back so I could see his face. "The negative spirits that once plagued the estate have moved on. Franklin and Marsh are gone. I can't live in that huge place with only poor Elliot as company."

"Wait, what are you saying? They're all going *live* there?"

"Hell yeah. We're gonna be neighbors!" Ethan proclaimed, his eyes alight with joy.

"After talking to the guys, uh, the boys," Alexander corrected, "I realized how much they could help out. I've decided to take them on as partners in the running of Morgan Manor. So, yeah, they're moving in."

"As a matter of fact," Nicolae cut in, "we should get packing. I want to get to the manor asap. That way, we'll be back before the pitchforks arrive."

"We'll be back before you know it," Gregory said with an encouraging smile.

And with that declaration, the boys left, each kissing my cheek on his way out.

Not to be outdone, Alexander kissed me full on the lips. He poured his soul into that kiss, his urgency and passion. "I won't be long, my love."

My heart leapt at his words, but I couldn't let down my guard. Mia had revealed the truth behind his treatment of me, but I couldn't just flip a switch. And I didn't have the luxury of time to unpack all the baggage encasing my heart. So I stubbornly shoved any sweet thoughts way down into my gut.

Keep your head on straight, Evangeline, I scolded myself. *Arbor's Most Moral don't give a shit that your heart's been put through a blender.*

With our guests off on their missions, Maggie, Adelaide, and I walked inside. A thick quiet blanketed the cottage. The stillness muffled my senses as if I'd been packed in cotton. I looked to my left to find my goddess-mother—eyes on the Aradia scroll. I looked to the right to find my high priestess—staring intently at her scrying mirror.

In that moment, a thought ricocheted through my brain. *Something's not right.* I blinked to clear my vision but could see nothing amiss. Maggie and Adelaide remained focused and diligent at their tasks. Neither showed cause for concern of imminent calamity. Yet my instincts kept screaming, *Something's not right.*

Meanwhile, I fell into Alexander's preferred method of deliberation—I paced. My brain fixated on creating a list of my friends and loved ones, where they were at that moment and how long until they might return. Then I took inventory of those who considered me an enemy. This list was longer and incomplete. The innumerable, often anonymous, online threats coupled with the average citizens of Arbor who railed against me in the privacy of their homes created a coalition of hate.

Agitated, I trudged across the cottage floor and muttered to myself as I deliberated. My temperature rose. Sweat broke out along my brow and the back of my neck.

"Something's not right, dammit," I blurted.

Maggie and Adelaide looked to me with wide eyes and dropped chins.

"What in the name of the Goddess are you on about, Evangeline? Whatever it is, can you please keep it down? Scrying takes concentration," Adelaide scolded.

"You don't understand, I—" I began.

"Darling, I know things are crazy right now, but that's why we need to focus," Maggie cut me off sweetly.

"But I—" I tried again to speak, only to be interrupted once more.

"That is enough, child!" Adelaide shrieked. "Do you have any idea of the gravity of the situation we're in?"

"Actually, I do!" I hollered back.

Suddenly, the temperature dropped, and an overwhelming scent of orange blossoms filled the air.

We turned toward the gallery to see my mother emerge. She stormed up to Adelaide. "For the love of the Goddess, will you listen to my daughter? She's trying to warn you!"

No one moved. Until, that is, Maggie fainted. I tried to catch her, but I missed. And she hit her head on the kitchen counter. Adelaide and I immediately fell to our knees to help her.

"Grab me a cloth and some—" Adelaide started to say, until my mother's corporeal ghost stepped between us.

"You need to leave. Now!" she screamed. And when still no one moved, she hauled Adelaide and me to our feet. Then, after hoisting her unconscious love over her shoulder and taking off out the door, she yelled, "Run!"

Adelaide and I followed, hot on their heels, toward the cover of the forest. I quickly outpaced the elderly high priestess. Calling out mentally to the familiars, I directed Shasta to help Adelaide and asked Rocky to head to the skies.

"Please, my friend, I need you to warn Mia and Celeste that danger approaches. They're somewhere on the property setting up a glamour. And then I need you to keep an eye out for approaching enemies."

"Too late, Evangeline," Rocky said in a dead voice. *"The enemy is already here."*

I ran under the cover of the oak and aspen, then tucked myself behind a nest of brambles and looked back. The scene laid out before me would be forever branded into my memory. Stuart hobbled on one crutch beside the reverend's silver Cadillac, tossing Fledermous, limp and lifeless into the trunk. He turned around holding a .357 Magnum at his side. A menacing sneer contorted Stuart's sallow face, and the putrid green aura of hatred reverberated around him.

In the middle of the yard, Jay gripped Adelaide's frail arms behind her back and snapped plastic zip ties around her wrists. She didn't cry out. She didn't resist. Instead, a blank, shell-shocked expression fell over her and all the color drained from her cheeks. Hunched and haggard, her powers made impotent, Adelaide gave herself over to Jay's onslaught. Her familiar was dead. There was no greater pain for a witch.

"Eva! Here witchy, witchy, witchy, witchy. I know you're out there. Tell your teddy bear to step off," Bunny called out toward the general direction of the woods. Her frizzed-out blonde hair and two-inch-long nails complemented her bubblegum-pop attire in true Bunny fashion. This sappy sweetness made the .270 Winchester rifle she aimed at Shasta's head—not twenty feet away from her—all the more grotesque.

"Attack her or run away, Shasta! Please. Why the hell are you just standing there?" My voice cracked. Panic surged through my veins.

"If I move, she shoots. She's got the muzzle of that gun trained to my brain like a laser beam, and it's bound to blow my mind."

"You can't hide forever, Eva. Though I can see why you'd want to. I mean, damn. I'd always known you were a freak, but I never realized just how fucked up you were. No wonder you spent our entire friendship pretending." Her hands trembled on the weapon as she spoke. "You made a fool out of me, you bitch," she said through clenched teeth. "You were supposed to be my friend, but you were nothing but a phony."

She was right. I'd been a crappy friend. Maggie had warned me that my treatment of Bunny would come back to bite me. The Law of Three approached, and as I saw my lies and secrets, every incident of disrespect and contempt with morbid clarity, I knew there was no escape from magic's most essential rule.

But if I'm going down, I'm going down fighting.

As I made this declaration, a felt a searing heat consume me. I looked down at my hands and arms and legs in astonishment. I'd begun to blaze and smolder like molten lava from within. A guttural scream ripped from my throat. A war cry. With my Goddess in my heart, I called forth all the flora and fauna of the woods. Their energies swelled, rising to meet my call to action. And together with Rocky, we burst out from the forest into the yard.

Rocky led flocks of robins and sparrows in an aerial attack on Jay. Their bared claws and sharpened beaks left bloody gashes on his face. Jay let go of Adelaide to swat away at the birds. While my feathered friends chased him off down the driveway, my once-mighty high priestess fell limp upon the grass. She was unable to muster even an instant's strength to save herself. Her familiar was gone. Adelaide was pain. Adelaide was loss.

Setting my sights on Stuart, I flicked my fingers and directed vines and tree roots to bind him. When they took his legs out from under him, Stuart fell hard on his face, breaking his pointed nose. The blood pooling around Stuart's ginger head mesmerized me. I'd seen it pool like that once before when Alexander charged in and saved the day.

Bunny's frantic howls called my attention away from this sick fascination, onto a new terror. Spiders, beetles, chipmunks, and squirrels swarmed her. The creepy-crawlies and rabid fur balls wriggled, rippled over each other on their way up Bunny's legs and torso, biting and scratching as they swallowed her up.

Taking advantage of the distraction, Shasta charged her.

It was all too much for Bunny. She crumpled to the ground and fell on her weapon.

A single shot rang out.

I dropped to my knees and screamed. I screamed until I lost breath. I felt the bullet crack through my own head the moment it split open Shasta's skull. My vision blurred. There was a deafening buzz in my ears that grew louder and higher pitched until it became one, ceaseless pinging of metal against metal reverberating through my head. It felt like someone had drilled a hole through my skull and was searing my brain matter with a blowtorch. Every torment Shasta suffered, I suffered—only without the physical wounds to match.

With flesh and fur hanging from bare bone and her rich, magical blood oozing down her cheek, matting her fur, Shasta lumbered a step, two, three, before collapsing a few feet away from me. I dragged myself over to her through the grass and flung my arms around her warm, powerful body. I hid my face in her coarse fur and sobbed as great heaving waves of horror washed over me.

I hadn't cried this hard when my mother died. I hadn't cried at all when my mother died.

My momma bear, the one who comforted me then, when I was a little girl lost without her mother, the one who stood beside me in torment and suffering and heartache, the one who gave me strength, this tender spirit who had devoted her life to me, was slipping away. The rhythm of her heart slowed. Her breath grew shallow.

"You can't leave me." I clung to her, pleading. "I need you. I need you."

"No, you don't. You're strong. And don't forget Rocky. Together, you will soar. As I will it, so mote it be."

A sudden loss of breath tightened my chest. A lancing pain swept over me, from my heart outward.

Shasta rolled onto her side as she would in hibernation. *"I've just reached the place where the willow don't bend. I'm going. I'm going,"* she said and closed her soulful eyes one last time.

"I'm gone," I finished the line. *She quotes Dylan with her last breath. What a blessing, to deliver a smile even at the edge of death.*

Death claimed my friend, and the moment her spirit passed in delicate crystal light onto the next plane, my own spirit ripped from my body. I didn't move onward but upward. It was a bit like flying with Rocky except, of course, I wasn't tethered to my physical body. What could I do as a spirit? Adelaide needed me. Celeste and Mia and Maggie needed me. *Shit. Where the hell is Maggie?* I panicked until I remembered she'd been whisked away by my mother. My mother in corporal form.

And there I was, split in two—my body lying limp and lifeless atop the dead black bear and my spirit hovering overhead. Disembodied, I was powerless to do anything but watch the scene play out below me.

Without my magic to direct them, my defenders of the wood halted their assault and withdrew to their burrows and nests. Now undeterred, Stuart, Jay, and Bunny regrouped. And they were a fright to behold. Deep gashes and bright-red scratches sliced across Jay's face and head, permanently disfiguring the vain hipster. Blood coated Stuart's face and the front of his shirt, and his nose cocked awkwardly sideways. Bunny was unrecognizable— a bloated, battered ragdoll, caked in blood and dirt. And it was hatred, vengeance that drove them to brush themselves off and get back to work.

They snickered as they hauled Adelaide's unconscious body into the Cadillac's trunk.

"Crazy bitch," Jay muttered, with his typical smug smirk now monstrous.

Bunny grunted out an assenting laugh, but Stuart didn't respond. They shut the trunk, and Stuart charged over to my immobile form. He clenched his fists at his sides, and his mouth pulled tight in a grim line.

"I don't give a shit about the old hag. It's her," he spat on me. A feverish hunger burned in his eyes. His rabid lust hung thick like humidity in the sultry summer air. And the desire for something more—the desire for revenge—added fuel to the inferno I sensed churning within him.

Jay took a step toward me, and Stuart rounded on him. He kicked him over into the dirt.

"She's mine," he snarled.

"I thought you hated the slut. Now you're playing the knight?" Jay taunted from the ground.

"Oh, I'm gonna save her, all right," Stuart said with a satisfied sneer. "I'm saving her for myself. You got to fuck her for what, two years? That pussy's mine now."

Jay staggered to his friend's side and laid his hand on Stuart's shoulder. "No offense, my man, but Eva would ride your ass raw. No way you could please her."

Stuart's right eye twitched, and he balled his fists. "Do you think I give a fuck about pleasing this cunt?" He snarled and foamed at the mouth.

"Will you two keep your dicks in your pants, for fuckssake. Everybody's waiting for us. Get your asses in gear," Bunny said to the pair. Then she grabbed a hold of my hair and dragged me behind her. My body bounced and smacked again and again into the dirt and rocks.

Bunny threw my body in the back seat, and Stuart slid in beside me. "Don't worry, sweet thing. I'm going to take good care of you."

Those were the last words I heard before Bunny, Jay, and Stuart took off in the reverend's car.

Chapter Twenty-Six

Rocky. I need to find Rocky.

The thought drove me to soar in the opposite direction of the Cadillac. I had a pretty damn good idea where it was headed. If I could find Rocky, we could communicate. Then he could make sure the others knew I was alive and well. If a bit disjointed.

Rocky wasn't the sole object of my search. Maggie was out there somewhere, injured, with no one but my mother to protect her. And I had no idea if Mia and Celeste were safe, or if they too had been snatched. My search, however, proved fruitless and did nothing more than eat away precious time. So, after changing course in midair, I raced the wind to downtown Arbor.

My spirit soared over roofs and treetops. Arriving at my destination, a vulgar sight greeted me. The Great Pavilion, situated across Parson Street from the First Ecclesiastical Church of Arbor, was swathed in red, white, and blue. Banners with the tag "Vote Crandall" hung from every lamppost. Rows of picnic tables, heavy with greasy food, bland beer, and red, white, and blue balloon-bouquet centerpieces, provided rest and refreshment to the assembled. The parishioners of the First Ecclesiastical Church of Arbor weren't the only ones in attendance. At least half of the town packed the Pavilion. The carnival atmosphere acted as a twisted backdrop for the atrocity I next witnessed.

There, beside the arched, stained-glass doors and white steeple of the church, three wooden pyres had been erected. My lifeless form was tied to one of the rough, wooden beams by my wrists and ankles. Adelaide was bound beside me. The third pyre, positioned on the other side of Adelaide, was missing its witch.

They haven't found Maggie, thank the Goddess.

Alexander, Mia, Celeste, Gregory, Ethan, Nicolae, and Luca surrounded the base of the wicked spectacle looking fierce and seriously pissed-off. Our friends frantically cast protection spells and defensive charms. There was no sign, however, of Ayo, Maggie, or my mother among them.

The impatient Arbor citizens, eager for a show, pressed in closer. They cursed and spat and threw handfuls of gravel from the church parking lot at us. A few especially fervent young men climbed the pile of logs at my feet, but they didn't get far. Archie snarled and snapped at their legs until they retreated. And Rocky flew in circles above, defending us from the crazed zealots by clawing and pecking anyone who got too close.

"*Hey, Rocky!*" I shouted without a sound. Thankfully, my lack of vocal projection did nothing to damage the mental communication I had with Rocky. I was grateful and more than a little relieved. It made my situation a bit less horrifying.

"*Thank the Goddess! You've made it back safely. It was everything we could do to keep these disgraceful people from defiling your body while your spirit lingered elsewhere.*"

"*Thank you so very, very much. Now I need to ask more of you.*"

"*Of course. Anything. Always.*"

"*Tell Alexander I'm here. Like this. And have him ask Mia how the hell I get back in my body.*"

"*Sometimes, my dear witch, you miss what's right in front of you.*" Rocky shook his head and ruffled his feathers.

I squinted, confused.

"*Have you forgotten I can read your thoughts? I know your spirit is here. Somewhere,*" Alexander interrupted.

"*Alexander! How the hell can I hear Alexander? I've never been able to hear him before,*" I rambled.

"*Another trick I picked up in Italy. And a timely one. Are you okay? I mean, I know you're not okay, but are you okay? I was so fucking worried. I thought I'd lost you.*"

"*You still may. I'd be better if I could jump back into my body. Can you ask Mia how?*"

Alexander leaned over and whispered in Mia's ear. Her eyes popped and darted about in an attempt to catch a glimpse of my spirit form. When he finished speaking, Mia whispered back.

Then Alexander's voice came to me again. "*Mia says to surround your body with the light of your spirit, and you will become whole. But she cautions against returning to your body until you absolutely must. You're going to be in a lot of pain.*"

I took off like a dragonfly and landed deftly beside my still form. Ever so slowly, by degrees, my spirit merged with my flesh and bone. The moment I fully became myself again, my heart thrust jolts of electricity through my limbs and head and gut. The pain surged through me like jumper cables.

A scream threatened to burst from my throat, but I choked it back and squeezed my eyes shut. I used my remaining senses to determine the extent of my hellish circumstances. The first thing I noticed was the stench, like a cross between mold and pig excrement.

Dear Goddess, no. They used elder trees for the pyre wood.

Whenever an elder tree is desecrated, whether by cutting or burning, it releases an unholy stink. The fumes released when burned are toxic. The elder tree is known as the Goddess tree. The Wiccan Rede states, "Elder is the Lady's tree, burn it not or cursed you'll be."

Not like Arbor's Most Moral are reveling in the Goddess's favor as it is. If they set flame to these pyres, they will seal their fates.

A loud squeal and a crackly tap, tap, tap reverberated from ten yards or so to my left, interrupting my thoughts.

"Is this on? One two, one two." Mayor Doreen Crandall's amplified voice addressed the assembly. "Yes? Loud enough? Okay, great..."

I figured everyone's attention would be on the mayor, so I peeked my eyes open just a sliver as the sinful scheme unfolded.

"Good afternoon, folks! It warms my heart to see so many patriotic, God-fearing citizens here today." A raucous cheer responded to her. "And I know I'll see each and every one of you out on Election Day! Right?" She trilled a fake chuckle. "Am I right? Vote Crandall!" Then she pulled back the rah-rah vanity and replaced it with stern sobriety before continuing. "I'd like to thank Reverend Cudlow for his tireless leadership in this spiritual war. And of course, I'd be remiss if I didn't thank the reverend's dutiful wife, my dear friend and yours, Mrs. Gladys Cudlow. You'll be out of that wheelchair in no time!" She grinned through pinched lips. "You know, just last night, Gladys asked if I worried that today's burning might dash my election hopes. And given our state's proclivity for liberal snowflakes, her question is a valid one. But you all must realize that we are no longer a silent majority! Every time a baker refuses to sell a rainbow wedding cake, every time a cemetery refuses to put a pentagram on a tombstone, every teacher who prays with her students in school, these small but righteous acts embolden and amplify the voices of the like-minded around us. Every act of holy defiance demonstrates to the uncertain of the flock that we are in this together, and we mean business! We are blessed to have such magnanimous leadership in Washington, and I have no doubt they would support our efforts here today!"

She's out of her fucking mind.

The mayor paused to take an overdramatic breath into the microphone and invited Reverend Cudlow to say a few words.

The reverend stepped up to his portable pulpit. With a somber mien, he opened his Bible, put on his reading glasses, and cleared his throat. "Let us pray," he said, bowing his head. "Heavenly Father, we are gathered here today to restore our community, to cleanse our town of a terrible evil that has taken root. We need you to pray, folks."

The reverend raised his Bible in his hand. I noticed a cross-shaped spot where the red leather was torn away.

"We need you to pray for our government. Call out on behalf of our elected leaders. Because, you know what? There is a tipping point. The tides of wickedness are rising. We must ensure that the depth of our faith rises even higher! We must root out the gays and bisexuals and transsexuals. We must root out illegals. We must root out the Muslims, Papists, Atheists, and witches. We must root out all influences of the Evil One from every facet of life. They must be rooted out and destroyed! And their destruction begins today!"

The "Amens" rang out from every direction.

Holy crap. They are all out of their minds.

Mayor Crandall returned to the mic.

But I couldn't let this go on. I knew I had to speak. It was now or never.

"My good neighbors!" I called out, to the shock of the crowd. "Your own religious tradition dictates that love is a moral imperative. How can one love their neighbor and justify allowing them to be strapped to a pyre? Even if you call us enemies, your Christ commanded that you love your enemies. But we have done nothing wrong. There is no justifiable reason for me or Ms. Good to be tortured in this way." I looked over at Doreen Crandall. "The desire for power and control has brought us here." I looked to the reverend and Gladys. "Ignorance and fear brought us here." And then I, once again, addressed the crowd. "We've done nothing wrong. We have not bewitched anyone. We have not harmed a soul. We aren't converting or indoctrinating anyone. We are not your enemies! We are your neighbors!"

My voice, strained and dry, gave out. Not like I knew what else to say. How does one convince a mass of people not to condemn you to death—or worse, not to light the match themselves?

That's when Celeste's voice rang out.

"Bide the Wiccan law I must
In perfect love and perfect trust.
With these Eight words the Rede fulfill
An ye harm none, do what ye will.
What ye send forth comes back to thee,
So ever mind the Law of Three.
With naught but love within my heart
Merry we meet, and merry we part."

Celeste fell to her knees before the pyre. "Please forgive me, Eva! I'm sorry. I'm so, so sorry," she wailed. Tears streaked her face.

A chorus of mocking laughter reverberated through the crowd as they pelted her with rocks. Instead of covering herself, Celeste opened her arms, inviting the punishment. Showing extraordinary empathy, Alexander lifted her from her knees and tucked her into the crook of his arm to protect her from the onslaught.

"Okay. Okay, then. That's enough of that." Doreen Crandall laughed and again took control of the gathering. "I'd say we have all heard quite enough from these heathens. And as you can see, Adelaide Good and Evangeline Clarion have called more deviants to their side. They've even corrupted the heir of Morgan Manor! Oh, yes, they are actively fighting against the good people of Arbor. This is exactly what we have been warning of! But, have no fear. We will not let them get away with it, will we?"

"No!" the rabble replied with vigor.

"There are witches before you," the mayor spoke sotto voce to lend impact to her words. "They have poisoned our fine little town. But, no longer. Their evil will torment us no more. This ends today!" She ended with force.

"Burn them," someone called out.

"Burn the witches! Burn the witches! Burn the witches!" the crowd took up the chant; repeating it over and over again.

And then they lit their torches.

"Arrest the accomplices and then burn the bitches," Mayor Crandall commanded, before coolly stepping aside to let others do her dirty work. Beside her, Reverend and Gladys Cudlow looked over at their parishioners and neighbors, smug and self-satisfied.

I expected Chief Harrison to come bounding through the crowd to offer the mayor a good-natured chastisement and a crash course on the illegality of her actions. But the Arbor police were nowhere to be found. Instead, a squadron of soldiers in head-to-toe battle gear marched in lockstep and surrounded my friends. With high-powered weapons trained on their chests, one by one, they were handcuffed and led away.

Unobstructed, Stuart and Jay and Bunny—still bloodied from our battle—led the parade of citizenry, each dropping their torches to the kindling at our feet.

When the first lick of fire touched my flesh, a primal scream ripped from Alexander's throat and echoed over the melee. Not even the rabid cries for blood from the enraptured minions could drown out the anguish in Alexander's voice.

"No! Evangeline, save yourself. Get yourself down from there. Please, Great Goddess save her!" Whether through his newfound magic or sheer force of will, Alexander broke free from his handcuffs and free from the soldiers' grasp. He crumpled to his knees before me and raised his tear-stained face to the heavens.

His voice cracked in despair as he called out, "I can't lose her! I can't lose her yet." He tore at his hair and beat his chest. Archie, ever loyal, howled mournfully by his side.

"I'm okay! The fire doesn't hurt me," I cried. "Please, save Adelaide!"

But Alexander, overcome with anguish, didn't seem to hear me.

The blaze swelled. The flames crept up my legs, crackling and spitting as it burned away my clothes. Its noxious smoke coated my throat and stung my eyes. Soot blackened my skin, but my flesh was unharmed. I'd been reborn in the Midsummer fire, and this pyre didn't hold a candle to the Goddess's incandescence.

Still, Alexander howled his torturous grief.

"I'm all right! Alexander, please, I'm okay." No reply. *"You have to save Adelaide!"* Not a flicker of recognition.

I tried to produce a mighty wind to blow out the flames, but I couldn't create a single breeze. I tried to draw the fire away from Adelaide and toward me, but that too proved ineffective. I simply couldn't manifest my magic while so anxious and agitated. Having my hands tied around an elder tree pyre didn't help matters.

"Rocky, make him—and the others—understand that I won't burn!"

Rocky flew up to the church eaves to avoid the growing inferno. *"Alexander's heart has shattered, Evangeline. He hears nothing. And the mayor's para-military guard knocked Mia out when she produced fountains of water from her palms. The others understand you will not burn, but it doesn't make it any easier to watch. Every witch is trying to use their powers to save the high priestess, but nothing is proving effective."*

An agonizing cry erupted from Adelaide. She'd remained unconscious until this point, but the searing pain must have woken her. Her eyes peeled wide with horror as another inhuman shriek ripped from her throat. Her skirt already shredded away, the flesh of her feet and legs blistered and blackened and peeled off her bones. The flames licked upward, engulfing Adelaide's shoulders and singing her hair. Her face contorted in freakish anguish.

The acrid reek of burning elder wood mingling with Adelaide's charred flesh was too gruesome to bear. "No! Goddess, no!" I wailed. *She can't die. Not like this. No. This is not happening.*

I closed my eyes, and called on my memories of Adelaide, her lectures on life, her sharp-tongued quips, and I channeled them through the magic in my veins. I felt the Goddess's energy heating me from within. And as I let lose a maniacal howl straight from the pit of my soul, I ripped my hands free from the pyre and kicked my feet loose, shredding the ropes that bound me and tearing away skin from my wrists and ankles. I threw my hands wide and called on the rain to save Adelaide.

Nothing.

I hadn't calmed myself enough, so I tried again.

Nothing.

Like a living torch, I fell to my knees before Adelaide's blackened, blistering misery. Guilt sliced through me like a hatchet to the chest. My heart refused to accept what my mind comprehended on the spot. Adelaide's life was fading away, and I was too weak to do a damn thing about it. Every lesson on spellcraft and scrying, every late-night chat over tea, every crude remark and witticism and nugget of wisdom Adelaide had ever imparted, played out before me. The spirit of the once brash, feisty, defiant, fearless, potent high priestess surrendered to the depravity of hate and ignorance. Her soul rose and disappeared in the thickening clouds.

And seeing Adelaide's head slump, lifeless on her neck, the sick, sadistic citizens of Arbor roared their approval.

Maddened by the twisted wickedness of it all, Alexander spread his arms wide, and with all the sorrow in his soul, he cursed Arbor. "If they burn, you will all burn with them!"

And then he called down the lightning.

Grumbling thunder preceded a momentous, eardrum-shattering *crack*. The ground shook as the first strike hit the church steeple, instantly setting it ablaze. It shook again seconds later when another bolt hit the Great Pavilion, just feet away from Doreen Crandall. The blast knocked the mayor off her feet, and her head slammed against the pavement.

There was a collective inhalation of breath—followed by shrieks of panic.

And then Reverend Cudlow's mind snapped before our eyes. He'd been standing just beside Crandall, his partner in crime. When she collapsed, he gawked down at the mayor and the blood that puddled around her head and laughed. Buckling over, the reverend slapped his knee repeatedly as a deranged, maniacal fit rocked him. With a demented smile stretching his mouth wide over his teeth, he pointed at the fallen mayor and at the flames that churned around them—and around his beloved church—and he sputtered out a sickening belly laugh.

The reverend's behavior was so disturbed that even Alexander stopped to stare. But only for a moment. He flashed his gaze to me, then to Adelaide's unrecognizable corpse, and back to the hosts of the evening's morbid festivities. And he continued his assault, directing bolt after bolt, fury and grief fueling his destruction.

Individual lightning fires merged, and the undulating mass writhed its way down Parson Street. It leveled the church and the Great Pavilion. It crept along, devouring the flower shop and Ebenezer's Café with meticulous precision, leaving behind blackened, skeletal frames.

Chaos reigned. Townspeople screeched and scattered. Even Crandall's hired guns abandoned their posts and prisoners and ran to save themselves. Celeste and the boys were too busy working to free themselves from their handcuffs to be of any aid. It was up to me. If I didn't act quickly, the entire downtown would be engulfed. So I pushed aside everything that weighed me down. I released the rage and sorrow. I let my mind go blank. Empty. Calm. And this time when I called down the rain, it came. The clouds tumbled and billowed as they shed their tears upon the scorched and the soul-weary.

But it wasn't enough. Arbor still burned.

I dug deeper. I put my trust and faith in myself and in the magic that flowed through my veins. Raising my hands above my head, I commanded the waters of the Ausable River, and all its streams and creeks, to heed my call. I drew forth their waters and ordered them to douse the flames. The torrent crashed in wave upon wave of drenching relief. Only when I felt confident every last ember had been extinguished, did I relent and send the waters back to their beds.

Celeste ran to me and threw her slim arms around my naked, soot-covered shoulders. She burrowed her face into my neck and wept.

"Shh, I know. I'm here," I said softly to soothe her. "I wish I could pluck out your pain and leave you with a lighter heart. But I don't have that power."

Her weeping stopped mid-sob. Celeste raised her head and hastily wiped away her tears. "You're the strongest woman I've ever known," she said. "I need you in my life, and you need me in yours—as a friend or something more. But I'm not going anywhere. Please. Please don't send me away." A glimmer of hope brightened her eyes.

"You manipulated me, Celeste. And Alexander. I don't know what I feel right now, but I'd be lying if I said I didn't still care about you." I pulled her back into my arms, and we stayed that way until we heard the wail of sirens rip through the acrid air. Chief Harrison's police cruiser led a battalion of fire trucks and ambulances screaming down Parson Street.

Harrison gawked in slack-jawed awe as he exited his vehicle and assessed the scene. "What in blazes..." he began to say before he noticed Doreen Crandall lying in a pool of blood beside the mad-eyed reverend. He rushed to her side and felt for a pulse. "Let's get some EMTs over here. Now!" He called out his orders, and in seconds, medics were attending to the mayor. The chief's knees cracked as he stood, but he had his handcuffs at the ready. "Reverend Cudlow, you have the right to remain silent..."

With the reverend secured in the back of his cruiser, Harrison returned holding a pile of thick woolen blankets in his arms. "Miss Eva, let me cover you," he said kindly and wrapped one of the blankets around my shoulders.

"Thank you," I said, sucking back tears. "Are you the only sane one in this town?"

"Well, I know of a couple others."

He stepped aside to reveal Ayo and Maggie. They knelt down and wrapped their arms around me. And I choked back another sob.

"What happened? Are you okay? Is my mother still with you?" I whispered in Maggie's ear.

"She's gone. I don't know how, but she healed me. Then she hid me in the forest, searched out Ayo, and brought her to me." Maggie stopped and looked lovingly into Ayo's dark eyes.

Ayo took up the story without releasing Maggie's stare, "I found your goddess-mother in the woods beside the cottage. Once she came to, we found the evidence of your struggle littering the grounds. And we found Shasta, of course."

"We needed the police—well, we needed *Harrison*. But when no one answered at the station, we knew something was wrong," Maggie added.

"Mayor Crandall went off the deep end this afternoon," the chief explained. "She was spoutin' about havin' to snuff out the evil and purge the town of its sinfulness. When I challenged her, she had her thugs lock me and my deputies up… in my own jail! I had an appointment scheduled with Ms. Kehinde, so when she and Ms. Maramma came along, they sprung us loose. If not for them, we'd have served a life sentence! Once they filled me in, and Ms. Kehinde showed me the evidence your boys found, we rushed down here."

Words failed me, so instead of a poor attempt at a thank-you, I hugged Chief Harrison with my last ounce of strength.

"There, there now. Just doing my job, miss," he said, blushing. But the color drained from his cheeks when he caught sight of Adelaide, burned upon the pyre. "Dear God, what have they done?"

Alexander and the boys climbed the steaming logs and reverently lowered Adelaide's body to the ground.

"Don't look. It's too much," Alexander warned.

"Fuck that!" My scream shocked me as much as those around me. "We have to look. Fear killed our friends! Hate killed our friends! Adelaide and Fled and Shasta. This should be seared into everyone's brains. We can never forget this. *I* will never forget this."

"But is she *really* gone?" Alexander asked as he tried to find a pulse. "Shit, I can't tell."

He placed his hands upon Adelaide's scorched flesh and attempted to draw on his new powers to jump-start her heart, to heal her. One by one, Maggie, Ayo, Mia, the boys—even Celeste—followed his example and laid their hands upon the high priestess. I held my breath and prayed for the Goddess's intercession. But when Maggie broke down and buried her face in Ayo's shoulder, I knew Adelaide was really gone.

Chief Harrison laid one of his woolen blankets over her corpse. "Can't tell ya how sorry I am. Ms. Good and I go way back. She was one hell of a woman." He wiped a stray tear with a starched white handkerchief.

His words shook me from my grief, and I pulled myself to my feet. I looked to Maggie and all my gathered loved ones, and they met me with expectant hope. With Adelaide gone, I was truly their high priestess. They didn't turn to me because I was some sainted figure. My pride and my reckless, vengeful use of magic had a hand in this chaos and destruction. They didn't look to me because of my power, for they'd seen me at my weakest. I was unable to escape magic's most essential rule: what one projects into the Universe will return threefold. I'd learned my lessons the hard way—that every action has a reaction, although rarely in equal measure. In the end, they chose me to lead them because, despite the obstacles, I was stubborn, relentless. A fire burned within me that hatred and ignorance and fear could not extinguish.

"Let's go. We've got work to do."

Epilogue

Ethan's fae ancestry was on full display. A shock of silver hair caught the candlelight as it skimmed along his sharp cheekbones. He leaned over and slid the sleek, shimmering leotard up his dancer's legs. It hugged every inch of corded muscle. The iridescent top, glinting in shades of green and silver, molded onto his flat stomach and arched outward into full gossamer wings at his shoulder blades. The costume was an impressive bit of craftsmanship. I'd worked on it every evening for a month.

Ethan shivered with nervous energy. In an attempt to distract the jittery lovebird, Alexander clapped him on the back, hard.

"So, a fairy and a druid walk into a bar..."

"Don't start with me, Alex. It's going to be a long night, and I'm edgy enough as it is." Ethan huffed and rolled his eyes at the dashing host of the evening's festivities.

"That's enough, gentlemen," I scolded with an indulgent smile.

I rose from the settee in the corner of Ethan's well-appointed suite. It was one of the largest bedrooms in Morgan Manor. Ethan had chosen it for its spectacular views of Gothics Peak. All the boys had taken up residence at the manor in return for their employment at the estate.

"Do you need us for anything else before we head out? The musicians, performers, and artists must be sharp and in position by the time we open up those doors. Are you sure you have everything under control?" I asked with a skeptical eye that Ethan did not deserve.

He really was a pro. His contract paperwork for each entertainer had all of its *I*s dotted and *T*s crossed. The office area he'd set up for himself in the far corner of his room boasted a fevered efficiency, not a pencil out of place or file askew.

"Everything is set. The entertainers are in position both inside and out, and the artists' exhibits are in place. I'll do a final review before we kick things off."

"I hope you have enough time. We'll need to see you downstairs in...how much time do we have before we open the doors, Alexander?"

"Half an hour, and there are easily a few hundred people waiting out front already," Alexander said as he looked down from the window, his forehead pressed against the glass, at the Who's Who of the arts and magic communities milling about with the Arbor citizenry on his lawn.

"Okay, so you'll need to be in position in twenty," I said. "Will that be enough time?"

"Just enough," Ethan said as he lifted my chin. "I've got this. It's going to be a great night. I promise."

I kissed the fae on both cheeks.

Ethan clasped a tendril of my hair and allowed it to run like silk through his fingers. "Alexander, make sure you look after this one tonight. She is wicked hot, and someone's bound to get burned."

My black hair swept up in a chignon with strategically chosen loose locks. My eyes were dark, and my lips popped with burgundy. The garnet Dilek Hanif gown rustled as I moved. It hugged my curves, and accentuated every asset. The fabric weighed a ton, but it lent the feeling of nobility. It was the most elegant garment I'd ever worn.

"Don't worry, Fae," Alexander replied with a wide, easy, Hollywood grin. "I'm not letting this witch out of my sight."

"Who's worried? This is going to be spectacular!" he said and surprised Alexander with a kiss. "Now, get along with you!"

We left Ethan to finish preparing for his role in our big night. We made it a whopping three feet down the hallway before Alexander backed me into a darkened corner. Looming over me with hooded eyes, he pressed me against the wall. He leaned down and bit along my neck. Shivers of pleasure shot through me.

"Do you realize how beautiful you are? And delicious. Your skin tastes like warm peaches," he growled as he nibbled. "I'd devour those lips too if I thought I'd be able to stop there," he said and leaned his chin on the top of my head.

With my cheek against his chest, I could feel the rapid pulse of his heartbeat and his labored breath. "You're insatiable." I smirked, then shook my head to clear his spell. "Come on. They'll send out a search party soon." I took his hand and led him down the wide, marbled staircase.

Before we turned into the kitchen, where the staff awaited our final review, Alexander pulled me aside again. "I have something to confess," he said with his head bowed and his long, dark waves hiding his eyes.

"What is it? Are you okay?" I ran my hands up his powerful arms.

"I'm nervous as hell," he said and peeked up at me through thick lashes.

I couldn't help but smile. Alexander rarely showed his vulnerable side, and it was kinda hot. "You have nothing to worry about. We've covered our bases. Everything's in place. And we'll stick together."

"You're a tough cookie, Ms. Evangeline Clarion. You know that?"

"Oh, I do. Now, let's make sure the staff knows it too. I want no slacking this evening. There's too much at stake."

"Well then, lead the way."

But before we could take a step, Celeste, the evening's Mistress of Ceremonies, caught up to us, panting to catch her breath. "There you two are. I was about to send out a search party."

Alexander and I shared a secret smile.

"The natives are getting restless," Celeste said in a fevered pitch. "At last count, we're looking at five hundred folks breathing down our necks. Nicolae and Luca are manning the entrance. They're doing their best to hold them back, but I don't know how much longer they can keep the peace."

"Is the violinist playing?" Alexander asked.

"Yes, but—" Celeste replied.

"Is the bubbly flowing?"

"Yes, of course, but—" Celeste began.

"Are there plenty of hors d'oeuvres?"

"Yes, but—" Celeste tried again.

"Then don't worry," Alexander said, his easy confidence firmly back in place. "Eva and I are going to touch base with Gregory and the kitchen staff. Then, as soon as Ethan checks in, we'll be good to go."

"I just don't think we can wait that long, Alex." Celeste stood strong and defiant, not wavering an inch underneath Alexander's glare—especially brazen since he was, once again, her employer.

I grinned at her sass. One couldn't help admire her strong will and tenacity. It was her cunning I hadn't yet learned to forgive. She'd worked tirelessly to restore her integrity and prove her steady reliability. And devotion. And I was grateful for the truce she and Alexander seemed to have forged, however tenuous. Yet while our relationship remained friendly, and I couldn't deny my attraction to her, there existed a layer of caution that hadn't been there before.

"Those doors won't open a second before eight o'clock. We have all worked too damn hard to rush and fuck things up at the last second." Alexander would not budge.

Although obviously perturbed, Celeste gave him a sharp nod. "Got it, boss." Turning her attention to me, Celeste softened. "You look stunning, every bit the high priestess."

"Thanks. You look rather breathtaking, yourself. The navy was the perfect choice." The shimmering gown played perfectly against her fair skin. "Is there anything else I can do for you?"

"Not at the moment. Later, though…" She let the flirtation linger, and with a cheeky wink for me, and a saucy eye roll for Alexander, Celeste made her way to the foyer.

Our review of the catering moved quickly. Gregory directed the kitchen with military precision. He, too, was in costume, cloaked in a heavy, hooded, black-linen robe that crisscrossed his chest, and was cinched at the waist with a cord of black leather. Black leather pants and steel-toed shitkickers made him look badass. A long, bone-white beaded necklace with a Star of Ur amulet, hung from Gregory's neck. He was dressed as dominance incarnate.

Ethan's going to pass out when he sees him.

"I was thinking the same thing," Alexander said with a wink.

We checked back in with Ethan, and he gave us the final all-clear we needed to kick things off. Before I knew it, I stood in my choreographed position with Alexander, back at the top of the staircase, awaiting our cue. On the other side of the manor's iron doors milled hundreds of guests, including most of Arbor's residents; all eager to glimpse the Witches of Arbor.

It was Samhain and the grand opening of Arbor's newest gallery, the Manor Arts.

It had been four months since the burning of Arbor. Alexander invested a massive sum of money into the cleanup and restoration of downtown Arbor. He felt it his duty. He blamed himself for the fires that destroyed the Great Pavilion and damaged many of the businesses along Parson Street. The First Ecclesiastical Church of Arbor had been leveled too, but since the Cudlows were behind bars, no one seemed in a huge rush to rebuild it. Doreen joined her son and the Cudlows in prison after she was released from the hospital. And it was Bunny's testimony that did them all in. She'd taken a plea deal that ensured the Crandalls and Cudlows would spend a good long time in jail. But Bunny, the one responsible for my familiar's death, would escape punishment for her crime.

Upon the bones of the church's ashes, we planted three elder trees, one for each of the friends that had been taken from us.

Alexander worked closely with Arbor's newly elected mayor, Jonathan Riddle, a good man, strong and honest and fair. He won the special election to replace Doreen Crandall as mayor in a landslide. Together, Alexander and Mayor Riddle laid out a vision for the community that was more inclusive and progressive. But we weren't fools. We knew hearts and minds didn't change overnight. And that was exactly why the Manor Arts was so important. Along with honoring the memory of Alexander's eccentric late great-grandfather Cain, it was a way of forgiving the community, asking the community for forgiveness, and atoning for our collective guilt.

My only disappointment was that Maggie and Ayo weren't there to witness the culmination of our work. They took off after Adelaide's Summerland Rite. Maggie went to fulfill Aradia's wish. She became La Belle Pellegrina, the beautiful pilgrim, who cares for the afflicted and aids her fellow witch. And Maggie and Ayo set out to warn covens and solitary practitioners alike of this radical fundamentalist ideology, the kind that fueled the hatred that sparked the Arbor witch-hunt.

Without Maggie, the cottage's lavender fields and gardens could have gone neglected. Thankfully, Mia agreed to stay at the cottage until Maggie's return. Her presence maintained the magical bond struck between the first Arbor witch and the land. And Mia's magic was spectacular. She'd stand at the end of each row of lavender or tomatoes or blueberries as if she was a conductor. The round, wrinkled witch orchestrated the weeding and pruning and harvesting with her fingertips. Those herbs used solely for magic making, on the other hand, she tended more personally. She dug in the dirt and cared for their roots. She caressed each leaf. It seemed as if the plants spoke to her, like they told her exactly what they needed and when they were ready for picking. The potions and elixirs made from these herbs were infused with the magic from her fingertips.

"Are you ready, Evangeline?" Alexander asked, waking me from my reverie.

After a deep breath and a quick kiss, I answered, "Yep. Let's do this."

Alexander cued Celeste, who cued the brothers outside. Following our strict choreography and dressed in exquisite, identical suits of shining armor, Nicolae and Luca raised their swords. Trumpeters opened the front doors wide and heralded Celeste's appearance. She dazzled under the brothers' raised swords, looking nothing like the meek, frail girl I'd first met.

She raised a microphone to her lips, and addressed the crowd in a clear, commanding voice. "Welcome to Morgan Manor and welcome to the grand opening of the Manor Arts! A blessed Samhain to you all, and a happy Halloween. My name is Celeste Galehorn, and I will be your Mistress of Ceremonies. This evening you will be treated to a feast for the senses, from the tantalizing fare to the enchanting music. There are illusionists, crystal ball and tarot readers, and of course, the highlight of the evening's festivities, art exhibits in every conceivable medium.

"There are treats to be found around every corner, but mind your step. Steer clear of the shadows, for tricks abound, and not only from the illusionists. Consider yourselves warned." Celeste paused for dramatic effect. The guests waited with inhaled breath. "And now, without further ado, I have the great pleasure of introducing your host and hostess, Mr. Alexander Morgan and Ms. Evangeline Clarion."

There was a polite round of applause. Alexander and I slowly descended the staircase, visible to most of the crowd on the front lawn. I flicked my right wrist slightly and produced a fluffy, low hanging fog that wafted at our feet. With a flick of my left wrist, I turned the fog blood red. I made it grow and snake along before us into the crowd. Neither movement was pronounced enough for the assembled to catch, so to them, it was all just part of the show. That fact didn't lessen their dread. The crowd withdrew as we approached. Alexander and I stopped just outside the manor doors under the brothers' outstretched swords.

Celeste handed Alexander the mic. "Welcome to Morgan Manor, and welcome to the grand opening of the Manor Arts." He kept his voice even and pleasant, as if he were speaking to one person instead of five hundred. "The Morgan family has lived in the community of Arbor since before the dawn of the twentieth century. In the early eighteen-eighties, the residents of Arbor began construction on the manor. Fifty years later, along with the rest of the nation, Arbor was hit by the Great Depression. That is when these ten-foot stone walls were erected around the estate, not to keep people out, but to give the men of Arbor the dignity of a day's work for a day's fair wages. Their very sweat and blood lives within these hallowed walls. Many years later, my great-grandfather, Cain Morgan, began a tradition of opening his home to the public every Halloween. Many of you knew my great-grandfather. You saw throughout his home his love for the unique and his passion for and celebration of creativity. Today, over a hundred and twenty years after Morgan Manor's completion, I have the honor of rededicating my family's home to the citizens of Arbor, the Manor Arts!"

Alexander had charmed them, and they lavished him with thunderous applause.

I took the mic and a half step forward to speak. I cleared my throat, and the crowd hushed.

"This is no ordinary evening. It is the Feast of all Souls. It is Halloween. It is the Day of the Dead. It is Samhain. There is magic in the air, palpable, tangible. Ghosts and goblins and sprites, and mischief-makers of all shapes and sizes linger in the manor's darkened hallways and shadowy corners. You are wise to keep your eyes opened should one of these choose you as their next victim of trickery. You will encounter sights and sounds and smells and tastes that may seem strange or foreign to you. We encourage you to embrace these new experiences.

"Alexander and I invited you here this evening to celebrate creativity in all its manifestations. Allow yourselves for a moment to appreciate the vulnerability and daring inherent in artists. The Manor Arts will be an open, welcoming space; a safe haven for creative thinkers to test the limits of their abilities. Tonight we celebrate these risk takers and rule breakers. As you make your way through the grounds, amid the gardens and groves, through the many concert rooms swelling with vibrato and bass, through the art exhibits, some stark, some ferocious, some delicate, as you dine with us on the bounty and abundance of Autumn's harvest, allow yourselves a moment or two to think of those who have gone before us. And remember the legacies they've left behind."

The crowd's hearty applause surprised me, and I had to choke back tears before continuing.

"Ms. Galehorn, Mr. Morgan, and I will be here throughout the evening to answer any questions or assist you in any way. We hope you enjoy."

Alexander stepped to my side and called out, "Let it be known that the Manor Arts is officially open!"

Before I could join the surge of guests inside, Alexander pulled me close. "You're one hell of a witch."

I threw my left arm around him and my right around Celeste who had come to stand beside me. I kissed them each on the cheek and smiled.

"Let the revelry begin."

About the Author

J.L. Brown is the mother of two boys and the wife of a musician. She's a nature lover, a die-hard Phish Chick, and Suburban Sensi momma. She reads Poe and Anne Rice, and has a serious Jane Austen habit. She lives in a little old home in Jersey, where she drinks too much coffee and enjoys good wine. She is often found raving about politics, and believes chocolate can cure most ills.

Email: 1authorjlbrown@gmail.com

Facebook: www.facebook.com/AuthorJLBrown

Twitter: @AuthorJLBrown

Website: www.jlbrownbooks.com

Also Available from NineStar Press

Connect with NineStar Press

www.ninestarpress.com

www.facebook.com/ninestarpress

www.facebook.com/groups/NineStarNiche

www.twitter.com/ninestarpress

www.tumblr.com/blog/ninestarpress